Heaven Expedition

Joshua Giem

Copyright © 2020 Joshua Giem
All rights reserved.
ISBN: 9798620327539

For Liz and Jess.

ACKNOWLEDGMENTS

This book would not have been possible without my kind reviewers and editors: Marla, Allene, Tobias, James, Julia, Elizabeth. Thank you from the bottom of my heart for spending countless hours helping me improve my craft.

My thanks also go out to Alessandra Suppo, whose cover illustration is astoundingly beautiful.

CHAPTER 1

A split-second after I caught sight of the woman's face through the entryway, my twelve-shot was raised, cocked and aimed squarely at her forehead.

I was enjoying some time alone in one of the private rooms at the smoke-house in the Yin town of Yaxiang that I had lodged for the evening. I wasn't supposed to be disturbed. This fact made the weathered woman's sudden appearance through the beads covering the doorway instantly threatening. An unfamiliar voice emerged from the woman. "Are you Haye Zintan?"

The end of my hookah had been thrown to the floor, all thoughts of blowing smoke rings towards the ornate, geometrically-patterned ceiling gone from my mind. My face remained static. "No. Mind leaving before you get some lead between the eyes?"

"There's no need for the hostility, Ms. Zintan. I've no harmful intentions." The woman shakily raised her hands. "Would you care to join our group in the Purple Room? We've an offer you might be interested in. Nothing..." she paused, "...in your usual line of work."

My trigger finger twitched. "What do you know about my work?"

Her voice softened. "All I need to know is that you've been up to the base of the Great Ranges, and you're the quickest shot in Yin. We require your expertise."

I snorted. "Yeah. And you also require that I walk out that door into the waiting arms of the Yinda's enforcement."

The woman's blue eyes widened. "Furthest thing from what I was thinking."

I dropped the barrel of my gun as I stood up. Curiosity finally overcame my caution, as I lowered my revolver completely. "What's the job? Pitch it fast, I'm in no mood for chit-chat."

"My group is organizing an expedition beyond the Great Ranges."

After an incredulous laugh, I looked back at her face and realized she was serious. "Listen here ma'am," I began.

"Doctor."

"Listen here, *Doctor* Ma'am, which blend are you smoking? I feel as if I'm missing out."

"I don't partake," she vacillated. "I'm telling you the truth."

I considered her. She wasn't Yin - that was for sure. No epicanthal folds around her eyes. Her eyelids also had bumps on them, like an animal hide. She was a Beltlander through and through – her days had been largely dominated by the sun hovering on the distant horizon. She seemed more darkward in ancestry than me, since her face was too squarely shaped. If I had to guess, she was from some place near one of the Unknown Seas. She was close to two meters, about the height I would expect of someone from that area, wearing a jacket lined with several pockets and dark gray trousers that partly concealed the tops of her heavy boots.

I decided to heed my curiosity and follow her. "One wrong move." I holstered my revolver as I warned her. "That's all it takes. I shoot first."

I found the Purple Room deserted except for two figures reclining in the corner on separate divans. One was a middle-aged woman wearing a brown fedora and field jacket with black pants, possessing similar features to the woman who had led me here, filtered through a couple of decades. More eye-bumps. The other was a young man who avoided eye contact and pondered the floor. His muscles presented through the thin material of his shirt, which upped his threat level in my mind. My intruder sat down next to them, but I didn't follow suit. My hands went to my hips as I stared them down.

"So what is this?"

The middle-aged woman spoke. "Would you care to take a seat? I promise I'll try to keep this as short as possible."

I was stock-still. "I'll stand. What's this about an expedition?"

She folded her hands and began. "I am Dr. Hennir, professor of archaeology at Inninger University. This is my colleague, Dr. Ininsir," she gestured at the woman who had disturbed my relaxation before she shifted her hand to the man, "and my assistant Yensir." How familiar are you with the Forebear settlement recently found in the Yten mountains?"

"I don't follow Beltlander affairs, Doctor."

The doctor paused only briefly to assimilate this information. "A year back, a team from Inninger University uncovered remnants of a gigantic ancient outpost dating back several millennia. The team, myself included also found a map that depicts a massive Forebear city."

Hennir continued. "Nothing in the field of archaeology ever prepared us for this find. All we've ever excavated are remnants of small towns dotted across the Beltlands. If something even larger were ever discovered, it could be the find of the century. With the technology found in that city, we could advance humanity's progress by centuries, if not millennia."

Ininsir interjected, raising her finger , "There's just one catch. The map points sunward, beyond the Great Ranges, to the very sunward pole of the world."

After I'd had a minute to mull over what the two strangers had said, I asked the obvious, most important question.

"What's in it for me?"

"Payment will be in Aulan Rubles. We'll give you two thousand now, plus fifteen thousand monthly," Hennir said.

"Not good enough." By the look on her face, I could tell Hennir was taken aback. The sum would make me a rich woman, but nobody had ever gone to the very sunward pole of the world. "Listen up, Doctor Hennir. This is a lunatic mission I'm not convinced will succeed. Going up to the sunward pole involves several risks you haven't addressed. There's pack animals, protection from the heat, armament... and if you think I'm going to take fifteen grand a month and handle all of those issues..."

"We're handling those as we speak," her startled expression faded slowly. "And I think you'll be more than pleased to know we won't be going on foot."

***

It was a week by andironback out to Mansu. From there by the newly built sunward rail line to the airport of Kinyu, it was only six hours. The Yin steppe was slowly but gradually being tamed. Barbed wire fences lined the whole length of the railroad, caging in the formerly wild frontier. I suppose, in the end, that was one reason I joined the doctors' mad endeavor. As industry spread to the Yin, the open road faded with it.

On the other hand, being chased from town to town by the most ruthless bounty hunters in the steppe would provide some extra motivation. Sunward was perhaps the best direction to go at that time.

The Airship Destiny, I was told, was the top of the line, cutting edge. She was built to withstand severe weather and temperatures. Below her decks were stables to hold ten outraptors, the feed needed to sustain them, crew quarters and food, ballast, and even a fully-equipped scientific laboratory. As for speed, she could hold forty knots at full impulse via a new fuel called diesel. To top it off, she was commanded by the best captain in the Aery, Ila Nome.

Kinyu is the most sunward of the Yin prefectures. About fifty kilometers beyond, the imposing ten-kilometer height of Great Range foothills casts a never-ending shadow on the town. Within this great darkness, the temperature plummets compared to the rest of Yin. An eternal glacier covers the ground, from which only the occasional melt flows darkward along the path of least resistance.

As it happened, the only ship in the airfield when we arrived was the Destiny itself. I was immediately impressed with her size. From bow to stern, the ship's gondola must have been a hundred meters lengthwise, and her canopy at least twice that. I can't overstate how much volume the airship occupied; she dwarfed the small circle of buildings that constituted the town of Kinyu. Intrigued locals sat in the doorway of their huts gazing up at her bulk, tracing her red-and-white banded hull with their eyes. It was quite evident that nothing of this size had ever landed at Kinyu; the ship had been angled at catty-corners to the landing rectangle in order to fit.

No sooner had we exited the train than a figure cloaked in an Aery overcoat and an officer's bicorn walked onto the station to greet us. Captain Ila Nome was a grizzled woman with short gray hair and pock-marked skin. Since she lacked the features common to the two doctors, I surmised that she was a fellow Nordecker. Her lip was permanently twisted downward into a slight scowl, and her hands were stuffed into the pockets of her overcoat.

"Gentlewomen, good end-rhythm to you. Welcome to Kinyu," she growled.

The two doctors shook her hand while Yensir struggled with our luggage. I folded my arms, sizing the woman up.

The captain turned to me. "I see you are our guide for the first section of our journey. Will you recognize our path from the air?"

I shrugged. "There's only one place I've found that divides the foothills. It should be easy to see."

"Let's hope it continues beyond the foothills, otherwise we'll need to backtrack," Captain Nome answered firmly. "I'll show you your quarters; we're readying for late end-rhythm takeoff."

Getting used to the Aery's division of the rhythm into 25 hours instead of 26 was going to be an adjustment. May as well have gone from one calendar to another.

We left the platform and strolled towards the airship. As we did so, I noticed a row of four cannons jutting from gun ports along the side of the ship, one deck below the top.

Dr. Hennir spoke up. "I see you have armament."

"If we run into flyers, we can manage three shots every minute. And we have excellent maneuverability for each cannon as well."

Hennir smiled. "I can see why you told me you were happy with her."

The captain's scowl briefly flickered with pride. "Destiny is the top of her line. I'm very pleased with her weapons."

I broke in. "How does your gun crew handle three shots a minute?"

"Rear-loading." The captain turned to me and raised an eyebrow. "My understanding is that rear-loaded cannon aren't commonplace among the Yin?"

"I'm afraid not. Are you going to let me have a look-see at those?"

The captain nodded. "That can definitely be arranged."

A voice from our left interrupted us. "The ship's blessing has concluded, captain."

I turned to catch a glimpse of a man slowly walking towards us, dressed in a well-pressed but simple black priestly robe. A long, gray beard stretched down onto his chest, and he held a cup of holy paint in his left hand. His right was held outward, the two fingers used in the ritual of consecration painted various dark colors. If it was possible, his face was even more pock-marked than the captain's. I sensed Hennir suddenly tense in his presence, and a brief flicker of anxiety crossed Dr. Ininsir's face as she glanced at the older doctor.

The captain was unfazed. "I'm glad to hear it. Have you

communed with the River yet?"

The priest, who was apparently the ship's chaplain, nodded solemnly. "Yes. The River spoke to me, and told me of a travail that was very soon to come after the ship's departure, but that Destiny would see it through. Moreover, the River also impressed upon me the importance of the crew's piety. It has been displeased with the rationing of alcohol among the airmen, and wishes a moderate decrease in their share."

Dr. Hennir had started climbing up the ladder over the side of Destiny's gondola while the chaplain and the captain were talking. Dr. Ininsir followed suit, with a puzzlingly nervous expression on her face. I knew there must have been some history between the doctors and the chaplain, but pushed the thought from my mind as the captain continued talking to the chaplain.

"Can you be any more specific about what will befall the ship?"

The chaplain shook his head. "I leave its message up to you to interpret. The River does not take kindly to those of my order who ask beyond the Veil, as I'm sure you're already aware."

The captain frowned, but nodded. "I'm aware. Forgive my inquiry, I don't intend to ask you to go beyond what was given to you by the River. Are the crew aboard? Aside from the loaders and ourselves of course."

"All except for the... engineer." The chaplain's nose wrinkled and anger flashed in his eyes. "Yuri Aldarin, I believe his name is?"

A flash of recognition passed through me. I knew that name.

I stepped forward and asked the chaplain, "Where is he?"

The chaplain flipped his thumb back towards the airport drinking hall with an expression of disgust on his face. "He's over there, getting drunk as usual."

***

When I entered, I found the drinking hall to be mostly deserted. There was a fire pit in the middle of the room, from which heat radiated outwards to fill that cavernous space. Yin geometric designs were embossed into the building's wood, with long chains of triangles snaking around its many pillars. The barkeep was slumped against the wall with his eyes shut, clearly off-rhythm from everyone else. I warily eyed him. I might have been an outlaw, but at least I knew what time of the rhythm was for sleeping, and what time was for wakefulness. There were a few Yin huddled around a table at the far end, laying dominoes together to pass the time.

Through the smoke in the room's center, I caught a glimpse of a pair of bright eyes flashing in my direction as I entered. They were joined by the sound of wood scraping against wood as the person arose to meet me.

Yuri Aldarin's ruddy face beamed with warmth on seeing me. A daft grin plastered itself across his expression, and he bounced towards me with surprising alacrity. I barely had time to brace myself before he threw his arms around me with a boisterous laugh and proceeded to crush my ribs.

"Haye! Six months! Six months since I've heard from you! You turn up in the strangest of places, sir!"

I gingerly returned the hug, and tapped my chin on his bald head briefly. I whispered, "Please, I'm glad to see you, but can you not shout my name?"

He abruptly broke the hug, and looked up at me worriedly. "Again? What happened this time?"

"Long story. Let's sit down."

Yuri's table was, thankfully, distant from the other people, and his outburst hadn't woken the barkeep. Contrary to what the ship's chaplain had said, Yuri wasn't surrounded by empty glasses. Instead, the stone table was bare except for several design blueprints he had obviously been obsessing over. It fit with what I remembered of him.

"The chaplain seems to be under the impression that you're drinking yourself under." I smirked slightly.

Yuri snorted. "He wouldn't leave me alone otherwise. Bastard doesn't think highly of drink, or those who partake of it."

I sat opposite the engineer, leaning myself into the wall as he cleared his schematics from the table. "You're on the Destiny. Why'd you accept their offer?"

Yuri shrugged. "You and me, we're in this for the same reason. We can't stand anything too crowded, and Yin's getting crowded of late. Have you seen the fences?"

I nodded. "Mansu's streets are slowly being paved over. It's the same in Yinau. Pretty soon the only place left for me will be sunward."

"At least you'll still be following your childhood dreams." Yuri noted.

He'd hit it. I had to be free. I'd left civilization in search of freedom many years ago, and never looked back. An overbearing father, a society that viewed me as second-best, dreams that couldn't be realized under the restrictions society had put on me. Nordecker women were supposed to be subservient and submissive. Already in the more enlightened parts of the Beltlands, this attitude had long disappeared, but the aristocracy of Nordecker held out against all change. If Yin modernized to that extent, there was no question the Yinda would have the power to enforce similar distasteful norms on the people.

And there was another reason I'd joined. Ever since I'd first looked out towards the sun that hung endlessly at one point in the sky, I'd felt the sunward pole of the world calling to me. It tantalized me with visions of celestial weirdness that faded and shifted together in my dreams.

The short man sighed through his nose in frustration. "People like us, we're becoming obsolete. You may have to take up a profession, like book-writing."

"If I had to, I could do worse." Books were rejected in Yin as sources of Beltlander corruption.

Yuri's eyes narrowed. "Haye, I was joking."

My expression turned to mock sadness. "Oh, but, here I was thinking, I'm getting tired of the life. I've wanted to get out of the business for a while now and..."

I didn't even finish my sarcasm. Yuri's head went immediately to his palm as he recalled our former business partner. "He really was a piece of work, wasn't he?"

We both laughed.

Yuri finally interrupted his laughter long enough to ask, "So, what did they want you to do on the ship? I mean, for me it's obvious, but a polymath like you..."

"Scout, apparently. Also weapons officer." My hand came to rest on my revolver holster. "And shipboard sheriff of sorts."

"Letting the outraptor guard the meat house." Yuri commented.

"Speak for yourself."

"True... Good point there. You'd better watch that I don't wreck the ship by stealing its gears off." His eyes twinkled with kleptomania.

Silence fell between us for a while as we both turned to watch smoke rise from the fire pit. It was broken by Yuri first.

"So, what was your long story?"

I folded my arms in front of me loosely. "You remember governor Tarwei of Ilu?"

His brow furrowed. "No."

"He was one of the Yinda's advisors who supported banning books in the first place. The foremost of the gang of five."

Yuri's brow softened. "Continue..."

"I was in Ilu, smuggling for some idealistic group. They had an outrageous plan to smuggle books into the governor's palace to several... interested parties. I had to play as one of the suitors to the governor's daughter."

"I can see where this is going. Why'd you accept the mission?"

I sighed with regret. "It seemed like a good idea at the time. And the money was good."

"How good?" Yuri raised an eyebrow.

I nodded with satisfaction. "Extremely good. 50 grand worth of Yinlus."

Yuri whistled at that.

"I got caught in a compromising situation I'd rather not talk about, and now I've got the Yinda's men *and* several mercenaries, including the White Hats, after me for smuggling books."

The White Hats were the most notoriously effective bounty hunters in the entire Yin steppe. They were vicious and methodical. Nobody had escaped their reach yet. One man tried, went out to the far end of the steppe into uncharted highlands. The White Hats had returned with his head stuffed in a bag.

"And also hunting me for, eh... *that*."

"You didn't?" Yuri chuckled.

"No!" I punched his shoulder. "You know me, it was nothing quite... exactly... like that."

"You stole a kiss?"

"I absolutely did. I'm not going to blow my own cover." Yuri nodded thoughtfully while I softly slumped against the wall.

More silence passed between us.

"Do you think you were followed to Kinyu?"

"Maybe. Thankfully we're taking off in a few hours. And after that, only the most foolhardy would follow us."

Yuri suddenly frowned. "I hear..." It was at that exact moment that I froze, and the door of the hall opened slowly.

I knew who the group was by their deliberate footsteps as they entered the hall.

Three figures entered the drinking hall, sauntering down the center and scanning the room. I covertly followed their movements. Three white-furred caps, with bronze points at their top. Mustaches impeccably groomed. Eyes that locked onto our position. They fanned out slowly among the spread out tables. The door was left hanging open.

The other group of Yin nervously crowded into a corner of the room behind their table, and the barkeep, now awake, took one look at his new guests and shouted "Can I help you?"

One of the White Hats spared him a cold glance, which quickly drained the blood from his face, and he slowly lowered himself behind the cover of the bar. He knew what was about to happen.

When the White Hats had finally cornered their prey, they usually offered them time to kill themselves before they started a shootout. Some twisted code of honor thing that allowed the prospective victims an alternative to being mercilessly tortured to death. I'd managed to evade their tracking until now. Once they'd made their presence known, there were three options: suicide, fighting, or running. Options one and two were practically the same thing. Nobody outshot the White Hats. Period.

I tensed up and began whispering quietly to Yuri as his face grew focused. "Count of three. Upend the table for cover." He nodded quickly.

"One."

The footsteps of the White Hats stopped. They lined up in the center of the hall, their revolvers drawn and their left hands folded around them at their waists.

"Two."

The chamber was deathly quiet. The only sound came from a small snull that had settled on the hole in the hall's roof, which fluttered away.

"Three."

Yuri and I jumped backwards out of our seats, and shoved the stone table over into a covering position. The White Hats brought their guns to aim a split second too late. Bullets hit the stone surface of the table, cracking it, but not going through to our side.

The White Hats began to move sideways, seeking to flank us,

but Yuri drew a new-fangled automatic rifle from under his coat, and opened fire over the top of the table. The White Hats frantically moved to cover.

I slapped Yuri's shoulder and nodded at the window twenty paces to our right. He caught the hint.

The White Hats conserved their ammunition, waiting for us to make the next move.

Simultaneously, I broke my cover and sprinted towards the window, and Yuri began laying down another field of suppressing fire. As I ran, I had my own revolver drawn, and slung a few bullets towards the White Hats. One of them caught a bullet in the shoulder, but the other two shot towards me with trained accuracy. Had I been moving slower, I would most certainly have been hit.

Yuri followed along behind me at a slower pace, keeping the White Hats heads down with some well-placed bursts.

I jumped and slammed through the window glass. It shattered, and I felt the impact of tens of tiny shards breaking my skin. I slammed into the ground beyond with an uncomfortable finality as Yuri made his jump as well.

We didn't have much time to recover, but adrenaline was pumping through my system by this time. I grabbed Yuri by the shoulder and hoisted him up so we could sprint towards the Destiny.

The White Hats weren't far behind. We hadn't gotten far when they burst out the door, and raised their guns at us again. I began swerving from side to side to throw their aim off. Bullets whistled past us. Yuri fired a few shots behind him again before his rifle ran out of ammunition.

Destiny's crew heard the shots, and her airmen scrambled into action.

Thankfully, the White Hats had to reload. We made it to the airship with time to spare as the bounty hunters started to run to catch up with us.

A cannon blast sounded, and a shot flew over our heads towards the White Hats, missing them, but stopping them in their tracks.

We stormed up the ladder onto the deck of the airship. Captain Nome turned towards me, her eyes searching for an explanation.

"Captain, sir, recommend we leave." I breathlessly heaved out.

Captain Nome made a quick decision. "Master of Altitude," she called out firmly, "prepare ballast for takeoff." She turned to another officer. "Mr. Pullnir, all hands aboard. Now."

In the few seconds it took for the ship's anchor lines to be separated and the few loaders to scramble up the ladder, the rest of Kinyu suddenly exploded in a flurry of activity as villagers took cover from the sudden shootout.

A loud voice called up from one of the White Hats. "Captain Nome, deliver your scout, or you will be charged with aiding and abetting a fugitive."

Captain Nome remained stoic.

The Destiny began to rise slowly as the ladder was drawn up. A volley of bullets flew upward to stop her rise, but only succeeded in drawing a withering burst of cannon from port, starboard, and, I realized then, the front and back of the ship.

The Destiny was soon at ten meters, twenty meters, thirty meters... her rise accelerated. Then the massive diesel turbine under her kicked into high gear, whining as it pushed her to full impulse.

Suddenly, I heard a series of awful clangs above me. "Canopy hit!" someone yelled out.

I turned upward to see no less than six bullet holes caused by revolver fire. The White Hats had hit us. We were losing air.

We were still rising, and by now well out of range of ground fire, but for how long?

CHAPTER 2

Captain Nome was the first to react. "Master of Altitude! Report!"

"Upward acceleration decreasing, captain! She won't be in the air for long!"

The captain's voice remained steely. "Helm, maximum impulse. Get us as far away from the town as possible. Repair teams to the rigging!"

"The port rigging's left behind captain! We didn't manage to load it in time!"

Nome's expression soured, and she paused.

I don't generally consider myself a mechanic, but I've made airtight repairs before. Back in darkward Yin, I'd welded metal patches onto water towers, iron bars together, that sort of thing. Yuri was by far someone more skilled in understanding how things fit together, and what gears went where, but a simple welding job? I could do that.

Mind you, it was a slightly different prospect doing that job without rigging.

I saw my opportunity in several elements simultaneously. One was a rope laying coiled up next to the edge of the deck. Another was one of the airmen holding a welding torch and mask with several bits of spare metal. The final element was the metal rung, which jutted out from the side of the Destiny, formerly used to hold rigging.

I didn't ask for permission. That isn't my style. I grabbed the mask, metal patches, and torch forcibly, secured the mask to my head, then began tying the rope into a lasso. Around me, few of the airmen noticed.

Captain Nome was beginning to speak when I completed the lasso. "Repair crews, prepare for..." She stopped when the head of the lasso flew into the air.

The loop flew upwards perfectly, wrapping snugly around the rigging rung, where I pulled it tight. Taking a breath, I grabbed the rope tightly, and began to climb. In retrospect, I should have secured the other end of the rope first.

I swung out over the edge of the ship, dangling over several hundred meters of cool, mountain-shadowed air. A crippling sensation of vertigo trickled up my spine, but I suppressed its influence to the best of my abilities.

I was a few meters up before the crew on the deck below me attempted to grab the other end of the rope. The hard point where it was fastened to was a good ten meters horizontally from the side of the gondola, which meant that I had swung out almost twenty over to port. I was making good progress upwards, but the climb was exhausting. Occasionally I caught shouts from below, but the majority of them were drowned out by the scream of the turbines. Air whipped past me at a ferocious speed. Thankfully, I had the presence of mind to not look down.

I finally climbed far enough to the point where I was level with the bullet holes. Gas was leaking fast out of the compartment. I had to close it soon.

I began swinging over towards the Destiny, the rope beneath me curling in a serpentine pattern. I swung increasingly closer. Five meters, three, one...

At one meter away, I began scrabbling for a handhold on the ship. I was unsuccessful, and swung backward over the abyss below me. My left hand, taxed with holding a blowtorch and the rope at the same time, slipped a few centimeters before I grabbed hold of the rope again with my other hand.

I swung in a second time. This time, I was able to grab on to the red-banded underside of the Destiny's canopy. Thankfully, the bullets themselves had left only the tiniest of breaches in the metal, so I was able to weld them directly shut with the blowtorch.

I spied another hard point closer to where the damage was, and looped the side of the rope through it as I held on to my handhold. As I slid the helmet's cover over my eyes, the screaming air current buffeted my legs about and threatened to yank me off the rope. The new position of the rope meant that I only had to hang on to the rope with one hand, but it still wasn't easy to aim the welder.

I sealed holes one through five with some difficulty. Six proved to be a problem. Its repair burst halfway through completion, and then refused to close as the hole became wider and wider from my fumbling.

A constant stream of curses left my mouth as I wrestled with the leak. Finally, I became so fed up, as the air knocked my blowtorch off course yet again, that I jammed the torch inside the bullet hole.

Liquid metal flew back towards the outside of the hole, becoming caked around the nozzle of the torch. I quickly pulled the torch back before it could be stuck inside the hole, and was rewarded for my efforts by an imperfect, but holding, seal over the bullet hole.

I felt the rope jerk beneath me, and finally it went taut as the last of the holes was sealed shut. The crew had finally grabbed hold of the other end and secured it. I paused for a moment to make sure that the repair had been complete, before raising the cover from my helmet and sliding down the rope.

I don't really know what I expected waiting for me as I descended. A fair number of airmen stood agape when I hit the deck. There wasn't any applause, just a strange reverent silence.

A smile flickered briefly across my face before I looked at captain Nome. It was clear that two conflicting emotions were running through her head as she decided how to respond.

On the one hand, I sensed she was as impressed as everyone else at how I had saved her ship.

On the other hand, she must have remembered who put her ship in that position.

I decided to break the ice by deferring to her. "Orders, captain?"

She didn't miss a beat before responding. "Ms. Zintan, in my ready room." She turned to her first lieutenant. "Mr. Pullnir, keep the ship on her current heading; rise to the highest altitude her buoyancy will let her. And see to it the spare rigging is fastened."

She turned back to me as the lieutenant began barking orders. It was written large in her eyes, even if she didn't say it. *You've a lot of explaining to do.*

***

Ten minutes later, absolute silence had finally fallen.

I was in the captain's ready room. There were three circular windows built into the far bulkhead, and these provided the majority of the light in the room. Nome herself was backlit impressively. No doubt the authoritative effect was intentional. She sat calmly at her desk with her hands folded, musing over my story.

Beside my seat stood Yuri, obviously feeling anxious over what had transpired. For reasons unknown, the two doctors were there as well. Dr. Ininsir appeared to share Yuri's anxiety, but Dr. Hennir was quite calm, standing with her hands stuffed firmly in the pockets of her field jacket.

Through the brightness that shielded her expression, Captain Nome finally spoke. "Dr. Hennir, first of all, I'm not angry at you."

I was bewildered. "Captain -"

"Ms. Zintan, please help your case by remaining silent."

I responded by glowering at her.

The captain massaged her temples. "So." She breathed in deeply. "Doctor. Do you make a habit of hiring wanted criminals? This is the first I've heard of it if you do."

Dr. Hennir responded quite calmly. "Ms. Zintan knows the area better than anyone either here or in the Beltlands. She understands the native ecology of the Great Range. Without her, the expedition remains at a disadvantage. I might add that some among your airmen have similar criminal records."

"The Aery runs a strict indentured rehabilitation program with airships like the Destiny. Airmen are only commuted to our tier after three years' service in the Aery." She motioned at me. "Last I checked, Ms. Zintan, you didn't have any record of service."

I smiled acerbically. "Show me the money, captain, and I'll be more upstanding and useful than all your Aery lieutenants combined."

"Or disloyal, provided someone else pays more."

"I saved your ship, captain."

"What do you want, a trophy? You saved your own ass, and you know that."

Yuri spoke up. "If you don't like Haye on your ship, captain, you may have to be down an engineer as well."

The captain ignored him. "The Destiny can't maintain enough of an altitude to make it over the Great Range. We've lost too much helium. We will alter course to fly alongside the Great Range until we can make it around Yin, and back towards the Beltlands. We will then hand Ms. Zintan over into the custody of the Yin authorities and make preparations for a second trip sunward."

Dr. Hennir's voice was still calm. "You know we can't do that, captain."

"Give me one good reason we can't." Nome was growing more irritated, but still retained a firm command of her expression.

"You fired on the Yinda's men. They'll be looking along the ranges for you."

That statement hung in the air for a while.

Dr. Ininsir broke in. "It would seem the only way is forward."

Looking at the captain, I sensed an opportunity to keep the expedition going without having to leave it. That would protect me from the White Hats. "Captain, the White Hats are on your tail. Anyone who's defended a target of the White Hats has ended up dead. One had his head nailed to a noticeboard. Another, poisoned, then had bulls' testicles jammed down her throat." I paused for effect. "It's not the Yinda you should be afraid of here. The only escape for both you, and me, much as you may not like it, is beyond the Great Range."

"Save your stories, Ms. Zintan." The captain folded her hands again as someone knocked on the door. "Enter."

It was her first lieutenant, Mr. Pullnir. "Altitude is stable, Captain. She's holding at seven kilometers."

The captain nodded, and then dismissed him. "That's not enough to make it over the foothills. Let alone whatever might be beyond them."

"Perhaps I can be of assistance, captain." Dr. Ininsir took a timorous step forward.

"I'm listening."

"The Great Range itself has an abundance of untapped mineral deposits. If we can find a vein containing pitchblende, I could synthesize helium in the laboratory."

"Would we find it just lying about on the surface?"

"The range is metamorphic. A good amount of deep-surface minerals could be found closer to the surface. It's been documented in the Aras Range, and in the Yten formation. Both of those are metamorphic. Current geological models generally hypothesize scaling that up on a gigantic level in the case of the Great Range. I would, of course, require the help of our chief engineer to set up the synthesizing apparatus."

"How much time are we talking?"

"Unfortunately, pitchblende only contains a small amount of helium. But, if we have magnesium sulfate... Darkward salts, pardon... I could speed the process up. We would lose a few rhythms." The doctor folded her hands behind her. "At this point, it's our best option."

There was a short pause before the captain spoke again. "Make it so. But." She turned towards me. "This isn't over. You've put my ship and my crew in danger. When we find a way to return from our expedition, I will hand you over to the Yinda myself. If you don't like that, you should have thought twice before joining."

I looked her dead in the eye. "I'll shoot you before that happens."

"I'm in command of this ship." Her nostrils flared. "I suggest you not threaten me."

***

Two hours later, I was staring over the side of the ship and the massive distance beneath us. My stomach churned as I looked down. The farthest up I'd ever had the unpleasant experience of being was a couple hundred meters back in Yin. Beneath me was three kilometers of air. I had been ruminating on that fact for a while.

Only a short distance under the gondola, white clouds streamed out from the foothills of the Great Range like some ocean-river. They were perfectly flat, and calm; the aphelion blizzards wouldn't arrive for several months, but still the ground below was covered in ice. These two layers of white provided the illusion of a single rumpled carpet extending across the land for kilometers back towards Kinyu. It also left me feeling that the Destiny was very exposed to attack up here. Her red bands stood out against the white backdrop, though thankfully not as much as they would in full sunlight.

The foothills of the Great Range were getting closer. At this height, I saw that their massive craggy bulks were themselves shrouded in a great darkness. My unease grew as I recalled what I had heard of the titans beyond.

No one had ever up to this point ventured beyond the Great Range, which ringed the entire world, cutting a divide between the Sunward Expanse and the lands beyond. The reason for this was the gargantuan height of the Range. Their foothills, themselves the tallest mountains ever to be discovered, rose ten kilometers. Those who wrote in legendary texts concerning the height of the giants beyond described colossal peaks whose shadow spread for an incalculable distance. Here, the temperature from mountain-shadow became ever more frigid and the air thinned to the point where one's body would mummify from the lack of pressure.

The more talkative of those who roamed the steppes darkward often told of horrors hidden within the stoic faces of the mountains; great malevolences that manifested themselves to each person as their own internal fears given form to walk upon the world. Those who wandered far up into the Great Range would be consumed by their own madness.

I, of course, didn't put any stock in those stories. Perhaps there was a grain of truth to them, but it was so tiny as to be microscopic at best.

The most concerning thought I had was not the drunken tales of people who had never even been as close to this place as I was, but rather the unsettling idea of finding a way through the Great Range, only to be accosted by an even more gargantuan procession of monstrosities. What if a never-ending series of ranges grew ever taller, and trailed off to one giant peak at the Sunward Pole?

I knew that wasn't possible. But somehow, as irrational a fear as it was, it was still more sensible than old explorer's tales.

I had become accustomed to the comfortable hum of the ship and its various personalities. Order was not something I actively sought in my life, and yet, faced with the tremendous drop below, it felt like something I could play off against the unease from being so high, and having no access to the water pipe.

The other officers mostly avoided me at that time. I must have intimidated them. Nonetheless, I learned their names and positions through eavesdropping frequently. Mr. Pullnir was the first lieutenant of the ship, and one step above me. I instantly disliked that. Unlike the other officers, he didn't have an edge to him, which meant we shared no common ground. He largely stepped in time with the captain's orders, and was conservative and cautious in his actions. Must have been why she selected him out of her crew for that position.

He currently stood at the rear of the gondola, eyeing the ship's aft view, obviously watching for pursuers. All I could see of him was a brown ponytail that jutted out the back of his officer's bicorn, and rough hands clasped behind his back.

The Master of Altitude, Tian' Xi, was sprightly, as most Yin were. She was the polar opposite in character to Mr. Pullnir. She eschewed the officer's uniform in favor of a dirty long-sleeved shirt that was stained with grease. She hung in the ship's rigging, coordinating with her airmen.

Hans Evinsir, the Master of Navigation, was bent over the main control panel for the ship. In addition to the ship's wheel, a number of blinking LEDs and switches for the diesel engines of the ship splayed out along the panel. His craggy, white-bearded face screwed up in concentration as he directed the ship under less-than-full buoyancy.

Finally, the Master of Semaphore lounged in a hammock on the left side of the ship. I couldn't look in to see her face, but I would get the chance to make her acquaintance later.

The sudden arrival of Dr. Ininsir at the rail disturbed my reverie. I hadn't heard her approach – not good. This thin air played havoc with my focus. She peered ahead at the mountains and wrote quick notes in a weathered journal.

I figured I'd inquire about something that was bugging me. "Pitchblende."

"Yes?"

I stepped back from the edge and stretched. "Isn't helium uncommon in pitchblende?"

"Yes."

"You lied to the captain?"

"No, I exaggerated a bit. There is a process which separates out the various components of pitchblende by exposure to darkward salts. Some minerals with strange properties recombine with the darkward salts to form a toxic salt, and that can be used to create helium."

I scoffed. "People say the River can create from nothing, and I don't put much stock in them."

"I'm serious. Helium might be created out of nothing..."

"I'll believe it when I see it."

The Doctor sighed. "You're right though. The process will take several more rhythms than I gave the captain. I hope I can stall her until we've created enough helium to get us over the Range."

"We're just going to fly straight over it?"

"No. There's something on the map Dr. Hennir found, a pass.

It'll be a tight squeeze at the lowest altitude though." She turned to me. "It's more of a crevasse."

The hairs on my neck stood just thinking about the insanity of what we were about to do.

Dr. Ininsir turned back to her journal. "You should head belowdecks. I think I can see a flat plateau just below the mountains. We'll need that away team ready to go."

"Care to tell me what pitchblende looks like in the ground?"

"I'll be going with you to find it."

***

The time arrived for our departure. As I made my way to the outraptor bay, I kept a wary eye on the Beltlander crew.

Some tension over the end-rhythm's events still remained, but the crew seemed to be coping. Jokes rang out through the corridors as I passed by the mess area.

The end-rhythm meal had just begun. I smelled cooked grains, roots, tubors, pemmican, and a variety of enticing spices that were less familiar to me. My stomach growled, but I kept my distance. The Beltlanders acted funny. Some of them grabbed other airmen's dishes from the same table to bring them back to the cook. Others took up the mops along the wall of their own accord and began cleaning up the floor. It was all too nice. Maybe there was something in the food.

The crew drew from many different Beltlander nationalities. Some were Nordecker like myself. We almost uniformly had smooth rounded faces - similar to the Yin. Other airmen were clearly from Aula - the same place the doctors hailed from. You could tell by their eyebumps. Apparently they were cosmetic. Still others were from Ijritan, Drei, and a few were from the opposite side of the world. I couldn't begin to fathom the politics involved in keeping people from rival countries, like Aula and Nordecker, working together side-by-side in the Aery.

When I finally stood in the outraptor bay at the base of the gondola, I stared my personal outraptor down. Her long, sinuous neck bent and curved as she sized me up. She had beautiful emerald-green scales, black eyes, and a curious, black forked tongue that flickered out of her mouth as she continued to scan me.

She was tied up. Her gangly bird-legs extended and her tail swished from side to side impatiently. I allowed her to get closer and more comfortable with me. For now, I was her master – it made sense to have a good rapport with her. She snaked her thin neck over my shoulder, and then looped it around and over my other shoulder. I patted her head reassuringly.

After a few minutes of this, it was time. She was saddled up and ready to go, so I gently pushed her diamond-shaped head away, and swung myself up.

It was a small team. Dr. Ininsir, Yuri, and three midshipmen with their own outraptors. Yuri was having some difficulty in mounting his.

I clicked my mount forward as the outraptor bay doors opened, exposing the interior to positively freezing temperatures. The cold was deathly, easily colder than the steppe darkward at aphelion. My outraptor hissed grumpily at the chill and darkness, and hesitated. I reached into my saddlebag and brought out a long tube of fur, setting it around her neck, which she warbled pleasantly at.

All six of us urged our animals forward into the cold air.

Here at the base of the foothills, the mountain-shadow was most severe. We couldn't see a meter in front of us.

"Flares." I shouted out.

The light from six magnesium flares burst into existence.

The ground was packed with ice that twisted into lifeless fern-like forms that sprouted leafy fractal patterns. Larger ice crystals bushed up and outward like pictures of trees I had once seen long ago. Dead silence hung in the air. The only sound came from the Destiny's deck: airmen's shouts, swinging rigging, and the gurgle of diesel being loaded into her turbines. The sounds were dampened somehow, as if they were being absorbed into the ice beneath us. It was like the stillness of an icy tomb.

The others in the group took in the strange and alien view, amazed by what they saw. I breathed in deeply, tasting the cold air. I'd been here once before several years ago.

Not here exactly, but it was in this environment that I'd found the white tribespeople. My memory stirred, bringing those primordial faces back into the front of my mind.

I briefly fingered my twelve-shot revolver and drew a machete from my other side.

Then I urged my beast forward into the dark, as I cut through the jungle of ice.

***

A few hours later I heard a call from behind where Dr. Ininsir was riding many paces behind.

"Zintan! Over there!"

We had reached a point where the relative flatness of the plateau curved upward into a mountain cliff face. Through the creep of ice-plants up the side of the mountain, I saw gigantic rolling waves of rock that folded themselves into immense curves, reminding me of the old Nordecker bread loaves from my childhood. The concentration of ice formations was getting thinner here, which was a mercy to my wrist – now exhausted from slashing through the "undergrowth".

I had fared better than my companions though. Past experience served me well; the midshipmen shivered visibly. We'd been slowed significantly until I ordered the party into single file. I'd positioned the midshipmen in the middle of the group, huddling into their jackets and fingering their revolvers.

I hacked through one ice-vine in my way, pausing then to see what Dr. Ininsir was calling out about.

"Where?" I called back.

"In the mountain face!"

She was right. There, just barely perceptible through a sheet of ice, stood the entrance to a tunnel, visible because certain sections of the ice covering it had caved in, giving it a surface not unlike a rotten sponge.

I nodded. A good place for finding our quarry. Lucky we'd found this on the first rhythm.

I sensed Dr. Ininsir squeeze up the line to ride beside me.

"In there. That might run along under the mountain for a ways. That's our best shot."

"I agree. Yuri? Thoughts?"

Yuri was right behind me. As the party filed out of the path I'd made through the ice into the relative clearing ahead, he pulled up on my other side, his face doubtful. "We shouldn't go too far inside. I don't know about you, but I want more supplies carried here before we follow along the whole length. We might run out of torches..."

"I doubt it." I fingered my rucksack. There were at least two dozen in there.

Yuri nodded. "As long as you're good with it. Boys!" He

shouted the midshipmen out of their stupor. "Fasten the outraptors. Benson, Aldir, Wait outside for us. Hapsman, follow us in."

A few minutes later, we'd dismounted our beasts. Mine warbled again at me, her curious eyes ringed by her black-furred neck covering. I patted her reassuringly.

The ice sheet in front of us stood only a fourth of a meter thick at the thickest. I unstrapped an ice pick from my back and began cutting into it. The sound of the pick reverberated off the cliff, and this amplified it in the quiet air. Each hit felt like a gunshot. It sent prickles up my arms.

One section of the sheet finally collapsed, and a view of the tunnel beyond gaped before me.

My magnesium flare only lit up a certain way inside the cave, but from what I could tell, it was long, cylindrical in nature, and almost perfectly horizontal. The deepness in front of me, coupled with the strange undulations along the wall, gave me the impression of a throat, or animal intestine stretching away for many meters.

I stepped in, and the trio behind me followed. Our footsteps echoed off the wall with incredible volume. After hacking through the silent forest behind me, the loud noise jarred me.

Strange patterns attracted my eye the deeper we plumbed. They could be natural; ominously geometric triangles linked to others. A few meters later it gradually dawned on me that they could be human-made.

Twenty meters.

Thirty meters.

Forty meters.

Shadows danced on the wall, looking like faces in the rock. Then one of the faces didn't disappear under the light of the flare. Like the rock around it, it was a dull brown. Its eyes were closed, and its mouth hung open as if in fright.

I paused, and tensed immediately, my hand reaching for my gun in an instant. The group beside me halted, and all sound died in the cave apart from the slow hiss of our flares.

My eyes probed the expression of this being. Our presence must have scared it, so I assumed that it could react with hostility. I myself was surprised that any humanoid was able to last this far from the light.

Until I took a few steps closer, I operated with caution. But then,

I saw that it didn't react to our presence whatsoever. Its face was distorted, as though it was...

Dead.

I stepped closer, illuminating the figure further. It was definitely human. Most of its clothes were preserved along with it, as it was draped in various leather rags. It was slumped against the wall, with its head lolling towards the entrance of the cave. I realized I had been scared by a cadaver.

Above the body was a shock of red along the wall. A painting, across which little depictions of humans crawled on all fours.

Dr. Ininsir broke the silence. "Interesting. He must be a native." She bent down to examine the fallen human. "Perfectly mummified from the cold. A man, must be thirty, forty. Dr. Hennir would have a ball with him."

Yuri grunted with displeasure at the surprise. "Why is he down here?"

The doctor looked up at the painting. "This seems to depict some form of gathering, but I can't understand what." She looked around the mummy's head. "There's a puncture wound in his head, a very deep one. I have a feeling he was murdered."

"Why?" My question hung in the air.

"Tribal rivalry?" Yuri helpfully added.

"I don't think so. There's a painting here. He's been placed in a very particular way. Notice how his hands are folded over. He's been deliberately put here."

"A burial?" I was uncomfortable with the idea of disturbing the dead and angering his kinsfolk.

"Maybe. He could have been a sacrifice."

I felt a wave of nausea come over me, and I wondered how that statement had such an effect on me. Everyone knew that the fringes of civilization held undesirable and uncivilized peoples, and I reveled in mingling with them. The Yin themselves were uncivilized by Beltlander standards. Why should I be so nervous from discovering the handiwork of these people? Why did it shock me? Better to be on your guard instead in case the pale demons came to get you. But my revulsion remained.

I shook my head to clear my mind, and spoke. "Let's continue."

Several more meters past the remains, the tube suddenly curved naturally upward at an almost ninety degree angle. I left my pack with the others, and grabbed a hold of one of the folds in the surface. It was cool to the touch, and I hastily clambered up the wall to the top of the rise. It was barely four or five meters above the rest of the tunnel before it leveled off. I rested my torso against the rise, noticing that the tube bent back downward on the other side, as if the tunnel had been bent by some great uplift. A wave of vertigo passed through me with an even greater intensity.

I rested my hand against the floor of the bend and blinked. Why was I so dizzy? I shook my head and looked back towards the others. "Something's... not right..."

My voice was unnaturally high. The thought clicked in my head immediately. Helium. We'd found it.

I scampered down from my position.

"I've got this."

The voice belonged to the doctor. I turned to her in confusion. She hastily rummaged through her rucksack.

Yuri's grouchy voice echoed around the increasingly tight cave section. "Haye, we need to keep down here, don't poke your head too high or you'll breathe more of it in."

"We should go back! I don't want to suffocate down here!" The midshipman cried out.

Ininsir finally stood up in triumph, struggling with some sort of mask. "Pull yourself together Hapsman. Haye, catch!"

She finally succeeded in pulling the most horrific apparatus I have ever seen over her head, and threw one just like it in my direction.

The nightmarish quality of the device started with the rubber mask that tightly fit her face. Her eyes were hidden behind darkened and scratched glass portholes engineered into the mask, which were uncomfortably large and vaguely arthropoid. A long, corrugated nose drooped down from where the mouth should have been, hooking into a small metal canister at its base.

From behind the mask, the doctor spoke again in a muffled voice. "There's two like this one in your rucksack, Hapsman."

The boy immediately began scrabbling with his pack, while Yuri coughed and stepped towards the midshipman, his disgruntlement growing. "Mind distributing them more evenly next time?"

Hapsman finally pulled out the two masks, and then fell against the boulder at his back, gasping with panic.

Dr. Ininsir ran towards him, closing the distance as I yanked the apparatus over my head. She spoke softly to the boy as I struggled with the folds of the mask. "Even breathing. Even breathing. Now here, slip it on like so..."

I finally managed to tame the fabric, and slid the goggle lenses up towards my face. I could barely see out, and the whole mask reeked of some loathsome musk. Gradually, the temperature rose inside the mask, and small prickles of claustrophobia tore at the sides of my consciousness. The doctor finished stuffing the midshipman's head inside his own helmet.

Hapsman tried to follow the doctor's directions. The oversized mask gave the illusion that his head was far too big for his body.

"That's good, keep your breathing at that rate. See?" Dr. Ininsir slapped the midshipman on the shoulder.

I glanced deeper into the tunnel. "Doctor, are we good to go?"

The doctor shook her head. "We should go deeper to determine if this is truly the highest concentration of helium, or if the source is located further on."

Yuri cut in. "Further in?"

"Yes."

Hapsman began hyperventilating again. Dr. Ininsir grabbed his shoulders. "Remember: calm, regulated breathing."

I walked over to them and kicked the midshipmen sharply in the leg. "Knock it off, boy."

The doctor turned around and stared at me. I couldn't see her expression through the mask, but I got the feeling I had upset her with something I did.

Yuri picked up one of the fallen magnesium flares. It flickered low. Some native oxygen permeated the cave air, but it wasn't enough to sustain as bright a reaction from the flare. "How effective are these things?" he said, tapping at the mask on his face.

The doctor stood up as she answered. "Very. They don't filter out gas from the air. That's your oxygen supply down at the end. They won't last terribly long though, so be conservative with your breathing."

"Great. How long is your best estimate?"

"Twenty or so minutes if you breathe properly."

I spoke up. "Forward then. On your feet, Hapsman!" I reached down and grabbed his shoulder, setting him upright."

"Ye... Yes ma'am!" He managed to gasp.

The tunnel curved around, cracks winding their way through the surface and breaking up the molded texture. Adrenaline still pumped through me. We'd been walking at a rapid pace for seven or eight minutes now. The entire group kept silent, conserving our air.

I knew that helium suffused the air around me. Likely some other gases too, and at least enough oxygen to support an extremely weak flame from the flares, but certainly not enough of it to be breathable for long. Nonetheless, it felt no different than if it had been regular air. There were no visible signs indicating that this little pocket of death might ultimately be my crypt.

The tunnel widened. Our dimmed lights couldn't fill the void in front of us.

Finally the tunnel opened into a chamber. Multiple tunnel mouths like the one we'd exited gaped around the room. Light glowed from some massive space ahead of us.

It was a very faint, almost gentle, blue ambience that glowed out from further on in the room. We approached it cautiously, and my foot splashed in a shallow puddle of water. We crested the edge of a great pit and saw an amazing sight in front of us.

For a distance of several hundred visible meters, a vast lake of water stretched across an oblong-shaped room, its edges vacillating with more curves. The ceiling wasn't visible. At the deepest point of this crystal-clear pool, thirty or forty meters down, we saw the outlines of strange veins in the rock. Crystals that cut the water like so many jagged teeth covered the bottom. Through the depth of the water, the crystals shone with an uncanny light, illuminating the still water as nothing I'd ever seen before.

What mineral could produce such a wisp-like light?

Dr. Ininsir stood entranced by the view. She peered over the edge seemingly in stupefied silence, her face unreadable through the mask.

"Fascinating!" she exclaimed, awe writ large in her voice.

Yuri murmured agreement. "I'll second that."

"That pool... This... Augh." She groaned with frustration for some inexplicable reason.

"What?"

"This rewrites a number of things about our understanding of how helium can break conservation of matter." She shook her head.

"Nothing I'd expect would interest you, but still..."

My voice turned sharp. "Shouldn't we be returning, doctor?"

"Yes." She replied with frustration.

As we left our discovery for the exit, the doctor took one last glance at the pool, as if she were trying to capture the image in her memory for future use.

CHAPTER 3

The hammock swung gently from side to side, slowly losing momentum and drifting to stillness. Exhaustion wracked my body. It was several hours into the off-rhythm, and I – like most others – don't consider myself an off-rhythmer.

We had returned to the Destiny by the same way that we'd cut through the ice forest. After our discovery of a ready resupply source for the canopy, it didn't make sense to remain longer. We barely spent time to map out the various entrances that lead to the central, helium-producing chamber. Throughout the trip, I had often glanced back at the tunnel, and hoped to the sunward side I'd never be asked to return there.

Captain Nome had listened to our debrief quietly, only asking the bare minimum of questions while we recounted the discovery. After that session, the senior staff drew up a plan.

In the span of twenty minutes, the Destiny was relocated nearer to the mountain. On touchdown, the crew ran long hoses, their helium-refilling duty usually reserved for when the Destiny landed or docked at airport, inside of the tunnel we had stumbled out of. Meanwhile, Yuri jury-rigged together some of the onboard ballast pumps at the other end of the hoses inside the tube, where the helium concentration skyrocketed. The process was extremely efficiently organized at all levels, and I had my hands full coordinating with the officers.

At the end, satisfaction filled me that we would be in the air by the time on-rhythm broke.

The officer's barracks were quiet for the most part. The outlights that funneled natural sunlight into the barracks sat darkened. A small carbide lamp remained, placed at the center of a round table in the corner. The other officers played rounds of three-track in the glow with hushed voices.

I've never been one to sit out a game of three-track. During my stays at Mansu, I'd developed a keen ability for reading the people on the other side of a bout. It made me an expert at the game, and more than a few angered enemies. I turned over in my mind whether or not I wanted to join the game.

Eventually, the hushed whispers of the group sneaked into my brain, corrupting my light sleep. I swung my legs over the side of the hammock, and walked towards the group. If I won a few rounds, they would lose interest in the game and shut up. Then I could sleep.

It made me slightly tetchy to think that the rest of the officers chose this moment, when I needed to rest, to gamble this way. They were used to ignoring the low background noise around them. I was not. The steppe is quiet, but the Destiny could be unbearably loud.

As I drew closer, everyone at the table turned towards me. I saw unsure expressions form across their faces as my footsteps came closer and closer... and contempt in the face of Pullnir. But... I smiled as I saw Yuri there, and he squeezed his portly frame over to the right as he saw me approach. I nodded my thanks, and turned to the current Seller, speaking shortly. "Deal me in."

The table was quiet. The Master of Semaphore hiccuped slightly, holding a drink in her hand. Good. My first target.

Pullnir leaned in. "Welcome to the game, Ms. Zintan. We're on the second Inning; the small pot is at fifty. Buy in is at twenty." His face returned to a neutral expression, but I could tell he would be gunning for me.

I pulled twenty worth of Yinlus out of my pocket, slapping them down perfunctorily. The Seller doled out five cards in my direction, and I had them organized in a few seconds.

I looked them over. Two of squares, three of wheels, six of cardinals, archbanner of squares, three of cardinals. One pair, high squares. I glanced over at the Master of Semaphore again. "So ma'am, I don't believe I caught your name."

"Alanin... hic... Dostwikr."

"Dostwikr eh?" I smiled again slightly. "Care for high trade?"

Pullnir narrowed his eyes at me. "The pit isn't open. And it's not your turn."

"I'm not going out of turn, just curious if she's up for it."

Yuri laughed with a mock exclamation. "Come on Haye, don't

ruin her!"

"Aery rules. No negotiated trading." Pullnir folded his arms in front of him. "I understand the Yin have different ideas, but this is a ship of the wall. We don't deal darkwardly here."

I folded my cards into a single stack. "I wouldn't suggest anything else." My smile intensified as I stared the first lieutenant in the eyes.

After a couple seconds of electric silence, the Seller, Tian' Xi, spoke up in a heavily Yin-accented voice "Open. Haye, you wanted a high trade?"

I smiled warmly at her, and replied in Yin, "I was going to try and give lieutenant Dostwikr a fighting chance, but sure, since you asked nicely." I pulled the six of cardinals out, and slipped it face down on the table over to her in return for another card.

Tian' Xi smiled back, replying in Yin. "Thank you. Sorry the first lieutenant is a fartbag."

My translation of her description was somewhat liberal.

Pullnir was incensed, even though he couldn't understand what we were saying. "In Simplified Standard, please."

Tian' Xi's smile disappeared from her face. "Sorry, lieutenant."

I flipped the card up so I could view it. Two of cardinals. I did my best to conceal my tics. Two pair. High squares.

Excellent.

Even better, I'd found out who I trusted to not place me at the top of their target list. That gave me room to compete for Dostwikr's buy-in, and deny it to Pullnir. I knew how defensively Yuri played. He would be a tough nut to crack, but ultimately one I'd cracked before. The Master of Navigation, Evinsir, he was the wild card. That put him in a good spot, but if I could draw him out... have him overplay his hand...

The early game unfolded like I expected it to. I laid low and allowed the others at the table to play aggressively. At the last moment, I swept in and took the "small" pot.

Given that everyone had themselves bet small amounts for the large pot, the small pot ended up being much bigger than the large pot. I smiled as I collected my winnings.

As the mid-game commenced however, I became acutely aware of a dark figure staring at us from the opposite corner of the room. I briefly glanced back at it, and saw the ship's chaplain. He had no expression on his face, but his eyes spoke volumes as he stared at us disapprovingly. Nonetheless, he made no movement to stop us or even protest our gambling. He simply stood there, straight as a rod, silent and almost barely perceptible in his black robe against the bulkhead of the ship.

I felt a moment of anger. Why was he here? Didn't he have anything better to do with his time?

The bets were heating up now. Like I had at first, I waited until the last moment to swoop in, and received a hefty prize from the small pot once again.

Pullnir got the large pot though. I felt a flash of annoyance course through me. Time to up my game.

By this time, both Tian' Xi and Dostwikr had folded for good. Evinsir held on, barely. I'd discovered he didn't like to bet too much regardless of the circumstances. Yuri played his usual game. Pullnir meanwhile, aggressively tapped his fingers on the table.

I took a brief moment to glance back over my shoulder. The chaplain still stood there. I bared my teeth and returned to the game.

I pulled out all the stops. Bet after bet raised between Pullnir and me. Finally, it came down to the two of us. I had the upper hand, and I knew it.

Our eyes were locked.

Finally, the lieutenant... folded.

I smiled in triumph, and slammed my card down onto the table in the middle of the third track, reaching for the small pot.

And suddenly realizing my mistake, I groaned inwardly.

Yuri and Evinsir high-fived and grinned as they each doled out half the large pot – thick with obscene bets from both Pullnir and me.

"Haye! I'm surprised at you!" Yuri laughed. "You're getting rusty!"

"Tough luck there first lieutenant sir." Evinsir's rasped out. "If we played with Yin rules, you might stand a better chance."

Across the table, Tian' Xi chuckled. Pullnir slumped back against the wall, completely silent.

I couldn't lose this way. This badly. This stupidly. "Third Inning." I demanded.

Evinsir grunted wearily at me. "Buy-in would be thirty."

I rummaged around in my pockets, only coming up with twenty-five. My mood soured even further.

Yuri noticed. "It was a good game, Haye. Leave it be." He patted a hand on my shoulder.

I nodded curtly and stood up abruptly. "A fine game. Good night."

As I walked stiffly back to my hammock, the priest had disappeared. My blood boiled. If he hadn't stood back there the whole time, boring into my back, I'd have won that game handily. I even had most of the players figured out.

Why did he care whether we gambled?

It wasn't his ship.

***

I woke hours later, the only change evident being the loud thump of sky boots on the deck above me as airmen went about the on-rhythm change of crew. The off-rhythmers would head downstairs in a bit, ensuring another hour of loudness on the deck below until the off-rhythmers went to sleep. I resolved to be on deck within five minutes.

When I pulled myself out of the fore hatch, the on-rhythmers were pulling up the remainder of the helium resupply hoses. Above the ship, the great bulk of the mountain loomed over us ominously, like a sword of Antir. If the cliff face were to fall down, triggered by another tremor, like the one in the tunnel, would there be any one of us left alive to limp back to civilization?

I surveyed the few airmen currently left out of the gondola, trying to gauge a time until we flew off into the sky. Out of the corner of my eye, I saw Yuri walking towards me from Destiny's aft deck, rubbing his hands - from the cold, I hoped, and not because he was extremely satisfied by last night's performance.

"So." He spoke as soon as he got to me. "Two hours rustwork. That's what I'm offering."

"For how much?" I snapped.

"Ten. That should get you into the buy-in for two Innings if you're smart about it."

My shoulders slumped. "One for five?"

"Sorry Haye, it's a package deal."

I leaned against the railing. "What could possibly be rusty on this rig? She's top-notch."

"Ah, but you haven't seen her steering mechanism." He shuddered. "Great piece of engineering. Horrible maintenance."

I remained silent.

"You know," he continued, "That rivalry between you and Pullnir is incredibly useful. If you keep that up, I'll definitely be the richest one aboard by the time we turn around." He chuckled, but then stopped once he saw my expression.

"So you won, congratulations. What's the score stand at now? Seventeen to thirty-six?"

"That's not the important thing, Haye." His tone became glum. "We're gears on this ship. Pullnir may be a bit bent out of shape, but he's the master gear. We've both been on jobs out there with more... eh... 'zhopoliski' at the helm."

He leaned on the railing next to me while inquiring, "How'd he piss in your brew?"

"He's the captain's good little boy. When I need to get away from the White Hats, he'll want to turn me over." I stared straight ahead.

"Ah. Fair point." Yuri nodded.

I shot him a glance, "I'd rather not give you all my spare pocket change."

We stared out at the ice for a while, taking in the silence. As the Destiny's canopy was sealed shut, creaks snapped along the hull as the ship's buoyancy pitted against the diesel ballast.

"So what did you think of our discovery in there?"

"Hmm?" I backed away from the railing and leaned against a nearby crate.

"The dead guy?" Yuri folded his arms in front of him.

"Oh. I thought you were talking about the pool."

"Naw." He waved a hand in my direction. "Savage, ain't it? Reminds me of that time we caught up to the guy who'd been rustling andironbacks? Head caved in and all. Imagine they do that all the time, the people that live here."

"Do what?" Dr. Ininsir had walked up behind us.

Both of us turned to stare at her.

"Uh..." She rubbed the back of her neck. "Just curious..."

Interest got the better of me. "Doctor. How did you know to pack those respirators?"

"Standard for delving into pitchblende-heavy places. The scientific community has long known of those kinds of helium pockets."

Yuri scoffed. "And you failed to mention it to us?"

"I was focused on other things." The doctor sniffed and poked her glasses higher on her nose. "I didn't have the time to orient you on all of the possible dangers."

I took a step forward, my eyes narrowing at her.

"But, nonetheless, I apologize. It was a bad slip of my memory."

"Gears, doctor!" Yuri groaned with frustration and abruptly sat down on the deck.

I regarded her for a moment, realizing that she wasn't going away. "What was in that pool? That glowing? It looked like a gas light."

"It's a phenomenon tentatively labeled 'lightrotting'. Its very existence is controversial." She suddenly rubbed her hands together in excitement. "Especially now that we can link it with helium generation! This raises all kinds of questions for my colleagues in Pesldin. That pool would be the target of its own expedition if I had my way. And just think!" She pointed in the direction of the Great Range. "That's only what we've discovered on the first leg of this journey! What more is waiting for us over that Range?"

My face remained firm at her enthusiasm, but in some senses I shared her curiosity.

The doctor's face fell as she saw Yuri stretching himself against the rail, and my stoic expression. She became annoyed. "Yes. Well then. I was told to relay that the captain wants you to become accustomed with the gun crews and our armament for the duration of your service on the Destiny."

I twitched slightly, but acknowledged the statement with a nod.

Ininsir sputtered some nonsense. "She looks after her crew..."

"Yes. I'm sure."

Yuri spoke up to me from his sitting position. "Remember our game, Haye."

For once in a good long while, I almost barked a curse at Yuri, but just as I was about to, a huge irregular rock plummeted out of the sky, and buried itself in the back of an airman to my left with a sickening, meaty thump. I jumped into a running sprint for cover.

The cry went up from the rigging, joined haltingly by a scattering of panicked voices. "Savages... Savages!"

I looked around the side of the crate I'd taken cover behind, and saw their faces peering through the ice ferns.

They were as I'd remembered them from my earlier expeditions up here. Strange pale faces that never knew the sun, the light from magnesium flares bouncing off their eyes in a menacing way. Heads shaved completely bald around the rims, with bones piercing their cheeks and tattoos in geometric patterns that crisscrossed their entire bodies. Furry rags wrapped around their entire bodies haphazardly, exposing many patches of flesh to the elements. Their hair hung in straight lines that shook as they crept out of the ice forest. They barely wore anything that resembled footwear, besides another clump of fur around their feet. They shook rocks and leather slings in their hands, but they were deathly quiet as they did so, like the expanse of white around them.

These were the white savages of the Great Range.

One of them at the forefront of their group began swinging a shot around his head, and I heard the whistling from my position several meters away.

The Destiny exploded into a frenzy of action. The lines holding her down were lifted rapidly, and those left on the ground scrambled to ascend into the gondola before she could take off. The aft hatchway opened, and Captain Nome burst out into the air as the crew swirled around her.

I figured I wouldn't allow the tribesman to get off another shot at us, so I drew my revolver, aimed, and fired for his torso. The shot went wide, but it caused him to halt from the sound long enough for me to fire off another shot. This one went home, and he suddenly clutched his abdomen and gave an unearthly howl as he dropped to the ice. Red blood flecked the ice-covered ground behind him.

The natives suddenly began to yip, hopping about as though they had suddenly gone mad. A few of them began charging up their own bullets to pelt at us.

And then, I saw them. Standing there in the middle of the native line, were the unmistakable tall forms of the White Hats.

A stunned thought pulsed through me in a split second: how did they get here!?

All three of them raised bolt-action rifles in unison, and aimed straight at me.

I rolled barely in time as their muzzles flashed. Three high-caliber bullets whistled through the space I had previously occupied. A couple of airmen unloaded disorganized fire on the troupe below.

That angered the natives more, and they charged forward towards the ship.

I felt the ship move beneath me, and she began to rise. I heard Captain Nome shouting orders.

"Engage the turbines. Get us as far away from their firing range as possible."

"But sir, we need more helium..." I didn't know who the voice belonged to.

"Do it now!"

"Yes sir."

"Dostwikr, douse the lights!"

The turbines engaged, and instantly their screech overwhelmed my hearing. The Destiny immediately began to pick up speed, and the mountain in front of us loomed even closer.

I ran to the aft of the ship, catching a glance at Evinsir's navigation pit. His eyes were wide open, focused intently on the view in front of him as he frantically turned the ship's wheel.

I made it to the aft as the ship reached an approach of 45 degrees with the cliff face. I searched for an object to brace myself against. I knew we would be impacting the cliff.

More shots rang out below us from the White Hats, but thankfully, they went wide this time.

We were now at 70 degrees. I closed my eyes and awaited the inevitable. Why did I ever agree to that job back in Ilu? Why did I agree to this mission?

The captain yelled out, "All hands brace for impact!"

Time stopped. I felt nothing but cold air on my skin, heard nothing but the frantic yells of airmen, smelled nothing but the scent of shadow-chilled air. Seconds passed.

I opened my eyes again.

We were traveling parallel to the cliff face. The collision had been averted. I sighed in relief.

More shots from several meters down below drew my attention again. I looked over the railing again at the rapidly fading area where we had been, still lit with flares we'd left behind. It was a pointless exercise to fire at us now. We saw them, and they couldn't see us. White natives swarmed the area, tearing at the supplies we'd left behind, poking at them, and burning their hands on the magnesium fires.

The Destiny began speeding away from the site quickly, and rounded the corner of the cliff, aiming for a pass between the two titans ahead of us.

When we were two minutes away, and fading into the shadowed mountains, I heard a blood-curdling shriek from our aft.

I heard more panicked screams from the airmen. "What was that!?"

"Where are they!?"

I knew they were after us again. In the darkward lands, they knew them as Shaffengur. The Beltlanders wove tales about how they would steal children from cribs, or even whole houses. The Yin, who'd never seen them, still repeated travelers' tales of giant monstrous beasts, whose form was too indescribably horrific to relate. A tangle of a thousand spindly limbs, grotesque and unordered, attached to an armored torso that lacked a body plan. And yet, somehow from this form sprouted wide, membranous wings that carried these creatures aloft.

I'd heard that scream once before, at the governor's palace in Mansu. Flickers of remembered images rippled through my mind. Long bony, multi-jointed fingers. A bulbous mass encased in chitin. A wrinkled, snarling head.

The White Hats were riding them. They were coming for us.

I grabbed one of the airmen assigned to the Destiny's gun crew. "Man the cannons," I ordered frantically.

The airman looked at me, at a loss for words. Fear overwhelmed him; throughout his time in the Aery, he had never heard a shriek to rival the one that had sounded to the ship's rear. And he was being ordered by someone he didn't know, who had never commanded him before, who, according to rumor across the ship, was a presumed criminal responsible for the situation they were in right now. I released my grip on his shoulders, and saw others from the gun crew standing around staring out at the blackness.

I decided to swallow my pride. I swiftly turned towards where the captain stood, and ran up to her. She had heard the Shaffengur cries, and her face searched the aft of the ship in vain for a glance at what pursued us.

I almost stumbled over my words as I spoke. "Captain, I need the gun crew to assemble at the aft guns."

Some small, distrustful part of me expected her to sneer at my request. That part of me disappeared when she nodded her approval, and called out a command with force behind her voice.

"Gun crew! Report to the aft cannons and follow your commanding officer's orders. NOW!"

The airmen jumped into action.

The captain turned her attention towards me. "Load tracers in the aft and fire at your discretion. Do *not* let them get close enough to cut us out of the sky."

She turned rapidly to Evinsir. "Master of Navigation, fly like hell!"

A crowd assembled at the aft hatchway, scrambling inside like the Nemesis itself followed after them. In the chaos, I shoved my way through the gun crew, and slipped down the ladder with great alacrity. Below decks, the sounds of airmen shouting resounded through the cramped space. The regular smell of diesel in the air melded with the disgusting odor of sweat from the crew. In the aft firing chamber, a third smell added to the vomit-inducing mix: gunpowder.

The barrels of the Destiny's cannons were massive compared to what I had seen previously among the Yin; they were definitely Beltlander make. Each of the twin aft guns fired shells of the twelve-iander. A ridiculous caliber of artillery for a ship. At the moment, I was as glad for the punch that they had as I was of the fact that they were mounted on pivots that gave them a more flexible range of fire. With practiced exactitude, two of the airmen unlatched the rears of the cannons in preparation to receive ammunition.

I called out in the tight space. "Load tracers, set for flak!"

The crew formed a line from the ammunition stored at the fore part of the chamber to the guns, and quickly passed forward two of the tracer shells.

Another scream sounded, this time much closer than the first.

The crew on the left fumbled with the shell, almost dropping it. The one on the right was ready first.

"Targeting?" The wincher on the right called out.

I furrowed my brow. The Shaffengur sounded as though it was barely a kilometer back. "Timer for one second. Aim at three degrees, ninety to ship's plane."

The wincher began cranking the cannon into position as the crew timed and loaded the shell. The rear of the gun slammed shut behind it.

I stepped up to the viewport in the center between the guns and peered out. Complete darkness filled the air behind the Destiny.

"On my mark."

The crew tensed. "Left gun ready!"

I slammed my hands over my ears. "Right gun fire!"

A great concussive rush of air filled the chamber as the muzzle to the right outside the viewport flared bright. The blast noise was deafening, only slightly muffled by my hands. I blinked, and saw the tracer round streak through the air briefly, before exploding in a brilliant flash of light far off.

The blast clearly fell behind our pursuers. The light of the flash backlit three silhouettes. Their bodies were long and sinuous, with limbs as grotesque as my memory related. These ones, in contrast to that recollection however, were fully grown. Some of their longer limbs trailed like thin, atrophied vines behind them.

The shriek sounded again, this time with considerable anger. As we'd opened fire, they had sighted us.

"Left gun, new angle! Minus two degrees, one hundred to ship's plane."

The left wincher cranked furiously. The right gun crew meanwhile opened the rear of the gun, allowing the smoking cartridge to fall outside onto the floor.

"Left gun fire!"

Another deafening blast, and our shot sailed through the air again before exploding closer to the Shaffengur, but still behind them.

The wincher on the right called out, her voice increasingly worried. "Right gun ready sir!"

"Angle: minus three, ninety-eight to ship's plane." The beasts were getting closer. If we didn't take them down in the next volley, they would be all over us.

"Fire!"

The shot flew further than the last shot. Our pursuers had zigzagged out of its path.

"Left gun jammed!"

My blood ran cold. The right gun couldn't reload in time. We had only seconds. I heard the beasts flapping as they closed the distance – they were only a third of a kilometer away.

"Right gun ready!"

I almost turned towards them, puzzled, but stopped myself, and instead calculated a shot. "Right gun, move to five degrees, ninety-five to ship's plane. Hold fire."

I looked through the viewport, calculating.

"Sir?"

A bead of sweat dripped down my forehead.

"Sir?"

"Hold fire!" I snarled, waiting until they were closer.

"Orders, sir?!"

"OPEN FIRE!" I yelled out.

The right gun sang its powerful song, and the shot flew through the air in half a second, finally hitting home and striking the creature in among its tangled mass of limbs. The shockwave ripped many of them off, leaving trails of some sort of black ichor before the vision faded.

Intense agony filled the shriek, this time.

To my relief the sound of their gargantuan wings faded, presumably as the other White Hats descended to help their leader. After several seconds, when the noise had finally faded away, one of the gun crew cried out, "They're gone!"

Immediately, cheers and yells of "UURRRAAAAH" broke out among the crew of the Destiny, which rivaled the firing of her guns for volume of sound.

CHAPTER 4

Many hours into on-rhythm, I still stared out into the void behind the Destiny with my back against a secured crate. I leaned cross-legged and nervous; the albedo from the red crescent outside the mountain-shadow, reflected more light further up from the ground. We were no longer in pitch blackness. In one sense, this comforted me, since the White Hats couldn't get the jump on us again. On the other hand, we were more exposed up here.

And they would be back. While their delay may be considerable, the White Hats' creature would be fully healed in three rhythms, perhaps two if we were unlucky. Then, they would do what they always did with their marks. Even if this map of Dr. Hennir's really did drive us over the Great Range, it wouldn't matter. They would hunt us down to the very Sunward Pole itself.

A shiver of mixed anger and fear poured through me as I contemplated my pursuers.

At the very least, I knew how they would plan their next moves now. If we were to make it over the Range, we would be in sunlight again. The only reason they were bold enough to attempt an all-out assault against the Destiny this time was that they had the darkward advantage. Over the Range, they wouldn't risk such a tactic again.

The Destiny was now the andironback to their pack of outraptors. They would be watching, following. If they saw an opportunity – low on supplies, landed, or something else – that is when they would strike, just as outraptors do to exhausted or sick andironbacks.

My mind raced as I thought through points where we would be the most vulnerable. We needed a plan to defend ourselves from them. If we couldn't do that, we at least needed to lose them for a while if we had to gather supplies from the land. I knew, without knowing what awaited us over the Range, that we would need to do that at some point. If we didn't manage to lose them or fend them off, we would be dead within the next few weeks.

This reminded me of the incident in the gun chamber. The left gun needed maintenance. And that gun crew needed more training; they had fumbled after all. We couldn't have the cannon locking up in the middle of a fight again.

I heard the soft pitter-patter of feet behind me, and looked around to see Hapsman, the midshipman, approaching. "Zintan sir, the captain wants to see you in her ready room."

***

It was strange being in Captain Nome's ready room again so soon after our harrowing escape. For one thing, I was completely alone with her. The crowd of faces around me that had characterized my last tense visit were absent. Mind you, I still didn't trust the captain, so my hair almost stood on end when I walked into the room.

For another thing, aside from a gas light on her desk, the room lacked all illumination. The three windows at the back were almost pitch black, only letting in the barest of ambient lighting.

I sat across from her, silent while she wrote something in the ship's log. Finally, she looked up at me and folded her hands, searching my expression for something.

It was a tense few moments before I decided that I'd had enough with her trying to intimidate me.

"The gun crews need more training on the ship's battery. I had one team mess up this rhythm."

The captain didn't blink. "I heard a cannon jammed?"

"That's not the problem, even though the guns could use more maintenance." I leaned back and put my hands behind my head. "No. The team was fumbling about when it came time to load the flak. Almost dropped the shell. Their reload time was also significantly worse than the other team's."

"You should reserve time over the upcoming ten-rhythm to drill them."

"I was going to do that, yes."

Another silence passed between us.

Finally, I snarled out in irritation, "Why did you call me down here?"

Captain Nome suddenly stood up. "First of all, that is not how you talk to me on this ship, or anywhere else for that matter. You will address me as Captain, or Sir, and you *will* work on that attitude." She briefly flashed me a look of anger... before surprisingly softening her gaze. "Now. I have called you down here to inform you of an important change of policy."

She walked over to a shelf on the wall, on which stood various miniature models of airships, glistening with chrome finish. Their names were embossed below them on little plaques: *Aeon, Zeir, Constellation, Entrepreneur... Destiny.*

Wait, I'd never noticed that before...

Below her model collection hung a shelf holding nothing but a series of leather-bound books, worn from frequent use. She pulled one out from the end and held it up in front of her.

"Dr. Hennir has loaned me a book from her personal collection detailing an almanac of sorts on the groups operating in the Yin steppe. You'll be glad to hear that it details the activities of the White Hats in quite gruesome detail."

I squinted. "What are you getting at?"

"I've had a change of heart, Haye Zintan, and I'd like to make it clear that I have no intention of handing you over to the Yinda's men, or to the White Hats at any point now or after the expedition." She turned to face me. "Do I make myself clear?"

I sat there stunned, and more than a little distrustful. "That's not what I heard the last time I sat here."

"What you heard were the words of a captain concerned for the well-being of her crew, and perceiving a potential threat on board her ship." She finally blinked. "Incidentally, why does the Yinda want you dead so badly? You had mentioned a past incident vaguely, but never explained it to me in full. I took it to be something horrendous."

"Book-running job gone wrong. Long story." I folded my arms in front of me.

Her hand ran softly down the spine of the volume she held. "Book-running..." she mused.

"Yes."

"Well then, there are a few things I will insist on for the duration of this expedition in return for my leniency. One: every first-rhythm, you will consult with the ship's chaplain, and he will spiritually educate you to the best of his ability."

Very few things in life jar me. Being ordered to visit a priest is somewhere on that list however. My jaw dropped. "What!?"

"Yes. I am very concerned for the ultimate fate of your soul. Even if you are telling the truth about your book-running, something that can hardly be called a crime, I know from Dr. Hennir that you have a reputation as an outlaw. If I am to take you aboard as a crew member, and forgive all that you've put the Destiny through, I must demand that you are held to the same standard – higher even – as any common airman."

My face contorted into a snarl. "You can't do this. This is pointless. I don't believe."

"In time you will. Or perhaps you won't. Nonetheless, I have faith that you will take from his lessons a sense of what is morally expected of you on this ship. I must again state that this is something I demand of every airman on my ship. I am not singling you out as an unbeliever." She returned to her desk and sat down. "The next thing I must demand of you is that you not cheat at cards when you bout with your fellow officers. Very bad form." Her expression remained deadpan.

"I... what?"

"You heard me. At multiple points during three-track last night, you advertised high trades when you had significantly better cards to offer. While not technically cheating, it is highly frowned upon by officers of the Aery. You'll want to pass that message on to your colleague Yuri Aldarin as well, though his behavior certainly isn't as egregious."

"How did you..." My anger faded back into unease.

The captain smiled at that point. "I have many eyes around the ship. A captain who does not know what her crew is up to can hardly be considered a captain at all."

I suddenly realized. The chaplain. I had to be careful around him.

"And that list extends beyond just the chaplain, in case you think you've figured it out." The captain folded her hands again. "I think we're done here for the moment. Here is your agenda." She opened a separate notebook from the ship's log.

"Item one. As previously mentioned, train the ship's gun crew. Make sure we are not caught in a situation like we were a few hours ago. I leave it to your discretion as to how you will schedule training.

"Item two. Organize a resupply team for hunting expeditions. In one month's time, the ship should make a landing on the other side of the Great Range in order to resupply the ship's stores. As you are our wilderness survival expert, I expect you to lead this effort.

"Item three. Attend first-rhythm meeting with the ship's chaplain.

"Item four. Attend airman first class Jif Turndr's memorial service next rhythm at mid-bells. I have just received word of his death from the ship's barber twenty minutes ago."

A series of conflicting emotions were running through my head. "He didn't make it?"

A shadow passed over Nome's face. "No. He didn't."

I sat there contemplating it. The Destiny's first death. The first of many. Nothing I hadn't been exposed to before, but it affected the captain quite deeply.

The captain straightened in her chair before speaking again. "That will be all."

I stood up, eager to leave the chamber before the captain unloaded any other demands on me. As I reached the door however, I heard her speak at my turned back. "One last thing."

I paused. "Yes?"

"Good shooting."

***

Several hours later into on-rhythm, I was squeezing through the depths below decks, inside the cramped space that held the Destiny's steering mechanism.

"Remind me why I need to be in here with you?"

Yuri continued rummaging around the oily tangle of gears and pistons that continued to operate centimeters from his face. "Hold up a second." His face contorted into a grimace as he narrowly avoided having his fingers crushed beneath the operating machinery. Finally, something clicked, and his face brightened as he retracted his limbs in possession of a rod encrusted on every surface with tarnish. "All right! There we go. Molodyets!"

He pushed himself away from the mechanism, and leaned his bulk against the back wall while wiping his brow. He chuckled. "Now you see what I mean!"

"Uh..." I peered at the still operating mechanism. "That wasn't an important part, was it?"

"What? No!" He laughed. "I had Evinsir switch to the redundant system for now so that we could work on this beauty here. At least, I think I did..." he scratched his head while I narrowed my eyes at him.

He looked at me and snickered. "Just kidding!"

I punched him in the shoulder lightly.

Once he'd gotten over his 'joke', he continued. "So, this is the first component, I'll bring the second one out to you in a bit, but you can get started now. The bucket and brush are outside."

I groaned. "Why'd you make me come in here then?"

"So that I don't have to make a second trip in here." He slapped his belly. "Something of a tight squeeze."

I rolled my eyes and began sliding my way over to the crawlspace's exit, taking care not to entangle my shirt in the rapidly clanking pistons – a task easier conceived than carried out.

A small, lithe hand greeted me at the exit to the crawlspace. "Need help with that?" I recoiled at first, but then, recognizing Tian' Xi's outstretched palm, handed over the rusted metal part before carefully extracting myself from the crawlspace and into the hallway beyond.

I staggered slightly before regaining my balance, and glanced at her before proceeding to dust myself off. "Thank you. What brings you here?"

She raised an eyebrow at me. "Two hours rustwork for ten worth of Yinlus. Wait." She smiled. "He gave you the same deal?"

I nodded.

"Son of a bitch. That has to be over a quarter of his winnings." She snapped her fingers while peering back through the crawlspace.

Something about her demeanor was infectious, and I found amusement flicker across my face briefly as I rubbed the back of my neck.

"Hallo! What was that something about my winnings?" Yuri's ruddy face suddenly popped into view.

Tian' Xi ignored the question. "I tried to convince Dostwikr to take up your offer. She didn't bite."

"Aw." Yuri pouted. "It appears I will have to take the third bucket after all."

"Come on, you loaf." I was sorely tempted to punch him again.

All three of us grabbed the buckets and brushes Yuri had stashed down besides the crawlspace, and set to work on the parts he had supplied. The smell of brinefruit juice hung thick in the air.

We talked briefly in between scrubbings. I loosened up to the Master of Altitude after a while; she seemed like she had a head on her shoulders.

"So I heard the captain gave you a talking to." She said at one of our many intervals.

"Yeah."

"What happened?"

"Among other things, in return for immunity from our trackers, I'm to see the ship's chaplain."

Yuri briefly snorted before a quick look in my eyes silenced him.

"Ah." Tian' Xi smiled dolefully.

"She said something about being held to the same standard as every airman. Bullcrap is what I think of that."

"No, she only sends officers to the chaplain if they've been cheating at cards."

Yuri definitely snickered in full this time. I opened my mouth in protest. "Now hold on..."

"Oh what? You think I didn't know?" The Master of Altitude snapped a wry look at me. "Really? Now I *am* offended."

"I didn't..."

"No, you did, and it was obvious." She grinned and switched to speaking Yin. "I let you get away with it because it was fun watching you stand up to the first lieutenant like that. It's not good having someone like that as your commanding officer."

"He doesn't seem to like you or anyone from the steppe much."

"No. He doesn't."

A frustrated shout from Yuri at our unintelligible conversation interrupted us. "Oi! Speak normal, yes?"

I patted his shoulder. "Ponjatno."

The engineer threw up his hands in mock frustration. "I give up. We're on the ship of the River now, with as many tongues and speeches in one rhythm as the Basilica hears in a year."

Now it was my turn to chuckle.

"You know." Tian' Xi stopped in the middle of her work. "That is interesting. What languages do you know besides Yin and Standard?"

When she didn't get an answer, she glanced over at me. "Zintan?"

I wasn't listening to her. My ears had picked up a noise from the deck.

A loud drumroll came from up top. Snare drums. Followed by a loud voice, faintly discernible against the background noise of the ships turbines.

"All hands to quarters! All hands to quarters!"

***

I took one look around after I'd pulled myself through the fore hatchway, and was stunned at the progress we'd made in the course of half a rhythm. The foothills were almost behind us, a remnant of their bulk slithering forward like a snull into the horizon ahead of us.

We were encased in an orange gleam of light that only affected the Destiny. Mountain shadow hid everything else around us. I tried to scry its source.

Then, the ship's lookout called out from the fore rigging. "Thar she rises! Say your prayers to the River, lads and lasses!"

I suddenly felt an urge to run towards the fore of the ship. With great excitement, I almost sprinted the short distance to the gondola's head, and peered out into the ray of light that surrounded the ship.

I first noticed that the ground and the fast-flowing river of clouds below were illuminated with the same light in a spectacularly straight line across the ground kilometers below. Shadow fell around it. Deep shadow. Colossal shadow. The great absence of light that characterized almost everywhere else in this forsaken place, became pitch black ahead of us to the sides.

Then, my gaze swept upward in the blink of an eye, suddenly my excitement turned to awe.

Above me at an incalculable distance in kilometers, a red band streaked through the sky. The sun's rays in the black above us, shining over the tops of indescribably titanic peaks, appeared like a bright squiggle of a rogue penman, jutting out the form of one mountain after another. I couldn't see the faces of the Great Range, except from what penumbra radiated out from the strange light ray that encompassed us. That bare glimpse revealed worn and wrinkled rock that had been rolled by the same forces as the cliff side that we had witnessed in the foothills. Underlying the stillness of the silhouettes in front of us, a distant, but clearly loud roar of wind, separated the deathly quiet foothills behind us from my mind completely.

The light directly ahead of us in that line was so bright. Punishingly so. My eyes fell to squinting as I strained to glimpse what lay ahead of us. My skin felt the Sun's natural warmth for the first time since boarding the train to Kinyu. A range of emotions passed through me. Exhilaration, awe, dread at the godlike forms ahead of me, and... longing. The sunward side called to me from beyond the Great Range.

Since I couldn't see what lay ahead, I looked backwards, and saw that the line of light shone directly into the back of one of the enormous foothills behind us. Nobody had discovered it until now. Now we were truly treading into the unknown. Sailing on forbidden winds.

I couldn't contain myself. I let out an ululating cheer of anticipation, before I realized that no one else shared in my feelings. Or perhaps, no one else cared to scream as I did.

I looked around at the many pairs of eyes staring at me from the common airmen.

"What are you looking at?" I blustered.

The airmen resumed their tasks. The captain called out, "Master of the Battery, to the aft."

I walked briskly away from the view up front, trying to hide any embarrassment in my walk. When I arrived aft, I saw the captain and the two doctors, along with the rest of the officers gathered in a circle. Dr. Hennir held open a hefty volume containing what appeared to be a section of a map, drawn in a highly stylized form.

They knew this was here. I furrowed my brow.

Captain Nome barely paid me any notice before posing a question to the doctor. "What time estimate do you have? Or if you can't give me that, can you give me a distance at least?"

"Twelve kilometers. We should be there in little under half an hour if you throttle up to top speed." The doctor firmly answered.

"With the wind against us? Your estimate accounts for that, right?" Nome scratched her chin.

"We picked the time when the passage was the least turbulent. We are confident within a standard deviation of two minutes."

"Ara, I'm trusting you." She looked meaningfully at the doctor. "I'm trusting you to be right about this."

The doctor nodded stoically.

"All right. Evinsir, we're going to need maximum drive on the turbines."

The Master of Navigation saluted as smartly as his aging fingers would allow.

"Master of Engineering. Have you finished with the maintenance on steering yet?"

"Forgive me, sir; we were halfway through the process when we beat to quarters." Yuri interjected.

"Replace the parts and switch back to the primary mechanism, job finished or not. Are the turbine modifications ready for the crossing attempt?"

"Yes sir, but you'll only get a few more knots out of her for a lot more diesel. I don't advise it unless the winds are too strong."

"Noted." The captain rubbed her hands together before a brief silence took hold of the gathered company. "Well crew, you all know the risks. Dr. Hennir should have explained that the passage we were seeking to go through might be turbulent when you signed up. I'm hoping you all took that warning to heart."

Her gaze drifted over each of us. I boiled inside. No. They hadn't mentioned this to me.

"I'm not one for speeches, so I'll make this brief: Say your prayers, hold your charms, do your job, and we might make it out the other side of this. May the River be with you."

She suddenly called out loudly, "CLEAR SKIES!"

The refrain rang out from the other officers, "THE AERY FLIES!"

***

The next few minutes were spent – for me at least - tensely waiting, peering up at the front of the gondola as we approached the passage.

The strangeness of what I beheld continually amazed me while the Great Range drew closer and closer. From the very base of the titanic formation beneath the brilliant orange cloud layer to its absolute crest kilometers above in airless ether, an almost perfect vertical split in the rock cleft the range in two. It was as if some monstrous giant had stood above the kilometers of rock, and sliced through it with a meat cleaver. As the kilometers flew behind us, the massive roar of wind whipping through the cut grew steadily louder in my ears.

I struggled to keep my jaw in place as I wondered by what process such an unnatural feature had formed.

Once the Destiny flew closer to the rift, I saw beneath us that the river of clouds streaming from the brightly-lit opening in the rock increased in tempo to a raging current. The wind against us, even though we were several meters above the cloud tops, suddenly increased in strength. It was like a hammer of air beating repeatedly into my face. The Destiny struggled to stay on course.

Finally, the call went out: "Master of Navigation! Full impulse! Take us in!"

The turbines kicked into overdrive, and the wind against us grew even stronger. The sense of trepidation that swam so neatly with the rest of my emotions marched to the front of my mind.

We were close to the titans now.

One hundred meters.

A tremendous gust of wind rattled through the ship, causing many to grab hold of something to brace themselves on. The Destiny settled back to its original path.

Fifty meters.

The gondola swayed immensely in thirty-degree arcs with the motion of the wind. I became increasingly sick.

Ten meters.

We were almost to the rock face, and I looked up in awe as we were enveloped on both sides by a mighty wall of rock that seemed to stretch infinitely up to the heavens except for one sliver of light at the top.

The entire ship rattled as we made our way inside this strange world. I couldn't do anything but look on in awe and terror at how small we were compared to the amount of rock that stretched above us.

We had flown a kilometer inside in two minutes. Behind me faded the now-comforting darkness of the world behind. All I had ever known lay beyond that sliver. All the Yin steppe, considered so wild and untamed by the rest of civilization, was now behind me.

A humongous grin broke out on my face, which mixed poorly with the sickly green of my expression, and I spread my arms, welcoming the new world ahead of us.

My eyes drifted over the right side of the passage. Eyes.

Multiple pairs, arranged monstrously on top of each other and oozing with alien coolness staring at us.

    I was shocked and blinked. They were gone. Had I imagined it?

CHAPTER 5

Several minutes later, I realized the wind had begun to whip against my face faster, and the passage had narrowed slightly. The Destiny slowed in response. The airship shuddered violently with each gust that poured through the way ahead.

Finally almost ten kilometers in, we were at a standstill. The orange sun filtered through the passage tantalizingly. I could tell that we were a majority of the way through, but the Destiny's turbines couldn't overcome the wind speed ahead of us.

I caught sight of Captain Nome walking aft with the two doctors and the first lieutenant. She shouted over the noise, "... that's with the modifications we made to the turbines. How do we get past this?"

Dr. Ininsir responded emphatically. "We need to find the still layer. It must be further up in altitude..."

"Do you know how high up we are?"

The roar of the wind drowned out the conversation momentarily. I walked over to the trio.

Captain Nome spoke again. "Doctor, my crew are seasoned, but there is a limit to how far up they're conditioned to go."

"It's the only way I can think of getting us through here."

"Doctor..."

"We may only need to fly up just over four kilometers..."

"Doctor."

"There might even be ways to mitigate..."

"Doctor!" The captain snapped. "I appreciate the gravity of the mission, but four kilometers is the Aery limit for safe travel. Any further and we risk asphyxiation."

I intervened. "Dr. Ininsir, how many of those respirators did you bring?"

The group regarded me with surprise at my interruption. The

doctor quickly responded, "Eight? With several canisters."

"Captain, we can distribute those to key crew members to work on the deck. The rest of us can take shelter below decks. The air won't drain as fast down there."

Nome contemplated the move. "The Destiny isn't airtight. If she stays up there too long, the crew will asphyxiate anyhow." She said.

"All we need is a few minutes." Dr. Hennir helpfully added.

An extremely long pause stretched between the group before the captain nodded. "If this doesn't work, the expedition will be abandoned. Do it Mr. Pullnir."

I felt a tremor of anticipation flow through me again. There was still hope to see the sunward side.

Orders were relayed, and masks handed out. In the space of a couple of minutes, most of the crew were below decks. As I was packed again into that revolting space, I hoped against hope that we would succeed. Adrenaline coursed through me with each beat of my heart.

Finally, a few minutes after preparations had begun, the command sounded to ascend and I felt the deck move underneath me disconcertingly. The ship turned her nose upward at a sharp angle, and I braced myself against the bulkhead.

I positioned myself next to a viewport out to the Destiny's starboard side. As I felt the force of the acceleration upwards, the sides of the passage appeared to be moving downward at a great speed. This was an illusion, but it still made my stomach churn.

Altitude measurements filtered down from instrument observers. They were relayed by airmen shouting one after another in a long succession, carrying the word back towards their fellows.

It took a little over five minutes for us to reach that threatening ceiling of four kilometers. I didn't see any changes in the rock face outside. I angled my face up from the bottom of the viewport, and saw that the cavernous passageway still continued up into the ether. We had barely brought the peaks of the mountains above us any closer at all.

We continued upward. I looked below and saw the cloud tops fade much further away. They whipped and churned below us like rapids in a stream. I also noticed that the rock face appeared to be moving sideways. We were going forward.

After five more minutes, the hold grew darker. I wondered

who'd turned the gas lights down, as their flames flickered lower and lower. I glanced out the viewport again and saw that our ascent had slowed. Did we lose some turbine power? Or buoyancy? The ship angled up sharply, so we were still on a good navigational heading.

I began feeling drowsy, and rubbed my eyes to get that strange blackness out of their corners. I needed sleep. The whole endeavor took its toll on my mind. I considered curling up against the wall, just before I realized that it was strange to feel tired at a time like this when the unknown lay before us. I blinked. Why did I feel so tired?

Suddenly, the ship's angle altered so that she pointed straight ahead. We gained an enormous amount of speed all at once. The room swirled into a blur of lines and color.

I glanced again out the window, and saw moving from left to right a great trio of interlocked triangles, grouped tightly around a common center, etched into the cliff face of the Great Range. I shook my head to clear my eyes, and they became natural veins of granite in the rock. They reformed in my mind to the interlocked triangles however, and remained there no matter how much I tried to shake them out of my consciousness. It was a beautiful design, but it couldn't really be there, could it?

In a moment, the vision vanished, replaced in a hurried blur by... sunlight! We'd turned left for some reason. I smiled as I felt the warmth of an extremely high sun on my skin. The feeling was indescribable.

I felt the deck drop beneath me, and struggled to balance myself. My body trembled moderately from the sensation of vertigo. Were we descending? Oddly enough, I couldn't tell. The deck felt as though it floated kilometers below me. My legs stretched out into that distance, like twin noodles for all they could support me. My brow furrowed, and the sensation fell away. We were actually descending.

Quite rapidly.

The Destiny floundered, and the downward draft of air that came suddenly along the far side of the Great Range steadily pulled her along.

I stumbled through the halls as our descent accelerated. I began climbing up the hatchway – I needed air! I felt as though my lungs were burning.

Once on deck however, it took a minute before I felt the

claustrophobic sensation to fade. I stared at the mountain side and heard shouts surrounding me. I couldn't hear what they were saying.

As I watched, our descent slowed, and the Destiny gently began maneuvering towards a small grotto that indented into the mountainside. Its floor tilted at a very slight angle, but it would provide us with enough shelter until we figured out how to escape this mysterious downdraft.

I shivered when I comprehended that I'd nearly asphyxiated.

***

I walked down the spaces below decks, limbering myself as I went, and trying to shake off the experience I'd just had. It unnerved me how many times in the span of two rhythms I'd come toe-to-toe with death. Normally I'd be able to shake off the feeling. There were shoot-outs aplenty where a bullet had grazed me. I'd seen war – albeit briefly, from afar, and against spears and pikes. I'd acquired the ability to push most of those experiences to the back of my head given time.

I counted five times now in this rhythm and the previous one where my life hung in the balance. It had a draining effect on me.

My fists clenched. I was tougher than this. I needed to choose a task for myself, or else I would have the captain on my back again. That was the last thing I needed. It galled me bad enough having to visit the chaplain every first-rhythm. I forced myself not to imagine what other demands she would make of me.

Off-rhythm had arrived. Most of the on-rhythmers had fallen back to their hammocks, which meant that organizing the muscle of a resupply party would have to wait. Training the guns couldn't happen until the Destiny took off from her shelter.

I remembered that there was something I had wanted to do. It made me more annoyed to think about it.

I found my way to the laboratory Dr. Ininsir had set up in the hold, one deck above the outraptor stables. As I approached, I heard an exclamation from beyond the door.

"Yes!"

Without knocking, I pushed my way in. Dr. Ininsir was frozen in the middle of a strange maneuver. Her right hand was balled up near her chest, while she crouched with a face that was best described as jubilant. A bevy of chemicals and minerals were crammed along two desks that had been hastily set up in opposite corners of the room, and a single square table occupied the center, with only three chairs surrounding it. Otherwise, the lab was empty, lit by an extremely bright outlight.

I paused, bemused.

She noticed me and straightened out immediately. "Can I help you?"

"Happy about something?"

Her arms crossed in front of her. "It wouldn't interest you, no doubt."

I needed her on the resupply team. As much as I knew the lay of the wilderness, she was clearly one of the more useful people aboard. She at least had the foresight to bring along respirators on our previous away mission, even if she didn't forewarn me. My mind wandered back to when I had to ally with more unscrupulous people. As partners go, Ininsir wouldn't be as difficult a person to work with.

Or at least she shouldn't be. I found her frustrating at times, but I could teach her to get on my good side.

First step: get on her good side. "No, go ahead; tell me."

"It's very rude to just barge in like that and then demand that someone tell you what's on their mind."

"Fine. I'll start first then. I need people for the next resupply mission. You're on my list with Yuri and the Master of Altitude."

"And if I don't want to?"

My eyes narrowed. "You'd pass up exploring the new world in depth just to get back at me for barging in?"

"It isn't just that, Ms. Zintan. I find you an extremely disagreeable person to be around."

I threw my hands up briefly before letting them fall at my sides with exasperation. "Why?"

"I can't..." she slapped a palm to her head and sighed in frustration. "You don't understand. See that's... part of the problem. You don't really care about the people around you Haye Zintan. Not one bit. And it filters into the way you talk to people, act around them..."

"Hey!" I raised my voice. "I'm not the one who forgot to inform my team about the risks involved with walking into tubes that just might contain helium-producing ore. Or about the little fact that respirators might be necessary in that case. Or for that matter, about the fun idea that we might be traveling over a mountain pass with the wind blowing against us, which might lead to us getting smashed against the rocks."

She hesitated. "You were informed of the Line Channel, weren't you?"

I stared her down. "You know what the difference is between you and me, Dr. Ininsir? I'm efficient. I get the job done, and I do things my way. If that rubs some people wrong, fine. I can live with that. It's not my job to make people feel good."

She shook her head. "Maybe, but don't expect many people to help you of their own accord if you take that outlook."

I tried to continue my line of thought, ignoring what she just said. "*I* wouldn't have forgotten to inform my team leader about certain critical information."

"All right then." She stepped forward, dusting herself off. "I'm sorry. It was a mistake; I apologize and will work towards it not happening in the future. You may leave now." She met my gaze expectantly.

I paused. "What?"

She just stood there for a second. "I'm not going with you unless you agree to stop being..." she struggled to say the word. "...an asshole."

I considered it for a second. I wasn't entirely sure what she meant. On the Yin steppe, the outlaws definitely took my way as the norm. I supposed she meant for me to act more civilized. It was a small price to pay for having her along.

I relented, "Very well."

"You agree then?"

"Yes, as much as I'm able."

"Good." She turned her back towards me, her previous animosity gone, and curiosity overtook me.

"So what were you so ecstatic about?"

She whipped around, her previous expression replaced with a broad smile, recapturing what I'd interrupted. The sudden change of mood surprised me. "My theory was proven correct. There are darkward tides."

"You'll need to explain." I scratched my head.

"Definitely. Airship captains have known about the seaward tides ever since the time of Tindalus. When the first air galleys cranked their way up and towards the sky, wind patterns were observed that gravitated towards the Unknown Seas. Above a certain level, the air has been almost completely still, but occasionally layers of cloud drift over this still layer that fly contrary to the Seaward Tides."

She puffed up proudly. "My colleagues and I have a model that we've put forward – a hypothesis if you will - that the seaward tides are part of a global wind current. In fact, if this model is correct, the seaward tides are actually sunward sides that float below a higher layer, the darkward tides, which we encountered when we flew into the Line Channel."

I cocked my head to the side. "That was what we flew into?"

"Yes. This suggests something profoundly map-changing for science. It suggests that the Unknown Seas are actually hiding massive gaps in the Great Range. Whenever a seaship sets sail and is lost to the Seaward Tides, they are actually carried beyond the Great Range into the unknown lands beyond. The wind simply becomes too strong for them to tack against. This goes for airships too."

"Unless they were to fly high enough." She smacked her hands together for emphasis. "At which time they would encounter the darkward tides and be carried the other direction. They would be blown in the same way that the rain that sustains the world moves down from the sunward side to the Beltlands."

"We actually flew with the wind at our backs from Kinyu to the foothills. I don't know if you noticed the change once we came closer to the Line Channel. That could be proof of the darkward tides."

I regarded her for a second. Her passion for the subject was evident. "So now you have your proof. No one can argue with you."

Her expression turned to bitterness, and she straightened out her lab coat. "Perhaps now. That didn't stop the meteorological community from shouting us down when we first proposed the idea. Apparently scientific orthodoxy is more important to some people than a new framework. It's like we live in the times when the Basilica was run by priests."

I raised an eyebrow. "You're sure that's not an exaggeration?"

"Quite."

"Interesting." It wasn't exactly a true statement on my part.

Suddenly, a really interesting idea occurred to me. It was all I could do to prevent a devious smile from crossing my face.

"Say doctor, I would love to continue this conversation, but there's a bout of three-track with my name on it waiting for me in the officer's barracks."

"Oh. Right then. As you will."

"Listen, if you want to come along and join, I can teach you the ropes. Might be a bit more relaxed than... whatever it is you're doing." I waved my hands at the table.

Her smile stayed firm. "I appreciate the offer, and I'll definitely take it up next time. Right now, I'm trying to organize my observations on the wind in the Line Channel."

I briefly wondered whether she saw through my attempt to gamble the money out of her. Best not to push it, there was always next time.

"I'll see you around then."

She nodded in response and shifted her attention back to the notes on the table. I turned around and left the lab behind me.

***

The next rhythm found the officers of the Destiny gathered around the rectangular conference table in the briefing room. Like many other spaces aboard, austerity suffused the space; I was beginning to notice a pattern. Six outlights illuminated the interior, three on each side of the chamber, but they were small. The whole room was dingy and bunker-like.

All five of the senior officers were gathered at one end, while the captain sat at the other with one doctor at each of her sides. The ship's chaplain stood behind her almost menacingly. The others were listening intently to Dr. Ininsir's report. I had to keep myself from yawning.

"...which means that the further down the side of the mountain we fly, the more favorable the winds become. Should we choose to, we could forego the use of the turbines, since the winds will be stronger on this side of the Great Range."

"Coasting." The captain mused. "That's all well and good, but how do we avoid being dashed against the side of the range from the downdraft? I don't believe the Aery has ever encountered anything quite like it."

Pullnir spoke up for the first time the whole meeting. "The turbines should be set to full for the duration of our descent. We need to angle away from the range and put as much distance as we can between ourselves and the slope."

Nome nodded. "Otherwise we risk slamming into the cliff before we are caught by the sunward tide."

Evinsir's scratchy voice added, "We would be able to control the speed of our descent a little better if we angle the Destiny up just slightly as we go. That might be more useful than flying straight out."

"No." said Tian' Xi, "The draft is too powerful. If we do that, it'll just take time away from gaining distance."

"Indeed." The captain's voice grew curious. "By the way doctor Hennir, seeing as how you're an archaeologist, you saw that pattern on the wall of the Line Channel?"

I perked up. So it hadn't been part of my imagination after all!

"Yes, it appears to be a copy of a glyph we've found in Site 23. Clearly the Channel was made by the Forebears, though the process it took to make such a colossal trench remains unknown to science."

She faltered. "I can't even fathom how such a thing could be constructed. There isn't a single legitimate scientific hypothesis for it."

The table fell silent, contemplating the magnitude what the doctor had just said.

"Well then crew, be prepared to take the doctor's recommended actions once we lift off. In the meantime, I believe there are other matters to attend to within the next bell." She looked behind her meaningfully at the chaplain.

He was soft-spoken in his response. "All the preparations have been made."

***

The crew stood assembled at attention on deck. The off-rhythmers were fighting off the clutches of their normal sleep with a mixed range of success. The on-rhythmers, in contrast, were bowed from a different cause. Sadness was etched across their faces; apparently airmen Turndr had been well-liked.

At Destiny's fore, the captain and the chaplain stood side by side. There was no perceptible change in the captain's attire, apart from prayer lines etched in sacred paint along her hands. The chaplain had the same lines, except that they stretched not just over his hands, but also crisscrossed his face. He held a cup of sacred paint in his hands.

I and the other officers were situated near to the fore. I had a very good view of the whole thing. Not that I wanted to have one; it was uncomfortable to be trapped at the funeral of someone I didn't know. It didn't help that I had no reference for what was happening. The Yin cared for their dead differently.

The Destiny's drummer sounded off a volley of beats, and bearers carried the dead man from aft to fore slowly on some type of stretcher. The cold blue hue and stiffness of death embraced his form. I recognized the firm, boxy face of the man that had been hit in the back with the native sling-stone, and instantly felt strange. It hit me how often I'd seen the dead, and how they'd never been memorialized in this foreign Beltlander way.

The drums rang out again, and then fell into complete silence. I didn't hear a single sound apart from the howling of the wind outside the enclave.

The chaplain stepped forward. Dipping his left index finger in the red bowl of paint, he traced lines on the dead man's face, drawing an intricate and complex symmetrical pattern. When he had finished, he stepped back and began to speak.

"From the River all things flow, to the River, all things return.

"This stream of life exited the River's embrace some twenty-aught perihelions past. For the earliest course of its flow, the streambed was rocky. Sharp corners cut the stream and chopped it into boiling rapids. The course of many other streams that ran in parallel, meandered away, into the wilds beyond. This stream was left alone to cut a path through a jagged canyon, where landslides threatened to block up the stream.

"The stream took on an aggressive flow, unnavigable by any boat. Its waters were so troubled that they threatened to fracture apart into many streams, each one too weak to continue without returning to the River.

"Finally, the stream's course came upon a flat plain, where channels had been dug for it to flow into. As it filled these channels, its waters were tamed, and made the surrounding land fruitful, supplying the plain's shores with many bountiful harvests. As it flowed onward it was joined by others, whose banks ran close to its shores.

"Together, the stream and its companions set out on a great journey through a mountain range so high, its expanse was unmeasured. As they began to approach that insurmountable obstacle, its path diverged from that of its companions.

"And so it was that the stream returned then to its great Originator and Protector, and is now safe within its endless waves, never again to be tormented by the rapids that plagued it for so long."

The chaplain stood back and looked over those present. "The promise of the River is to hold our many varying brooks and streams in its loving embrace, and bring tranquility and order after our allotted time on this world is through. That promise is the promise of the eternal flowing Originator, from whom all things do indeed flow.

"It is to the River that we submit our conscious bonds to airman Jif Turndr, and turn his body over to corruption – looking for the time beyond time when we might join him in the River's kind envelopment."

The chaplain sung out in one long monotonous note. "Peace be with you, and upon your family, and upon all who travel upon the winds."

The crew replied. Their singing ability varied greatly, so a cloud of notes were flung up that hurt my ears with its dissonance. "Flow well."

"In the name of the holy and ever-extending River, flow well."

The priest stopped speaking and stepped back. In response, the pallbearers again took hold of the stretcher with another drumroll. Alone, they lowered the dead man over the Destiny's side, setting him gently down on the hard, slightly angled ground.

One man had visible tears in his eyes.

A last drumroll indicated the conclusion of the ceremony. I breathed out as the rest of the crew returned to their duties with solemn expressions.

I found myself meandering to the side of the ship, and looking over at the man beneath. The light from the sun that filtered through the clouds shone on his face without breaking, coloring his dead blue skin orange with its intensity. The red paint streaks across his face remained unaffected for now. That would likely continue on for many decades to come as he lay up here; it was unlikely that he would rot for some time. We were too high up. No flora or fauna dwelled here that would be tempted to consume him. The pallbearers had left a variety of small artifacts with him. I saw a drinking canteen – silver, very expensive. A picture of someone. A book. A...

ragdoll?

I blinked at that. A weird feeling crept through me as I wondered what kind of life he had led. It was a strange feeling that I'd never felt before. Most people in the steppe lived and died without such trinkets. Why'd he get so attached to them?

My eyes drifted up from the body, and my memory triggered before I recognized what I saw.

Cool, silently measuring eyes loomed out of the fog. There were multiple pairs of them, eight in total, stacked on top of each other like some monstrous tower of orbs. They looked like a horrific crossbreed of an insect's compound organ and a great predator's vertically slit iris. Briefly, an elongated and bullet-shaped head gained form out of the fog, but as suddenly as it arrived, it disappeared along with the eyes.

Both my hands fell onto the railing, and I frantically examined the void to find the creature's form, but it had departed like a mirage.

Something apart from the White Hats was following us.

My priorities shifted to letting the captain know of our observer. I turned swiftly on my heel, and walked briskly over to the ship's fore where the captain was washing her hands of paint in a ceremonial brass basin.

"We're being watched."

Her eyes met mine questioningly. "Report."

"I've seen a creature in the fog twice now. Once while we were in the Line Channel, and once now, just over starboard."

"Is it predatory?"

"Yes."

I did my best to describe it briefly.

"We move immediately then."

Pullnir, still at her side, nodded and called out the order. "All hands prepare for liftoff!"

As I checked my revolver's bullets, the captain took one last saddened look at the body below.

The ship angled for departure, and the turbines engaged. As we departed, the fog soon swallowed the grotto and the lone figure within it.

CHAPTER 6

As soon as we exited the mouth of the enclave, the ship plunged downward at a terrifying speed. Even at full impulse, some eddies in the air pushed us back towards the range slightly. The rock face behind us loomed outward through the fog as we descended the sheer slope, degenerating into crags the further down we fell. Smooth stone gave way to heavily worn rock and treacherous terrain.

At last, the wind began to flow away from the mountain, and I understood that Dr. Ininsir was correct in her hypothesis.

We descended with astonishing rapidity. In ten minutes we had covered several kilometers, and flew a good deal lower than we had been before. The orange light of the sun dimmed considerably, and the air chilled again. This wasn't mountain-shadow; this was the chill of a cloud-shadow.

We finally hit a point where the air current gracefully shifted straight Sunward. I felt a small drop of water on my forehead and blinked. All around us, condensate fell onto the ship, and I shivered as the temperature dropped even further. The rain picked up and held a steady pace, making a significant change in soundscape from the howl of the Line Channel.

Suddenly, I could see below us. We were now flying under the cloud layer.

The range gently sloped downward into low-lying ground. The rain around us obscured part of our view of the distance, but an enormous river coalesced around the base, where multiple ferocious streams ran together into the greater stream. Faintly visible on the horizon, similar rivers ran Sunward.

Along the banks of these lumbering waters, tightly-packed stalk-like trees stretched as far as my eye could discern. They bent slightly towards the sun, and broad, black leaves that spiked outward ringed each. These leaves spiraled up the central stalk in a helix, ending in a point at the top. Each tree must have reached eighty meters at the least, and some easily stretched over a hundred.

In among the forest, dotting the swampy ground, strange spiraling columns of grimy stone twisted and bent into the sky far above the strange plants. As we flew beneath one that formed an arc with its other end, I noticed with much perturbation that a writhing, boiling mass of polyp-like creatures covered it. They squirmed over one another, as though fighting for space on the rock. After a deeper inspection, spent partially fighting a sudden feeling of nausea, I saw instead that they were cooperating. Many carried large pieces of fauna, firmly grasped by their tentacles, into holes in the rock.

With each raindrop, I became increasingly ill at ease to think of the vast quantity of life we'd found. Each raindrop felt like a bug latching onto my skin. In the span of two hours, we'd gone from barren, desolate mountain-top to lush swamp-forest. Like going from a sterile clinic in Mansu to the street gutter outside.

Nonetheless I wondered at the alien landscape we found ourselves in, and hoped we wouldn't encounter another predator to replace the mysterious one we'd left behind.

***

I spent most of the rhythm on deck watching the new land. Dr. Ininsir and Dr. Hennir were on deck with me, frantically scribbling notes and sketches of the new biome, doing their best to shelter their notebooks from the endless rain which blew in sideways. Awed and uneasy exclamations erupted from the crew, especially whenever the Destiny flew close to one of the polyp colonies.

At the behest of the doctors, the ship made several approaches to within a hundred meters of a colony. As the rhythm neared its end, that I decided to tear myself away from the sight, and find lieutenant Dostwikr.

I couldn't always bring Yuri with me. Dostwikr was a natural choice for the resupply party if Tian' Xi wasn't able. I figured it would maximize utility, since there weren't any ships around to communicate with.

I found her beneath decks in a side hallway, swinging in her hammock. She never slept in one place.

She was curled up, her legs tucked in with her kneecaps under her chin, and her brown hair obscuring her features. When I approached, she didn't move at all.

I cleared my throat. "Dostwikr?"

"No."

"Are you all right?"

"No."

"I..." I paused, slightly frustrated. "I know you don't have much to do apart from cards, would you be interested in joining the resupply party?"

"No."

"Why?"

"They're out there."

I leaned against the bulkhead. "The... White Hats?"

"No. Those gross squid things. Not interested."

I nodded. "Fair enough, but we're not landing for a few weeks at least. We would be beyond them by that time. Let me know if you change your mind."

I turned around and walked away, but something made me stop in my tracks. It was the feeling I'd had when Tian' Xi was talking about Pullnir.

I faced Dostwikr again. "You'll be joining us for cards tonight, I hope?"

"No. Please go away."

I paused; something was wrong here.

"Are you sure?"

"Yes." She breathed in heavily. "Zintan?"

"Yeah?"

"I'm sorry I'm a horrible person, and that I can't join the resupply mission."

That came out of nowhere. "Uh... You're not? It's not a big deal. I'll find someone else."

Silence. I took the moment to leave the hallway, before things got weirder.

***

There weren't enough people for three-track, so it was tabled.

I didn't sleep well in the off-rhythm. Something about Dostwikr's statement bothered me, though I couldn't put my finger on it. It just seemed like such a non-sequitur.

When I woke at rhythm's change, it was first-rhythm. That meant a charming visit to the chaplain.

I cursed as I swung my legs over the side of my hammock. I needed something to clear my mind before I endured the captain's order. I decided to enact another order of hers; gun practice was now officially scheduled for this hour. I stomped down the corridors of the Destiny, my annoyance growing by the minute. I stopped an airman, and told him to pass the word to the captain that the gun crews would be training momentarily.

When I reached the cramped crew barracks, the smell appalled me. Thankfully I'd spent enough time on ship now that I'd gotten at least partially used to its presence, but the sheer concentration here made me pause before I entered the room.

The barracks were long, divided into non-demarcated sections that housed different crew segments. Since we weren't beat to quarters, the aft gun crew loafed in their hammocks, trading jokes and in a few cases snoring to raise the dead. They were the only occupants of the entire deck.

I walked up to one – I recognized him as one of the airmen stationed on the left gun – and kneed him in the back as he lay in his hammock. "Up."

The airman flinched in his hammock out of pain and surprise, and ended up tumbling over the side. As he collected himself from the floor, the segment where the aft gun crew was bunked quieted down. Only a few residual conversations continued on oblivious to my presence.

"Officer on deck!"

The call had come from a young airman, her voice loud over the hushed murmur of her fellows. She can't have been a rhythm over twenty, and yet the aft gun crew followed the command and snapped to attention. A brief flurry of activity exploded as a handful of figures flung themselves out of their hammocks and stepped into the line. The resulting formation didn't extend very far, only amounting to about twenty airmen.

I focused my attention on the airman who had called out. "And you are?"

"Airman first-class Yudina. Battery specialist, sir!"

I measured her voice. Disciplined, calm, useful. "Airman Yudina, where is the rest of my gun crew? I only see the aft battery represented."

"We are the only airmen assigned to the battery on a permanent basis. Non-specialist airmen are required to support a full port or starboard broadside, sir!"

Great, so I was understaffed. I pushed the thought aside as I realized I hadn't considered how to go about training the gun crews. An awkward pause. I decided to get tough with them. That was what these Aery types were all about, right?

"All stationed on the left aft cannon during our encounter with the White Hats, step forward."

Half the assembled airmen stepped forward.

I breathed in before tore into them. "You people are shit."

You could have heard a pin drop on deck. I almost let a smile flicker across my face.

"I don't have words for what I saw from you. First, you nearly drop a shell. If the fuse had been lit, you would all be giblets by now. Then your cannon locks up. I don't think that's a coincidence. In all my years, I've never come across a bunch of loons like you."

My voice grew louder. "All you gutter lickers better straighten up your act, or else I will set this entire deck to side-scrubbing duty for the next week; you'll be up to your elbows in shit. Fortunately, we're going to remedy this situation right now. Firing exercises start immediately on the aft guns."

I strolled down the line, looking each one of the airmen in the eye carefully, doing my best to intimidate them.

I stopped and waited for a few seconds. "Now! GO!"

The crew sprang into action, and I happily watched them rush to the exit towards the Destiny's aft. It was cathartic to finally let loose like that.

As I followed along behind the crew, the young airman shouted out orders to her fellow crewmates. I couldn't hear what she yelled over the loud stomps of twenty-odd pairs of feet, but I supposed that the exact details didn't matter as much.

When the crew finally crowded into the aft gun bank, a line formed towards the ammunition boxes stowed at the back. Déjà vu trickled through my awareness. Airman Yudina took up a position as the wincher for the right gun, and assumed my position at the central viewport.

I called out initial orders. "Load blanks and prepare to receive firing angles!"

A commotion erupted as blank shells were hastily pulled out of their casing, and started to make their way down the fire-line, passed quickly from hand to hand. I heard at the same time drums rattling above decks, notifying the crew that the cannon fire was an exercise, and that the ship was not under any threat. Or I hoped that was what the drumroll indicated.

The shells reached the battery in a few seconds, and were loaded just as quickly.

The two winchers called out nearly simultaneously.

"Left gun ready sir!"

"Right gun ready sir!"

I decided to give them a lower angle, simulating an attack against the ship's underside. "Minus twenty, eighty-five to ship's plane left, and ninety-five to ship's plane right."

I heard a frenetic amount of cranking from the wincher's positions.

"Fire!"

The guns fired simultaneously. A deafening blast. I cursed under my breath; I'd forgotten to cover my ears. I rubbed my head trying to get the ringing out of them.

When my hearing returned to normal a few seconds later, I heard the call: "Right cannon ready sir!"

I paused. The left crew wasn't ready. Many seconds passed before the left wincher began to relay the left gun's status. "Left gun..."

He didn't get far. I rounded on the left gun crew, looking for an easy target. I saw the airman at the front of the fire line. He was, like Yudina, young. About the same age as the midshipman Hapsman, and yet one of his hands had been replaced by a brass hook. He had been at this station when the left gun crew fumbled their shot in action.

I focused on him, interrupting the left wincher. "Airman."

He visibly shivered and snapped to attention. "Sir!"

"What are you doing?"

"Passing ammunition..."

"*Why* are you doing that?"

"I've been stationed on the fire line... sir!" His voice was quaking.

I stared at him meaningfully, a wrathful expression chiseled onto my face. I didn't blink, I didn't ask further questions; I just stared him down.

"I take responsibility for his posting, sir!" It was Yudina's voice.

I wheeled around to meet the right wincher as she left her position and stood at attention in front of me. So she was responsible for this whelp being stationed at such a critical position? "Explain."

"Airman Vickir has not acquired experience on cannon operation. I have assigned him to the fire line in order to improve firing rate."

I searched her eyes. Was she challenging me? On the steppe, people who spoke up like that against the outlaw leaders were asking for a fight. I didn't know how to interpret what she said.

I decided to go with my gut and take her down a peg. "Airman Yudina, I admire your honesty. Unfortunately, honesty alone does not a fine team leader make. This airman is a drag on his team. Why is he even on the gun crew? Shouldn't you have recognized this before now?"

Her jaw remained clenched. "Yes sir."

"You had best rearrange the left gun crew, or so help me I will assign you side-scrubbing duty with your tongue." I continued to raise my voice. "From here on out, firing exercises will be scheduled whenever I feel like it. You will get no advance warning of these exercises. By the time the next one rolls around, the left gun crew performance had better match the right gun crew in every way. Do I make myself clear? Do I, Airman?"

A pause. "Yes... sir."

I turned back to the main viewport, satisfied that I'd gotten my point across.

"Crew! Unload and return ammunition to the rear. Repeat loading. Again!"

***

Several hours later, I stood in front of the chaplain's quarters, rolling my neck around to iron out the cricks. The early rhythm's events satisfied me. The gun crew was terrified of me. Apparently experience on the steppe translated well into an Aery environment.

I should really make it a habit to hold firing exercises on first-rhythm. It left me completely at ease to face the chaplain.

I drew one hand up to the door, but before I could knock, The low tones of the chaplain's voice anticipated my action. "Enter."

I shrugged. He must have heard my footsteps. I grabbed the door handle and swung it inward, revealing the most curious room I had ever seen.

The Nordecker strain of the Riverrun I remembered to be very austere, especially what I recalled of the women's chapel at my father's house. It felt a world apart from the darkened room I walked into. There were points of contact between the two worlds, such as the priest's simple black robe, and the incense burner sitting on the floor next to him, spewing a woody, foreign smoke.

The similarities were overwhelmed by the differences. Where the gatherhouses of my youth were barren of decoration, the chaplain's quarters were festooned with colorful paintings in the stylized form of the Auridans. Books were stacked against the wall, categorized by the language they were written in. A variety of ritual materials formed a semicircle around the chaplain as he sat cross-legged on the floor, each contained in a colored jar of material. There were a variety of colors: turquoise, crimson, violet, deep blue... even with the dim illumination of a particularly small outlight, the array of hues was at least pleasing.

The man himself, and the authority he represented, were less so. His eyes were closed, and prayer lines played across his hands, forming a series of triangles that interwove with one another up towards his arms. It reminded me of an imitation of those Yin patterns I'd seen somewhere.

I sat down in front of the chaplain cross-legged as well, on top of a small rug set out for me. Faded red geometric shapes whirled about its surface. A shame for it to be stuck here, in the solemn if colorful quarters of a priest.

The chaplain muttered under his breath, "Flow well." He opened his eyes and spoke directly to me. "I'm glad you came."

I sniffed slightly, my confidence still high. "I didn't come of my own accord."

"No one really does." He folded his hands together. "The River directs them towards where they may profit from learning."

I eyed him. "Does the River direct you to spy on my card playing?"

"Yes, through its servant the captain."

"What business is it of yours or the captain's if I choose to bend a few rules in a friendly game with my peers?"

"Of course it is our business. I tend to the spiritual well-being of the crew; she tends to their physical well-being. Our goals and duties merge from moment to moment. If our congregants are being taken advantage of, it is our joint concern that the situation be rectified."

I was about to negate his statement, when he suddenly stretched. "You should be aware that these quarters are built directly above the aft battery. I hear all that transpires there. I will be reporting your exercise of the gun crew to her directly."

My hackles rose. "And what exactly will you be reporting?"

"You have much to learn about the distinction between discipline and barking orders, though I don't blame you so much for not understanding that difference. The life of the outlaw is indeed different to the life of the ordered stream."

"Now just a minute..."

"No. Your instruction begins now." His voice was firm.

My anger was getting the best of me, but I found that the more irate I grew, the dizzier I became from the fumes of incense boiling out of the burner.

I decided to try and regain the upper hand. "Whatever you say, I don't believe."

"Why?"

"Because the River is a fiction told by senile geezers to get power over people too stupid to know when they're being sold a lie."

"Does that fit with the third precept of the Riverrun, which is to turn from prideful love of the self?" He raised his eyebrows. "Would a power-hungry priest deliver such a teaching? Would he or she commit to a life of celibacy? Would he or she accept the vows of poverty common to all the Orders?"

"Yes?" I honestly had no idea.

"Hmm. Maybe." The priest tapped his fingers together. "Even among the River's most faithful servants, there is a tendency towards pride in piety. And we ourselves embrace pride by treading on heaven's shores."

I didn't know how to respond to that. He had changed sides in the middle of the argument.

"Now. We begin at the beginning of all beginnings." He stood up, and gently bent over to a bookshelf directly behind him, picking up one of the older tomes. When he turned around, I saw the title of the book in his hand. It was the Testament of the River. I had only seen the bare, ascetic copies used for the Nordecker women, so I was unprepared for the beauty of this book.

Gilt illumination filled every inch of its cover. A stylized script in some language I didn't understand flitted about the top of the cover, and below it was Yin lettering – again stylized – of the name. The chaplain opened the book to the first page. It was done in a traditional Yin style, and I recognized that the entire book must have illustrations completely done by hand.

"I have figured, based on your faint accent, that the language you live and think in is clearly the Yin tongue. Therefore, respecting that characteristic of yours, it is prudent for your spiritual instruction to take place in that language."

To my surprise, he switched to a mellifluous artisan's dialect of Yin. "For now, read the first division out loud. I will wait through however long it takes you to finish." He held out the book towards me.

He wasn't wrong that I'd "gone native", so to speak. Nordecker was almost a distant memory for me. It did annoy me how easily he'd figured it out, however.

I have a failing for the Yin arts. Partly because I've been involved with their black-market trade a few times. Whenever I'd run a painting through from one city to the next, I gained a respect for how much work went into it, and how much expression of the individual would be found if you looked closely at it. Some artists were frilly in their design, others more minimalist. Some valued a multitude of colors, whereas some obsessed over one color almost exclusively.

I had wondered sometimes if I could imitate that art, but had never tried myself.

I took the book out of the priest's hands, purely to examine the illustrations within. It was interesting to me to see what the Yin take on the Riverrun would be.

I wasn't disappointed. There were so few rivers in the Yin steppe, so the depiction of the eternal river was instead a portrayal of small, grass-covered hills, each colored a deep blue. This must have been the closest thing that missionaries from the Beltland could use to describe to the artisan who had never been to the far corners of the Yinda's land.

"When you're ready."

My anger hadn't faded against the priest, but the book intrigued me for its own artistic value. Maybe I would get an opportunity to "borrow" it for a while if I played along.

So I gave one last glare at the priest before I began reading.

"In the time before time began, there was no land but the mountain. The eternal river sprang from a well on this peak, and all things were held in its embrace..."

CHAPTER 7

The first precept was to love the River, and to love your fellow human. This was demonstrated supposedly through the River's outflowing to create new life, out of love and respect for its more rebellious currents.

The sickeningly saccharine nature of that precept nauseated me. I've seen enough of it for one lifetime. It was the kind of thing that made you weak to the pressures of the steppe, caused you to end up six feet under well before your time.

It did nothing even for my mother, whose love was the truest for me. In the end, her love had done nothing to prevent my father from attempting to force me to marry. Relations between people always fell before the barrel of a revolver.

This made it all the more strange that these people would obsess over so ineffective an emotion. Obviously the ship ran on force of arms, not love.

It was end-rhythm by the time I'd managed to argue my way out of the chaplain's quarters. He hadn't loaned me the book, no matter how much I tried to wheedle him out of it. I didn't care an ounce for the book's words, but the pictures. I would have gladly read each page over many times if only for the art within.

I walked past a starboard viewport, and peered outside at the forest. My eyes traced over the strange tree forms, and the alien polyp hives in the distance, and finally found focus on a bare patch of ground that was practically underwater. Tree roots spread out in a branching pattern from each tree, giving them the appearance of being lifted on stilts. The water there was murky with a strange black covering that I took to be plant life. In among the pads that coated the surface, strange snulls flitted from platform to platform, snapping unknown wriggling organisms out of the water.

There, that was what the world truly revolved around. I wondered what the creatures of the rainforest would think about the chaplain's precious first precept.

Fog had enveloped the deck of the Destiny when I arrived there. Tian' Xi joined me as soon as she saw me. I could scarcely see the underside of the ship's canopy. As a consequence, we thrust at a much slower pace through the rain, which by now swept violently from starboard. Water drenched the gondola. The air was humid and warm. I felt like crawling out of my skin.

I raised my voice to be heard over the growing sound of rain and thunder. "Does Evinsir know where we're going!?"

"He's got a compass you know!" Tian' Xi yelled back.

"What if we smack into a polyp colony!?"

"That's why we're going slowly!"

"River take this." I hissed this into the wind.

"What!?"

"We're going to hit something! I just know it!"

"How do you know that!?"

"With *our* luck!? Let's see: assaulted by natives, check! Assaulted twice again by bounty hunters famous for never stopping at anything to kill their targets, check! Nearly asphyxiated, check! At this point, I would be surprised if the Destiny managed to stay afloat the next hour!"

"Cheer up! We've got the world's best engineer keeping her in the air!"

From near our side, Yuri grinned at the mention. "I'll keep her flying, even if we do bang into those suckers!"

A grin that matched his briefly shone across my face, before fading at the sight of something at the fore of the ship.

A lone figure precariously balanced at the ship's head. It hung on by one hand to the rigging, and the other swung over kilometers of open air. It leaned over, as if getting itself used to the idea of the air below it.

I made my way forward, Yuri and Tian' Xi following my sudden change of pace. When I arrived, I still couldn't make out who it was until I got within ten meters. "Airman!" I yelled out.

The figure didn't respond. Something was very wrong about this.

"Airman! Turn around and identify yourself!"

The figure turned to look at me, and I saw with shock that it was the master of semaphore, Lieutenant Alanin Dostwickr.

The rain had soaked her through. Even so, I could make out tears in her eyes as she shuddered. It wasn't cold. She shuddered in fear. She cut a sad, lonely figure out there on the bowsprit, hanging with one hand on the rigging, clearly terrified. Her lean off to one side of the bowsprit instinctively made me want to run out there and grab her from where she stood.

I'm not generally good at reading people who aren't Yin. However, some expressions are universal between different cultures. I know despair when I see it. I know how to read hopelessness in a person's eyes. In that moment, Dostwickr didn't need to say anything for me to understand her. Many things tumbled into place as I realized the bigger picture. And I cared.

I paused for all of two seconds. Then I held out my hand. "Alanin, come here, I want to talk to you."

Dostwickr didn't move.

"Alanin?"

She briefly looked down at the air beneath her, then looked back at where the three of us stood. A small group of airmen started to gather at my back as I continued to extend my hand.

The master of semaphore violently shook her head.

A new voice popped in from my right: Tian' Xi's. "Hey Alanin, come back here, we need you."

"Why?" Dostwickr's response was so quiet I almost didn't hear it over the rain.

"We just do. Trust me."

Dostwickr's face contorted with indecision. She gave one last look at the foggy air below her, and a final emotion emerged at last: fear. Fear of death, of heights, and of many other things I could only guess at.

Her free hand suddenly grabbed ahold of the rigging above, and she gingerly started making her way back towards the deck.

***

I was back in the officer's barracks, sitting and twiddling my thumbs uncomfortably as Yuri, Tian' Xi, and Evinsir attempted to console Dostwickr.

Only a handful of airmen had seen the incident, and I was glad for that. The last thing we needed was for the whole ship to have confirmation that a senior officer had attempted suicide. Rumors at least could be quashed, though not without much headache.

A small mug of hot drink – some variety of Yin tea – sat in front of each person at the table. As I sipped in its bitter and pungent flavor, I quietly regarded Dostwickr.

She was young for a senior officer. Definitely at least five years younger than me, couldn't guess further than that. It didn't strike me the first time I met her, but now that I devoted some thought to it, I would have expected her rank to be senior midshipman at the highest. How had she reached the rank of master of semaphore? There was also in her a fragility which simultaneously repulsed and concerned me. She had been, even prior to the rhythm's events, always anxious except when drinking. Right now, her eyes were dead-set on the table before her.

"Please talk to us." Tian' Xi said.

"I don't want to."

Yuri and Tian' Xi shared a nervous glance.

"I'm an embarrassment and shame to my family and crew. I can't even kill myself properly." Dostwickr sniffed and a fresh path of tears made its way down the side of her face.

It was Yuri's turn to speak. "Perhaps that last bit's truth falsifies the first bit."

"You wouldn't say that if you knew me."

"I would say that of anyone."

"Not me. I'm a failure."

I broke in. "I've contemplated the same thing you've tried this rhythm. Does that make me a failure?"

"I don't know..."

"Great, thanks."

Tian' Xi interrupted. "I want you to know, Alanin, that you are not a failure as a member of this crew..."

"How would *you* know!?" she screeched out through tears, causing me to grimace. "This ship hasn't seen another in six rhythms! This whole expedition, we're not going to see anyone for kilometers and kilometers. That's why I'm here; I can't do anything, and I won't be asked to do anything. I'm useless."

The table was forced into silence as she continued.

"I barely passed Aery training. The grandmasters were going to place me as midshipman, but I come from a long line of lieutenants in the Aery, so my family didn't want to have to deal with one of their own being lesser than her parents. They got me this post on the Destiny.

"I didn't get here by merit. That's what the Aery is supposed to base its officers on, right? I got here because my father's rich, and has many friends among the grandmasters. I'm not even supposed to be here.

"I can't read or write, the letters just end up looking jumbled to me. They gave me a book on semaphore, I can't read it. I've only learned from watching other masters of semaphore.

"I can't do complicated signals. I know, I've tried. Multiple times. Every time I do, it just ends up wrong.

"My parents knew this, and that's why I'm here. This is my first assignment, and also probably my last."

Before I could stop myself, I blurted, "I can't read or write in Simplified Standard."

All eyes turned to me.

I cursed inwardly as I realized the embarrassing fact I'd revealed. "What? Never needed to. Learned Nordecker as a child, Yin later on. My point is this: you're not dumb or useless for not learning Simplified Standard. Stupid spelling system anyhow."

"What Haye means," Tian' Xi continued, shifting her gaze back to the distressed Dostwickr, "is that your problem can be managed, and we can help you..."

"Didn't you hear what I said? I said I can't do complicated signals! That's most of what my job is supposed to be!"

"...I was going to say..."

"Forget it! There's no getting out of this for me. I know you all are trying to help me, but it'll never work. I'm a disgrace to my family." She leaped out of her chair, and took off running away from the officers' barracks.

Everyone ran out after her except Yuri and me.

After a bit, I found it within myself to speak my thoughts. "I've been there. We can try, but there's not much we can say that will help her. Certainly not instantaneously." I snapped my fingers for emphasis.

Yuri nodded. "It'll be something she has to live with."

"I can remember wanting to off myself. It was for a different reason; I'd gotten to Mansu, couldn't feed myself. Was starving for three rhythms. I wanted to end my suffering. Nothing anybody said to me made me feel better. Only my own decision to live helped me."

Yuri finally left to run after the others, and I was left there, staring at a corner of the room, feeling much more angry, annoyed, and saddened at the whole situation.

***

The call went out from the crew at the Destiny's fore: "Contact aforeship!"

A massive structure loomed in the distance over the surrounding forest. It was perfectly vertical and looked like a great rod of silver metal. It stretched into the sky far higher than anything surrounding it, though I couldn't tell its exact height. Coils of strange interweaving metallic braids intermingled on its surface, and some sort of engraved curvatures that resembled lettering distorted around the sides of the entire structure. As I watched, a massive chain of lightning streaked across the sky and struck the structure, leaving it unchanged.

The clap of thunder that resulted was itself interrupted by the cry of a strange figure flying in from the distance ahead of us. As it grew closer, its features gained distinction. A glider, made from ripped and tattered animal skin wound a path through the sky. The creature underneath it captured my notice immediately; it wasn't human.

Humanoid, to be sure, but not human. Brownish-orange fur completely covered its body, and it was easily taller than a human by half a meter. The giant had both elongated limbs and neck, with hands populated with several spindly digits. The head, meanwhile, took the form of a predator, with four eyes above a jawless maw lined with snag-teeth and fangs that lacked a symmetry. This new creature only wore a belt, out of which a crude but effective axe with a head made from a blackish stone dangled.

Its maw opened, and I heard a wheezing screech. In the distance, a whole swarm of hang gliders closed in on the Destiny from all directions. I drew my twelve-shot, knowing full well what this meant.

Hollow screams echoed around the airship from our interlopers. I immediately heard the captain shout, "Crew! Prepare to repel boarders!"

The command echoed down the entire length of the ship.

"Repel boarders!"

I felt a shiver of adrenaline.

"Repel boarders!"

The creature in front of me landed on the deck of the ship, dropping from its glider. It drew its axe and prepared to swing at me. I shot it between the eyes, causing a greenish mist to spray behind it.

The other attackers were not far behind. A frantic scramble broke out for guns. Drumrolls began to manically beat and echo across the ship. An airman next to me took aim with a bolt-action rifle and shot one of the creatures out of the air.

Someone tossed me a rifle, and I snatched it, priming it and taking aim at the nearest of our attackers. One shot, one foe dropped.

All around me, the sounds of gunfire joined the drumbeat as airmen took aim at our interlopers. Five of the enemy died all at once. The circle continued to draw tighter.

I heard a burst of repeater fire next to me, and saw Yuri, his face grim, taking out a massive section of our attackers.

Seven dropped onto the deck. Four went down almost instantly. Two were cut down by sabre. One grappled with an unfortunate airman, and appeared to overwhelm him.

A volley of spears whistled towards the deck from the air. In the blink of an eye, I managed to roll to the side as it hit the metal plates where I'd been standing.

Chaos enveloped the deck.

Nine more of the creatures dropped onto the floor, this time so close as to be able to engage the crew in close quarters. They towered over the deck and pouncing on the crew with lightning speed.

The deck quickly became congested. Rifle fire continued, sometimes dropping the flyers before they approached the ship, sometimes in an attempt to kill those already on deck. I slipped on a puddle of greenish blood, and heard a scream – human – to my side. I snarled, and turned towards that way in time to see one of the savages raise a massive club over its head to smash the airman's head in. I raised my rifle and shot its torso. It fell over backwards, drooling green, viscous blood from its maw.

I saw a sabre lying on the ground, and snatched it up. One of the creatures confronted me straight on, lunging forward with animal ferocity. I couldn't dodge in time and felt a sharp object shove into my left arm. I grimaced before cutting upwards from the other direction, lodging the sabre in the muscled side of the beast, two inches into the cut. I dislodged it with difficulty, and the beast kept its four eyes fixated on me, while coming back for another blow.

A bullet impacted it from the side. It was Pullnir, who promptly turned towards another creature and felled it with another bolt-action shot. I saw through the corner of my eye, the head of one of the creatures come sailing through the air, decapitated, trailing that greenish mucus.

A cannon burst sounded and one of the flyers exploded in the air, very close to the ship. The blast was deafening.

Several guns discharge at once, and their targets howled as they were struck in their peripheral anatomy, or fell gurgling to the deck.

Captain Nome stood her ground at the fore of the ship, engaged in mortal combat with one of the creatures. She darted forward with amazing speed for her age, and sliced the creature's left wrist almost clean off with a flash of her sabre. It hung by a tendon.

The creature was not deterred. It swung the axe in its right hand downward, but Captain Nome sidestepped and plunged her sabre into the creature's neck, cutting through what appeared to be several arteries and supporting tendons.

A rifle blast sounded right next to me. My ears rang.

Just as I turned to look, another cannon blast exploded close to the ship. The remaining creatures flying around the ship's deck retreated with angered screeches, swooped low into the tree line, and were lost to my sight. A few scattered shots rang out, and the last of the attackers were dead – I counted twenty four bodies in total. I stood staring around; the sudden end to the fighting gave me pause. My boots were splashed with green blood, which stuck to my boots and slurped as I walked towards where Yuri stood, his machine gun still cocked.

The captain recovered quickly. "Damage and casualty report! Mr. Evinsir, forward impulse at full. Master of Altitude, raise the ship!"

I rushed over to the captain. As I did so, the intense pain in my arm finally triumphed over the adrenaline pumping through me, and I clutched at the nasty-looking puncture that went clear through the skin of my left arm.

Captain Nome took one look. "Lieutenant Zintan, report to the ship's barber immediately."

I grimaced and kicked one of the bodies of the creatures nearby as anger coursed through me. Those assholes stabbed me.

As I retreated down below decks, questions popped into my mind. What were they? Where did they come from?

***

The barber judged my wound as non-threatening. After sterilizing it and stitching it together, he dismissed me in favor of the other casualties that had been the result of the battle. I was disappointed at his job; it looked like hackwork, and felt like it too.

I walked back to the deck with my arm bandaged, trying not to move it too much. I had to see where we were going. That building in the distance didn't look anything like what we had seen earlier. Judging by the technological state of the natives we had encountered, they couldn't have built it, which meant that it must have been abandoned for them to venture so close.

I found the two doctors at the fore of the ship, hastily detailing the impressive tower in their notebooks. I stood behind them a distance, musing on the same subject as we drew nearer. A small crowd of gawkers gathered behind me.

The structure gradually gained definition out of the rainy haze as we drew closer. It was much taller and thicker than it looked from a distance; a square prism about a half a ship's length wide. The coils on its surface, I discovered much to my surprise, were most definitely alive. They were vines, with shimmering trunks that appeared to be metallic. Tiny black leaves sprouted from their main body, oriented in the direction of the sun.

Under the plant cover, I could barely make out glimpses of the tower's surface itself. It was apparent then that its silvery appearance from afar was due to the plants; the tower itself had a much duller, browned and rusted appearance than the vines that enveloped it. The snatches of surface that I saw included those curving elements I had seen before. They still appeared to me like letters in an unknown language with strange and alien geometries.

As I watched, the rain around us decreased in intensity before it faded and disappeared altogether. I blinked, and saw a small parting open in the clouds far to our right. The sun hung high in the sky, and rays of light broke out at a steep angle over the forest. I felt a tingle of appreciation at the sight before me, and the break in the clouds grew larger and larger with each passing minute until it finally passed over where we were holding still. Two things struck me about the sight: one, the sun was high enough in the sky that the Destiny's canopy barely shaded me. Two, while a shroud of darkness fell on the wetlands around us, there were areas of contrasting light that shone with a brilliant orange. The effect created a jagged colorscape of alternately bright and dark areas.

Once the darkness around the tower had lifted, I also caught a glimpse of colored panels in the interior of the structure through deep dark holes in the side. The panels were faded, but I could make out that they depicted a myriad of stylized scenes in dark and ancient hues. The perforations through which I viewed these depictions were the result of the tower eroding away; they weren't designed.

I ventured to look down, and noticed that similar ruins spread out around the ground at the base of the tower, each flooded by water, and covered by the same metallic plant species. This ancient settlement spread out for kilometers, gradually breaking down into smaller and smaller remnants of the buildings. On the very edge of the city, a plethora of simple mud-daub huts ringed the entire site. They were thankfully vacated.

A short time later, the Destiny began to descend from its position near the tower. We were coming in for a landing.

***

When I stepped off the last rung of the ladder, I was immediately met with murky black water that swallowed my feet. Around me, airmen stepped off the deck of the Destiny and looked around warily at the flooded ruins around us. Gone were the sounds of the rain, even though the clouds above still intermittently passed over the sun, shrouding the area in intense darkness before suddenly receding and covering everything in orange light again. An uncountable number of bestial sounds erupting from all sides replaced the susurration of the rain. Both predator and prey were very well represented in the surrounding forest.

Soon after we had landed, word had been passed to me that an away party had been organized to head into the tower. By her request, Dr. Hennir and her assistant had been attached to the team.

I knew that the expedition couldn't have given up on the opportunity to study these ruins, whatever the risk of another attack would have been. To do so would be to ignore the mission. I didn't complain as much as I could have. I wanted to go in there, more than anyone aboard.

The captain had given us one hour to collect as much information as possible, and so I had requisitioned as many able hands as I was able. Twenty-five airmen in all.

Yuri slogged through the water with his rifle slung over his shoulder in front of me. Around his belt swung two replacement ammunition drums.

To my left the Master of Altitude had a violently disgusted expression on her face as black pond scum squished under her boots. She had tucked two revolvers into her belt.

Lastly, as I moved forward, the middle-aged Dr. Hennir splashed down into the water somewhat clumsily. Her servant Yensir followed her. The man was burdened with Hennir's suitcase, which he carefully held close to his chest as he stepped into the water.

I pointed my twelve-shot downward with the safety on, drawn and at the ready. I had no faith that those creatures wouldn't return. Around me, many in the party were armed with rifles and revolvers.

The group didn't need much prodding from me to head in the direction of the tower's base. We were too tense from our battle in the sky a few hours ago, and so silence reigned on the ground among us.

The tower base itself was an impressive sight. It stood upright on a pyramidal set of stairs, cracked with age, and partly submerged under the water. As we walked up the steps towards the building, the water at our feet withdrew with the rising ground, and it became easier to walk. As we finally stepped onto dry land, the sky overhead again darkened. This time, however, it was for the duration. The breaks in the cloud layer were sealing up.

In front of us, five rectangular pillars split the base of the tower at the pedestal's top, four at the outside corners, and one central pillar with a cuboidal, rail-less staircase chiseled into it. The roots of those strange metallic vines dropped from the side of the tower above the entrance into this room. They were coiled about all over the inside floor and along the pyramidal steps outside. I could barely see them; only ambient lighting illuminated the darkness inside.

I turned to get one last look at the abandoned city before the unending cloud cover again shrouded the sun. Patches of buildings were still lit by orange sunlight, and I could make out geometric statuettes carved into the sides of the buildings, each one a caricature of a humanoid form. They were frozen, staring over their decaying empire, slaves to the material they were built from.

I stepped inside the room carefully, walking slowly and deliberately over the coils of plant that obscured the entrance. To better see, I lit a magnesium flare.

Rubble from the outside lay scattered across the floor. Piles of broken stone, bones, and decaying plant matter filled the air with the warmth of decomposition, as well as its stench. What immediately struck me was the regularity of these clumps. They were lined up in rows that radiated outward from the central staircase. Clearly they were artificial.

We crossed the room towards the center, and I examined whether the staircase would hold our weight or not. Thankfully, whatever strange alloy it had been constructed from didn't crumble under my foot, despite the eons of time through which it must have existed. I turned towards one of the airmen and motioned him up the stairs.

All of us followed tentatively, aware of the possibility at any moment of the savages' return.

Above, another room presented itself, this one more complex in design than the last. We fanned out across the space, and Dr. Hennir practically ripped her sketchbook from her pocket, quickly taking down drawings of the chamber.

A distance of fifteen meters split the room's center from its sides. Twisted and tangled forms crafted from metal whose exterior was scaled like a fish filled this space. The taller specimens near the sides of the room towered over us with a height comparable to our earlier interlopers. Those nearer to us hunched like stumpy, malevolent goblins. Their form was indecipherable to me. At first glance, these statues resembled a living creature, but when given a closer examination, they were deformed with gross asymmetry. Where at first I thought a leg, or perhaps an arm grew, instead the limb transformed itself as my eyes followed it into another torso. None of these forms had any semblance of eyes. Where their "head" was, a single void opened in the top section, sometimes dividing itself by a small, sunken line into four empty sockets.

The room was decorated with more of those painted niches I'd seen earlier. I discovered – much to my amazement - that the media on which they had been painted was some strange, fibrous and semi-rigid cloth. I couldn't understand how they hadn't rotted away after all this time in such a humid environment.

I approached one of them, squeezing my way past the nightmarish monstrosities that ringed the room, and held my torch up. It was a depiction of rolling hills, across which a sea of blue triangular forms sprung up between blades of grass. The entire artwork was constructed in such a way that the lines between colors were well-distinguished. Instead of blending seamlessly into each other, a stark division separated the gold of the hills from the blue of the geometric forms within them. The blue of the sky was a different hue than the blue of the forms below. A flash of ochre shone out of a series of three interlocked triangles. Was this the sun?

I became lost in thought staring at the painting. Who made it? What were they trying to express? We were so far from any hint of the landscape it represented. It seemed as though it was a memory of some distant time - some vague and half-remembered image from the painter's childhood. Or perhaps a representation of the land before this forest came and swallowed the civilization that had produced this work of art.

I lost track of time, and the echoes from my team-mates poking about in the chamber behind me became background noise. Their steps sounded distant, like the rain pattering on the roof of the gondola.

Suddenly while I stood there, I heard a different sound; a low rumble from right behind me. I turned around, and came face to face with that familiar form.

Eight eyes, stacked on top of each other.

It was six inches from me, standing perfectly still.

I wanted to react. My mind screamed at me to move, but some mysterious outside force slowed that response. It was as if I was trying to push through a brick wall. The creature loomed over me briefly before flying at breathtaking speed up towards a hole in the roof of the chamber. My eyes processed a mass of sinuous tails flowing through the air in utter silence.

Finally after it had left, I gave a strange half-yelp, half-gasp. I had regained control over my body. The call echoed off the walls of the chamber and faded quickly.

Everyone turned to look at me in surprise. None of them had

seen the malformed creature. After a pause, I heard Tian' Xi's inquiring voice. "Ms. Zintan? Are you all right?"

I shivered. "No one else saw that?"

"Saw what?"

I pointed to where the creature had been, taking measured breaths. "It was right there in front of me. A creature..."

From my side, Tian' Xi shook her head slowly. "No?"

The airmen in the squad took me more seriously. As soon as I had related the creature's existence, they began silently surveying the room, and in particular the hole in the ceiling that the creature had floated up through. Muted calls of "Clear" filled the room.

Yuri trotted up to me, scratching his bald head pointedly. "Should we move?"

Dr. Hennir joined the group forming around me. "We've barely started. This tower is the most important archaeological find since site 23."

I blinked at her. "Dr... Are you aware that we are in the same building as an apex predator?"

"If it had wanted to kill you, it would have done it a few seconds ago. Its behavior seems to be more in line with a curious creature than a hunting one."

Yuri chewed his lip. "Maybe it likes to play with its food before it eats it?"

The group pondered this for a moment, before our silence was interrupted by an airman yelling from the side of the room: "We've got a problem!"

We ran over at a brisk pace, edging our way past gargantuan statues. The airman in question stared out through a crack in the wall through which vines probed their way into the building. I pushed him out of the way and took his place. Outside, I caught the form of the Destiny ascending from the ground. At first, I was struck with disbelief that the airship would leave us here, but then I saw the ground beneath it.

Hundreds upon hundreds of the native monsters were swarming below where she had been, chattering in some disgusting language that oozed and slurped from their toothy sphincters. There were too many to estimate; a thick mat of them carpeted the ground. In frustration, they massed around where the airship had been and shook their fists defiantly at her receding form. Finally, one of them dressed in a vivid array of crab-shell parts stood straight on a rock which protruded from the stagnant water below and screeched.

"Fglitahwwww!"

The masses below us lurched away from the landing site, and teamed towards the entrance to the tower. I realized there was no escape downwards.

We had to move. Now. "Staircase!" I yelled. "Now! Let's go!"

The next few minutes were a blur. We passed room after room filled with the same silent watchmen that we had encountered previously. I leapt up the giant steps two at a time, so I wasn't paying much attention to the individual characteristics of each chamber. However, the grotesque guardians became more threatening with each room we went through. I could have sworn they were looking towards the stairs at us with each step we ran.

The whole party was in a panic, throwing frightened glances backwards as the sound of the horde below grew louder and echoed up the staircase.

It was a long and grueling climb. Occasionally I caught glimpses of inset carvings along the wall, depicting strangely enough exactly the position we were in at the moment; a horde of creatures – similar to the ones we were running from – were pursuing a differently colored group of them up these stairs, killing them either on the stairs, or as soon as they reached the top and there was nowhere else to go.

It was a ritual. A reenactment.

We were sacrifices.

I grit my teeth and put more energy into my legs. I didn't know how far it was until we got to the top, but I wasn't about to let my fear bog me down.

An eon passed on those stairs. Only once did someone lose their footing. It was Yuri. I yanked him up from the floor as I passed him with a yell of "Come on!"

We burst out into the open air through a massive doorway. My lungs were burning from the marathon we'd just run. I collapsed to the ground in pain.

The wind blowing past the top of the tower buffeted me and I shivered with the cold. Out of the corner of my eye, I saw the Destiny, floating off to the side. In that moment, she was the most beautiful thing I'd ever seen. The team around me scrambled towards her. I pushed myself up again with some difficulty, and tried to run forward before stumbling down. My arm screamed with pain from where it had been stabbed.

Every part of me was hurting like a hot poker had been stabbed into it. All my adrenaline stores had been used up. I was conscious of Yuri screaming at me to run, and saw the captain on the deck of her ship, readying a rifle to shoot at the monsters that were now spewing forth from the entrance we had left such a short time ago.

I made the conscious decision that I would live. As the Destiny began to swing away from the side of the tower, with the last of the group besides myself aboard, I stood up.

I ran as hard as my legs could carry me, covering the remaining distance in a few seconds and leaping into the free air just as the Destiny began to ascend again. A weird, strange sort of peace flowed through me in the moments I was airborne, before I slammed into the deck of the airship ungracefully.

CHAPTER 8

I shivered in my hammock from the cold, each tremor rippling through my body and causing me intense pain. I had broken something, I just didn't know what.

From time to time, indistinguishable forms had haunted my nightmares, chasing me through stairs and endless corridors. Their shapes shifted into twisted and malevolent configurations, endlessly morphing into each other. In their heads, those twisted, empty eye-sockets. Sometimes eight, stacked on top of each other.

I wasn't alone in the room. Off to the side, slumped against the wall, was the small, exhausted form of Yuri, from which comforting snores emitted. When I woke up, there were extra blankets tucked in around me, colored with the Bezlander patterns I had come to know belonged to the engineer.

I smiled weakly to myself. Old, loveable bastard.

The rain tapped against the side of the ship, and occasionally dripped down the window over the outlight, causing strange patterns to swirl about on the opposite wall. Combined with the stale, musty air of the officer's barracks, the sight threw me into a contemplative mood.

What was that being? Why did nobody else see it?

Questions like those sent a shudder through me. I thought I'd seen most of what could be seen in the Yin steppe. Imagining a beast with the power to immobilize and selectively appear to me unnerved me. I began to contemplate the supernatural for one second before I dismissed the thought. If Dr. Ininsir said it was scientifically possible for things to spontaneously appear, perhaps that could explain this creature. Had I just been immobilized by fear?

I grumbled to myself. That was even less likely than some supernatural explanation. And it didn't explain why the creature wasn't visible to the others.

The door to the barracks squeaked open, and I heard footsteps. Through my half-closed eyes, I saw Tian' Xi sneak in. She carried a bowl of gruel. "I know you're awake."

I opened my eyes wider. "I'm not feeling good."

"You took a pretty bad hit on the deck there. I brought you some food. Compliments of the chef."

I sat straighter in the hammock with some difficulty and set about devouring the porridge she'd handed to me. "Did all of us make it?"

"Amazingly yes."

I was relieved. "Where are we now?"

The Master of Altitude cocked her head at me. "Speeding away at top velocity. Do you remember anything?"

"No."

"You were going on about some creature you'd seen in the building. You said it was floating near the rear of the ship, but I didn't see anything."

I paused, spoon frozen midway between the bowl and my mouth.

Tian' Xi looked at me uneasily. "Are you sure you're well?"

I couldn't answer. My spoon fell back into its original place. It was here. Around us. Somewhere.

Tian' Xi sat down as she waited for me to say something. She tried to hide it, but I saw her hands tracing prayer lines on her arm. I didn't have the energy or peace of mind to tell her what I thought of the Riverrun's superstition.

"Haye, would you like me to pray for you?"

I shook my head.

"Is there anything I can do to help?"

I looked her in the eye. Her expression betrayed concern as if I was her friend. I blinked. I hadn't known her for as long as I'd known Yuri. I didn't know if I would be able to call her a friend.

She continued, "I know there's not much I can do, but if you're seeing things, I'd rather not leave you alone to fester with that thought. Senior lieutenant's duty and all that." She attempted a smile.

I growled at her and turned over. I did not want to deal with these emotions at the moment.

***

It was another rhythm before I attempted to walk again. Fortunately my earlier assessment of having broken something turned out to be false. The ship's barber still wanted to keep an eye on me, to ensure that my wounds didn't become gangrenous, but I was able to hobble my way around the ship.

The next rhythm, I stared out at the endless forest, watching as a slow drizzle poured around the ship. A severe fog shrouded the land, so I couldn't see far into the helix trees, as the crew was beginning to call them. Nonetheless, the sound of the wildlife, if not the sight of the wildlife, still reverberated in the air. More of the polyp colonies loomed in the distance. The Destiny took special care to avoid them. We weren't making any more stops for a while. Not after the last expedition.

I couldn't sleep during off-rhythm. Our stalker was out there somewhere. A persistent rumor had started among the airmen that I was insane, haunted by some fury of my past. It didn't help that I'd been a hard driver for the gun crews.

I prowled around the ship, without direction, scanning for the creature I knew was hiding out there somewhere, tracking us. I felt anger course through me from time to time in place of my fear. Surely I did look like a madwoman from the outside, chasing phantoms that drifted out of the fog.

It was at the end of the next rhythm that I overheard the end of a heated conversation between the two doctors around a corner.

"...so of course, the answer is no." It was Dr. Hennir's voice.

Dr. Ininsir spluttered, "I'm not asking for his thoughts or anything, only his resources."

"As far as I'm concerned, all literature that one draws on is flawed. As a rational scientist of the Academy, I cannot agree with your hypothesis." Dr. Hennir scolded.

I turned the bend towards where the racket was coming from, annoyed at the intrusion into my futile search. Dr. Ininsir was tapping her notebook frantically.

"I know your politics concerning it, but wouldn't you be at least interested to see if there's any correlation between the two? I'm not advocating..."

"What you are advocating is an explicit rejection of the scientific method." Hennir had a stern look on her face. "I quote: We now know that all works of pre-Academy Basilica history are irreversibly tainted by the biases of their authors, and as such are unreliable for any serious scholarly study."

Dr. Ininsir frowned. "Why would you be willing to support unorthodox ideas such as the Sunward Tides, but not this?"

"I don't have to answer that. I'm your colleague now, not your mentor. Choose how you spend your time, but don't expect me to support a case like that in front of the Basilica." She walked away abruptly, ending the conversation.

Dr. Ininsir looked for a moment as if she wanted to follow after her, before turning away with a dejected look on her face.

I butted in. "So what's her problem?"

Dr. Ininsir's hand went to her chin. "I've finally proposed something she doesn't like."

I raised an eyebrow.

"But that's not going to stop me looking into it. If I'm right in my thinking, this does have implications for our understanding of prehistory and the Forebears."

"I'm not following."

"No." her hand balled up into a fist. "I suppose not."

I was about to leave, when she spoke up again. "Can you do me a favor?"

"What sort?"

"Next time you see the chaplain, can you extract a specific book from him?"

"Which?"

Dr. Ininsir became quiet. Her eyes shifted from left to right, betraying a sudden paranoid thought. She hurriedly tore a scrap of paper from her notebook and wrote down the name before handing it to me.

"Tell nobody. We might cause a religious panic otherwise."

"What..." was all I could muster before the doctor swiftly placed a finger on her lips and moved to go belowdecks.

***

I had the doctor asking me for favors now. That meant she trusted me, but on my end that also meant more annoying errands.

Dr. Ininsir wanted the book *History and Genealogy of Aula*, though she still hadn't explained why.

I'd handle that the next time I went in for my counseling session.

I was in the rear gun chamber, staring out the viewport at the clouds. The temperature difference between the inside and outside of the ship's underdecks fogged the glass. I idly traced patterns on the viewport. Three interlocked triangles, helixes that trailed up the side, eight dots in two rows...

Beside me, Yuri was concentrating hard on his next move. Somehow, he'd managed to "requisition" some spare parts and crafted them into baji pieces. I would win; I'd predetermined the outcome in the first few turns.

I don't know why Yuri still gambled with baji. I'd pretty much mastered the game; maybe it reminded him of his past? We were playing with a Bezlander variant.

He finally laid down his final piece and awaited my move. "Your turn."

I didn't have the heart in me. My mind was elsewhere, and his loss was inevitable. I always felt wrong somehow playing baji with Yuri. I continued to stare out the window.

Yuri cocked his head to the side. "Your marbles still in there? You got conked hard, I dunno."

I interrupted before he could chuckle at his own joke. "They all think I'm crazy."

He paused at this, and leaned back against the wall. "Eh. Not the captain, that's for sure. Maybe the Master of Altitude, and certainly Pullnir; but I doubt you care much for his opinion anyway."

I finally returned my attention to the game and fingered the winning piece. "The captain?"

"She's posted extra detail at night on the chaplain's recommendation."

"How do you know this?"

A weary smile came up from Yuri. "Through the extreme sport of talking to people."

I snorted. "Humpf." Promptly, I put down the last piece.

Yuri's voice became congested with phlegm. "Good game." He rose to stretch himself and gathered his pieces.

"You owe me twenty worth of Yinlus." My hand shot forward and I motioned with my fingers. "Pay up."

Yuri didn't complain as he handed me my winnings. "So, what was this creature like?"

I described it to him as he scratched his head.

"Why?" My curiosity was piqued.

"Well... both the captain and the chaplain think there might be some sort of supernatural explanation for this creature. I was wondering..." Yuri's arms fell to his sides in exasperation. "Blast it all Haye, do you remember Kriton? Two years back?"

"Yeah, I don't see where this is going?" I knew exactly where it was going.

"Kriton and I were friends. Real close. He took the Aurora blend. I know, because I was there smoking with him."

There was a very pregnant silence between us.

"He was fine, for the first few rhythms. Afterwards, he started having memories of the stables job, the one in the governor's palace-"

"I know the job." I interrupted tersely.

Yuri started speaking several times before he finally brought himself to say his piece. "He died, Haye. He died screaming mad. But not before he had killed several people."

"You do too, then." I was disappointed.

"I don't think you're crazy, I think the stables job is coming back to haunt you."

"It's not a Shaffengur." I snapped. "And I never smoked the Aurora blend because I'm not stupid, Yuri. I know what that stuff does."

He threw up his hands. "Maybe it's like that shell-sickness? The one the Beltlanders found?"

I was enraged. "I know what I saw, and I saw what I saw. Get..."

"Haye!" He grabbed my shoulders and shook me. "No! I'm trying to help you. Nobody else saw what you did."

I was about to punch him when I saw something in his eyes that startled me. There were tears, barely detectable. My fist relaxed a little.

"My friend died like this, and I had to put the bullet in him. I don't want to do that ever again."

My hand fell to my side.

"I still have nightmares about the stables job myself Haye. If you ever want to talk, I'm here."

I was suddenly uncomfortable, and looked away, giving Yuri the opportunity to bear-hug me. I returned it, if only to calm the poor man down.

"I'll be ok Yuri. I'll be ok."

***

I huddled into myself after he left.

What if he was right? What if I was going mad somehow? My talk with him allowed doubt to fill my entire being. It hurt.

The distant hum of the ship meshed with the sound of the rain, which intensified outside. The viewport had finally fully fogged up, leaving me with no sight of the outside. My earlier doodles had faded entirely with the rising cold outside.

I became aware of how strange it was that the temperature was cooling as much as it did. As we got closer to the Sunward Pole, everything was getting much hotter. What was the source of this freeze? I reached out to touch the glass of the viewport.

In surprise, I withdrew my hand at lightning speed. The viewport's surface was cold enough to burn my skin.

Sudden dread spread through me as the indistinct but familiar form of my tormenter loomed large in the viewport. Four familiar pairs of eyes stared in malevolently at me.

I drew my revolver and aimed it squarely at the glass. "Leave. Me. Alone." I growled out, my hand shaking.

It was then that I first heard the Voice. It rumbled through me seismically. Every bone in my body, including the bruised ones, felt its impact. If I had to draw an exact comparison, it was as if a volcano, or the whole titanic mass of the earth were speaking. Its tone was curious as much as it sounded frighteningly ill-intentioned.

"Where goest thou?"

My trigger finger pulled itself reflexively. One shot rang out from my revolver.

CHAPTER 9

I stared straight ahead. A swirl of quick thoughts and muttered statements surrounded me on all sides from the assembled group. I didn't pay them any attention at first. I couldn't. My mind drifted in an agonizing state of paranoia and anxiety.

"Haye?"

"Ms. Zintan?"

At last my attention drifted back to those present. The group that occupied Captain Nome's ready room looked at me expectantly. I shook my head. "Yes, I'm here."

"The voice? Did you recognize it at all?"

I shook my head. "No."

The chaplain tapped his fingers on the captain's desk. "There is a certain list of criteria for Biehs possession. With your permission captain, I would like to examine Ms. Zintan and assess the need for an exorcism."

A fist slammed down on the opposite side. Dr. Hennir barely restrained her voice. "Now is not the time for superstition. Ms. Zintan must be confined to the brig until such time as she can undergo a full medical examination."

"What sort of medical examination do you propose?" the captain said.

"Phrenological. We can determine if she has a propensity towards psychoses by measuring her parietal and frontal plates."

The chaplain stood stiffly. "An exorcism is hardly mere superstition. Phrenological science on the other hand, represents a gross departure from reality."

A sneer from the doctor met this statement. "A priest of the Riverrun, lecturing me on gross departures from reality?"

The captain merely waved her hand to silence the two. "Both of these approaches are valid at this point. We simply cannot afford to be wrong either way. Whether she truly is possessed by a Biehs or suffering from psychosis, the whole ship is in danger."

My conversation with Yuri drifted to the forefront of my mind. Of all the people on board, he was the one I trusted with little qualm. If he was concerned about my situation, I decided that I needed to trust his judgment on this one. He'd worried I would snap. I didn't want to do that with him aboard.

"I have a request, captain." I said.

Three sets of eyes fixed on me. "Yes?"

"Lock me up until this thing goes away." I met Captain Nome's eyes. "Lock me up good and don't let me out."

***

The ship's brig reeked of outraptor manure and had a single cot to the side, without sheets or stuffing. It was completely closed off to the outside world except for a single outlight. Rust caked the rivets, and the door shrieked every time an airman came in with the rhythm's rations.

I huddled against the wall, my knees drawn inward under my chin and my arms clamped tightly around my legs. Outside, I heard the muffled patter of the eternal sunward rain through several layers of steel. Only the hum of the Destiny's turbines and the quiet warbling from the outraptors next door sounded louder.

Somewhere, a leak. Every ten seconds or so, a drip resonated within the cell.

I'd never seriously considered the possibility of the supernatural before the last few rhythms. There was a small chance that I was insane, and I wasn't entirely willing to discount that. However, to have stood there, and felt the Voice rippling through me, was to have known a great cosmic terror that was more real than reality itself. To have known the Voice, and touched its very essence as much as it touched mine, was to have been convinced of airmen's claims that beyond the Great Range lay mysterious supernatural beasts and unguessed-at monstrous evils.

Which is why, when the chaplain arrived with a rucksack to commence his examination, I jumped from my fetal position to meet him.

"What," I asked first, "exactly, is a Biehs?"

He answered without missing a beat. "The adversaries of the

River. There are seventeen levels of Biehs, each responsible for different aspects of channeling the River's streams away from rejoining it. I am here to assess two of those levels directly."

I nodded and spread my arms. "Assess away. Get rid of this thing, whatever it is."

The chaplain raised an eyebrow. "And here I thought you had dismissed the whole idea of anything immaterial."

"Not after my experience, no."

"I understand." He nodded thoughtfully, and I ascertained an irritating presumption in his voice. "I have felt the River's presence from beyond as I have communed with it. Sometimes, I have even felt Biehs, tempting me from my sides, whispering lies and deceit in my ear. It is truly a terrible thing to come in contact with divine, or infernal, forces."

"You haven't felt anything at all."

The chaplain closed his mouth with displeasure.

"Not until you've heard that... thing."

"On the contrary, I have. But I don't expect you to understand or appreciate that with your limited experience of these matters."

He rifled through the rucksack and set at his sides two incense burners leaking an unplaceable odor. A bowl filled with granular aquamarine sand followed suit. After pouring a dubious liquid into the bowl, he proceeded to mix the two substances with a pestle.

I wondered whether the examination would have any effect.

"If a Biehs is tormenting you, you should know that it is not entirely your fault." I heard intent to comfort in his voice.

"Why?"

"I have a growing suspicion that we are treading where we are not supposed to."

"Explain."

"There are four theological interpretations of the River's existence. Firstly, that it exists as an idea across multiple persons, and is manifested in human memory only. This interpretation," he added with a snort of disgust, "is much too profane for my taste.

"Secondly, that it exists as a metaphysical and extra-physical manifestation. That is to say, it has no recognizable form, but is tangible in its effects on the world."

"Aren't those two the same statement?" I said.

"You miss the nuance of the ideas. One says it is a mere idea, the other says that it exists, yet not physically."

"The third option, opted for by a long line of orthodox theologians, myself included, is that the River has physical form, yet is not comprehensible to humans. It exists, yet we do not see it, owing to human incapacity.

"The fourth option is that the River exists physically, with a material presence perceivable by the human eye, and that it has a specific location. It is this interpretation that I am beginning to fear is correct." The chaplain began grinding the pestle harder.

"Why so?"

"Because, young Zintan, if that interpretation is true, then we tread on Heaven's very shores."

The chaplain let that statement hang in the air for a while before following it up. "There are a growing number of things that convince me of this conclusion. We were almost killed twice by the bounty hunters that seek you. An airman was lost to the savages. We have seen the River's will manifested in the mountain that almost smashed our ship for daring to travel through the Range. We have felt the divine breath of the River pushing us back through that great chasm. We have been swarmed by the wild here. We have seen Biehs given physical form and beheld their legions at the city. At every step, new forces from around us are arising to keep us from reaching further sunward. Omens, like flies off a carcass, swarm through my dreams at night.

"And now, a piece of evidence that seals my conviction: you are quite likely being haunted by a more powerful Biehs than any I have heard of."

He finished his mixing of paint, and began applying more intricate prayer lines than I have ever seen across his palms.

"Heaven?" I blinked. "Heaven is sunward?"

"That interpretation is mentioned several times in *History and Genealogy of Aula*. Only a few of my colleagues have ever given serious thought to..."

"Oh! That book!"

The priest lifted his gaze from applying his prayer lines. "Yes? What do you know of it?"

The words bluntly tumbled out of my mouth. "I need it!"

"Why?"

"To look something up. Something... uh... something about my family name. Yeah. That."

"Dr. Ininsir put you up to this?" His face was blank.

"No, No! Of course not! Why would she do that?"

"She might."

"Aw come on," I smiled as sincerely as I could, "would I lie to a holy man like you, who's exorcising such a powerful Biehs from me?"

"Yes."

Yeah. Shouldn't have tried. Never good at lying under circumstances like these.

He continued applying prayer lines. "You may have it for now. Perhaps Dr. Ininsir will find something of use. Or maybe it will convince her that we should turn around now before something even more disastrous happens."

My smile grew wider. "Thank you! I'll tell... I mean, I was planning to use it for..."

"Don't insult my intelligence, Ms. Zintan," he growled, "I've already had enough of that from our scientific guests."

He looked up again. "If I find any of my pages missing, or torn, or scribbled on, or otherwise damaged in any way, I will request the River to visit you with seventeen times as many Biehs as you have suffered throughout your entire life."

***

I heard a polite knock on the door. A welcome difference from the poking, prodding, and interrogation of the chaplain. I grumbled my assent.

The door squealed open slowly, as it had for my previous visitor. It was Dr. Ininsir. "Come and gone, I see?"

I nodded. "Is it really common practice for exorcists to poke you to determine if you are possessed?"

She nodded the affirmative.

"Literally poke you?"

Again she nodded.

"As in, poke-poke?"

She sighed. "I'm here to do a phrenological exam. I see you managed to get the book off him."

This time it was my turn to nod, and point triumphantly at the big, musty volume at my side.

"Excellent. This may help in determining a few eerie things I've noticed." Her expression turned sad. "Though it won't, I'm afraid, help with determining what you saw." The slow drip-drip of the water punctuated her actions as she pulled out a battered chart from the pocket of her field jacket.

I croaked, "So doc... do you think I'm mad as a hatter?"

"No."

I sighed with relief.

"I think what you saw was a hallucination, but that does not mean you qualify as psychotic."

"*What?*"

"There have been plenty of people who experience audio-visual hallucinations, even repeatedly, and lead otherwise normal lives. I think you may be suffering from something similar."

"I *felt* it, doc. I didn't just hear and see it."

"Feeling is one of the many senses that can be tricked into perceiving things that aren't there. One of the more commonly retold instances of hallucination is the feeling of insects crawling under one's skin."

"You think I *tricked* myself!?"

"No." I quieted as her expression remained compassionate. "I think your physiology is playing an extremely cruel trick on your mind. I'm here to help you overcome this cruel trick and be your ally against it." She continued to hold my gaze. "I'm not here to judge, condemn, or label you. Only to help you.

"I am, of course, obliged to administer a phrenological exam, but I don't think I'll find anything unusual. What will likely be the case is that you will need psycho-analytic care."

I scratched my head as my anger subsided into confusion. "What sort of scientist are you again? Don't you have a specialization?"

"I have four doctorates in Geology, Chemistry, Thermodynamics, and Meteorology. Additionally, I have studied under the master of Psychoanalysis herself, Teane Ilinir."

That put me to silence once more.

"Allow me to begin my first exam. This will only take a moment." Her hands came up towards my head, and I grudgingly complied as she felt her way across my skull. Enough with the prodding already; I'd had enough for one rhythm.

She was correct about one thing. It only took a moment for her to conclude that I was phrenologically sound. "We'll continue with my next exam then. I advise you to make yourself as comfortable as you can."

As I settled back on the cot with my arms crossed behind my head, I had the presence of mind to ask about the book I'd acquired for her. "So the book. Are you thinking the same thing the chaplain thinks?"

"What does the chaplain think?"

"He thinks we're headed towards Heaven. Real actual physical Heaven. That we shouldn't be here."

"I figured he'd jump to that conclusion sooner or later. The answer is no."

The doctor settled on the floor. "But there is a grain of truth to his sources if my idea is correct. That book you helped acquire contains a recording of a recording of an alleged account of the settlement of the Beltlands by servants of the River, who later became humanity as it is now. They came, so the account claims, from beyond the Great Range. If true, that would account for the innumerable cultural similarities I am seeing between Forebear symbols, pre-classical era art, Yin folk art, and the amazing new relics I have had the honor of seeing along this journey."

"What similarities?"

"There is a recurring motif in all four of those sources of the perfect equilateral triangle being used as an abstract representation for a material or metaphysical object of any kind. The Yin use long chains of it to supposedly grant mystic integrity to their buildings, since the chain of triangles represents strength. Pre-classical era artwork uses it to signify great rulers, especially using three interlocking triangles. That same knot of triangles has been found at ancient Forebear sites infrequently below the Great Range, but now, I see it everywhere. In the Line Channel, carved into the rock above where it has no justification to be. At that Forebear tower, in the artwork, where it represents the sun. And below it, little triangles representing green rolling hills!" Her excitement grew with each word.

"What does that mean?"

"It means that we are inheritors of a great legacy, that we are the descendants of the Forebears. And that within us is the potential to reclaim that legacy. To build their civilization again. Just imagine the technological greatness it must have taken to carve that channel through the Great Range! Imagine what our society would be like if we were able to harness that power!"

"Huh." I imagined it. "Probably not much different than it is now."

I clearly had annoyed her. "Oh, fie! Trying to get you excited about science is like..."

"Pissing against the wind, doc." I smiled. "No, but really, weren't we headed to that level of technology anyhow? Aren't there steam engines drawing horseless carriages back down where you're from? How does knowing we're descended from the Forebears change that?"

"It confirms that it's possible for us to understand their technology. Some – I'm not naming names – but some," she sniffed, "within the Academy believe that it's not possible for us to understand Forebear technology because they are a presence entirely alien to this world. From beyond the ether. This would prove them wrong once and for all."

"Hmm."

"Yes. Well." She sat cross-legged on the cell floor with her back to the wall. "Perhaps it is time we begin your second examination."

"Get on with it." I rapidly grew tired of her prattle.

She pulled out a different notebook from her field jacket. "Tell me about your father..."

***

When the third knock came at my door, I exhaustedly snapped, "Go away."

Instead the door squealed open yet again, and in walked two familiar figures. I groaned, and turned away from the door in frustration.

Yuri's voice was close to breaking. "Hey Haye. You turn up in the wonkiest of places, sir."

Tian' Xi spoke in a soothing voice. "We brought you a roll-up from Pullnir's stash."

My eyes popped open at that. It had been many rhythms since my last smoke. "What kind?"

"Jinberry and Landir. I know it's frou-frou, but at least it's something. I heard you like the water pipe."

"Yeah I do." I immediately rolled over and sat up. "Seriously? Pullnir smokes that aristocratic loam?"

Tian' Xi smiled knowingly. "Fancies himself a blueblood it seems."

"How did you get it?" I accepted the heavily ornamented paper with the herbs firmly secured inside.

The master of altitude replied in lieu of Yuri, who stood quite lamely to the side. "Borrowed it. I can return it after you're done if you like."

I chuckled. "Nah, let him wonder where it went. Light?"

Yuri fumbled in his front pockets, and finally produced a match and a matchbox. One strike later, and I breathed in the stuffy taste of Jinberry.

"How'd it go?"

"Interesting. Too much physical contact though."

"Anything else?"

"Yeah." My brow furrowed. "Kind of important. Not about me, though."

Tian' Xi sat down. "Care to talk about it?"

"Sure, why not. Yuri, you ok?"

He sat down next to the master of altitude. "I'm... fine."

He wasn't. But I didn't quite know how to set his mind at ease. Hell, I didn't know how to set my own mind at ease.

I took a long drag before I spoke. "The chaplain thinks we're headed towards Heaven. Actual literal Heaven. The doc thinks we're headed towards evidence that the Forebears were our ancestors. Each one wants to go the opposite direction from the other. There's going to be conflict. If word of this goes through the ship, it'll be two sides against each other."

"More like one side against a handful of influential people." Tian' Xi nodded grimly. "Airmen are a notoriously superstitious lot. There'll be a mutiny if we're not careful. First I'd heard of the literal Heaven being sunward though."

"Apparently it's a fringe interpretation among the Riverrun." I took another drag. "Nobody ever succeeded in going through the Great Range before us, so it didn't really come up in a big way."

"Heaven. Huh."

"Yeah."

"So that makes this an expedition to Heaven then?"

"No. The chaplain just believes that because he's scared." Smoke filled the cell. "Yuri? What's your take on this?"

"I want to know about you. Did they find anything wrong with you?"

I sighed. "No, Yuri. I'm not psychotic, and I'm not infested by scary ghosties."

"Was less concerned about the second bit, but glad to know the ghosties are leaving you alone." He gave a weak chuckle.

"Although that doesn't stop that idiot chaplain from believing I've got a Biehs haunting me. He just thinks it's too powerful to be categorized normally. In short, he sees what he wants to see. I'm starting to believe Dr. Ininsir has the same problem with her psycho-whatnot."

Both of them digested this information. Smoke continued to fill the space, causing Tian' Xi to begin coughing. "Well. Seeing as how you're ok at the moment, what do you say to some time above decks? The captain authorized me to take you there for a breather, we just have to keep an eye on you."

I nodded. "It'd be nice."

They both stood up.

"And Tian' Xi?" When she turned, I waved the burnt roll-up. "Thanks for this."

She smiled again. "Don't mention it. Seriously, don't. If Pullnir knows I got into his supply, I'm in for it."

CHAPTER 10

The next rhythm, the good Dr. Ininsir joined our little trio in my brig cell after the on-rhythmers had finished their shift. We played cards.

"So what made you join the Aery?" I asked Tian' Xi as I sorted my hand.

"Education." She considered her options. "Mansu isn't really the place to be if you want to study something apart from the Dictates of the First Yinda. I wanted to learn about the world, maybe rise above my family's stonework to something more. I went with the first Aery recruiter that came along. My family disowned me, so the only way left was forward."

I played my hand. "I'm from Nordecker. Similar story, except I headed sunward with one of the caravans out from Vosterdon. Snuck away in the night from my father."

"I see."

"Are you happy in the Aery?"

She nodded. "Never been happier. Once you hit a certain number of years served, they'll support a truncated course for officers at one of the universities. You can go to Ininger, Yten, Caudisri... Anensorg in Nordecker if you're into that. Some of the recruits even attend one of the Basilica-affiliated universities. There's also lots of opportunities for advancement. I'd like to captain my own ship someday. Earn the respect of my crew like Captain Nome has."

Dr. Ininsir spoke up, "Are you planning to go to Ininger? I'm currently studying there with Dr. Hennir."

Tian Xi' shook her head. "Already studied, doc. I went to Caudisri. Studied ballistics and world history."

Yuri looked intrigued. "Interesting combination."

"Everybody's got to have a hobby." She smiled, and laid down her hand.

I sighed. Loss again. "Fine." I waved my hand dismissively. As the cards were shuffled back into the deck, I briefly mused, "It's an interesting thing getting all these people from different places to work together on a ship like this. You wouldn't see this in Yin."

"Yes." Tian' Xi replied. "Take Aula and Ijritan for example. Big rivals, almost on the brink of war most of the time. And yet there are people on this ship from both empires."

"How does that happen?"

"The Aery isn't tied to the military of any of the Octant Empires. Aula, Nordecker, Ijritan, Drei… none of them have control over us. We're directly funded by the Academy of the Basilica and the Hierarchs of the Riverrun. Consequently, we can draw from an international group that pledges its allegiance to the ideals of the Riverrun."

Dr. Ininsir broke in again "And science."

"Yes, that goes with the Academy."

I wryly looked at Tian' Xi. "So you know more about my home country's history than I do. Tell me what you know about Nordecker."

"Rival to Aula, third largest of the Octant, behind the Drei Ascendancy. Currently ruled by an Autarch, one of a long succession of dynasties that has ruled the deserts darkward of Yin for millenia. Noted for having a strongly conservative outlook on modernization."

Dr. Ininsir reshuffled her cards. "Aula is better than most, but I've still run into some of my colleagues who think male gonads are a prerequisite for having something interesting to say. Yes. Conservative against modernization. Something I would do away with in all the Octant lands if I could."

"That makes two of us." I mumbled.

"Three." Tian' Xi added.

"Four! Don't leave me out of this!" Yuri grimaced. "Does a lifetime of my family being chased from town to town just because we're Bezlanders mean I can join the anti-anti-modern club?"

I smiled. "Yes, Yuri, it does."

Someone banged on the door of the cell sharply. "Ms. Zintan? The captain wishes to speak privately to you."

***

I had stepped into an access-way that ran along the length of the gondola. It was completely deserted, which made strange the loud echoes of conversation on the metallic walls. Someone had left half the outlights covered in this section of the ship, which spoke to an airman neglecting their duty.

As I drew closer to the discussion's source, the people driving it grew more and more insistent. I recognized three distinct voices. One was a deep voice, clearly one of the more burly airmen. I had a vague recollection of the owner, even though I couldn't put a face to him. The second voice was a young boy's; I recognized him immediately as someone belonging to the gun crew. Wasn't one of his hands a hook?

The third voice took me a little bit longer, but I eventually placed it as airman Yudina, the Bezlander who headed one of my squads. I then recognized that the entire group was from the gun crew. My demeanor changed, and I started searching for the source of the sound. I should listen in to what the gun crew talked about. It had been a while since I'd paid them a visit.

I finally found a grate in the deck through which the sounds emitted. I crouched down quietly; if I could hear the three of them, nothing stopped them from hearing me.

The boy spoke. "It was right there, I saw it. The outlaw lady convinced the semaphore lieutenant off the ship's bowsprit."

"I wonder what Dostwickr's problem is." Yudina mused. "She's new, so I haven't heard much about her. A position like that is quite cushy, under the circumstances. Can't have been stress."

"Guilty conscience is what I say." It was the brawny voice.

"Guilty?"

"You can run from something for a while, but eventually it gets to you. River knows I've seen some hard men take their own lives from guilt."

"Do you really think the lieutenant's a hard woman?" I detected a note of sarcasm. "Zintan fancies herself that type, so I'm willing to give the name to her. Dostwickr not so much."

"T'aint no other explanation. Unless you wanna give her shell-sickness instead."

"No, I don't. Something else is going on with Dostwickr. I can't figure it out."

The boy broke in with a scared voice. "What if she's possessed?

What if she's the source of our troubles?"

"Uthir, have you ever seen a possession? They look different."

"I heard Zintan was possessed, maybe it jumped from her to Dostwickr!"

"Hmm... no."

A chuckle, punctuated by coughs, resounded out from the male airman.

Yudina continued. "Dostwickr has something else going on with her. I don't know what it is, but it sure isn't possession. Zintan, however, is possessed."

The male airman finally stopped coughing. "You think? There are so many contradictions in that woman; she might just simply be crazy."

"The difference between possession and insanity is harder to draw." There was a slight pause. "You're right though, she is strangely contradictory. If she did convince Dostwickr off the front of the ship, that doesn't fit with what we know of her."

"She wasn't very nice to you." The boy said.

"Exactly."

The brawny voice coughed again. "She doesn't have a clue how to lead. That's what that is."

"She's a selfish, arrogant, darkward person. She thinks the Aery is just like some lord's army, and so feels like she can beat us around as much as she wants."

"I wonder if she'll get told off for it."

"We should pray she doesn't. She'll just take it out on us more. Especially with all this talk of possession going around about her."

"Again though, she helped Dostwickr out, maybe she'll be changing?"

"I hope so."

I pulled back from the grating quietly as I heard the group exit the other end of the corridor below. With a certain amount of queasiness at the general opinion of me, I leaned against the wall and thought about what I'd just heard.

It seemed as though the crew didn't like me that much. That worried me. I must have been just too different from the Beltlander folk with their strange customs and fondness for civilization that they would never accept me. Clearly, everything I'd done so far for the ship should have validated me in their eyes.

Then my mind turned to the next implication of what they'd said, and I shuddered. Was I going soft? They had been conflicted as to whether or not to trust me, and it wasn't anything to do with how helpful I'd been around the ship, but the situation with Dostwickr. How did they think they knew anything about Dostwickr, or her situation? How did they think that showing weakness, as I did at the bow of the ship, was somehow a stronger indication that they could trust me?

I couldn't make heads or tails of it. Stupid Beltlanders and their stupid obsession with people who coddled them. I kicked the wall out of frustration.

I had a feeling that the captain would sooner or later feel the need to talk to me about this, if she didn't already plan on doing just that.

***

Two minutes later, and I stood in front of the captain's ready room door. I tentatively knocked. Had she decided to lock me up permanently?

I heard her voice from the other side. "Enter."

She wasn't alone. Hapsman the midshipman stood at her side, apparently just finishing a report on some issue. At the moment, that wasn't important to me. Although the captain looked at her timepiece and half-listened to the midshipman, I sensed a powerful mixture of anger underneath her expression. This time, I was hesitant to step forward. Something had really ticked her off.

She looked up at me and motioned for me to shut the door. I complied, and she interrupted the midshipman, who simply trailed off. "Come forward and sit down."

I did as I was asked, my trepidation growing immensely.

"You are an extremely strange person, Ms. Zintan. I have just heard from Hapsman here about the situation with Dostwickr. Understand for the moment, it is being handled. Your involvement in it is suspended until further notice."

"Why?"

"Because, simply put, you're not the most graceful or thoughtful person when you speak. Prolonged exposure to you is not something I would purposefully inflict on lieutenant Dostwickr."

"Having said that, thank you for talking her down."

I wasn't letting my guard down. "There's a 'but' coming, isn't there?"

"But."

She stood up and placed her palms on the table in front of her.

"I'm removing you from the post of master of battery temporarily."

"Good." I exhaled. That could have gone much worse.

The captain blinked. "Excuse me?"

"The gun crew doesn't like my leadership style, apparently. You made a mistake putting me there."

"You're wrong about that," she shot accusatively down at me, "I put you there to test your ability to lead and your ability to adapt to ship's function. You have failed the first of these two tests."

"The gun crew and I are just not a good match."

"Wrong again." She crisply stated.

The captain searched my eyes. I couldn't figure out what she looked for until she spoke again. "Rarely am I incorrect about these things. You wouldn't agree, but I know there is leadership underneath those layers of arrogance you've built up over the years."

Frustration overtook me. "I gave you steppe leadership. If that's not good enough for you Beltlanders, I don't know what is."

"I'm half-tempted to increase the frequency of your first-rhythm moral instruction. There's evidently something lacking with the current level." She sighed before continuing.

"Leadership, Ms. Zintan, is not merely barking orders. It is not pummeling your command into submission. It is not breaking your crew down and leaving them to build themselves back up again. Discipline is an important part of leadership, but so is understanding your crew. So is sharing in their struggle."

She spoke softer, "This is what went wrong with your attempt to train the gun crew: you gave them too firm a rod without giving them any reward for success. In the short term, this might produce results. In the long term, it affects morale. Under the current circumstances, morale is vital to the survival of this mission. You might not see it, but the crew is seething with discontent. They've already endured severe danger in coming here. A martinet for a master of battery will only stir those waters further."

"So you've removed me from command to solve that issue. I don't see any problem with that."

For the first time, a smirk briefly started to form at the captain's lips. "What if I told you that affected your pay?"

I felt a rush of anger, but suppressed it. "Fine by me. No job is worth..."

"Worth what?"

"...Becoming a Beltlander. Going soft." I snapped back.

"Caring about someone other than yourself?"

"...Sure. We'll call it that."

"Why?"

"Because that's not who I am."

"We are who we choose to be."

"And I choose not to be a Beltlander. I've had enough of that life."

"Explain."

I hesitated before I responded. At first I was tempted to ignore that command. Why did she need to know my thoughts? I figured that the captain had enough faith in me up until now. She could have thrown me off her ship when the Yinda's men came after me. I owed her an explanation.

"When I was in Nordecker, everyone talked all the time about how much the collective was more important than the individual. There's a Nordecker saying about how 'one grain of sand is insignificant, but ten thousand-thousand make a sandstorm.' I believed that. It seemed like it had the ring of truth. Wisdom, however, is usually meted out by the powerful to control those without power.

"Anyone can sell a wisdom. If I say to you: seize the rhythm and live life for the here and now. Don't worry about what comes after this life, just be good. Perhaps that sounds wise? On the other hand, I can sell it the other way: live life with an eye on the future afterlife, be pious, and do good, so you will receive your just rewards from the River. Perhaps that sounds wise instead?

"Both statements have the same ring of wisdom, but cause one to support different ideas. This is the underlying truth of wisdom: it means nothing."

The captain sardonically interjected, "What a wise thing to say."

I continued, trying to ignore her interruption. "In the case of the Beltlander ethic, there's something similar going on: try to have empathy. Learn to live with others. Try to understand them.

"My father would sternly uphold that idea when talking with

other men. When it came to us women, however, that idea went out the door. You see: we were supposed to be even more altruistic than him. Women could give more, and so more was asked of them. It was just the natural order of things." My voice dripped with sarcasm as I said this last bit. "If you hold to the Beltlander ethic, you are soft. Easy prey to be manipulated. That thing you said, about leadership being understanding? That's just not true. Leadership is domination. Being a Beltlander will make you a slave. The only way to avoid that is to be self-interested.

"My self-interest led me to escape from Nordecker and a forced marriage. It led me to success on the steppe. It freed me. You want to tell me I shouldn't have done those things?

"Where does Beltlander understanding stop? How do you know when someone makes an unreasonable request of you? You can't. Everything is justified under the banner of 'you should be nicer to people'. Well, damn being nice. Damn the crew if they can't take a hard driver. Damn the Destiny, love boat that she is. Damn every bit of it."

As I finished speaking, I folded my arms. Likely, the captain wouldn't even take any part of my thoughts into account. It felt good to get that off my chest though; if Nome really wanted to criticize the way I handled the gun crew, she should've found someone else in the first place to handle that position. A smirk at her absurdity crept over my lip.

My thoughts were soon troubled by my realization that Nome hadn't been listening for the past few seconds.

A terrifyingly familiar chill had fallen over the room. I'd felt it once before. In the battery.

The Voice was here. In this very room.

I opened my mouth falteringly. "Captain, it's here."

"I know. I can see it."

Puzzlement overtook me. The captain had her eyes locked on the door. I followed her gaze, but couldn't see the monster. I knew it was here though. I sensed it instinctively.

The captain didn't move. The creature had immobilized her, as it had me the last time. I followed the captain's gaze, and in an attempt to help her, threw a punch through the air. My fist met only the slightest bit more resistance than normal. Adrenaline coursed through me.

Frost formed at the edges of the captain's desk, tendrils of it starting to reach slowly for the center between Nome and me. I shivered, and glanced nervously around. Somehow the outlights had become obscured and the room had dimmed.

At that instant, a strange blue cloud began to creep in from the outlights. It was thick, billowing, and completely opaque. With great rapidity, it flowed around the captain's shelf, and then listed towards the desk. I rose to my feet as the cloud wrapped itself around my legs. My legs screamed at me from the pain of the cold.

The cloud passed me and continued on to Hapsman, enveloping him and causing him to suddenly begin shaking. He jerked from side to side as he was swallowed from view by the cloud. I heard a frantic and distorted scream from inside his new cocoon.

The captain, for her part now fully mobile again, leapt out of her seat and reached into the cloud to drag the boy out of its grasp. She withdrew with a grimace of rage, fear, and pain as soon as her palm met the cloud's surface. Marks of frostbite crossed the surface of her hand.

The scream was cut short, and the cloud faded. After it lifted, I saw Hapsman's body underneath. He lived, but something was off about him. I expected him to shiver from his experience, or remark about how cold he felt, or continue screaming. Anything but just stand there and look suddenly indifferently at us.

There were no markings on him. No changes in his appearance. But he was different. Whoever, or whatever, stood before us had his body, but I sensed immediately that this wasn't Hapsman. The hairs on the back of my neck stood on end, and I backed away immediately towards the opposite side of the room from this abomination.

He looked up simply and slowly. To have a child give me that cold look was unutterably terrifying.

Then the Voice returned. As last time, I felt it ripple outward through my body. This time, it mixed in with the midshipman's voice. It spoke entirely in Archaic Aulan, saying various idioms and phrases I had never heard spoken, only read.

"I am not thy enemy."

Hapsman stood there, as if awaiting a response.

"What have you done to my crew member?" the tenor of Captain Nome's response shocked me out of my horror. In the face of this obviously supernatural terror, her expression remained defiant and fearless.

"Thy servant will be returned after I speak with thee. Thou trespassest in my house."

"We are on a mission of peaceful exploration to expand the boundaries of science. We do not intend to engage in conflict with anyone, but if you do not return the body of my crew member and leave my ship..."

"I will question thee at my pleasure."

"I will withhold my answers to your questions then, until you learn to respect the boundaries of my ship."

"And if I should pass from thy servant into thee to gaze upon thy mind?"

Captain Nome didn't hesitate. "If you could do that, wouldn't you do that already with him?"

The Voice's rasping laughter rattled through me. "Thy arrogance waxes hot. When we meet again, intruder, perhaps thou wilt better satisfy my curiosity."

Suddenly, Hapsman's eyes rolled into the back of his head, and he fell backward onto his chair after giving one last gasping breath.

CHAPTER 11

The side of the barber's area was too cramped for me to fully stand in. As a result, I remained seated on a three-legged stool I had requisitioned from the ship's hold. The Destiny's turbines were only separated from the chamber by a thin layer of metal, which gave the room a low, resonant hum. It sounded vaguely like some musical drone, playing interminably on the same, strangely high note. Amid the alcohol-laced smell that wafted through the room, I caught other odors of presumably medical compounds.

I attempted to push these sensations out of my focus of concentration. The midshipman Hapsman lay before me in the recovery cot, alive and yet on death's door.

Almost a full rhythm had passed between the incident in the captain's quarters and that moment, sitting at the midshipman's side. The young boy had slipped into a coma, and beads of sweat formed along his forehead. When the captain and I had carried him down to the barber, I had felt an intense fever that radiated from him. Sweat had soaked the sheets encasing him.

The barber did not have confidence that the boy would live two more rhythms.

I didn't really know why I stood here. It was evident to both the captain and me by now that locking me up wouldn't help the situation. Nonetheless, I wanted to be alone, and I found myself missing the quietness of the ship's brig. People hustled about everywhere else apart from here at Hapsman's side. The barber himself had excused watching over the boy, claiming that it didn't make much difference if he were present or not. Sooner or later, the lad would breathe his final breath, and that would be that.

Truth be told, for the second time since Dostwickr's attempted suicide, I had actually felt sorry for someone on this ship. It wasn't a good habit of thought to have, but at the same time I realized that Hapsman, more so than I, had come in complete contact with the Voice. Knowing how terrifying it was to just *listen* to the Voice made me feel for the kid.

If the midshipman died, it was a reminder that there was little we could do to protect ourselves from the Voice's possession. The thought angered me. We were mere playthings in the face of this being, helpless to defend ourselves.

That didn't stop the captain from trying. One of her first directives after the event last rhythm had been to set the chaplain about to painting prayer lines along the interior bulkheads. Protection and warding symbols had been drawn at key junctures of the ship, I learned after a brief visit from Yuri. At one point, the chaplain's path had even taken him into this room, where he took an hour to draw an intricate, multilayered sigil in the center and around Hapsman's cot. He hadn't disturbed me thankfully.

Other responses to the event were more opaque to me. Dr. Hennir had apparently locked herself in her room, and wasn't speaking to anyone. When Dr. Ininsir had attempted to engage her in conversation, there had been extremely laconic responses. Something about looking into the matter from an objective viewpoint.

Most of the officers agreed to keep this matter quiet in an attempt to dampen the fires of discontent that spread among the crew. It wouldn't work, of course.

Meanwhile, I had sat all rhythm in contemplation.

I hadn't slept. Having rested poorly for a number of off-rhythms, this pushed me over the edge to the point where I drifted in a slight daze. The deck moved beneath me, literally and from my off-kilter perception. From time to time, the small gaslight in the center of the room danced in my vision, lagging behind my perception of its surroundings.

A sudden ragged intake of breath from Hapsman jerked me out of my sleepless stupor. I blinked, and the boy started shaking violently. This lasted for a few seconds while I considered it. I wasn't sure what to do about it, and so stood up as much as I could.

Finally the boy opened his eyes and yelled loudly while lurching forward.

I blinked again.

Hapsman glanced around, and realized he was safe from

whatever haunted him. Then he saw me, and closed his eyes again while setting himself back into the cot. A quiet, relieved sigh escaped his lips.

I didn't quite know how to respond to that situation. "How do you feel?"

"Not good ma'am." His voice was scratchy with dehydration.

I held out a canteen of water. "Try this."

He nodded his thanks, and proceeded to gulp down the contents. "What did you see?"

He shook his head, repeating the word "No." He turned away from me.

"Hey, boy, you can tell me."

I shook him a little, and then heard a muffled whimper from the other side of the bed. This situation became more and more uncomfortable by the moment.

"We need to know."

He briefly paused before turning back towards me. He contemplated something, and a look passed through his eyes as though he had aged several years while he slept. At last, he looked at me, and spoke with some finality in his voice. "Yes, you do."

***

"Here you go, midshipman."

The mug that the captain handed to Hapsman was filled with a liquid I didn't care to identify. The boy greedily accepted the mug and drank it in one swig. Since waking up, his fever had diminished greatly, all that remained was rehydrating him and stuffing food down his gullet.

The entirety of the ship's senior staff had joined me at his cot: officers, the chaplain, Dr. Ininsir, the captain. And that one man, whose name I kept forgetting. Yensir.

Hapsman, for his part, took his time in starting to speak. He collected his thoughts, figuring out the best way to relate what he had experienced.

"Well?" I stood with my arms crossed, getting tired of all the waiting.

The captain insistently motioned me to silence.

Hapsman cleared his throat, preparing his voice. He looked up at us, and his tone was oddly calm.

"I saw two things, at different times. I guess?

"The first bit," he gesticulated with his hands, "was when the thing came into your quarters, cap'n. It was really cold for a bit, and then I could see myself doing stuff I wasn't making myself to do. I also felt the thing speaking. Felt like an earthquake.

"Thing is: I also felt myself thinking... I could feel what it was feeling. It's a bit difficult to take apart the two, which is the strangest thing. It was the feeling of curiosity, really deep. Curious like you wouldn't believe. Sort of, more curious than the most curious feeling I've had.

"After it left me, I blanked out. I don't really know how much time passed; Haye here says it was a whole rhythm. I remember a few weird images, and then I was in that place down below." He gestured down towards the jungle. "I knew something was following me, so I had to start running.

"It was really strange; it wasn't a usual dream, sir. It was really vivid, and I couldn't tell whether I was awake or not. I don't know if I was, maybe? It felt like it was real. All the trees around me were made of triangles, I remember that. I remember the ground had triangles on it. The rocks were triangles, the air was filled with little tiny white triangles if I squinted my eyes right. Really tiny ones. Kind of like the same thing you see if you stare at a dark place for too long. Those multicolored things?

"Well anyway, I kept running. I knew there was something behind me, but I couldn't look. All I knew was just to keep running. The edges of my vision started getting all dark-like, but just as it looked like I was gonna collapse, the trees started to thin.

"I broke out of the forest, and into a weird open space. There were still a few trees, but these were different. Kinda stumpy. It was all wide-open.

"I remember those giant rivers we saw. Those got even bigger, but the rain stopped. It was really hot, too. There were three triangles in the sky, giving off a lot of light through the clouds. I started to run faster and faster, and as I did, I started to get bigger and bigger. I was a giant."

Hapsman paused at the ridiculousness of what he had said, and laughed a little.

"I must have run a ways, when I finally saw something in the distance. It was a small black speck, which looked sunk into the ground. It was much bigger than it looked from a ways off. I was towering over it; it was a perfect miniature model of a giant basin.

"I heard a voice then, a curious one."

The captain interjected. "Was it the one we heard earlier?"

"No, this was one that was completely different. It didn't roll through me like that one did. I remember what it said: 'Where goest thou?'

"I looked back, and a whole army of those native beasts was closing in from behind me. My memory's a bit foggy, but I remember that I was safe because something stopped them. I'm sorry I don't know what it was. I don't remember."

When Hapsman had finished, the captain quickly confirmed with a glance that Dr. Ininsir had been taking down the boy's statement in her notepad. She nodded at the midshipman. "Thank you, Hapsman, you've provided us with vital clues about our pursuer."

The boy's expression turned anxious. "I can't feel my legs, ma'am. I didn't want to bring that up before now. Didn't seem important enough. I can't move them either."

The captain and Dr. Ininsir exchanged a worried glance.

"Will I be ok?"

The doctor stepped in with an overly-hopeful statement. "There's a good chance your legs will return to you. We just got you out of a profoundly deep coma. Your legs could just be slower to wake up."

Hapsman looked crestfallen. "Maybe not though..."

"I'll examine you after we've had a talk with the captain so we can determine what the source of that problem is, ok?" The doctor attempted an encouraging smile.

"Ok ma'am, I guess."

The captain had pulled herself away from the cot's side and left the barber's. Her actions had an effect on the rest of us, and as one unit, we left the boy's bedside.

As soon as we were out of earshot, the captain stopped and turned around shortly.

"Your opinions on the reliability of the boy's account?" she queried.

The chaplain's swiftly replied, "I don't doubt he experienced what he said. Whether we can trust the vision granted to him is another matter."

Nome pushed her hand into her captain's jacket. "It bears the hallmarks of a vision from the River, doesn't it?"

"Certainly many, but the boy is not a priest of the Riverrun. We can't necessarily trust that some of the meaning wasn't garbled by his own interpretation or memory."

"Perhaps the River had some reason for giving him the vision instead?"

"Preposterous!" the chaplain guffawed.

"You're not seriously considering looking for the basin Hapsman saw?" Dr. Ininsir said incredulously. "It was a fevered dream. Even if it was a vision, what's to say it wasn't a vision from our pursuer? I recall it saying the exact thing: 'where goest thou'."

The captain addressed the chaplain ignoring Ininsir's input, "You said you had difficulty in classifying our pursuer? If it is one of the First Biehs, we can't hold it off by our own effort. Even your skills may be inadequate. We need to try and find this safe place, wherever it is."

Evinsir spoke up. "That might lose us a few rhythms looking for it."

"They will be rhythms well-spent." She turned to me. "I assume you'll have a resupply team ready by that time?"

I glanced back at the other officers before answering. "Yeah, I have a special request for the team. I would appreciate lieutenant Dostwickr being assigned to resupply."

***

I was getting sick of the Destiny by now. For three rhythms straight since the captain's meeting with the Voice, I'd been either trapped in the cramped spaces below deck, or wandering above decks aimlessly. I'd occasionally scanned the horizon for interlopers, but since our last encounter, I hadn't seen anything to break the monotony of ship life. We were now a full ten-rhythm into the journey, and I knew we hadn't yet gotten to the halfway point sunward. I felt as though I was slowly being suffocated from boredom. At times, I regretted my decision to join this crew, but then I promptly remembered the bounty hunters who, doubtless, waited for me when I returned darkward.

On the exact tenth rhythm since our departure from Kinyu I stood yet again on deck, peering behind us over the ceaseless jungle that grew ever patchier below us. The Great Range was well out of sight, leaving me with only fetid streams to focus my attention on. They wound in strange patterns that felt more appropriate for ferns than natural water features: weird spirals and tendrils that flowed outward from a single spring. The wind picked up as we continued, each cloud being more turbulent than the last. I spied Yuri losing his lunch over the side while Dr. Ininsir prattled to him, oblivious of his situation.

"That's why they thought of it that way. Perhaps that was why early classical philosophers would conflate the two?"

I wandered down towards the duo, and butted into the conversation. "What?"

"I was just explaining to Yuri here that the sun was thought of in terms of a river flowing across the sunward horizon from the Nemasian to anti-Nemasian side of the world. Early Beltlanders couldn't of course see the sun's orb, so perhaps that explains some of the references in the book you acquired for me to the River being sunward."

"Have you found anything you like in there yet?"

"Yes actually!" A grin spread across her face. "I've found references to Aulan nobility being descended directly from a group of 'Noble Beings' who came from the River's land. It fits my theory perfectly!"

"Isn't that book somewhat frowned on?"

"Only because people aren't willing to consider ancient historians as reliable sources." She sniffed one of her indignant sniffs.

"And those creatures at the city? How do they fit in with this theory?"

"Their existence doesn't disprove my idea! On the contrary, I have a working hypothesis that they descended from a common ancestor they share with humanity."

"And the Voice?"

"I'm still convinced there are some strange psycho-disruptive effects aboard this ship. I'm not exactly sure how that can be the case, only that it must be. Dr. Hennir is working through some possible explanations, including some unknown pathogen in the sunward air. I've personally noticed some strange effects in my radio-lab. Lightrot intensity seems to be increasing as we get closer to the sun. We now know that Lightrot has some psycho-dynamic qualities, this could be the source of the hallucinations."

I looked at her in disbelief, not quite knowing what to say.

Yuri's exclamation of surprise interrupted me, "Hey, look down below!"

"I don't want to see your barf, Yuri."

"Not that! The jungle's disappearing!"

It was true. As I looked over the side of the gondola, trying not to breathe in the smell of the ship's sides, there was a precipitous decline in the thick shroud that up until now had hidden the ground, which was carpeted by a thick mossy coat of black lichen. The tree line was sharp. In half a kilometer, the trees thinned in a smooth gradient to a small collection of stubby helix-bushes that dotted the landscape like spice granules.

The ground also sloped downward as a whole, and then immediately loomed back up, leaving a gently sloping deep valley that spanned a quarter-kilometer. This feature repeated itself for many more iterations before I realized that it bore resemblance to the ripple marks I'd seen made by children using sand and water. On this grand scale, however, the size of them overwhelmed me. What titanic force had swept through this landscape to leave such a monstrous mark? It must have continued, concealed underneath the growth behind us.

Whatever power had been through here couldn't have been that far into the past. The never-ending rain on this side of the Great Range would have washed these formations away.

Suddenly to the fore of the Destiny, the fog cleared and the rain stopped again. As it did, I could see for miles on the horizon. A massive wall of rock, sharply uplifted from the ground, loomed up before us. Had I not seen the outlines and terrifying forms of the Great Range itself previously, I would surely have gasped. The wall of rock thrust a kilometer into the air, something we could easily pass over. The formation curved away from us, a crescent whose bow we faced.

It took a short time to pass over this new and unexpected mountain range. As we did so, it became clear that the crescent I had formerly identified nearly completed as a circle on the opposite side of the range. The ground, too, sunk much lower than the ground behind us. It was a... basin? It spanned around fifty kilometers in total, and beyond it I saw my first sight in person of something I'd seen only in photographs.

A vast ocean, stretching further into the distance than I could comprehend. The clouds had broken; behind us one giant arm of clouds extended across the sky. Ahead of us, another cloud shadowed the way ahead, disguising the true extent of the ocean beyond. The darkness of rainfall concealed the way forward in a menacing shroud.

Above us, the sun shone as brightly as it ever had, illuminating the ground below in a brilliant orange tint.

The basin's ground was stunningly beautiful. Where black lichen covered the flatlands outside, the interior was sprinkled with pools of water. A purple plant covered the surface of each. It gave the surface a brilliant and vibrant hue that I felt a sense of awe at.

Was this the basin from Hapsman's vision? Were we safe here?

***

Two hours later, and I sat on my outraptor next to one of those primordial pools, letting her drink. She chirruped pleasantly as she drank in the clear, fresh water, nosing away the violet buds that obstructed her access.

The great benefit of outraptors, as opposed to other forms of transport, is that their maintenance is practically non-existent. They recapture most of the water they excrete, and they eat once per every ten-rhythm. As such, my outraptor hadn't had a drink in a while. I had decided to let her at the water pool for a treat.

The plants that covered the basin had a firm-stemmed center, with little spherical buds that spread outwards from the middle stalk in fractal patterns. The water was almost completely covered with them. It took quite a bit of prodding by my outraptor to separate the foliage and gain access to the freshwater beneath.

Behind me, I heard the other members of my small team. We were only a scout team, not on resupply work. Four had been selected besides me: Yuri, Dr. Ininsir, Tian' Xi, and of course, Dostwickr.

Yuri was having some trouble with his outraptor. "Now, steady there girl! Hold up!"

I looked up and pondered the land before us. Except for the cheese-holes where water pools stagnated, the land was fairly rocky. Closer to the ocean, the ground became more sandy. I figured we would avoid that area. Predators could hide beneath the sand.

I heard a cry of revulsion behind me, and turned in my saddle to see a hand-sized arthropod crawling out of the pool to my side. It had innumerable legs. Yuri's outraptor had started from the sudden intruder, lurching backward with an outraptor cry of alarm. I reached down with my walking stick and impaled the offending creature. It writhed, trying to escape my grasp.

"Disgusting." I pulled it up to my face and looked it over.

"Well, that's one water source we're not drinking." Dr. Ininsir replied.

"Tell me about it."

"I imagine they lay their eggs in that water. Drinking from there will involve some ingestion of potential parasites."

My face contorted into a grimace, and I threw the dying creature back into the water, nudging my outraptor away from its edge.

"Where to?" asked Tian' Xi.

I looked around again. A small rolling lump in the land rose gently about a kilometer from our location. "There." I felt it as good a place to investigate as any.

As we wandered over, I noticed that the lump had an almost animal-like form. It must have been a figment of my imagination, already taxed with encountering mythical beasts. Nonetheless, the resemblance was uncanny: the head of the "animal" swung away from the center of the basin, with some long trunk-like protrusion snaking away into the distance. Towards the base, a tail, thicker than an andironback's, sloped gently with the beginning of the basin's inner curve. The animal, if it had existed, would have been huge. It would have easily surpassed even the mighty Es-erdon in size.

I blinked, and my interpretation of its shape vanished.

We crested the top, and suddenly stopped, as a sudden vertical drop stretched about three meters below. Yet another surprise presented itself as I surveyed the scene before us.

An explosion presented itself of different, cold colors in the cleft of this dune-like structure. Shocks of blue arose in regular, ordered rectangles, alongside more obviously unkempt fields of purple. Several rows of some strange, alien cultivar happily grew alongside helix-bushes. A small cottage stood in the center, though not a cottage built in the same manner as the primitive village we had encountered before. It was a building made from stone slabs, repeatedly stacked on top of each other and sealed together with mortar. The roof of the hut, which was made from thin tubular plants, sloped upward in a conical fashion, with eaves that drooped down over the walls of the building like oversized bangs.

A well topped by a hand-crank system stood nearby, and a stone pen full of indistinct and scaled forms that were dormant, unaware of our presence. I saw a line full of clothing, withered and tattered, but still retaining some of its original luster. Various serfs' tools lined the cottage, built for farming, and quite rusted.

Why hadn't we seen this from the air?

In the middle of this bizarre alien oasis was a man, sleeping with his back to a helix-bush quite contentedly, oblivious of everything around him.

CHAPTER 12

I scanned the surrounding area. There weren't any threats in our immediate vicinity, but who knew if someone or *something* lay in wait in this man's field. Or perhaps his pen, or his house. I couldn't see any other cover that an enemy could hope to use against us.

"By the River..." Yuri breathlessly exclaimed behind me.

"Shh. We could be watched." I hissed in reply.

All of us backed our mounts away from the side of the hill. I heard the scribble of a pencil from Dr. Ininsir taking notes.

"Thoughts, doc?" I inquired.

"It seems we may have found someone who preceded us. It could be useful to talk to him."

I glanced over at her briefly. "What makes you think he'll want to talk?"

"We have civilized food and shelter, and failing that, guns."

An unwilling grin spread across my face.

"What?"

"Nothing, doc. I agree completely."

Dostwickr shivered despite the heat. "I don't like it." She said.

"I'm with Dostwickr on this one." Tian' Xi said. "Anyone else notice how bright this place is? We would have seen it from the air. Something's definitely off about this place. It's a trap."

"No question, definitely a trap." Calm laced my reply. "But we're armed, and on outraptors. We can pull out easily if someone jumps at us from the field, and chances are we could outrun them."

Yuri scratched his head. At this point, I was amazed his jerkin didn't have more dandruff than it did. "All the same Haye, this place ain't natural."

"Duh."

"No, I mean," he sighed in frustration, "it has a weird feeling to it. Before that incident with Hapsman, I wouldn't have thought nothing of it, but this place definitely feels like... do you hear that?"

His sudden shift in subject caught me off guard. "What?"

"That..."

Now that I thought of it, I did hear a sound in the distance. I drew my revolver and cocked it in response. It was a single tone, very faintly and endlessly playing. It felt near and far at the same time; I couldn't place its location. It sounded similar to an organ. It felt vaguely like the Voice, but it didn't intrude as much on my consciousness. Occasionally, faint prehistoric echoes would chime in on the same chord. The whole arrangement had a weirdly reverent air to it, as if some distant and primeval composer had poured their life's efforts into the worship of some forgotten god, and this was the last chord of their last piece, eternally sounding out throughout the ages.

It startled me how it had crept up on us. We hadn't been hearing it when we trekked up here. Only gradually had it filtered into my conscience; I had dismissed it as the sound of the wind at first. It didn't grow any louder, but remained at a low volume.

"I hear it!" Tian' Xi's exclamation was filled with unease.

My expression soured. "Don't shout."

"We should head back." Yuri glanced back at the relative safety of the Destiny.

"We have no indication there's a threat present, and this is by far the most interesting thing for miles around. If we didn't investigate, we'd be disregarding our duty." Dr. Ininsir spoke without breaking her concentration on sketching. She had already captured about half the details of the farm below. "I say we go down there."

Dostwickr and Tian' Xi looked to me. I in turn returned my gaze to the lonely figure at the base of the helix-bush. After a long pause, I made my choice. "Weapons at the ready. We'll skirt around the perimeter first, scout the place out. If anything jumps out at us, we leave for the Destiny at top speed."

I heard an assortment of sounds: the twist of a leather strap as Yuri unslung his automatic rifle from its position on his back, Tian' Xi drawing a revolver and flicking the safety off, Dostwickr fumbling with hers. I directed my outraptor towards the right side of the bulge we stood on, and we set off at a mild canter.

From the sides of the farm, I got to see more of the settlement. It was surprisingly austere; none of the implements one would normally expect would be required to tend crops were present. A plow leaned up against the back wall of the cottage of course, but I didn't see an attached seeder, or any animal that could draw the plow behind itself. The more I looked, the more the whole scene suggested some improbable parody of a farm. A "rustic" painting of one, or what a city-dweller might imagine a farm to look like. It made my hackles rise as I realized that someone had made a strong effort to make this entire setup appear very like what they expected a farm to look like.

Whoever had designed this place, however, did have some off-the-wall notions of human architecture. A cascade of steps led up from a flat area behind the hut. All of these steps were almost a half-meter high, leading me to think at first they were gardening terraces. The hut too, I finally managed to see, had both front and back doors that stretched up well over three meters. Whoever had built this was either a giant, or had no reference for a normal human door.

A part of me wondered how much of this was paranoia on my part. That possibility struck me as less and less valid with each waking second.

When we had fully circled this uncanny outpost, I wordlessly spurred my outraptor towards the hut, along a cobbled path that led between the alien fields. The others followed me single-file with their weapons raised, scanning the tall flora for an attack.

We approached slowly and surely, listening for rustles among the farmland. That infernally steady tone still haunted our ears. I found myself wondering if it masked the movement of an ambush. It neither increased nor decreased in decibel level.

Finally, we reached the owner of this mirage, perhaps its architect. He lay on a level dirt landing immediately below the hut, still resting as peacefully as he did before. As I dismounted and handed my reins to Dostwickr to take a closer look at him, he remained oblivious to my approach.

He was a gangly specimen. There was a wisp-like quality about him that left me questioning how much of a real fight he could put up. Underneath the baggy folds of his clothing I saw a frame that was slight, almost starved. His silver hair hung in tatters down the sides of his head, except at the top, where a broad patch of baldness betrayed a withered and mole-ridden skin. Likewise a long, ragged and curly beard made its way down his chin. He had propped his back up against the helix-bush behind him. His hands were folded neatly in his lap, and a placid expression was frozen on his face as he continued his slumber. Like the rest of us, his skin was dark, a welcome change from the whiteskins we'd encountered on the darkward side of the Range.

Hints of archaic symbols had been embroidered into the hems and extremities of his rags. Every time I looked at them, I couldn't quite grasp their form. Partly this was due to their faded nature, but partly it was because they shifted with every change in perspective. Optical illusions wove their way through the fabric.

I stepped closer, blocking the sun's rays over the man. Instinctively, I kicked him sharply in the shins, drawing a gasp of disapproval from behind me.

He didn't move an inch, or react in any way. Either he was an accomplished actor, or he was *out*.

"Should we really be waking him?" Dostwickr whispered timidly.

"Doesn't look like we can."

"Was it really necessary to do that?" I heard a sniff from Dr. Ininsir.

Annoyed, I faced her. "Why is it every time I do something rough to anyone, you always step in and complain about it?"

She turned back to her notepad. Yuri and Tian' Xi both dismounted and joined me. Dostwickr remained there lamely, holding three sets of outraptor reins in her hand. She couldn't hold all of them if they bolted.

Yuri leaned down and examined the sleeper as I had. "Seems a strange fellow... What do you think he's out from?"

I shrugged. "Who cares? We should check the rest of this place and see if there's anything valuable to provision ourselves with."

"Not the best way to win friends."

I shrugged. "This guy isn't waking up any time soon. We'll be long gone before he comes around."

"Still, awful bad manners." Tian' Xi crouched down beside the slumbering farmer. "There's something else to consider: taking stuff from here might be a bad idea. We don't know if this guy eats the same food we do. *And,*" she emphasized the word, "we don't know if he has friends waiting inside the house. We should leave."

I frowned. "We're going to at least look inside. Yuri, scope the pen, will you?"

Yuri gave me an uneasy look, but moved to comply.

"Haye."

For the first time since I'd joined the expedition, the master of altitude gave me a strongly annoyed look.

"Tian' Xi."

"I'm serious, if we want to restock on provisions, we should look elsewhere."

I matched her stare. She wanted to question my authority? Fine. I was in command of this squad, and she should have understood that.

She returned to her outraptor and mounted it. I turned with her movement, my back now to the helix-bush.

I threw my arms outward. "There is no elsewhere. I'm not willing to test those purple buds out on anyone, and it looks like they're the only plant around for miles besides these ones. There's definitely food here, ripe for the taking. So I'm overriding your intuitions on this one. We've got no other choice.

"Besides," I added with finality, "This guy's not waking up any time soon. It's easy pickings out here."

From behind me, a wizened, gentle, and mildly amused voice spoke. "Or so you say."

***

I started immediately from my position and spun around, both hands on my revolver, bringing it level to my chest as the rest of the group stepped back in fright. I looked, but the man wasn't standing yet. He remained sprawled luxuriantly against the helix-bush, his eyes blinking and a knowing smile spread across his lips. I lowered my gun to aim at him on the floor.

"Who are you?" I demanded.

He yawned disinterestedly and stretched his arms from their position on his lap. "I should be asking you the same question, if I didn't already know the answer."

"I'll ask the questions, thank you very much."

"My my! Such rudeness! And to think I was going to offer you my hospitality willingly." With some difficulty the man stood up. My revolver barrel tracked his movement as he patted down the back of his clothes. Despite his lanky build, he moved quite quickly for an old man.

He finished removing the majority of the dust from his robes and raised an eyebrow at me. "Will you put that crude thing away? I doubt it would even scratch my nose if you fired it."

My gun remained raised. "Name?"

He threw up his arms. "Fine. Do whatever makes you feel comfortable. You should know how impolite you're being though."

"Haye?" Dr. Ininsir inquired. I glanced back at her, and saw a look that said more than can be said in words.

Reluctantly, I safetied and holstered my weapon.

The old man rumbled pleasantly. "Thank you. At least someone here has some sense of common civility."

"You still haven't answered my question." I shot an accusatory glance back at him.

"Ah yes, that. Excuse me one moment." He clapped his hands together, and immediately the drone in the background ceased, leaving only the sound of wind whistling through the sides of the basin. "Can't believe I left that dreary thing on."

"What is it? And how did you do that?" the doctor immediately inquired.

"It helps the delvers hibernate." he said matter-of-factly, "They get a little cranky if left untended for too long. Can't have them digging under their fence. As for your last question..." he smiled, "I'm afraid that is far beyond your limited comprehension."

She sniffed. "I'm a scientist. Try me."

From the animal pen, a sudden chorus of angry grunts and frightened yelps erupted. A few moments later, Yuri came running around the corner holding his rear. I saw a very sizeable tear in the seat of his pants, but no flesh wounds thankfully.

I scowled. "Warn us before you do something like that again."

The man sighed. "Not my fault your comrade was poking around back there. How was I to know he'd be snooping where he wasn't wanted?"

"Don't get smart with me. You knew he was back there. After all, you know who we are, don't you?"

"Yes." He nodded the affirmative.

"And yet we don't know a single thing about you. You're not in cahoots with the Voice are you?"

He suddenly beamed with an unnatural joy. "I *like* that name! It fits him!"

"How?"

"Getting him to stop speaking is a near-impossible task. Especially in that ridiculous manner." The man began flailing his arms and crossed his eyes. "'Thou art made of dust's excrement! I shall rewardest thy stupidity with more insane rambling!'"

Despite myself, I briefly cracked a smile before resuming a less trusting expression.

"Anyhow, I assume you've come here because your ship needs provisioning, and your friend-servant received my message. This is good. And very timely too."

"You were the one that sent the vision?"

Yuri kept rubbing his buttocks, as if nursing a grave injury. "Can you nix the skazki and just tell us who you are?" he said.

I made a slight addendum: "Do you mean us harm?"

"None. Nor particularly any good will, but you are an interesting lot. You bring back a lot of memories for me..." The old man fell silent for a bit.

A faraway look glimmered in his eye. A vague sadness played about his features as he turned away to look at the sun.

"I should say memories of memories," he finally said after a while, "and memories of memories of memories."

We all waited for an answer to the first question.

"I don't really remember my first name, given to me when all things were younger. I swore an oath at one time to forget it. Long story." He held up a hand. "That story doesn't concern you. I have, however, since taken up many monikers. You can call me Archivist if you want. Or Chronicler. I've been called both."

"Some chronicler you are if you can't remember your own name."

"You'll learn, if you've lived as long as I have, that names are meaningless syllables. I describe myself by my function in whichever eon I've lived. I've recorded many more important things than names in my mind.

"I've a finite amount of space in my memory, and each waking moment I lose the recollection of something that happened millennia ago. All that's left is the knowledge that there used to be a memory there. And so I am left with a memory of a memory." The Archivist folded his hands in front of him.

We sat there stunned. Tian' Xi managed to stutter out, "How...

long have you been alive?"

"I don't really remember." He chuckled. "Quite a while I think."

"Great." I irreverently quipped, "So have you ever thought about writing anything down?"

"Yes, actually. Not the way you think, but yes." He lifted his tunic, and I saw alien hieroglyphs tattooed across his ancient torso. "All paper molds and decays. Every metal rusts, even gold. Or, it can be destroyed by the enemies of history. My body?" He thrust his tunic back down. "It seems it is indestructible. That is the burden I've had to bear for many years."

"What's written there?"

"Stories from rhythms long past. Battles fought between our kind. Pointless clashes with no bloodshed and no victor. Cycles and recycles of history lived and breathed by the same two hundred cursed minds over and over and over again. The entire well of endless time. In no less than five separate languages of course." He chuckled again. "I seem to have forgotten the method of reading the first two, of course. You're right, I'm a terrible Archivist.

"But I've since stopped feeling bad about it, of course. I beat myself black and blue for nearly two centuries after losing the first tongue. Literally went to the highest mountain back there and cast myself off it. It failed, of course. All I succeeded in doing was crushing a poor delver that had the temerity to follow me and stand beneath my jumping spot to save its master. Poor thing."

His expression didn't change, but his words sent trickles of ice down my spine.

"I'm not buying it."

I looked back at the speaker. It was the doctor.

"I'm not buying that you're immortal. I refuse to believe it."

"Well then, how do you explain this?" he clapped his hands and a jaunty tavern theme began playing from nowhere. The Archivist began dancing a lively jig to the triple-beat while clapping his hands.

"Are you taking requests?" Yuri's voice sounded amused.

"Why yes! What would you like to hear?" The Archivist laughed madly.

"Can you play that one song... how does it go?"

"Indeed I can!" The Archivist clapped again and the music changed to balalaika and accordion. He hopped up and down after the manner of the Bezlanders.

Yuri's eyes went wide with shock. "Well I'll be! You really can read our minds!"

"No mind reading necessary, old chap!" The Archivist cried cheerfully. "It's written on your expression!"

The doctor yelled over the carnival. "Any sufficiently advanced technology is indistinguishable from magic!"

The Archivist continued dancing. "So perhaps I have some hitherto unknown technology you don't know of! What difference does it make! Come dance with me!" His laugh became more boisterous. "It's been a long time since I've had visitors!"

"WAIT A MINUTE!" I commanded.

The Archivist looked dejected and clapped his hands again. "Your type are no fun. I wish I had remembered that."

"Tell us right now who you are, what you mean by that vision, who the Voice is, and do *not* start up that awful noise again." I scowled at him. Out of the corner of my eye, I saw Yuri wince a little.

The man looked playfully at me. "Do you prefer Nemasian swing?"

"No."

"Aulan opera?"

"No!"

"Nordecker chant?"

"No!"

"Commonwealth cat-wailing, help me out here!"

"NO! I prefer a straight answer from you!"

"Ok, ok! No need to shout! If you had wanted the whole thing now, you should have said so! Or maybe you did, I don't really remember..."

I felt my anger boiling over.

The Archivist grinned. "Temper yourself, youngling. Your life is short. You should be merrier. In any case, I think it best if you take me to your leader."

His expression became more serious. "There will be trouble coming this way, very soon."

***

Deathly quiet filled the briefing room as the Archivist sipped at the vanishingly small glass of water in front of him. A crowd of airmen had gathered outside the room, and while I couldn't see them through the door, their presence was palpable.

The Archivist wasn't the least bit perturbed by the sight of the entire senior staff of the Destiny eyeing him. He looked briefly into the glass, examining its contents quite thoroughly. At last, he spoke up.

"Quite good. Twelve millennia, fine year. Excellent vintage. Bit more fresh than I'm accustomed to, but hey, to each their own."

Nobody responded. Across the table, the captain gave him a cold stare.

The Archivist downed the glass in one fell swoop before gasping as if drinking strong vodka. "Ah! That hits the spot."

"Who are you and what are you doing here?" The captain said quietly.

"Can I just say that, the whole time I've been aboard your ship, captain, nobody aboard has been the least bit welcoming to me? Where's your sense of hospitality?" A moping, mock-sad expression plastered itself on his face.

"I've no time to waste on your games. Either you tell us your piece, or you leave the ship."

The Archivist nodded in defeat. "Oh very well. Have it your way." He looked up at the ceiling. "The question is where to begin?"

Yuri waggled his eyebrows. "You could begin at the beginning?"

"Why that's a fine idea!" The Archivist chortled. "In the time before time began, there was no land but the mountain..."

"Oh for the River's sake." My head fell to my hands.

"Ok, so maybe not the beginning-beginning, eh? Maybe think of that the next time before you make a dumb suggestion."

The captain aborted Yuri's protest. "Mr. Aldarin, please refrain from speaking."

She turned back towards the immortal. "We're listening."

The Archivist cricked his neck, and leaned forward, his eyes suddenly intent.

"I don't know how long I've been alive. I already told you that. All I know is that myself and one hundred and ninety nine of my brethren were awakened to this world many eons, epochs, and even more inconceivable cycles of time ago than you can possibly imagine with your limited brains. The closest words I have to describe these cycles is... not really existent. The very concept is unknown to your kind.

"What I can tell you is that an uncountable years' existence frays your mind unless you hold on to certain principles. I know for a fact that exactly sixty-six of my brethren have gone completely insane from the Long Awakeness. Whereas your kind was blessed with the Long Sleep, my kind is cursed with immortality. Cursed to remain alive until the very last stars blink from the night sky. Until this entire world is swallowed in flame and thrown off by her mother sun like some cast-off piece of garbage.

"My waking life is a nightmare. Every stale moment that I spend awake with you is a living hell."

The Archivist stood up suddenly and slammed his hands on the table. "My only blessing is a finite memory. Every moment I'm awake, something old is forgotten in my mind, leaving it able to be experienced again for the first time."

Anger filled his voice. "You don't have any idea what it's like to live like this, do you? With eternal boredom permeating your *every* step. Every square centimeter along this gigantic basin you see? I've walked over it. You privileged species. You arrogant, fortunate *insects*.

"I've walked the furthest reaches of this world from the sunward to darkward poles. I've even been further into what you call the ether, though my expeditions there have been curtailed for the time being. I cannot maintain my sanity at the sameness of the void beyond. Every rhythm that passes in that hellhole is even worse than if I'd lived here instead."

"It's true; there is a functionally infinite universe out there. But the attempt to explore it has driven sixty-six of my brethren mad. I, wisely, turned back with the others, leaving a third of my dearly-beloved siblings to their choice to descend into madness.

"The condition of your species is short, violent, and cruel. It has an end cut short in the prime of its youth, or in the almost-wisdom of "old" age." The Archivist laughed a pained laugh. "For us, there is only the promise of new things to get up for the next rhythm, and the next rhythm, and the next, and the next. And so on."

The Archivist shivered, before clenching his fists and grinning like a madman. "Yes! I'm feeling anger for the first time in millennia! By the primeval times, yes! I hate you! I hate you all!" He laughed maniacally, before slumping back into his chair, and starting to cry with joy. "You have no idea how good that feels! Ah!"

He sobbed and sobbed. "Does anyone have a handkerchief?" Yuri threw him his own. "Thank you." He blew his nose, and giant strings of snot flew out of his nose past the handkerchief, and onto the tabletop where it remained in a disgusting puddle.

He held up the soaked rag. "Will... will you be wanting this back?"

Yuri rapidly shook his head. "Keep it."

"Ok." A dejected look spread across his face. "Sorry for messing it up."

An unsettling feeling had begun to bubble in my mind as to this creature's predicament. Obviously he was in a great deal of pain, but the alien nature of his thoughts gave me the jitters.

The Archivist cleared his expression. "Pardon me; I must be too mercurial for you. I'm a bad Archivist, and it seems I'm a bad personality too."

A quiet voice spoke across the table. "You're not as bad as you think."

Everyone turned to look. It was Dostwickr. She suddenly flinched at the attention, and we all pretended to look elsewhere.

A smile popped onto the Archivist's face. "Thank you child. It's the thought of meeting civil, polite people like you that keeps me going."

Dostwickr hid her face, and I couldn't tell what she felt.

The Archivist continued. "Again pardon me. I should tell you what bearing this has on your situation.

"That creature pursuing you? He's one of ours. He's not evil, honest. He's just curious like the rest of us. He spends most of his time up on the mountains, alone. Hasn't had much time to spend on social skills. Doesn't know where his boundaries are. If I was telling you the truth, I think that's because he doesn't pay much attention to our collective subconscious."

"You have a collective subconscious?" Tian' Xi exclaimed.

The immortal creature paused. "Did I not mention that? Yes!" He slapped his hands to his head. "Oh, how could I not mention that? Bad Archivist! Bad!" He began slamming his head into the table.

The captain interrupted, yelling. "Mr. Archivist! You will desist from wrecking this ship's furniture!"

The Archivist paused. "Yes, I'm sorry. Quite sorry about that."

He patted his clothes down before continuing.

"We dream together, so I know his intentions.

"He's lashing out like a child. He doesn't know any different. He's completely forgotten how to behave in proper society. If he can't find out who you are, and somehow find out something new from you, he'll try and..." he pounded one fist into the palm of the other to indicate what he said.

The room was noiseless for only a few seconds before Dr. Hennir spoke. "Strange."

She walked around the side of the table and held an examining scope in the creature's eye. "There's no increased dilation in his eyes, captain. He certainly believes he's telling the truth. I can't guess what the cause of his particular form of psychosis is. I've never seen it so strong in disturbed individuals before."

"Psychosis!" An enraged shout came from the chaplain. "Captain, throw this foul Biehs off the ship! Begone you evil creature!" He made a sign of prayer lines on his palms.

The Archivist looked curiously up at Dr. Hennir. "I like you! Not so much him, but you I can get behind!"

"Patient is most likely suffering from severe effects of lightrot from prolonged exposure to the sun. I suggest we halt our progress until we can figure out how to counter the effects."

I started in. "Doctor, he's not crazy..."

In a flash, she hurried across the table and peered at my face through an oversize lens. "Intriguing. It seems it doesn't take long for the lightrot exposure to take effect. I'll have to begin a clinical record. With your permission, captain, I would like to examine both patients personally."

"I warn you, creature, come out of this man's body! In the name of the River, I cast you out, vile..." The chaplain raised a shaking finger towards the Archivist as he said this.

The chaplain didn't get any further. Nome gave an enraged shout that cut him off. "Both of you, shut up! If I hear one more peep from either of you, you'll be spending the remaining expedition in the ship's brig."

Silence reigned once more at the table. Nome breathed out while continuing to question the Archivist. "What exactly was the substance of your message to us? Are you offering us protection from our pursuer?"

"Yes!" The Archivist nodded enthusiastically. "The others and I have dreamt a solution to the problem. It's been the most intriguing council we've held in over a thousand years, let me tell you..."

"Get to the point."

"I was just getting to that, don't panic! He needs some form of discipline. He's played with his toys for too long, and that gives him a god complex. We've all come to the conclusion that it's high time we straighten him out. Set him on the narrow. Learn him some-"

"And?"

"He'll be bringing his toys along to assault the airship, since he's not powerful enough to take it by himself. Long story. It involves some family business I'd rather not get into.

"We're forming a different group of creatures to fight his group. They'll beat him for sure; we have the strength of numbers. But, there's a catch: they'll be here within about four hours."

My brow furrowed. "How is that a catch?"

The Archivist started and stopped speaking multiple times. "His army..."

"Yes?" I demanded.

He continued hemming and hawing. Captain Nome wasn't having any of that. "Speak quickly."

I knew where this was going. I knew exactly where this was going.

The Archivist finally relented. "His minions will be here within two hours. You're going to have to hold him off for that amount of time."

Suddenly, a commotion exploded at the rear of the chamber. An airman rushed in. "Captain! The ship's turbines are frozen! A solid cube of ice!"

The Archivist met the captain's gaze. "And that, is why."

CHAPTER 13

The drums beat considerably louder than I'd come to expect over my duration with this ship. A frenetic energy in their sound threatened to overwhelm the drummers' discipline. They were scared.

I couldn't blame them. Although I'd made peace with the situation a few minutes ago, mostly to make room in my mind for thoughts of how we were going to defend the ship, the fight or flight response still lingered in me.

It also caused problems for the crew's preparations. Everywhere I saw airmen making mistakes and miscommunicating.

After exhausting every option to raise the ship's altitude without the turbines, captain Nome had reluctantly conceded that the ship needed to fight. A strong possibility existed of losing some of her crew in the process, and I had briefly perceived her hatred at the thought.

Once the decision had been made to hold out, any reservations she had disappeared. She had experienced war before. She relocated the entire senior staff to the aft of the gondola's deck, where an extremely good view of the surrounding area stretched out before us.

We had several advantages. The ground around us was rocky and unforgiving. While scouting, I had for the most part stayed mounted on my outraptor for this reason. Outraptors are sure-footed; humans are not. The hope was that the enemy force would stumble and fall over the sharp terrain, breaking their charge. A clear lack of cover also acted to our advantage; not a single tree grew in this desolate basin.

The downside of defending here were the depressions containing those purple-foliaged ponds. Each of them fell about a meter or so below ground level. Two of them were particularly close to the ship:

one about twenty meters from the Destiny's front port side, one about thirty from its aft port. If the enemy took shelter from our fire in there, they would have defensible positions very close to our ship.

We had oriented the Destiny so its port side faced the opposite end of the basin. This was the direction that the enemy would approach from. Already, I saw a rapidly expanding orange blob kicking up dust in the distance. It appeared as if they were popping out of the ground - there was no pass through the basin's outer slope. At this distance, I couldn't tell how they were mysteriously appearing like that, but I could hear them. A faint rumble echoed off the mountains, coupled with primordial cries of anger.

The captain placed both hands on the guardrail. "We need to keep them at range. They don't have sophisticated ballistic weapons, so they will attempt to charge the ship and close the distance. Pullnir, thoughts?"

"The cannons can do significant damage, but their firing rate won't be enough to stall a charge. We can fire one, maybe two broadsides before they close distance." Pullnir responded.

"Small arms and bayonets readied for close-quarters, captain." Yuri said while loading bullets into an automatic rifle drum.

"Again, they'll overwhelm us if we don't change the battlefield in our favor, sir." Pullnir said.

The captain glanced over at the pond depressions and pointed at them calmly. "We need to secure those. Master of Engineering, are your satchels ready?"

"Ready and waiting sir."

"Saturate those ponds. They'll likely go for them. We can spring the trap on them when those positions are full."

I shook my head. Yuri's "satchels" as he called them were defensive charges that could be placed as mines. Each would only give us one blast. Useful, but not a game changer. "That's only going to delay us being overrun." I said.

Nome nodded. "Indeed. If only we had a repeater gun... Dr. Ininsir? Do you have anything to add?"

The doctor shook her head, but then reconsidered it and spoke. "I could synthesize a small amount of mulpherous gas from my stocks of sulfur dichloride and ethylene."

The captain frowned. "What exactly is that?"

"A very strong desiccant. Effects are particularly potent several hours after breathing it in..."

The captain shook her head. "Forget it. The weather gauge isn't consistently for us, and therefore we risk that blowing back in our face. We also need something more immediate."

I broke in. "Don't we have barbed wire below decks?"

"Yes. Not enough to surround the ship though. We'll have to place it at key junctions between those craters." Nome responded.

A quick suggestion came from Tian' Xi. "Couldn't we seal ourselves below decks? They wouldn't be able to get to us then."

The Archivist intruded into the group. "I'm afraid to say they're strong enough to rip through your hatchways. They may not be the most agile creatures, but my brother has designed them to be second to no animal in strength."

The captain's expression turned dark. "We've no choice then. We have to fight. If we break their charge, it'll take them some time to organize another."

***

A half-hour before the assault, I stood once more next to one of the pools. Above the depressions airmen frantically pulled lines of barbed wire to cover the distance between the two pools. Yuri meanwhile carefully disguised another row of his mines. We had thankfully finished up with the other minefield, which was just as well; my hands were stained muddy gray for a few rhythms from helping Yuri apply his camouflage to these satchels.

I felt impatient. Already those creatures had approached much closer than I was comfortable with. They had closed half the distance. Ten, perhaps fifteen kilometers. Their speed was unnervingly superhuman.

My voice cracked as I spoke. "How much longer?"

"Nearly there." Yuri leaned in again to apply another bit of waterproof gray sludge to this particular satchel. The curtain of rain I had seen earlier over the sea to our backs was coming in much quicker than I had anticipated. The darkward tides above were pushing the cloud layer to the shore, completely swallowing up the imposing ocean from view. In a short time, we would be enveloped in rainfall.

"Haye!"

I looked around for the person who shouted my name. It was Tian' Xi, jogging towards us through the throng of airmen. She held something aloft that I didn't recognize from a distance. As she came closer, I saw that it was another roll-up like the first one she gave me.

"Smoke before this goes down?" she said.

I accepted. I'd never refuse that kind of thing. "You're being weirdly nice, lieutenant."

"You're the best shot on the ship. Good to have you as calm as we can."

I shrugged my shoulders.

Yuri straightened out his back, and I heard a pop as he did so. He winced as he spoke. "Nothing for me? Ah, well. Can't be having too many of those go missing."

"You've got an automatic rifle to compensate for your aim, bud." I said with a smile. I knocked him on the arm gently.

He smiled up at me, but I sensed there was something pained in it. "I hope so."

I lit up my smoke. "What's on your mind?"

"We could die here."

"We've been in holdouts before." My tone was nonchalant. "Remember? We're sunward folk. Not like those Beltlanders back there."

Yuri shook his head. "Sunward or not, I don't think we can get out of this one."

"We've got guns." Tian' Xi interrupted. "They've got sticks and rocks."

"The point is," Yuri continued, "I have something to tell you that I owe you, Haye."

My eyebrow rose. "Yeah?"

"I'm sorry I doubted you about the Voice. I wasn't sure how to say it before now, but, well, we're this close to this thing, right?" He held his thumb and index finger close together to indicate how close we were. "This close to dying."

I took another puff as I considered his statement. "Don't worry too much about it. There was a moment where I doubted myself. You can hardly be expected to be better than me, can you?"

He smiled one of those weary smiles he'd developed since the expedition began. "I feel quite badly about it. You've gotten me out of more scrapes than I can remember. I should've trusted you."

"Like I said, don't worry about it." I puffed some more. "Tian' Xi, you came to help or what?"

"Well if we do go down," Tian' Xi paused as she said this, "I just want to say that I'm happy to have gotten this far with you. Sunward, I mean."

"Why are you so gloomy about this?" I said with frustration.

"Maybe because we don't have a smoke?" Yuri tried to crack a joke.

I finally decided to break the silence. "Well. It's been fun. This thing is far from decided, but if we don't make it here, I'll admit that you two have been solid."

"Have we managed to pull a tooth out of you?" Yuri grinned as he said this.

"I've never been this far towards the Sunward Sky. I've never fought creatures like that, or flown on a giant airship, or gone over the Great Range." I folded one arm under the other as I took another drag. "This whole affair is so bizarre, it's nice to have people you can count on."

"Likewise."

Tian' Xi closed the conversation with, "Cards at end-rhythm if we make it." I nodded my agreement.

At that moment, I felt a drop on my shoulder. A shadow fell over the ground as stormclouds blocked the sun's light. The rain had finally come. I let go of the roll-up after one last drag and ground it into the rock.

Yuri, Tian' Xi and I shared one last look, before all three of us shook hands and headed back towards the ship.

***

The captain could barely be heard over the falling rain as she spoke to the assembled crew.

"Crew of the Destiny!" She prowled down the front line of the crew as she spoke, her voice consistently rising in volume. "You are here to defend your ship. You are here to defend your fellow mates' lives. But most importantly..." She stopped in front of me, staring into my eyes. I couldn't tell what she was thinking. "You are here to defend civilization itself.

"Though those barbarians may crash against the side of this ship, you *will* repel boarders. You *will* show them force of arms. And you most certainly *will* survive this encounter.

"You will do these things because you are airmen. You are a part of the Aery. You are trained, and you are disciplined. You are

Beltlanders, most of you anyway, Whether Aulan, Commonwealth, Nordecker, Ijritani, Nemasian or Anti-Nemasian. You are the representatives of a greater and nobler tradition than those savages out there. Don't forget that." She drew a breath in and shouted. "CLEAR SKIES!"

A resounding reply came back from the crew. "THE AERY FLIES!"

"STORMY SKIES!"

"THE AERY FLIES!"

Just then, I felt a sudden chill. I knew the Voice was back before I saw him. I was somewhat surprised at his form however.

A single one of those monsters flew in from the distance on a hang glider, against the wind I noticed. I saw that hideous blue fog surrounding it. The captain held up her hand to the crew. "Hold your fire!"

The creature dropped clumsily off the glider onto the ship's deck, a few meters from captain Nome, who promptly drew her sabre. The glider sailed backward once it was freed from its owner, finally falling downward and clattering on the rocky ground.

The creature and the captain faced off with each other. The fog had faded by now, but I knew that the Voice stood in front of us. It spoke with the same intensity as it had before. This time however, its syllables were distorted as it spoke. Fleshy disgusting sounds punctuated its speech.

"Truly I keep my promises."

"And you still haven't learned yet to stay off my ship. Neither have you learned to stay out of someone's body."

"My servant is an empty vessel for my thoughts. Art thou ready?"

"Yes."

A nervous murmur went through the crew. They had only heard of the Voice through word of mouth. Several of them looked as though they wanted to step back and cover their ears. The captain's words did not make any sense to them.

"I ask thee again: where goest thou?" the Voice rumbled.

"To the very Sunward Pole of this world." came Nome's answer.

"What hopest thou to find there?"

"A great city, built by beings more powerful than us. A place where we can learn to be as great as those who came before us. I have told you previously; we are on a mission of peaceful intent. We do not want to be your enemy." Nome spoke firmly.

"Thou shalt have thy wish. Thou canst not hope to be my enemy. Thou art a small creature. Instead, thou shalt serve as a new test for my servants to face."

The captain stepped forward. "Why?"

"Why not? All thy lives are short and violent. My life stretcheth across eons. I am a god. A god doeth with his servant as he pleaseth."

"I do not believe that ethic." the captain said. "Though some have put forward that exact notion to me."

"Believe as thou must. I in turn must put an end to..."

From behind the ranks of airmen, I saw the Archivist step forward and start to speak. "Hello there, remember me?"

The Voice briefly fell silent. The captain raised her sabre at the beast. "We aren't toys for you to play with, no matter how imperious your voice is. The River alone is who we submit to." She held her blade steady. "And you will answer to that authority."

The Voice didn't have a rebuttal. The blue fog that characterized its appearance suddenly exploded out from the body of the creature, and dissipated into the air off to the port side. The creature, suddenly lacking an animating force, crumpled into a heap on the deck.

Dr. Ininsir rushed forward immediately, seizing the creature and pulling at it. "A little help here? This is the first intact specimen I've got my hands on, what with you morons tossing the rest overboard..."

I was about to help her, when a sudden cry rang out from somewhere on deck. "They're coming!"

A surge of readiness spread through the waiting defenders. Airmen rushed to their positions. I ran to the port side of the ship, grabbing a rifle from a nearby airman handing them out. I leaned against the railing and aimed.

They weren't far off now, still moving with that astonishing speed. I could even make out individuals among them. Some were armed with axes, others spears, and still others with slings. There were too many to count. The ground beneath us began to shake.

How did they not die of exhaustion? A run over a distance like that at that speed would have killed a human. Admittedly, they were much longer-legged, and each one of their strides was filled with much more power than I could exert in the same space, but that didn't account for it. They had machine-like endurance.

I saw the airman next to me quivering. I knocked him in the elbow to snap him out of it.

An order rang out from captain Nome. "First lieutenant, ready the ship's battery."

"Aye sir." The response came from the main hatchway. Pullnir was situated halfway below decks, relaying orders from above to the gun crew below.

I purposefully moderated my breathing. Inhale. Wait. Exhale. Wait.

Another order from the captain: "Don't fire until I give the word."

The walls of the basin were by now ringing with the sound of ten thousand of the monsters charging at us. They were starting to come in range of our guns, and I expected the captain to give the order for a full broadside any second now.

Any second now.

I saw their maws twitching as they came. They were just as I remembered them. Horrible sphincters full of jagged snaggle-teeth. They were foaming this time. Mucous and slime dribbled down their lower faces like the drool of a rabid dog.

A horrible cry abruptly went up from the onrushing horde. Various slurps mixed with yelping forcefully burst from the charge in a brew of sound that chilled me. It resounded loudly through the basin, becoming more and more amplified as old calls became entangled with new ones in the air.

My finger went to the trigger of my rifle. I was ready to fire. Inhale.

The monsters' charge continued, there were now giant amorphous formations of them within range of the cannon.

Exhale.

I didn't perceive the captain's orders to open fire with the port battery. My mind focused on my first target.

Inhale.

Shells slammed into the first of our attackers, scattering body parts and green blood across the rock.

Exhale.

I squeezed the trigger of my rifle. A single bullet sailed through the air in a split second, burying itself in the center of mass of my target.

Inhale.

My hand slammed the rifle bolt back, the bullet casing spiraling away to my side. In a split second, the bolt clanked back in place, a new cartridge ready to fire.

Exhale.

I squeezed the trigger again. The gun jammed.

My face contorted in anger as I cursed, my breath control lost. In the thirty seconds it took me to unjam the rifle, I heard gunfire crackle around me. With the offending rifle jam taken care of, I looked up just in time for the second volley of cannon fire.

Three shells flew towards the enemy, impacting at close range. The fourth shell never came. Twenty meters away, I saw a blinding flash that forced my eyes shut via reflexes. It was the satchels inside the first depression exploding from the impact of the shells. A hand from some unlucky creature in the blast radius flew past my head, along with rocky shrapnel flung in my direction. One of these bit into the side of my face and I winced in pain.

Below however, the unthinkable happened. That unending tide of beasts staggered, easy prey for airmen with rifles. I saw wave after wave of the creatures fall from precise gunfire. The river of creatures halted, and then reversed course as the lead creatures tried to escape our gunfire and slammed back into their following comrades.

It turned into a full blown rout. The monsters ebbed from the ship and the charge scattered across the basin in all directions.

A massive cheer broke out aboard the entire ship. In spite of myself, I grinned. Even though I knew they would regroup to try again, we'd beaten them back this time.

***

Little over an hour had passed, and I peered out at the rain-soaked land before us. My knees were gathered underneath my chin as I held my rifle close to my side. The period of time where nothing happened had slackened my will to remain alert. I saw forms, now more indistinct as the rain had grown heavier. They were gathering again for another attack from the same direction.

Funny, that. The Voice was obviously an extremely stupid commander, ordering his minions to charge directly into fire like that. I suppose he hadn't counted on them routing as easily as they had.

Beside me, I heard the sound of approaching footsteps. "Eh?" I grunted, not taking my eyes off the land before me.

"I want to shoot from here." It was Dostwickr's voice.

I glanced sideways at her. "More than enough room."

She sat next to me cross-legged. "Not a single death."

"They'll be coming, just you wait. They won't be routed as easily the next time."

"But they can be routed, right?"

"Right." I exhaled. Just one more hour now. One more. Less if we're lucky.

I heard another somewhat unwelcome voice behind me in the form of the Archivist. "It seems we have one up on that dastardly Voice! I can sense his plans. They're going to avoid the pond-beds from now on."

I pointed at the remains of the closest of the depressions. The rain was filling it nearly to the brim with water. "Does that look inviting to you? Of course they're going to avoid them now."

"True, true." The Archivist bubbled much too merrily. "Unfortunately that also means one of your traps has been lost."

"Yuri will find some way of retrieving it."

"Mmm. Perhaps." The annoying being briskly marched away, shouting vague epithets in an attempt to bolster the crew's spirits.

"I wonder why he doesn't help us fight." Dostwickr said.

I shrugged. "Do you want to give him a gun? Be my guest."

"It doesn't have to be that. He can't die, remember?"

"True. All the same: let him cower; I just want him to shut up. It's our lives on the line for these things' sick pleasure." I scratched my nose. "One of theirs, anyway. Forgive me if I don't feel exactly comfortable with his level of glee over our impending death." I decided to change the topic. "Why are you here at the railing?"

"I came to shoot."

"That it?"

She stuttered, "Well, that and I came to tell you thanks for talking to me when I... you know..."

I nodded. "Don't mention it."

She allowed that awkward statement to hang for a bit. "It means a lot to me. Even if I'm not going to make it through this."

I was going to say that she wouldn't die, but the words rang hollow to me as I thought about them. "You might not *necessarily* die."

"Even if I survive this, I'm done. I can't do it."

"I once starved for three rhythms in the capital of the Yin with food all around me on every street corner." I looked back at her. "If I can get out of that, I'm sure you can read a book."

She shook her head. "I'll be sure to go quietly."

Anger coursed through me. "No. If you want to go, go with a bang. Make sure everyone sees it. Don't you dare slip off quietly. Make the whole world see your choice and force them to deal with it."

A puzzled look crossed her face. "Why?"

"Because I said so." I wasn't even sure why I said what I said. It didn't sound rational at all, but I was fed up with her meek nature. If she wanted to end it all, the least she could do was own up to it.

My thoughts were interrupted by a lower call throughout the basin. It was more cautious, less vigorous than the full-throated battle cry we'd heard earlier, and much more scattered. I sensed weak resolve in that warbling rally call.

The captain's voice shouted out across the deck once more. "Crew! Aim for the lower abdomen! They've got a heart there!"

So the doctor's dissection had yielded some fruit.

I snapped upright and once more aimed my rifle toward the direction the sound had come from. I predicted that the main thrust of their attack would come from there.

I was correct in everything but the nature of the charge. It was disorganized. The attacking creatures stumbled on the rocky-ground, and over the dead bodies of their fellows. I saw several get tangled in the barbed wire we had set up between the overflowing pools of water.

Some of them had, interestingly, worked out the way around the other sides of the pools. They came in singles, or in pairs, and were shot down handily.

This "charge" lasted ten minutes. I realized that they were trying to avoid bunching their force together to present a target for our cannons. Somewhat clever, but their offensive lacked the blood rage that had characterized their earlier assault.

This limp attempt petered out. It didn't rout; it simply ended with a whimper. Scattered shots rang out as airmen attempted to pick off stragglers.

I realized then that it hadn't been a full-fledged assault. They were probing our defenses, trying to figure out where we were weak. A small amount of them had run around bow and stern of the Destiny before beating a hasty retreat. They were going to try something bigger.

***

A half hour later, they had massed all around us, having finally learned from their first two failed charges. We were surrounded. I saw their forms standing perfectly still in the rain, allowing the water to soak through their thick matted fur. Some new discipline animated them. I didn't know what its source was. I beat back desperate terror at the thought.

Altogether, the enemy casualties from their first two charges amounted to about three hundred total. Between the power of our cannons and the accuracy of our rifle fire, we had managed to stem their assaults quite well while suffering only minor injuries ourselves.

Long range fire would not save us this time however. The enemy had a vast advantage in terms of bodies they could fling at us. A veritable wave of the creatures would advance on us from every direction at once. We could still fire of course, but our fire rate couldn't keep up with the amount of force being directed at us.

At this point, there wasn't even a command given. I just saw airmen fixing bayonets to their rifles. Behind us, a second row of airmen materialized from the ranks that had previously remained in reserve, this time holding long pikes. A sharp spike and two axe blades attached in reverse to each other menaced at the end of each pike.

The Yin had a name for such a weapon, and in close quarters when your ammo ran low, there wasn't a single bladed tool to compare to it: the Shuiya. This was a Beltlander version, longer and with thicker blades.

I heard the command echoed down the length of the ship from the mouth of the captain, and repeated by midshipman: "Hold fast!" I joined in the call.

I glared out in attempted defiance at our enemy, but my resolve wavered briefly.

To look out and see an indistinct, motionless swarm of monsters staring at you from every direction at a distance of less than two hundred meters is an experience I'd not wish on my worst enemy.

We stood in readiness for a while before the third charge began.

Finally, a great drum sounded in the distance, calling out our impending doom. The loudest war cry that had yet blared out of the monstrosities soon followed. Then, they came.

The deck shook underneath me. The very speed of their attack was easily twice that of the first. Cannons fired from below decks, and a plethora of explosive thuds rocked the ground and slammed into their front ranks. Fiery plumes billowed skyward, rending their limb from limb. This did not stall their attack in the slightest.

I heard the order to fire and inhaled. Too late I realized I'd got my breathing wrong. I cursed inwardly before the rifle butt dug into my shoulder from the recoil, knocking some of the wind from me. One spent cartridge flew out of my rifle. I fired another shot. Another one.

Three shots. That was all I managed before the horde had completely closed the distance. They were at the foot of the gondola. I fired randomly down at the mess of alien bodies before I pulled out my twelve-shot and fired once more at the silhouette that leaped up from the ground in a single bound. The bullet caught it in the stomach, and it fell back down to the rain-soaked ground, writhing.

I managed to get out two more shots. Around me I heard the sounds of metal slicing through flesh as the aliens met our close-quarters blades. In the confusing and dark atmosphere, I also heard screams of pain from injured or dying airmen. After the third bullet, my gun clicked. Out of ammo.

I had no time to react as yet another of the beasts crossed over the railing and tackled me, pinning me to the floor with terrifying strength. Its maw opened wide, moving to engulf my head.

CHAPTER 14

The creature's head exploded on top of me. My eyes slammed shut as green blood and fragments of bone and flesh splattered my face. One chunk flew into my mouth. I tasted something metallic, gelatinous, and completely revolting. I shoved away the lifeless body and vomited my guts out.

The taste remained. I wiped my vision clear with a hand, and glanced up to see Dostwickr, rifle in hand. She repeatedly stabbed at the enemy with the bayonet, felling monster after monster as they attempted to scale the side of the gondola.

In the heat of battle, someone stepped on my hand and I screamed out a curse. I stood reached for the nearest weapon: a discarded rifle. A shadow loomed over me, and I turned to fire at its source. A creature was felled by the blast, a human arm in its hand, ripped clean from its owner's socket.

I lunged at another of the beasts that had overwhelmed Dostwickr. She had collapsed from its assault, and I hooked an arm under her shoulder to lift her up. As I did so, I felt something strange and lumpy underneath her shirt. Her clothes lifted slightly as I hoisted her up, and I saw several shells strapped to her torso with rigging-rope.

I spared only a slight glance at her in the confusion surrounding me. A look of calm determination remained on her face. Her eyes briefly met mine and I saw the faintest glimmer of a smile on her face.

Then, in the space of a moment, she had turned away. She ran towards port, speeding over the dead bodies of fallen creatures to gain height as she jumped over the railing. She was a blur; I barely had time to react.

Once she had disappeared, my gut wrenched. It took all of three seconds for me to reach the railing. A defiant cry rose from down below, though I couldn't discern the words.

The air rushed back around me, and I was blown backwards as though a giant had picked me up and thrown me across the deck. I felt a horrible pain in my chest and struggled to breathe. Through a series of strange white pops in my vision, I saw a huge ball of flame and smoke surge upward to tower over the deck. In the light of the explosion, I saw the swarm of monsters pause from their attack. In near-perfect silence apart from the ringing in my ears, the crew seized their opportunity to surge forward and drive the creatures off the deck.

I struggled to stand up, mind racing. Pain engulfed me, and I slumped against the fallen body of one of the airmen.

My hearing returned gradually, and I heard scattered shouts of triumph, but also cries of pain. The creature's charge had amazingly stalled.

I heard an order shouted over the din of battle: "DRIVE THEM BACK!"

The airmen swiftly reformed ranks and opened fire on the beasts that hadn't yet scaled the gondola's side. I heard a strange call of fear trickle through the attackers. They started to fall back as their casualties grew. They didn't retreat far. Fresh fighters from the rear ran into the front ranks yet again, and I saw some of the lead creatures get cut down by their comrades as they tried to flee. This scrum lasted for an interminable length of time.

Finally, the charge reformed, and rushed again at the side of the ship. The ground shook with an even greater intensity.

At first, I thought this was due to a much larger attack, but then I saw several points on the ground bulge outward around the Destiny. Within seconds, these massive hillocks burst upward, showering the area around them with gravel and rock, revealing Stygian horrors that took the shape of shell-less spine-covered mollusks. The moment these creatures burst forth they unleashed an endless stream of their kin from the new tunnels that laid into the front lines of our attackers with deadly efficiency. This stopped the fourth charge in its tracks, and caused a general rout of the enemy.

As they retreated I saw a mass of the same gray color as our allies burst forth at the rear of our enemy. The attacking army was caught between the two rings that encircled our ship. With no way out, panic spread through the creatures.

Frightened wails hung in the air. The crew stood mesmerized by how our allies shredded the enemy. Even when fighting alongside the Yinindai, I had never witnessed a slaughter like this. Bodies lay around the entire surrounding area, piled like so much lumber, left to rot.

The sound of the massacre continued for a long time.

***

The Voice's minions were crushed to a beast. Not a single member of the orange horde was left alive. Our saviors had retreated deep into the rocky ground.

I stood knee-deep in the dead. The smell was like a slaughterhouse.

For a ring of one hundred meter's thickness around the Destiny, bodies of the dead carpeted the ground. In some places the creatures were piled a meter deep. Nearer to the ship, fewer of the dead lay scattered more intricately. Some had drowned in pools of water. Others had been reduced to pieces from the multiple explosions. The few individuals entangled in barbed wire were lacerated beyond recognition.

The field of battle ran green. It could have been mistaken for a verdant carpet of moss. The thick blood stained the water pools a brilliant green.

The smell of decay hadn't yet set in. Instead, a plethora of different smells filled the air: sweat, organs, blood.

The Archivist led the way through the battlefield. The group, which consisted of the senior staff of the Destiny, sloshed single file through the maze of the dead. I had pulled my boots higher than usual.

We headed a half-kilometer out where a lone figure had materialized on a lump in the ground that gently sloped up from where we struggled through. The Archivist had insisted that we meet "someone".

I nearly stumbled a few times headfirst into the mire of bodies. This expedition just got worse and worse, and this nightmare was the latest to convince me of that trend.

At last, we broke through and began walking up the barely sloping ground. We heard only the whistle of the wind around us. No one spoke a word to each other. We were all of us in our own way overwhelmed. The rain had stopped, the weather on our side for the moment. I saw another curtain of rain approaching the ship.

The thing in front of us made no effort to run away or approach us. I felt distinct anger at having to wade through the morass while it remained there.

Within ten meters of the being, it held up what I took to be its arms in front of it as an indication that we were to stop. Or as a greeting? Or as a warning? I couldn't read its body language. Its movements were fluid and elegant, simultaneously intriguing and unnerving. Regardless, we stopped and waited for it to speak.

It had multi-digit hands. Its fingers were too numerous for it to be human, or of human appearance, like the Archivist. The fingers of these hands were jointed in all the wrong places, sometimes at odds with each other, so as to form a spring. Easily twenty sprung from each hand, some sprouting from the middle of its palms. It appeared like someone had taken a hand and modeled it after a sprig from a coniferous tree. In one of these hands, it cradled a severed head of one of the monsters. In death it became more terrifying. Above the other hand floated an orb that emitted a yellow-green glow.

The creature held this orb perfectly in line with its... head? I have great difficulty describing it here. There wasn't a visible head. Instead, the space where it should be was outlined by encircling biological horns protruding from its shoulders. This outline was much too big to suggest a human head. Something indistinct, but not air, filled that space. Something made of the same material as the being's clothes, which rippled and shimmered as though the space around the creature was on fire.

The being floated a meter above the ground. At the sight of this, the chaplain began making prayer signs with his hand. Dr. Hennir's expression was also deeply unsettled. Everyone was distinctly uncomfortable in the presence of this thing.

The Archivist didn't let out a single noise. He kept a reverent silence.

A voice flowed out of the creature, feeling very much akin to the voice of our attacker. It was less like an earthquake, and more like an onrushing tidal wave.

"I am not your enemy."

"I do not believe you are my friend either." The captain said.

"I have neither entered your crew, nor entered your ship, nor entered the area close to it. My actions speak for themselves."

"Your Archivist wanted us to speak with you. He was adamant we should do this. I assume you are our rescuer?"

"That I ultimately am not. But that is a mere technicality. I am the wave which has swept your pursuers aside."

"Well, you have my thanks." The captain said.

"Your thanks are taken, as meaningless as they are."

The captain paused. "I am..."

"Captain Nome. Commander of the darkward children's ship. I know who you are, young one."

"So you have entered into our minds instead of our bodies, then?"

"Your thoughts are written on your expression. It radiates from your face like a sunbeam. I perceive it whether I want to or not."

I took one step backward.

The captain continued, "I want to know who you truly are, and moreover, if that Voice will continue following us."

"He is confined, for now. I have him within my care." The being held up the glowing orb. "You already know what we know of ourselves if you have spoken to They-That-Plod-the-Ground."

"What do you call yourselves?"

"We do not know."

"Haven't you invented a name for yourselves?"

"Many times. But the exercise is pointless. The name, and the reason for its being, will be lost with time. I currently fulfill the role of They-That-Seek."

"*What* are you?" there was disquiet in the captain's voice.

They-That-Seek answered, "We are the many. The undying. Those who have been alive for longer than memory permits knowing. We are the ground beneath your feet, the sky above your head, and the flesh that machinates around your thoughts."

I finally summoned the will to interrupt. "Are you gods or something?"

The being hesitated. "No. And yes. It depends on what you perceive a god to be."

Dr. Ininsir in turn broke in. "What can you tell us of the Forebears?"

Surprisingly, the chaplain fielded another question. I heard his voice quake. "Are we headed towards Heaven?"

The response from the creature was instant this time. "I can tell you nothing of Heaven. Nor can I tell you of those who came and went many cycles ago, except to say that both might exist over that expanse." They-That-Seek motioned behind us towards the ocean.

"Surely if you've been alive for thousands of years, you would remember that." The captain testily said.

"No. The ones you call Forebears came to this world many millennia ago. We know not where they come from, but they were like you. As arrogant and short-lived. Many centuries passed, but we have not seen them for a long time. They left for somewhere, perhaps sunward."

"Did they look like us?" Dr. Ininsir said.

They-That-Seek laughed, a wave of energy that shook me to my bones. "There were similarities, I believe? I wish to think that they were better looking."

The captain spoke again. "Why didn't you follow them?"

"We were forbidden to."

The chaplain managed to find his voice again. "Who forbade you to follow them?"

"They-That-In-Perpetuity-Is-Common-Of-All-Three-Sevenths-In-Past-Present-Future."

My head cocked to the side in confusion. "What?" I let out.

"What he means is the Conjoined." The Archivist answered.

"That still isn't helping."

"The River." The chaplain breathed out.

They-That-Seeks rumbled, the intent of which I couldn't understand. "These are many names that inexactly describe the subject of conversation." It confirmed.

"So you can't even tell us what it is!" I felt frustration take over as I exclaimed this.

"To do so defies words. It would be fruitless of me to capture it in a sentence, especially a darkward one of your kind, as They-That-Plod-The-Ground can tell you."

"Very true!" came the cheerful rejoinder from the Archivist.

"What lies over that ocean?" The captain interrupted, pointing back towards the sinister breadth of sea.

"The center. We have not dared to go there for eons, as we have said. If They are still there, perhaps you will meet Them."

"Who are They? Are They the Forebears?"

They-That-Seeks rumbled again. "You bore me, young one. I saved you to sate my curiosity. I have read everything I need to know from your expression. Farewell." It began to float upwards, following the draft of the wind.

The captain's voice was uncharacteristically frantic. "Wait! We are curious as well. At least tell us who They are?"

"It is useless to tell you, young one. That knowledge will not save you from those who came beyond the mountains. They ride even now by wing and ship to find you and take you to the Long Sleep. I will not intervene again on your behalf."

"The White Hats!" I cried out in terror.

The ancient creature floated higher, casually letting go of the body part it had held in its hand. Only then did I realize it had been speaking to us through the decapitated head.

***

I sat alone, once more in the rear gun chamber, where the Voice had first terrorized me. In an immediate sense we were safer. In a greater sense we were being tracked even here by those vile bounty-hunters. There would be no respite for us, especially after we had been abandoned by the being. I had no doubt that his position reflected the rest of them. They were all assholes.

My inexhaustible desire to see the Sunward Side was fading by the rhythm. What lay ahead? Would we meet equally capricious beings there? It sounded more than possible in that moment. I would give anything to know who "They" were.

The Archivist's voice piped up from the doorway. "Trying to be alone, are we?"

"Go drown yourself in one of those lakes." I snapped.

"I would if I could, but I can't. Trust me, I really would."

I stood up angrily. "I don't believe you."

"Well, I certainly can't force you to believe something you don't want to."

"Why are you here? I thought we *bored* you." I marched over to him and looked him square in the eye.

He nodded. "You do, because you're predictable, but that's neither here nor there. I'm afraid the Seeker doesn't really see it that way, but trust me; I'm not about to bail on you! Very bad manners."

"I wish you would. You've been nothing but trouble for us ever since we found you this rhythm."

"Hey now! The general consensus in our dream was that we would not interfere with your business, before I put forward intervention. Without me, your ship would be crawling with the Voice's servants now."

I pushed him forcefully out of the way, and stomped down the access corridor. It was no use, he still followed me. I heard him sigh.

"I want to talk to you." His voice had resignation in it.

"What?" I snapped. I didn't stop walking.

"I want to know why you hate everyone."

"Go and kill yourself."

"I've already offered my crop to your captain. It's quite hard growing chitin-weed on the rocks, but I'm more than willing to part with the harvest. I didn't have to do that either. You don't figure you can trust me?"

"No. Don't you already know how I think? Isn't it written on my *expression*?"

"Yes, but I figured it would be nicer if I pretended that didn't exist."

"Not helping."

The Archivist suddenly grabbed my shoulder and turned me about. "Listen." He commanded.

I immediately grabbed the offending limb, and attempted to remove it. He had an inexplicably iron grip. My knee then thumped upward between his legs, hard. The only thing I succeeded in doing was bruising my knee, as the Archivist merely smiled.

"Nothing there." He said.

"Let. Go. Of. Me." I growled out.

"No. I've been giving gifts to your crew for most of this rhythm. Let me give something free to you: there are only a few people on this ship who like you. Plenty of them fear you. Only a few of them respect you. You in turn hate them because you think they're soft. That they're all sheep and you alone have a handle on things. That Voice, who terrorized you, thought the same thing. And we all know how well it served him in the end. The crew doesn't like you because *they can't rely on you*. You're too arrogant and selfish. You think that solves problems, but it usually causes more problems than it solves."

"Let go. Now."

He ignored me. "There's a lot more to life than looking out for yourself. I should know: I would have gone much more insane than I am now with the amount of time I've been alive, had it not been for the dream I share with my fellows. To live, here, and beyond that ocean, you are going to need to grow up. That's my gift. That's my advice. And now, I will let go. You may hit me if you wish."

He did release his arm, and thrust forth his chin. I didn't need a second invitation. I uppercut him on the offered target. He didn't move, and I bruised my hand this time. I cursed him to his face.

The Archivist clapped his hands together. "Now with that settled, shall we enter?" We were next to the barber's quarters.

I did follow him, but because I didn't want anything bad to happen to Hapsman and not because I felt like following the Archivist.

A different atmosphere permeated the barber's. The ship's hum had evaporated, leaving only the soft sound of the midshipman humming to himself in the corner. I didn't recognize the tune. When we entered, the boy looked up with clear sadness in his eyes. From the time he had been possessed by the Voice until this rhythm, he hadn't moved from his cot.

"How's the end-rhythm ma'am? I heard the battle." He looked more nervous as the Archivist approached. "Who's he?"

The Archivist gave a kind look at the boy. "A friend. We met before. I don't expect you to remember." The ancient creature said.

"I don't, sir?" Hapsman replied.

"That's all right. I'm here to help."

I seized the Archivist's hand and growled, "If you harm him..."

"Don't worry, I won't. Others of my kind might, but I wouldn't hurt a fly." The being held out a hand, palm first. "All right, youngest, if you would kindly lay back? This will only take a second." Hapsman complied, and the Archivist began making signs with his hands.

In my experience, there is a certain fluidity of motion exercised by priests of the Riverrun when they make prayer signs. The Archivist, however, outdid any of the priests I had seen for elegance. None of the signs were familiar, either. This process lasted a short time before he laid his right palm on the boy's head. He held it there for a longer time, not saying a word.

Finally, the Archivist moved back from his position, walked to the door and queried the boy. "Try that out, youngest one."

I turned back towards the boy. Hapsman was suddenly overcome with amazement. "I can feel my legs! Ma'am! I can feel my legs!" The boy shouted out.

I stood there perplexed, not sure what to make of the situation. "Consider this another small gift I offer to this ship."

I turned back to look at the Archivist, but he had disappeared.

***

Two rhythms passed there in the basin. I grew increasingly depressed as we stayed put, but we didn't have a choice. The Destiny's turbines had to be thawed out carefully and then repaired. I learned that some of the thawed water had dripped back into our diesel reservoir, which caused Yuri to scratch at his head more furiously in those two rhythms than I had ever seen him scratch.

I stayed out of it. For most of those rhythms, I found myself far from the ship and the increasingly horrendous stench that radiated from around our landing site. The captain mandated that the immediate area surrounding us be cleared of all debris. The waves of pouring rain that rushed in from the ocean made this all the more difficult. The Archivist, true to his word, healed the crew that were injured.

However there had still been casualties. And one casualty that was very hard for me to take.

I went to the service, which was held far away from the ship, between hastily erected tents. I felt dead as I saw each of the palls pass me by.

After the memorial had finished, the tents packed up, and most of the crew departed, I remained there. I knelt beside the dead crewmen. Nine total. All sat on makeshift palls. Their skin was colored blue, and in some cases their faces had been mauled.

Dostwickr's pall was empty. Nobody had found a single part of her body.

While the other palls were filled with objects from the life of the dead, as I had seen before on this expedition, this one was completely devoid of those memorials. None of the crew knew Dostwickr. Her personal effects amounted to the clothes on her back, several books, and a drinking mug. I had no idea she had been so frugal.

I felt surprised by Yuri and Tian' Xi, most of all. They had acquaintances at least among the other airmen who had died, and paid most of their attention to them. They were avoiding Dostwickr's pall. They couldn't even look at it.

I shifted from my kneeling position to sit at the foot of the empty pall, sitting in much the same way that Dostwickr had found me during the battle, remaining silent. Eventually, the last of the footsteps behind me faded. All except for a single pair, keeping vigil with me. I was expecting one of the officers, or the chaplain, but when the dignified form of captain Nome stepped up beside me, I was mildly startled.

She finally broke the silence. "Nothing to remember her by."

In spite of my dislike of the captain, I responded. "Yeah."

"I'm glad someone remembers her at least."

The words tumbled from me before I knew I'd said them. "I liked her."

"She was like you, yes?"

"Yeah. I moved beyond where she was, but she was like me. Never got a chance to believe in herself, that's the difference between us." I murmured.

"I think she did, at the end. She believed she could make things better for us."

"By killing herself." I shook my head. "Why are you talking to me?"

"I want to say thank you for talking her down when you did. Even though it only prolonged her life by a few rhythms, it was the right thing to do."

I recognized that the captain was attempting to hold out comfort, and my attitude towards her softened. "I failed to give her hope. Why was it the right thing to do if it didn't work?"

"Because you showed compassion. That is something that is highly uncharacteristic of you, and yet you managed to do it. In her final moments, I'm sure that was extremely significant to her."

"Don't start with that talk. I've already had enough of it from that annoying... Archivist. 'Don't be selfish' he says. 'Don't be like the Voice' he says." I spat on the ground.

"Well I certainly agree that he is a disrespectful individual, he's not entirely wrong."

"Again, don't start."

We remained there for a while, just listening to the wind, and the distant sound of work by the ship.

"I want you to take Dostwickr's position." the captain said.

"Alright, I'll take a useless job."

"Don't think that Master of Semaphore is useless aboard my ship, Ms. Zintan. When we inevitably return to civilization, we will need someone proficient at signals."

"If we return."

"When." The captain started walking away before stopping in her tracks to say something more. "There will come a time when you will understand the Beltlander ethic. It doesn't require you to obey every rule, or believe in everything that we do. It doesn't even require you to sacrifice all self-interest. All it requires is that you repeat what you did with lieutenant Dostwickr and apply it to everyone that you can."

She started and stopped again, adding a last addendum. "You still haven't learned to say 'sir' yet."

"Yes sir." I mumbled.

That was enough for her. She departed back to the ship, and I was finally alone with the empty pall.

I sat there for several minutes before I finally relented to the thought that had been growing in my mind: Dostwickr needed some sort of remembrance. There had to be something to stay here with the others, to remain as long as the wind and the rain permitted.

I didn't have anything to give her. She didn't have anything she would want from the ship, either. Her drinking glass perhaps, but I decided against that. I also wouldn't give her any of those stupid books that she hated.

And me? I had my guns, my clothes, and a few worth of Yinlus to my name. Not much to give, and it seemed a pointless act to just toss coins into that empty cot.

On impulse, I started arranging some nearby pebbles on her bed. When I was satisfied with my work, I stood up, bowed once as was the custom among the Yin, and departed.

I left behind an arrangement of the rocks in the three interlinked triangles that Dr. Ininsir said represented the sun. They were as good a representation as any of the Sunward Side, and I drew hope from them.

***

Off-rhythm came, and I found myself restless. Once again, there was nothing to do onboard. The smell from the battlefield had by now turned into a severe nuisance for me. It infiltrated the ship through multiple pores and vents, and I found that I couldn't sleep with that stench wafting through the ship.

I didn't tell anyone where I went. I only answered to the captain, under good conditions. Pullnir, in the past two rhythms, had attempted to give me an order, but I brushed him off. Yuri had managed to pacify that situation, but I left wondering how long it would be before the first lieutenant tried to come down hard on me.

I left for a spot closer to the ocean, to look out across it. I couldn't get to the shore, we were too far, but at least I would get to see a few sand-dunes. Something to take my mind off things.

The Yin steppes are full of many sunbaked plains and toughened plants. What they sorely lack that I remember only vaguely from my train ride through Nordecker all those years ago are the dunes that populate the Nordecker desert. These bore some resemblance to them, and so I was wary of them. Nordecker was not a pleasant memory for me.

I decided it best not to let that thought get a hold of me though. I purposefully strode towards them to sit and think.

When I neared the crest of one, I heard faint conversation from the other side. I hesitated before continuing. Who else besides me had escaped this far out from the Destiny?

I decided to not reveal myself. I had a sneaking suspicion that whatever this conversation was, the people involved were up to something. I crawled up the side of the small dune as quietly as I could, and peeked over at what lay beyond.

Two figures were at the base of the dune on the other side, sitting cross-legged and facing each other. One figure I instantly recognized as the Archivist. The other was cloaked, face obscured by some tan-colored cloth. It was a man, but I didn't recognize his voice.

"...by one of your own." the cloaked man said. "Will we be having any problems from the rest of the one hundred and thirty four?"

"No. I can't answer from the sixty six though. I haven't heard from them in a long time." The Archivist's answers were, as always, irritatingly cheerful.

"Good. Because we lost ground here. It'll be hell to make up that ground."

"You don't have faith in the expedition?"

"My faith has been shaken in the past few rhythms. For some reason, the land itself has been trying to kill us."

"Courtesy of my stupid, childish brother. But he's under control now. You won't have to deal with that anymore. Dealing with the Sun-storm on the other hand..."

"The passages you told us about? The sheltered ways? You're sure they still exist?"

"Even ten thousand years of wind and rain won't be enough to completely erode them. They exist. You can take them directly to your destination. Mind the wildlife, though. It can be even more temperamental than that which lies along the ring of the ocean."

"Fun."

"Did you have another reason to harangue me?"

"I need you to convince the others to delay the White Hats at any cost. If they catch up to us, they'll have wisened up to us. They aren't only coming for Haye Zintan. The Yinda has tasked them with taking us all down. We're all in his sights."

"Oh really?" The Archivist yawned. "I didn't know that."

"I don't really care what you do or don't know. I want to tell you that in person. This expedition will fail unless those men are stopped."

I saw from my limited vantage point that the Archivist shrugged. "I'll see what I can do."

A sigh came out of the unidentified man. "The Five never mentioned just exactly how unhelpful you were."

"I just said I'll see what I can do!" the Archivist spluttered.

"You don't seem very motivated."

"Well, hooray! There, is that any better?"

"Just... help us out."

"I will do my best, and nothing more."

This satisfied the other speaker, and he made motions as though he was preparing to leave.

The Archivist interrupted that departure. "Just out of curiosity, why does the Yinda want the whole expedition dead?"

"Under these circumstances, the excuse would be that we harbored Haye Zintan. But the Five have reason to suspect that Integer has begun execution. We don't know what stage it's at, probably in its infancy, but we have only a few centuries at most before its completion. The Yinda must have been recruited along with several other people in similar positions for Layer One. I can only guess how they managed to persuade him. He's gone over."

"A shame. You could have used him as an ally."

"Yes. Word from our agents in the Basilica is that something big is about to go down. If we can't get the support of the Yinda countering whatever it is that their friends are preparing, they might not even need Integer. He'll have to be," the figure made a throat-slicing motion, "taken care of."

"Brutal. The Five would outdo themselves if they pulled that off."

"I'm not looking forward to that time, when it comes. Wetwork and anything else remotely difficult always gets dumped on me. Look where I am now. The Five could have easily made this journey themselves. They have the records all stored away. Instead, they send Beltlander lackeys under *my* guidance. I have to tell you: holding this thing together and not being seen at the same time is a monstrously hard thing to do."

"I don't enjoy your wetwork, young one. Every time I hear of it, it causes me to believe less and less in the Five's cause."

"We have to force this thing to happen. And we have to force it to happen on our terms, not the opposition's. Any necessary sacrifice to meet that goal must be carried out."

"The Conjoined hopefully will see it that way."

The other speaker didn't have an answer for that statement. "I must return to the darkwarders' ship. Dream well, ancient one."

"Dream well to you." The Archivist chuckled.

As the two speakers parted ways, the one whose form was oddly familiar somehow passed by my hiding place atop the dune, just ten meters to my right. I hunched into the rock so as to appear to be part of it. The figure left, and swiftly scurried back towards the ship.

My mind raced. Someone on board wasn't who they said they were.

CHAPTER 15

The instant I returned to the ship, I found the nearest spot to isolate myself and think. I didn't know what the hell that conversation had been about, but I gathered two things. One, the conspirator wanted us to succeed; two, he knew the Archivist. The Archivist had a lot more experience with the world beyond the Great Range than he let on.

On the one hand, a part of me that wanted to believe that the conspirator wouldn't knowingly lead us towards our destruction. I couldn't count on that. I didn't know who the person was. I needed to find out as much as I could about him and what his plans were as unobtrusively as possible.

The references in their conversation were unfamiliar, besides the Yinda. I wouldn't put it past him to be heavily involved in some underground conspiracy. The rumor-mill around the Yin royal court had been well-developed, and past Yindi had been into a fair amount of secret societies.

Of note, the fact that the conspirator seemed to be working against the Yinda was enough to put him on certain pages of my good books. But then again, I remembered the words of They-That-Seek. "They" were waiting for us at the sunward pole, whoever "They" were. My mind immediately went to the possibility of the Forebears, the River, or something else more terrifying. It wasn't much of a leap to deduce that the Archivist knew the answer, however much he lied about how forgetful he was. The conspirator must have known as well.

Even before the events that had transpired in the basin, I had sensed a brewing storm between the chaplain and the doctors. Each had considerable influence over the captain, and each had contradictory interpretations about what awaited us at the sunward pole. Each would undoubtedly attempt to twist the knowledge of They-That-Seek to fit their own agenda. Dr. Hennir didn't worry me near as much as the chaplain. That man seemed too ready to believe ancient theology. Who knew when he would snap? I didn't know how he would interpret the existence of the Archivist and his ilk. It probably fit with some obscure theory of a long-dead navel-gazer.

Although, then again, maybe he was correct about the River's physical existence? I'd certainly seen some strange things this far sunward that had shaken my unbelief.

It was imperative that I sniff out this conspirator. Whatever he knew could be of infinite value to us.

One thing was for certain; I wasn't about to blab about what I'd heard around the ship, even to the captain. As much as she had more resources available to her that could be helpful, I didn't know who to trust. Pullnir was my first target. That man had been a bad apple since the first rhythm. Giving up the element of surprise wasn't a good idea here.

And so, I resolved to go about my business with both eyes open.

***

We departed the basin in the early hours of the next rhythm.

All hands were on deck, observing the takeoff of the Destiny. Instinctively, I scanned the basin for signs of the Archivist, even though I knew I wouldn't be able to find the creature. Both he and his house had disappeared overnight.

The Archivist hadn't said his farewells. One hour he had been there behaving as he usually did, and the next he was gone. The entire crew of the Destiny, by now grudgingly used to his presence, was set once more at unease by the sudden desertion, and even more so by the magical disappearing act his farm had pulled. Many returned to the now-familiar part of the basin where it should have been, and found nothing but hard ground, and a single, massive pool of water teeming with arthropods and fractal plants.

As the hours passed, something within me realized that a strong chance existed that the spy knew I had overheard their conversation. The Archivist could read minds. He would have relayed that information to my target. That meant that the spy had a leg up on me, and would likely be keeping low for right now.

Of course, there were more disturbing possibilities. He could be planning to kill me. It was in his line of work. With the disappearance of the Archivist, the search had become far more dangerous.

All I could do was hope that I hadn't had enough contact with the Archivist for that to happen. I certainly had made it my business to avoid him completely for that very reason.

"Captain on deck." Pullnir called out.

Nome exited the main hatchway and took a position at the head of the gondola. After a moment's consideration of the assembled crew, she spoke with great sincerity.

"Crew of the Destiny. We leave behind nine of our own here in this deserted place. These deaths weigh heavily on all our hearts. However, we must continue with our journey towards the sunward pole. Our stand to hold the line of civilization must not have been in vain. It is our duty as airmen to expand the borders of society to include all parts of the globe, including to these most sunward expanses."

The captain's voice shifted down in volume slightly. "Some of you may have heard rumors of our saviors. Some of these rumors are true, such as that they are not necessarily friendly. Many other rumors are not true. Many of them have been stated by our new acquaintances to be true, but are unsubstantiated. It is important to remember that these beings do not represent the final knowledge that awaits us at the sunward pole. All of us, and you personally, are advancing civilization to its highest levels of greatness. Whatever we find as we continue will uplift not just society as a whole, but also your families back home.

"In honor of those that have fallen for this great cause, and of one in particular without whom we would not be standing here, I have decided to invoke the ship's right of discovery, and give the name to this basin of Dostwickr.

"That is all."

A new voice rang out, that of Pullnir. "All hands, at attention for an honorary barrage for the fallen."

The side of the gondola lit up with a ceremonial broadside to mark the dead.

Briefly, a vivid memory flashed through my mind: Dostwickr jumping over the side of the ship. The flash from the guns synched perfectly with the massive explosion from my memory.

The turbines began to start up. After almost two rhythms of

repair, I heard hints of squealing as they whined louder and louder. The sound disappeared after they had reached full speed. The crew began swirling around me. Some general order had been given, but I hadn't heard it. Instead, I walked slowly to the railing as the airship began to tilt upward in preparation for ascent. I'd gotten used to walking on slight inclines by now for gaining and lowering altitude.

I looked out over Dostwickr Basin, and saw the line of memorials in the distance. They were left open to the air to decay. All except for Dostwickr herself. I couldn't make out the symbol I had left for her, but I felt satisfied that it was still there.

The Destiny began gaining more speed, traveling higher and higher in its spiral pattern upwards. As we turned, I repeatedly lost and gained sight of the palls. In their place whenever we turned, loomed the ocean. There would be no stopping in that desert of water. We'd gone one or two thousand kilometers already in twelve rhythms due to the slow speed through the jungle. Over the ocean, that speed was likely to increase because we were in less danger of hitting trees at our low altitude.

These alternating thoughts kept at me until we had climbed to our proper altitude: Dostwickr's memorial, and the way ahead. Part of me knew, deep down, that there was a high likelihood of many more deaths in the future.

***

Everyone at the table anticipated my next move, but none more than Evinsir, with whom I was locked in a duel.

Outside, that infernal rain returned hour after hour. Was it getting stronger? In front of me, Evinsir laid down a two pair of wheels. We were winding down the game. I wasn't fully committed to either the large or small pots, a fact that worried me.

As I came to understand the master of navigation's strategy further, I realized that he was playing this game at least conservatively. Major alliances hadn't materialized, leaving a stalemate at all four ends of the table.

Thankfully, one of us had removed Dostwickr's chair. It didn't feel right to have it nearby.

Pullnir was also nowhere to be seen. He must have been convening with the captain. This was both a blessing and a curse. Tonight, I didn't have to put up with him, but on the other hand, I couldn't gauge his reactions at cards. Cards tend to open a person up to inquiry, with or without drink. I had a theory that whoever the infiltrator of our ship was, it had to be someone with access to levers of power. That meant there had to be a link between them and captain Nome. Pullnir was a tempting target for investigation, but his voice didn't match the spy's. What if I hadn't heard that voice correctly?

The most significant other option was that the spy somehow influenced the ship's directions through the doctors. For some reason, ever since the Line Channel, the two women had uncanny foreknowledge of the way ahead. That alone was highly suspicious in light of my revelation. I knew Pullnir didn't pull that much weight with them.

Best to cover all bases.

A jolt went through the ship, which caused Evinsir to grimace slightly. "Daft off-rhythmers can't keep the ship straight."

"I hope their engineer is better than their navigator." Yuri answered. "I've started to find some of the side valves unset on the off-rhythmer's watch. Quite possible we'll stall out here."

I laid down a high two as I mused, "Isn't the first lieutenant supposed to have a sharp eye on the off-rhythmers?"

"What, more than on us?" said Yuri.

"Yeah. They're made from the more darkward elements in the crew." I shuffled in my seat a bit. "Just figured he'd be a bit more prone to keeping discipline up among them."

Yuri shook his head. "Nah, he wouldn't. Especially since you and I came on board, he's been more suspicious of us. Doesn't make much distinction between darkward and sunward, that one."

An idea occurred to me, one that would help me with my search for the spy on board. I smiled a false smile. "Tian' Xi?"

"Yeah?"

"Do you think you could introduce me to his roll-up stash sometime?"

"I haven't hooked you on that stuff, have I?"

"Not really. Smoking it is better than nothing for me, though."

"OK. Remember to take one or two of them. There's about two hundred a box; he'll notice if you take ten."

It was the perfect excuse to enlist Tian' Xi's help in searching through his stuff. I desperately hoped that if he was the spy, he would have some sort of plans or documentation that I could use to figure out his motives. If he didn't, or if they weren't stored with his roll-ups, that would cause problems for my investigation.

Yuri folded his arms. "I wonder where he is right now." he said.

"Filling out the first mate's section for yet another page of Dostwickr's death certificate." Evinsir said gloomily.

I crossed my arms, annoyed that every conversation went back to the former master of semaphore. "Hasn't that already been filled out for her? Seems like it should have been a priority a few rhythms ago."

Evinsir wiggled his fingers in the air, contemplating his next move in the game. "Where Aery and state meet, the bureaucracy only complicates things. Dostwickr was from one of those principalities near Basilica City I think. I can't pronounce its name for the life of me. Those places always have huge regulations on Aery membership." He scratched his jaw. "I'll bet they're barely on the twentieth page by now."

"We should talk about her." Tian' Xi said abruptly. When she saw that nobody at the table felt the need to respond, she floundered.

I stepped in. "No. We shouldn't." When she shot me a look, I asked, "What is there to talk about?"

"About how we feel."

I sat back in my chair. "I feel nothing. She's dead, and there isn't a *thing* talking about it will change."

"Could we have done anything more for her?" Yuri asked.

"We already talked about this, remember?" I replied. "You can't order somebody out of their funk. You can't wheedle them, you can't command them, *you* can't do anything. They have to do it themselves."

"She was too far gone to do much about, I think." Evinsir said. "There was an element of truth to what she thought about herself, and I don't think we're in the wrong over her decision."

I bristled a bit at his first suggestion. "Whatever truth there was in her thoughts is true only because she was put here by stubborn morons."

"I'm half-tempted to find where her parents live and break their jaws after this is all over." Yuri added.

"Make sure you bring along the brass knuckles. And leave one of their jaws unbroken for me." I fumed.

"There isn't anything more we could have done?" Tian' Xi

interrupted. It was a repeat question, but I understood why she would ask it.

I fiddled with a card. "No. We talked to her. She made her own choice to do what she did."

Tian' Xi slammed her hands down on the table in sudden outrage. "She didn't have to go out like that!"

I thought about that for a bit. "Perhaps it's best to leave that judgement to her."

We paused to digest this for a moment, but then our ears collectively perked up.

Once again, the drums were calling us above decks. From outside, I heard the boom of thunder, and saw bright light flashing through the outlights. The storm had gotten much worse.

***

The next wave of storm clouds was inbound. I saw the dark curtain underneath approaching faster and faster. I was out along the ship's makeshift port rigging, looking at my patch job from where the White Hats had shot through the canopy. Most of the holes had been welded and re-welded shut several times. All of them were sealed, except for one that kept springing minute leaks.

The wind was picking up again. Between the waves of rain that fell over the ship, the air currents died down, but that calm never lasted more than an hour at most. We were being buffeted from side to side, the gondola swinging below wildly. I wanted to puke.

I completed my patch job, and promptly lost my grip on the blowtorch.

I cursed as the tool went tumbling through the air below me, never to be seen again. I'm sure there were more blowtorches on board, but if somebody found out that I'd lost one, I'd have Yuri coming to me in tears. You'd think I'd have dropped a newborn child every time I lost a piece of equipment.

I made my way down the rigging, taking care not to lose my footing. The ropes beneath my feet had been requisitioned from below decks somewhere, so they weren't as strong as the starboard rigging. Some strange slippery grime covered them, which I couldn't identify. Very few airmen volunteered to do maintenance for the port side of the canopy as a result.

"Has anyone seen my blowtorch?" I heard an airman ask.

I took a moment to regain my bearings once back on deck. The attempt failed. The gondola swung a range of about 30 degrees. This was enough that my land-loving legs wobbled underneath me. Fortunately I was able to stand upright, but I knew I wouldn't be able to walk across the deck unless I took my steps carefully.

Fortunately, the crew had no such trouble. As I made my way towards the rear, I saw a multitude of them carrying crates up from down below. The crates were heavy. I saw many of them struggling to lift them, even though metal handles had been set into their sides. After they opened, I saw thick sheets of rubber being unpacked from them, which caused me some confusion. There were symbols punched into these mats which looked like the prayer lines the chaplain would have drawn. The crew began to distribute these rubber objects evenly across the surface of the gondola.

At the same time, I saw somewhat longer crates being brought up through the main hatchway. There were five of them. Within were long copper rods with a pitchfork design at their ends.

"Lightning rods." The sudden voice startled me, and I turned to see Dr. Ininsir standing ably nearby, with her hand gripping one of the taut attachment lines to the canopy. I sniffed. "I knew that."

She looked at me in a knowing manner. "There are five ports built into the canopy. One fore and aft for the majority of strikes, and one on top and two to the sides for all the rest." She said. "They affect aerodynamics, so we don't usually have them up there attached to the internal rods."

The crew scrambled to affix these rods to the ports via the rigging. They were able to work fast, and sped over the rigging much quicker than I could. I worried they would fall with the ship's lurching sideways movement, but they kept not only themselves on the rigging, but also somehow managed to keep hold of the rods. The whole process barely took a few minutes.

Of course, by then, the rain dashed nearly sideways. Due to the sunward tidal action in the air, it flew in from the ship's aft. The wind blew us forward at a fast pace, but the clouds above us were blowing out darkward. As a result, it appeared as though we were moving much faster than we actually were.

A brilliant blue flash, tinged with the faint color of the sun beyond the clouds, lit up a nearby cloud. Seconds later, the most tremendous sound yet rattled my eardrums. It was louder than any of the explosives we had used yet. For a moment, I blinked and rubbed my ears, trying to get the ringing out of them.

"Lightning rods in place!" came a call from one of the crew. It was relayed along the length of the gondola.

A few moments passed, and then another call went out: the captain was on deck. "All hands brace and prepare earplugs."

Many pairs of earplugs were passed around on deck, and I soon found myself the owner of a wax-encrusted pair carved and polished from wood. As much as I was disgusted by the fact that their previous user hadn't bothered to clean off their bodily emissions, I wiped off as much as I could and hurriedly placed them in my ears. If a strike happened on the canopy, I didn't want to even imagine what that would sound like without some sort of protection.

The deck descended into muffled sounds. All of the dialogue around me faded almost instantly.

The atmosphere turned surreal. I saw orders being relayed along the length of the deck by hand signals.

Then, without warning, I saw a brilliant flash of light that nearly blinded me. It burned afterimages into my eyes: brilliant blue and white tendrils that etched themselves into my sight even after I closed them. The whole canopy lit up as well, and I saw the outline of the many chambers within. I even saw a bright central column around which the canopy had been built. Evidently, this was the core of the lightning rod, and it was one of the brightest things I'd ever seen.

I didn't even have time to react and turn away. A horrendous and air-rending crack resounded throughout my skull and the atmosphere around me. I smelt ozone and felt my hair literally stand on end.

Then, the gondola began to list to starboard. In the confusion and after effects of the strike, I couldn't find the source of this strange slide, which was far more drastic than what had happened from the air buffeting us around.

My damaged eyesight fastened on a crate nearby, straining against its restraints. I saw written on its sides in a big stamp: SACRED INSULATION.

I ran immediately towards it, not bothering to think about what I could really do to secure it in the face of the nearly forty-degree slope that had suddenly appeared on the deck of the gondola. At this moment, when time slowed, my brain was operating on instinct, and my heart was pumping adrenaline.

I slapped my hand into place on the box, and felt it press against the folds of rope. I was suddenly trapped between the rope and the crate, and felt the rope bite into my hand quite harshly.

I saw, rather than heard, the other airmen who had suddenly let go of the crate began shouting at me. I thought I recognized some of them, but my memory didn't operate at full capacity in that moment of time.

In an instant, I realized something. This crate was big enough to hold at least half a ton of rubber in it. In fact, it was the exact same type of box that the crew had pulled those mats from. Some sense came to me as I realized that I couldn't hold it alone. Almost as soon as I had thought this, my other hand moved to free the hand that had been captured by the crate. I tried to free it, but to my astonishment, couldn't.

It was too late. As I watched with horror, the box slipped from its restraints, and slid against me, pushing me back with a steady but inevitable momentum behind it. I had the presence of mind to sidestep when I managed to gain a few inches, but my hand remained trapped in the rope, which was now tangled around the box. In horror, I realized that the crate was fast gaining speed.

I was swept off my feet and dragged behind the crate as it tumbled towards the railing. Splinters jammed into me from the box as we hurtled across the last remaining meters of the deck and slammed into the railing, breaking through it almost instantly.

On the other side was a two and a half kilometer drop into the ocean below.

I questioned my life. Why had I grabbed that container? I couldn't possibly hold its weight. Everything briefly flashed before my eyes before I felt the sinking feeling of resignation spread its way through my gut, followed closely by a resurgence of terror. The fall over the side of the ship loomed underneath me.

And with that, my hand broke free of the rope.

A hand grabbed the back of my shirt, yanking me back into real time, and back aboard the ship. I fell back onto the deck as it righted itself underneath me. I looked up and saw the canopy above, with its red and white bands running along its whole length. My mind traced entoptic patterns in the texture of the ship's material. I felt a wave of nausea pass over me and something like a full, eerie hum flowed through my head.

Then, the captain's stern face butted into my view of the canopy. "Are you all right Ms. Zintan?" she asked. I detected concern in her eyes. I realized it had been her who kept me from falling overboard. I couldn't hear her words through my earplugs, but I could read her lips. I gave her a thumbs-up, and pushed myself upright.

I heard and felt another deafening blast ripped through the Destiny. The crew hugged the deck, trying to keep low as another searing light flared through the canopy. All except for one. My mouth dropped open as I saw the chaplain's robed figure scrambling up the central rigging with that book, the Testament of the River. A look of absolute frenzy spread across his face.

He shouted at the canopy and held up the book against it. Multiple other flashes struck within the clouds near our ship, and I knew he needed to be yanked down from there. He was putting the ship in jeopardy; lightning could travel from the canopy through him to the deck, and from there to the rest of us.

I hadn't been the only one who immediately leapt to this conclusion. Dr. Hennir scrambled up after him. Where had she come from? She grabbed his ankle to pull him down, but he immediately kicked her hand away. She cursed and attempted to grab him again.

Just as her hand made contact with his foot a second time, I felt a familiar thump in the air, and smelled ozone again. The light blinded me, and I reacted to an expected shock on the deck. None followed. Instead, I opened my eyes to see the deck as normal, but with the addition of two burnt forms in the middle. One still held up the charred remains of his holy book, and the other crumpled in the fetal position.

A rush of crew swarmed into that space to transport the pair below decks. I remained strangely distant from it all, having almost witnessed my own death, I felt numb to the almost certain deaths of the two in front of me. Only after the stench of burnt flesh met my nostrils did I feel some semblance of confusion and amazement with the speed at which it had happened.

Around the ship, the lightning flashes faded, and the rain suddenly stopped as soon as it had started. We were in another break between the arms of cloud coming at us. I looked ahead, only to see more rain two hours out from our position.

CHAPTER 16

I wandered below decks for a half hour after that. I didn't know how the Destiny could possibly stay aloft in the coming storms. The further sunward we went, the greater their intensity. Three lightning strikes had hit us. Any more, and I was sure I would go deaf. Best to stay below decks.

After I'd passed the entrance to the crawlspace into the Destiny's steering mechanism, I heard a strange banging sound. I stopped in my tracks and gave the passage a second look. Someone was rhythmically banging a metal object against the wall inside. Yuri was the only person who had any knowledge of or desire to enter that space; I knew it was him.

I entered. It wasn't right to leave him without some sort of backup for whatever problem he had. What if the steering had been fried somehow by the lightning strikes? What if the canopy had been punctured?

I didn't have far to go into the passageway to find him. Further on, the pistons and gears inside became uncomfortably close, so he had slumped against the wall a few meters down the way, banging a massive wrench against the wall, listening to the sounds that resulted.

I raised my voice. "Mind telling me what you're doing?"

He held up a finger, and then slammed the wrench into the wall one more time.

A solid dent had appeared in the wall, nothing dangerous, but still a mark that was noticeable. Yuri's face was absolutely serious. There wasn't any humor left in it.

He leaned back and groaned. "The encabulator is broken."

"Oh." I said.

"It'll take too long to repair it, and we don't have any spares." He brought a hand to his forehead.

"Why can't it be repaired?"

"There's easily thirty or fifty moving parts inside one of those, depending on the model. Not counting the mechanical calculators inside. One for each sprocket. Those require a microscope to fix."

"How necessary is it?"

"We can deal with it for now, but its effects will add up over time. We'll go through our oil faster, might not even make it to civilization before the turbines stall out."

I nodded.

Yuri met this gesture with a sigh. "The ship's falling apart, Haye. It was supposed to be top of the line, but the maintenance I've seen... it's like a ship of twenty or thirty years that was tended to by amateurs. Communications lines haven't been replaced in a while - that's why the captain has to relay orders with voice relays. I'm starting to wonder how she was built. Seems strange to me." He suddenly slumped down.

"Yuri? Are you alright?" I worriedly asked.

He didn't answer, just drew his legs up under him.

I followed suit. "You said something a few rhythms back about the extreme sport of talking. Retired from it now?"

That drew a smile out of him. "And when did you start to take up conversation?"

"Right now. If there's something bigger that's wrong with the ship, I should know."

"It's not with the ship, it's with me." Yuri tapped his thumbs on his knee. "I still see them. In my dreams. That thing that just happened up there, that brought the memories of the stables job back. I hope you don't think I'm being like Tsu' Wei here."

I shook my head. "Tsu' Wei got cold feet because he couldn't handle even the most basic requirements for the job. I don't really see how you compare to him."

"He wasn't strong enough."

"Are you saying you're losing your nerve?"

"I'm serious. Every night we've been on this expedition, since I saw the White Hats flying those things, I haven't had a restful night."

"You old fool." I said softly. "If you keep repeating to yourself that you're afraid, you'll stay that way."

We remained that way for a bit, before I asked another question. "I wasn't inside the stables. What happened in there?"

"In five years I haven't said anything to you. I don't know if I can handle it." Yuri said.

"Maybe you can."

"I need some more time."

"OK. I'll wait." I responded after some consideration.

"Not now." He shook his head. "Sometime after we're back at civilization. Here, there's too much going on that reminds me of that rhythm. This place... it's too horrifying sometimes."

"We've got the White Hats after us. I don't think we'll have that much time."

"That's part of the point, and part of the problem."

I stared at the wall, my eyes tracing patterns in the dented metal as I stayed with the engineer for the next hour.

***

The ship's pace slowed in the face of the storms. Captain Nome mandated that we fly closer to the surface of the ocean in order to avoid more lightning strikes. On land, the maneuver wouldn't have helped avoid lightning strikes unless there were a nearby object higher than the airship's altitude. At this point, however, we were out of other ideas.

We left the ship's lightning rods up, just in case.

The ocean continued on. I found myself once again alone with my thoughts.

I saw the captain a few times, and remembered what had happened a few kilometers above: how she had saved my life. I didn't approach her.

My investigation of Pullnir turned up very little, aside from a crate full of roll-ups. As I had feared, there were no indications as to his plans, if he even was the spy. I decided that I would have to target another person with my investigation.

Only one moment stuck in my memory. A rhythm or two after our first trip through one of the storm-arms radiating out from the sunward pole, the waves grew choppier with the increase in wind and rain. Some were close to ten meters high, and as a result, we flew a greater altitude.

All of a sudden, a pod of strange creatures began to leap out of the water at high velocity. They resembled fish that had huge, inflated stomachs and six fins at their side and elongated, whip-like tails. Splotches of purple and white colored their sides. Two compound eyes were situated at their head, each of them swollen with some unidentifiable fluid that caused them to wobble when they jerked in midair.

The crew caught several, and pulled them aboard. Several hollers from joy erupted from their anticipation at eating something other than the hard cereals the Archivist had provided us. Once they cut them open, a foul-smelling yellowish liquid escaped from their bellies. It was sticky, and smelled like a mixture of lye, brine, and some other unidentifiable odor that made it stand out from the ocean.

My eyes watered. If the airmen felt comfortable eating that, or anything that had touched, they were free to do so. I would continue to eat the hard grains below deck.

The deck quickly became saturated with the smell. I passed through the outraptor hold shortly after that. It was the only smell that was both strong enough and rancid enough to wipe it from my nostrils.

I leaned back against the wall in the barber's as Dr. Ininsir kept taking notes. This place was once again a haven from the stir outside. The only other people in the room were the doctor and the two patients stowed at opposite ends of the room. The hum from the turbines ran at a lower pitch this time. Someone had placed an incense burner in the room with us. After the many odors from the ocean, it was a welcome change. A thin, unbroken line of smoke drifted upwards from the burner, drawn into meandering curves by the motion of the ship.

The doctor had drawn both patients on opposite pages in her notebook. In the margins, there were notes scribbled about their injuries, crammed together in an impossibly dense scrawl.

"How are they doing?" I finally said.

The doctor put down her notebook. "My colleague will recover. I can't say about him." She indicated the chaplain.

"I'm not so sure I'll be that devastated if he goes."

I heard sadness in her voice as she replied. "Perhaps you're right that we're better off without him, but I still don't feel good about the possibility of him dying."

I pushed myself gently away from the bulkhead at my back. "Sometimes I wish I knew what drives you Beltlanders. You're not the first person to care about someone you don't like dying."

Dr. Ininsir turned back towards me and blinked, awaiting an

explanation.

I shrugged. "A few rhythms back, the captain saved me. I don't really know why she finds my life valuable enough to risk being pulled overboard for me." I said.

"I don't have an answer for you. Maybe you should ask her?"

I smirked to myself as I imagined how that conversation would go. "When andironbacks fly."

The doctor returned to her sketches. "We're headed for trouble." She said.

"I know."

"It's only going to get worse. I've sketched out the meteorological implications of my atmospheric models of the sunward side. There's..." she stopped.

I raised an eyebrow. "Yes?"

"There's a gigantic storm on this side of the Great Range. A massive, circular system that defies all concepts of how big it is. If you thought the Great Range was massive, this storm measures easily eight thousand kilometers across."

"Shouldn't it end?"

"It's perpetual. The action of the sun evaporating the water in this massive sea keeps going forever."

"So what you're saying is that we're flying into the center of an eternal storm, and that the worst is yet to come."

"Right. I haven't a clue as to how to fly through it, either."

I remembered the conversation between the spy and the Archivist. They must have factored this into how they would advance the expedition.

"There's something else as well: the sunward lands look familiar to me. If there's ground ahead, I know I've seen that arrangement of land and sea somewhere, but I don't know how it formed. I know it must be the same arrangement though."

"You're losing me."

"Eh. I'll figure it out." The doctor said.

Silence reigned once more between us. I was about to doze off from the soft hum that surrounded us, when the doctor spoke again. "I talked with Dr. Hennir before this happened. She wanted to show me some of her notes. She still doesn't think the Forebears have any relation to early humans."

I stirred myself. "What did she make of the Archivist? And that other creature?"

"I don't know. She'll probably come around to my view, which is that they're using Forebear technology somehow."

I pressed further, "Do you think they're able to be trusted?"

"Perhaps. Most likely not. If they can't even remember how they came to use the Forebear technology, then they're unreliable at best."

"A very wise observation." I left out that I had doubts they were using technology, as opposed to being supernaturally gifted.

Dr. Ininsir's face brightened considerably. "Would you kindly bring those notes Hennir wanted to show me? They should be on top of her desk in her notebook. I know her too well: she keeps them all in the same place."

"You aren't going to get them yourself?"

"I want to stay here. Dr. Hennir was... is... something of a mentor to me. I want to make sure she recovers fully." As instantly as her expression lifted, it darkened again. "I still am concerned about her health."

I smiled. A perfect opportunity to investigate another lead.

"Give me the key to your quarters, and I'll gladly oblige."

***

The door to the doctor's cabin was locked. I regarded it carefully, planning my move.

The ship rocked furiously under the push and pull of another storm. The Destiny's turbines had increased again to the maximum. Somehow, Evinsir was compensating for the sideways motions with turbine thrusts. The increase in speed meant something else, I surmised. The winds behind us, drawing us in towards the center of the sunward storm, were getting to their strongest yet.

I didn't know if anyone stood inside the doctor's room. My sixth sense tingled. There were only a small number of people who could be connected to the spy, and Dr. Hennir was likely to be one of them. If that was the case, the man could be sitting in her quarters right now, waiting for me. He could know I was coming. My certainty about this grew with each passing moment.

He was getting prepared to remove me as a threat. My instincts were in full agreement about this.

As a precautionary measure, I peered through the keyhole. Unfortunately, the room beyond wasn't lit by any inside light source. Was that a boot in the corner? A desk? A chair leg? I couldn't be sure.

I hesitated for a bit. In that split second, I made up my mind to enter the room. I loosened my revolver from its holster, and quietly slipped the key into the lock.

I opened the door quietly. The smell of dusty books filled my nose as I quickly glanced over the entirety of the doctor's quarters. They were remarkably austere. There were two work desks and two simple cots in opposite corners. Apart from a single large chest and a couple of chemodans embossed with leafy patterns, there wasn't that much furniture in the room.

My attention passed over all of these in favor of the man that stood just inside.

In a second, I knew he was the infiltrator. He was the one who represented those who had machinated this foolhardy expedition into the unknown. He stood the same way as I had seen on the dunes back at Dostwickr Basin. His height was the same.

He was Yensir. That man who had never said a single word as long as I had seen him. The man I knew almost nothing about. He was always in the background, always skulking behind someone else, usually Dr. Hennir. He was her servant after all.

And most importantly, he held a derringer to his own head, his finger on the trigger, ready to pull.

CHAPTER 17

Yensir and I faced each other, weapons at the ready, although mine didn't do any good at the moment. No expression crossed Yensir's face. Not a single ounce of anger, or sadness, or concern. I could have heard a pin drop in that room, in spite of the raging storm outside.

"Tell me," he began slowly, "Do you know what a Kodjan is?"

I remained still, lest he stir from his rhetorical exercise and kill himself.

"It's an Ijritani concept. One of the few cultural items from the Nemasian side of the world that I admire. A man, usually, dedicates himself to the service of another for the entirety of his life. In return, the other grants... friendship to the man for life as well. It's not a marriage. It's roughly akin to an Aulan house-servant.

"I have pledged myself to the service of Dr. Hennir from the age of six, when she was twenty. She pulled me out of the slums of Da Faiq from a life of begging to a life of comfortable service. We have been together for over thirty years." He tapped the derringer with his thumb. "I wonder what sort of questions she might start asking if I was found with a bullet through my head. Especially if that bullet just so happened to be the same caliber as your revolver ammunition."

I wasn't fazed. "I also wonder what sort of questions she might start asking if she knew you were a member of the Five."

"Firstly, I don't think she'd take your word for it." He smiled nastily. "And secondly, you don't know enough to convince her even if she was inclined to trust you over her closest friend."

"Would you really blow your own brains to keep me from finding out what you're up to?" I asked. "Talk about cutting off your own nose to spite your face."

"There are events at work you can't possibly begin to understand." He narrowed his eyes slightly. "Or perhaps you do. Are you with the opposition?"

"Little old me?"

Yensir's eyes narrowed even more. "Don't get smart with me. The opposition has had operatives in much more deeply layered cover than you, if you are with them."

Maybe being conciliatory would work? "Let's start this conversation over. I'm not with the opposition." I said.

He considered the statement briefly. "That much I could believe, on further reflection. The opposition would not suffer someone with your ignorance among their ranks."

"So, are we going to stand here threatening each other, then?"

"I'm not threatening you, Ms. Zintan. You're threatening me. I'm merely acting on the protocols given to me under these circumstances. If you attempt to blow my cover, I will make that impossible. The only evidence you'll find inside this room to support your case is inside my head, which would be gone."

"What about the smoking gun?"

"They might believe I killed myself, but the rest of your story? They'll think you're crazy. And without me, you won't survive the sun-storm to get to the sunward pole. I'm the only one who knows the way. I'm not immediately pulling the trigger because I don't think we're necessarily enemies."

"Where have I heard that before..."

"I promise not to possess anyone or freeze the ship's turbines." He smiled again.

"So if we're not enemies, what are we?"

"I certainly haven't pointed this gun at you, have I?"

"Alright, point it elsewhere than your head. I want to know who you are, and you shooting yourself would complicate that."

"Stay on that side of the room, and close the door behind you." He ordered.

"Fine, but I'm keeping my gun out."

"Deal."

I stepped fully inside the doctors' quarters, and closed the door behind me, locking it as well. I pulled out one of the chairs currently situated at a desk on the left side of the room, and sat down, keeping my revolver leveled in front of me. Yensir, having seen this, took the two-shot pistol from his head and sat down on a chemodan. He kept his pistol in his hand, though he didn't aim it anywhere in particular, and his finger remained off the trigger.

"You should understand that I can't explain to you exactly who I serve, or what our goals are. Even if you aren't with the opposition, there's still a strong chance that they would gain high-level intelligence as to our operations from interrogating you." he said almost immediately.

I looked him straight in the eye. "Then you'd better come up with a way to convince me you aren't leading us to our deaths real quick."

"These are my low-level objectives: get to the sunward pole, retrieve my target, and return to civilization as quickly as possible. None of that involves killing the ship's crew, and by extension you."

"Is that 'something' you're looking for the same thing that Dr. Hennir is chasing?"

"Dr. Hennir believes that she'll discover the complete compendium of the ancient records of the Forebears, which explain their civilization. Dr. Ininsir hopes the same thing. I am searching for something completely different. That's all you need to know."

A sudden realization dawned on me. "You... led her to the map, didn't you? In Site twenty-three?"

"Among other things." Yensir replied. "How did she ever find out about the existence of the Line Channel, that it was a passage through the Great Range? I can guarantee you the map itself didn't include an explanation of that particular figure. As far as she knows, I'm only her helpful servant. In her mind, she's the driving figure behind this expedition."

My brow furrowed. "Why do you need her? Or any of us?"

"Because voyages like these are hard to conceal. Camouflaging our mission inside of a Basilica-sponsored expedition is much better than mounting one ourselves. The opposition would be that sloppy under certain circumstances, but we aren't."

"And your broader mission is?"

"Perhaps some future rhythm. For now, trust that I am already concerned that you know too much. I'm bending protocol here because you're some use to this expedition's survival. Don't be a liability to me." He tapped the derringer with his thumb for emphasis.

I considered what he had said. "It sounds as though we have a common goal then. But the first misstep from you and it'll be me shooting you, not the other way around."

We both relaxed a little. Yensir holstered his pistol, and I mirrored his action with my twelve-shot.

"One more thing: the White Hats have crossed the Great Range." Yensir said.

"I know."

"They have backup." He said flatly.

I cursed. "What kind?"

"Three frigate airships: the Death's Wing, the End of Joy, and the Bane. All commissioned from the dockyard at Suderzhir-Ingyan. All staffed with airmen of the opposition. All hidden at various locations across the globe before being assigned to track us across the Great Range. They represent the entire might of the opposition's clandestine air operations."

I regarded him with suspicion. "How do you know this?"

"Ask yourself, how do I know the Archivist so well?" He grinned.

"Fine then, don't tell me. How do we fight them?"

"That, unfortunately, I have no idea how to answer. I was hoping that one of the officers had a better idea of how we do that."

"Are you going to tell them that you got them into this mess? That's the only way you're going to get them to prepare for it."

"No. And anyway, I didn't get this expedition into this mess. You did, by drawing the Yinda's attention to it." Yensir glared at me before standing up and making his way towards the door. "This whole thing could have gone off quietly if you hadn't joined this expedition."

I coolly regarded him.

"The notes Dr. Ininsir will inevitably be looking for are over there on the desk."

"You *know* what, or who, is waiting for us at the sunward pole. Don't you?" I cocked my head at him.

He gave me one last look, as if to say: *That's for me to know, and you to wonder.*

***

I looked out at the ship's rear. Ahead of us, yet another lightning-filled wave of the storm approached. By this point, I found them boring and more of a nuisance than anything else.

I occasionally hallucinated shapes in the receding storm waves behind us. Were they actually hallucinations though? One cloud or the next appeared from this far away to be in the shape of a giant airship. The next moment, however, the cloud would change shape again to some impossibly convoluted and natural form; clearly not artificial.

I thought over Yensir's warning. Three frigates. All told, at least twenty or thirty guns each. From what I knew of airships, frigates were giant constructions. I didn't know exactly how big they were, but I did know that only the mighty dreadnought outclassed them. How in the world were we supposed to fight those things? With Shadow Flyers among them?

I was frustrated that I hadn't managed to wring an explanation from Yensir about his organization. That slimy bastard thought that I trusted him, but I didn't. I never would. Not even if he kept to his word, and kept us aloft for as long as it took to get back to civilization. I fully expected him to backstab us the moment that he got the chance. After all, I knew too much already.

It was clear now. I had stumbled onto something much greater than the expedition itself. Already, I felt the same curiosity pricking at my consciousness as I did when wondering what occupied the sunward pole. It gnawed at me.

When this was over, I knew I had to find out who held Yensir's leash.

"You spend too much time by yourself." Tian' Xi's sudden interjection stirred me from my thoughts as she swung down from the aft rigging to sit next to me.

I had gotten used to people randomly walking up behind me on this ship. It annoyed me to no end, but what could I do? "Speak for yourself."

"I've never seen you talking to any of the airmen. That's not really a good thing. Not for you, I mean. For the ship." she responded.

"Why?"

"Generally airmen in the Aery want their commanding officers to know what it's like to have a lower station. In your case, you need to talk to them in order to figure that out."

"I'm not much for talking. Sounds useless anyway to talk with them. Did you have to do that?"

"Nope! I was promoted from airman first class through to midshipman, and then to lieutenant. I know a lot of these guys from my time back then." She happily replied.

I knew automatically this was going to turn into another session where someone aboard the ship tried to lecture me. I'd had enough from everyone else; I wasn't in the mood for letting Tian' Xi get away with talking down to me. "How did you get from airman to midshipman?"

"I managed to raise the Destiny's altitude at a critical point during the last engagement we had. The previous master of altitude had been shot dead."

"And from midshipman to lieutenant?"

"I was officer of the watch when we got lost in fog. I was able to determine our altitude using some... unorthodox means." She smiled to herself.

"Ever think that you'd be where you were if you always thought first about everybody else?" I said pointedly.

"Yes? What kind of question is that?"

I growled with annoyance. Of course she must have thought about herself at some point in order to accept the promotions. "If any of you had spent any time where I've been, you'd agree with me."

"You think life is all sunshine and rum in the Aery, cupcake? It isn't, just letting you know. I've been in two separate aerial engagements with enemy ships. Let me tell you, the Beltlander ethic is the only thing that will truly help you in that situation. Just like how we stood together back at Dostwickr Basin. If everyone thought the way you did, the crew would have scattered from the ship, and been slaughtered."

I couldn't really argue with that. "You're still wrong." I finally retorted, lacking anything else to say.

"And that," she flicked her finger at me, "is one of your biggest problems right there. You don't know how to change your mind about things."

A call went through the length of the ship as I searched for a reply. "Land ahead! Land ahead!" I glanced back over my shoulder at the fore of the ship. Giant cliffs rose from the sea, almost enshrouded by the approaching rain. At last, the monotony of the past three rhythms was over.

At the seaside, black lichen clung to the rocky surface of the new place we'd discovered. Beyond, there was nothing but a solid plateau of pockmarked stone. The land was bare of vegetation. The terrain bore a significant resemblance to the ground we'd encountered at Dostwickr Basin, without the addition of any of those purple buds or insect-like creatures. Many waterfalls carved away at the rock through tunnels that emptied into the sea.

The air by now was so humid and so disgustingly hot that sweat regularly dripped down my face, and the faces of the airmen around me. The sun became uncomfortably bright, even through the layers and layers of thick cloud above us.

The Destiny tilted upward, and the turbines accelerated to full. As we climbed higher and higher, I saw something that took my breath away.

A multitude of shipwrecks dotted the rocky shoals beneath the cliffs. Some appeared to be from several hundred years ago. Scattered among the flotsam and jetsam were identifiable piles of bones, their owners long since decayed.

On the plateau above lay an assortment of airships. Many of them had been struck by lightning. All of them were derelicts. A massive, burnt-out corpse of a liner, some three hundred meters from end to end, lay to starboard. The landscape resembled one giant junkyard.

We'd found the final resting place of the missing ships that disappeared on the Unknown Seas.

***

After hours of looking down at faintly orange-lit desolation from barely one hundred meters up, I returned below decks to sit in one of the maintenance hallways. It was the same one where I'd overheard my prior gun crew talking behind my back. I knew that they would return at some point, since they thought they were safe from eavesdroppers here. I found Yensir there.

Before I could growl out a demand as to why he was here, he calmly pressed a finger to his lips and gestured towards the grate he squatted in front of. I heard voices coming from beyond.

"We're here?"

"Here."

"Here."

"I'm here."

The voices were a mangle. I couldn't tell who talked at which point. Clearly there were at least six speakers. The space beyond the grate fell silent for a while.

"This is nuts." A man finally said.

"Continuing on after what we've seen is nuts." Another speaker broke in. A woman.

"I agree."

"Hear, hear."

"Those ships down there could be us." The woman speaker said. "We've already been far enough, and I keep hearing rumors that the ship's been acting funny. Those doctors are intent on running us to the sunward pole even if it means killing us. They're not thinking straight. We should have turned back several rhythms ago. It's because of them we've lost eleven people."

"The crew's fixin' for a fight. They'll stand behind you." It was a burly voice I recognized from my previous eavesdropping.

"Exactly." The woman continued.

"Not all of them." The doubter said.

"Explain."

"You may not get this, since you're new around here, but captain Nome has commanded this ship for nearly twenty years. She's got the respect of the crew. In order to turn this ship around, you need to remove her from command. That's not something our fellows will do lightly."

Another voice spoke up, this one sounding like a young kid. "I'm sorry, but have we tried talking to her? She's a reasonable person. Maybe she could be convinced to..."

"...Abandon her friend's pet project? I've seen enough of her to know that she values her friendship over our lives. And if you want to go up and talk to her as a common airman and express your concerns, be my guest. I'd like to see how that goes."

When she was satisfied with the resulting silence, the woman started again.

"Now, the reason you're here is that we have a plan. The original idea called for an off-rhythm seizure of the ship's armory, followed by an appeal to the rest of the crew. We can adapt to the situation after that, but the outline is the same as when we met last time: we'll imprison the senior officers along with the captain and the doctors until we return back to Yin. At that point, the ship's crew will scatter and assume new identities.

"I'm calling a vote. Make your decisions quickly. All in favor? All against?"

The sound of shuffling erupted as the vote went around the conspirators.

"Three for, three abstentions... one against."

I heard a water drop somewhere in the hallway I sat in.

"This has to be unanimous."

"I know."

"You're still against?"

"I am."

"Care to explain?"

"If we don't have the full support of the crew, even half support from them, it'll be too bloody. That defeats the purpose of this thing, doesn't it?" The man paused. "We have to wait for the right moment."

"Fine." The speaker sounded defeated. "We'll postpone the action for a rhythm until you come to your senses. Be in readiness for when we move though. Back to stations."

I heard footsteps. The group was leaving. At the exact moment of their departure, Yensir wheeled to me and whispered urgently. "You should inform the captain."

I would have retorted that I wouldn't take instruction from him, but he didn't stick around for a conversation. If it had been a smaller group of conspirators, and half the crew hadn't given their support to them, I would have dealt with them myself. We needed to inform the captain of this.

***

The ship's ballast chamber was a long corridor that ran from aft to stern along the bottom of the ship. Stacked along both sides were ballast stones: meter-high boulders carved from granite into cubic shapes and neatly placed into notches in the bulkhead of the ship. A straight walkway led towards the fore of the ship, which I walked down. The absence of any outlights that would illuminate this section of the ship forced me to carry a lantern. Underneath me, the ship groaned and creaked with the force of the winds outside. Apart from that, it was quiet. The turbines were too far away from this section to be heard.

I knew the captain was here. I had first visited her ready-room.

When I hadn't found her there, I then inquired as to her whereabouts. The crewman stationed outside her room told me she was down here, but didn't know why.

I sniffed at the oily scent in the air. I didn't know why she was down here. Was there some ship's system she was inspecting? Did she, like me, need a place to be alone? She didn't strike me that way, but barring another explanation, it was the logical conclusion.

I briefly stopped in my tracks when the lantern peeked out of the far end of the ship. It was the captain, with a rare expression on her face. She was despondent.

I rushed towards her down the long hallway. As I drew near, she met my approach with an unchanging look.

"Mutiny." I blurted out in a hushed tone, my speech punctuated by hard breathing from running. "There's a plot to mutiny. I don't know who they were, but they've got support. All through the ship."

The captain nodded. "I've heard." She said.

"How?" I asked dumbfounded.

"You don't remember me saying that I've got eyes and ears throughout the ship, do you? I already know about their plans. I even know who the leaders are."

"Who?"

"A younger airman. She's been a troublemaker on other ships in the past, though I can't fathom what her reasoning is. She was a last-minute assignment. I still don't know who put her on my ship, but I certainly didn't ask for her."

"So why haven't you moved against her?"

"Because we haven't turned around yet."

I blinked. "What?"

I heard a groan from the ship's hull as the Destiny swayed.

"It's true. I didn't want to admit it until I saw the boneyard outside, but the expedition must return darkward. I can't ask the crew to fly blindly into that storm ahead of us. We've already seen what its outer edges look like. We won't survive the inner folds." the captain said.

"But... the expedition! The sunward pole!" I was furious. Was she really backing down now? After we'd gotten this far? I came all this way, to the Sunward Side I'd dreamed about as a child, and now it was to be taken away from me by some skittish crewmen? I searched for something that would goad her to continue. "The

Forebear city!"

"Is it worth sacrificing all of our lives? I respect the work of my friend Dr. Hennir, believe me. That said, I won't allow her work to jeopardize my ship. There are limits on what she can ask."

"So you're going to let your crew overrule the mission?"

"This isn't caving to the mutineers. It's a good command decision. I should have anticipated this over the ocean when we lost our chaplain and the good doctor herself. We won't be able to carry out any archaeological studies once we reach the Forebear city."

"We didn't lose her."

"My... friend... is not in a position to be continuing any of her work, therefore the mission has come to an end."

The finality she said that left no room for argument. I was still incensed, but it was clear that my desire to see the utmost of the Sunward reaches wouldn't be enough.

The captain started walking down towards the aft hatchway that led out from the ballast chamber. "Once I've announced we'll be turning around, the mutineers will be confined to the brig. Doing that now would be inadvisable given the current mindset of the crew."

"When will you announce that?" My voice was dripping with sullen anger.

"First hour of next rhythm. I want to say my prayers to the River first, and sleep. End-rhythm is not the time to be telling the crew that the sacrifice of their crewmates was in vain."

"You should be putting those troublemakers in the brig now. If you deal with them the right way, the rest of the crew would be scared into submission." I snarled.

She stopped.

"Not every decision one takes as a leader demands that you dominate your subordinates. Can't you see what effect that has?" she said.

Dead silence filled the air. I don't think the captain realized what she'd said to me.

A long time ago, so far back I didn't usually think about it, my mother had discovered a treasure trove of stolen money underneath my bed. She'd said the exact same thing. Even the intonation was the same. "Can't you see what effect that has?"

In that moment, I saw something different in the captain. It was past her stolid expression, past her hard-set eyes, past her uniform and the command it entailed. She'd saved my life in the storm because I meant something to her. I felt a brew of feeling overcoming me, and terror gripped me as I knew the captain would see my weakness.

I beat a hasty retreat. My face struggling to contain the intense cauldron of emotion brewing inside me.

CHAPTER 18

I needed to be alone. Somewhere. Anywhere. The barber's would do. No one would be in there besides the two patients. It was the only guaranteed spot where no one would bother me. I had to get there.

I halted as soon as I had reached the door. Unholy shrieks emitted from inside.

"Damnation! Damnation and eternal sundering! Repent! Repent of your transgressions lest we burn! Burn in the fires of Heaven!"

I remembered the chaplain's actions during the lightning storm and ran away from the barber's, and from him.

I couldn't bear to be near anyone. Captain Nome had awakened something inside me that I'd been running from for my whole life. I'd hidden from it in the various nooks and crannies of the Yin cities; in smokehouses and in underground chambers where the outlaw underbelly of Yin society met. I'd gone as far as the foothills of the Great Range to hide from it. Now, I was on an expedition to the very sunward pole for the same reason. Only this time, it had followed me.

I felt revolting weakness spread through my mind. It was the feeling of... homesickness? Nostalgia? A longing. A longing for my mother.

I burst out of the aft hatch onto the deck, breathing in air that still stifled with its humidity. The eternal orange sunlight blasted my face. Everything was too hot. Even the raindrops that were cascading over the ship as we hugged the landscape were close to boiling.

I ran to the starboard railing and looked over the wasteland we were flying over to try and clear my thoughts. A smooth, eroded surface of rock met my eyes, one that giant rivers were carving out as we continued to move sunward. Occasionally we passed the rusted hulk of another airship, its form barely recognizable from the years of rust that encrusted its surface. They were getting sparser now.

How many ships had been lost over the years? There had been an endless field of airships earlier. Their crews must have landed here to find something worth scavenging from the others. They were corpses each of them, cannibalizing their dead, eating components that were left on the dead ships.

I wondered whether I agreed with the captain. The air was becoming untenably hot. The intervals between the arms of the storm were getting shorter, and the lightning struck the ground with an intensity never seen further darkward. The orange tint that blanketed everything gave me the impression that the surrounding landscape was on fire.

And there were *things* ahead. Intelligent things. The hints we'd gleaned from They-That-Seeks and the Archivist were enough to give me pause. Even those ancient beings lived in fear of whatever existed at the sunward pole. I wondered what inspired that fear that lasted through endless cycles of time in those immortals.

In spite of all this, we couldn't go back. Not with our pursuers somewhere behind us.

These pressures only increased my longing for home as I mulled them over. I clenched my fists.

Some small, primitive part of my mind gnawed at me to return to safety back in Yin. It was like looking down a dark tunnel, your last torch burnt out, and only the sounds of heavy breathing emanating from its interior.

Safety? Where? To my mother? My mother couldn't keep me safe. I'd stumbled into a vast empty wilderness from which there was no escape. Even when the captain tried to turn around, she would run smack-dab into the White Hats.

The ship decelerated. Afore, the terrain sloped upward. A hill sat above the desolation, its top shielded by the stormy clouds that whipped up and over its massive bulk. A gaping, pitch-black maw, perfectly circular in size, sunk into its side. The hillside faced away from the sun; its interior completely shadowed. I couldn't see anything inside, though my eyes played tricks on me as forms from my memories of the past few rhythms shifted about my vision. Sometimes a creature appeared to dart out of that great shadow, but every time I blinked, the blackened shape had changed.

I felt the strongest intuition yet that we shouldn't enter. I knew that some malevolent force awaited us inside. That thought pounded away at my consciousness in the same way that the Voice had. This was not a good place.

***

The LEDs on Evinsir's control panel flickered with each passing flash of the lightning in the sky. The ship's controls were less and less reliable as we flew further sunward. Off-rhythm had come, and we were still next to the massive tunnel entrance. The rain had ceased briefly, but the air still felt suffocating.

I stared Pullnir down. The first lieutenant leaned with his back against the side of the panel, while Evinsir made preparations to navigate inside the tunnel. At our side, the midshipman Hapsman stood ready to take orders.

"So you want the ship to be destroyed by the sunstorm?" Pullnir asked matter-of-factly.

"We shouldn't be continuing without waking up the captain, and asking for her decision." I replied.

"Why? We've already lost significant progress. The captain's last directive was to get the ship into safety from the sunstorm."

"You don't know that her orders haven't changed."

"I do. That will be all." He waved his hand in an attempt to dismiss me.

"No, that won't be all. We don't have powerful enough lighting to see in there."

"Then we'll compensate by going slower."

How thick could you get, I asked myself. "We could still run into the walls if there's a sharp turn."

"Your objections will be noted in the ship's log." A twitch tugged at his lips.

I could seriously have punched him then and there. Regretfully, I didn't.

"You're going to get this entire ship killed because you want to play captain for the rhythm."

As I said this, the midshipman at our side gave a quick glance out towards the ship's aft.

"You're too much trouble, Ms. Zintan." Pullnir said to me, his face remaining motionless.

The midshipman pulled out a folding telescope from his jacket, and a look of disbelief crossed his face. He turned back towards us and stated insistently, "Sirs?"

"Is that so?" I replied to Pullnir.

"Sirs?" The midshipman tried to break in.

"Every time either the captain or I have tried to give you an order, you've been an insubordinate know-it-all that refuses to cooperate. You have no respect for your betters." Pullnir responded with a sneer. "Some fine rhythm, when this expedition is over, that will land you in hot water. I'll see to that myself."

"Unknown ship ten kilometers aft, sirs! What are your orders?" The midshipman finally shouted over our argument.

Pullnir was confused, but I recognized instantly the ship's significance. They'd finally caught up to us. I didn't know how they'd found us, but I knew that they were coming in for the kill.

I seized the telescope and peered in the same direction the midshipman had. It didn't take long for me to locate the ship. Even at this distance, I could easily tell that she was longer and heavier than the Destiny. Menacing patterns zigzagged across her hull. A trail of exhaust shimmered through the air from a full set of six turbines. I could barely see the crew; they looked like insects. The ship closed on us amazingly fast. It was likely she would be here within the hour.

"Someone followed us?" Pullnir stepped towards aft.

Two pinpricks of light briefly flared into existence at the front of the ship. Through the telescope, I saw huge white clouds billow out of two holes in the ship's fore.

"ALL HANDS TAKE COVER!" I screamed.

Confusion broke out on deck as the crew didn't see any immediate danger. Some followed the order, others didn't. I tried repeating the order, but it wasn't much use.

"Evinsir, take evasive action. Now." I commanded. The master of navigation moved to comply.

"Belay that..." Pullnir began. He never had a chance to complete his grandstanding.

The shells took a few seconds to arrive, during which time I heard them both whistling like a tea kettle as they drew nearer. When they arrived, they shook the deck beneath my feet. Massive explosions erupted a few dozen meters on either side of the ship. I saw the hull buckle from the force of the impact. Several airmen were blown overboard by the shockwave. I was lucky enough to be standing behind the control panel, whose lights flickered again in sympathy to the detonations.

Screams echoed across the deck. I saw several wounded, mostly from shrapnel, towards the ship's fore, where the artillery had been closer. Others yelled overboard at some of the more lucky airmen who had been wearing safety ropes and were dangling precariously over the side of the Destiny. I couldn't tell how many we'd lost.

It took my breath away momentarily to think about the sort of guns they might have aboard the frigate. They had fired over several kilometers, barely missed us, and at the same time fired artillery shells that were much higher explosive yield than I'd ever seen before.

A cascade of events happened immediately following our close encounter. I saw Pullnir crouch down behind the panel, along with the midshipman. The crew spun into action, and Evinsir's delayed evasive actions began. The ship pulled a hard left as Tian' Xi began maneuvering the Destiny downward. I hooked an arm under the first lieutenant and pulled him forcefully up. He was clearly shaken and temporarily deaf. In no position to be giving orders. I was fine with that.

"Hapsman," I called out, "send word for the captain."

A muffled "Aye." came back.

I paused. We were between a rock and a hard place. Going down meant going into the foreboding maw. Staying here meant being shot to pieces.

I made my first decision within a few seconds. "Full speed ahead Evinsir, get us over this ridge."

Pullnir had recovered by now, and had heard my orders. He grabbed the telescope from where it had fallen and caught sight of the pursuing frigate. He spoke up, and for once, it wasn't instantly condescending. "We can't outrun them."

I wheeled about to face him. "Why?" I asked.

"They've got six turbines. They're faster than us."

"They're a heavier ship! How can they possibly be faster than the Destiny?"

"We're not outrunning them."

"I..."

"For once, Ms. Zintan, trust that I have more airman's

experience than you?" A serious and frustrated look crossed his face.

I didn't want to admit that he was telling the truth, so I spat back at him, "So what to do?"

"We go down. Into the tunnel."

I paused just long enough to hear another pair of projectiles whistling overhead. The explosions were as big as the first pair, and hit only a few meters at best from where we originally were. Nonetheless, I saw ripples propagating through the canopy, and worried for a second that it would burst open from the pressure wave that had hit it. It held, barely.

There wasn't any way we could pull ourselves out of this situation, other than to go straight down, into the darkness. Where we couldn't see.

The Destiny fit inside the tunnel, but it was unlikely our pursuer would as well, given her massive size. With any luck, we'd be able to lose them in there.

I made my second decision. "Fine. We go in." I replied.

The Destiny entered into the darkness. Now was the time to run.

***

The darkness felt suffocating. We high-tailed it in with a speed that definitely made me uncomfortable. Just in time, too. Soon after we'd dropped out of view, two shells came whistling through the air where we had been, and slammed into the tunnel wall behind us, blasting out craters on the ceiling. I swore as I thought the tunnel entrance would collapse.

Thankfully, it didn't. We were able to escape into the darkness with relative ease.

A descent of forty-five degrees for about five hundred meters awaited us. We were significantly far below the surface. At this depth, the light from the surface couldn't reach down to us. My last order before the captain came to the deck was for magnesium flares to be lit along the sides of the ship. Our speed slowed to a crawl, and the deck fell silent as the wounded were carried below for the ship's barber. Pitch darkness surrounded us.

The captain ordered the ship to hug the tunnel floor, so as to have some surface we could orient ourselves with in the darkness. The ship, normally flying at incredible distances above the ground, was reduced to creeping along at almost ground level.

Nome stood calmly at the ship's aft, all of the lieutenants at her side. I detected tension in her posture. "Why wasn't I called the moment we encountered this tunnel?" She asked matter-of-factly.

"Apologies sir, we weren't able to get word to you." Pullnir responded. His palms were folded one over the other behind his back. She stepped up to him in front of us. Her brow furrowed as she tried to gauge him. "Something you want to add, lieutenant?"

He acted puzzled. "No sir?" he said.

"It's not like you to delay informing me of these kinds of things."

"It won't happen again."

Stiff silence fell over the gathered crew. I felt as though something was very wrong with this interaction, but I couldn't place my finger on exactly what. I glanced over to Yuri and Tian' Xi, but they just shrugged.

The captain pointed ahead. "There's no going back, but going forward in this dark is going to be difficult. Hapsman, pass the word: I want signal flares to be fired fore and aft by the minute. Evinsir, keep the ship steady at ten knots. Be prepared to slow down if we see anything ahead. Pullnir, I want a casualty report now."

I left for the ship's fore after the captain dismissed the gathering. The turbines quietly grumbled as we resumed our course. Inside the tunnel, the sound distantly echoed off the walls, betraying the vast and cavernous expanse that surrounded us. The tunnel was widening out.

I heard the first of the flares fired. The fuses were timed for three seconds before the flares lit up, lighting up the sides of the tunnel. I caught glimpses of carvings in the wall. These were clearly artificial: a weird tangle of triangles that depicted inhuman faces, but perhaps also human ones? They disappeared within mere seconds. I kept my eyes peeled for when the next set of flares would be fired.

We continued for some time with the minutes stretching on endlessly. I stood awake off-rhythm, but I didn't dare go to sleep. Not when we were in a place like this. I instead used the frigid air down here to assist in keeping me awake. The tunnel was cold enough that I saw my breath turning into fog.

We were several kilometers in when an uneasy but awed set of exclamations suddenly erupted across the deck in a wave. I turned to see what they were gasping at.

At first, I thought that they were small pricks of light. They looked like blue sparkling dots at that distance, each one shimmering slightly like lamplight reflecting off a lake. There were thousands of them, approaching from both sides of the ship. Another flare lighted, and I saw that the cavern had opened to the point that twin tunnels had forked off from ours. They were swarming out of these passageways.

Only when they came closer did I discern their true form. They were gelatinous, almost ethereal creatures whose indistinct shape phased in and out from one type to the next. I saw in quick succession tendrils, lobes, and ridges that swirled into other pulsating outlines whose nature I couldn't comprehend. They were floating towards us with uncanny speed.

The unease that permeated the deck increased in tempo as they approached. Several of the crew ran for weapons, as did I. There were rifles stowed inside a crate nearby, of which I grabbed the last one.

I aimed for one of the creatures, my hands firmly grasping the weapon. I decided that I would wait until they approached within fifteen meters, and then I would fire.

But then, I heard an order relayed down the length of the ship. "Hold fire."

I was bewildered. I couldn't comprehend it. Had the order come from the captain herself? Why was she ordering us not to fire? These things were going to overtake the ship, and we needed to defend ourselves.

I ran aft to determine what was going on. As I approached, I heard heated arguing among the congregated senior command, which died down as I arrived.

Before I could open my mouth, one of the creatures finally reached the aft section of the Destiny and paused. We stood staring at it, marveling at its alien shape-shifting quality. A crowd gathered around the aft section, some armed, some not.

Finally, it extended a tendril towards a young crew member. I recognized him as the boy who had previously served on my gun crew. The lad, unthinkingly, reached up to push the thing away as he stepped back.

On contact, I saw blue pulses of liquid flash in the center of the creature. They flew along the length of the extended tendril, and met the boy's arm.

On reaching him, it became apparent they were some sort of liquid that had been excreted from the interior of the creature. They splashed over his arm, covering it completely. I saw a look of shock cross the boy's face for a few seconds before his expression broke into a pained scream. I barely had time to see before others among the crew fruitlessly rushed to his aid and blocked my view; blue liquid had started to leak around his eyes. His hand had turned blue like death, and the venom crept up his arm. As it did, his arm melted as though it had been exposed to a powerful acid. The boy fell, and his scream was cut off. The creature flew backward from the boy's remains.

Upon witnessing this, the crew panicked. I thought they'd nearly panicked before when the abominations that the Voice had unleashed upon us had thundered through Dostwickr Basin. They hadn't. Or at least, they hadn't to this level. Absolute pandemonium gripped the deck.

Adrenaline, my old friend, coursed through my veins as time slowed. The creature that had attacked swooped forward again, extending several tendrils this time towards multiple targets. I raised the rifle I had commandeered, and fired a single shot into the center of the thing. It had no effect.

I cursed and slammed the bolt back for another shot. I noticed that there were lobes of pulsating flesh that occasionally materialized in the interior of the creature. My frantic mind zeroed in on them as a target. I aimed, waited one second for a lobe to appear, and fired.

The bullet pierced the beast, causing it to keel over to the side, and slump against the railing with a revolting squish. With the last of its strength, it slithered overboard, and landed on the cavern floor a moment later. Out of commission, I thought triumphantly.

Then I saw the rest of the creatures floating towards us. The closest individuals raised their tendrils threateningly, and I pivoted to shoot them.

On instinct, I clambered into the rigging and shouted out over the din, "All crew! Fire at will!"

The crew, to their credit, opened fire. I saw one or two of the creatures tumble end over end and fall to the ground.

"Aim for the lobes! Aim for the lobes!" I wildly cried out.

"Volley fire!" Rang out another command. I recognized the voice to be the captain's.

This got the crew's attention. I saw them line up against the railing, take careful aim, and fire in a disciplined way. Five more of the creatures went down.

A few reached the railing, where several crewmembers fell victim to their venom. I heard screams as the crew prepared to rout. I sighted one of the monsters at the railings and fired, felling it, and accidentally causing one of the crew to be dragged overboard with it.

There was no way we would hold out against this tide of lightning blue death. I prepared to meet my end, or the River, if it existed.

The things slowed, however, and finally stopped. The creatures stood at a distance, as if regarding us. It was clear they had second thoughts about attacking the ship. One by one, they began drifting behind the ship as we increased our forward speed. At last, they fully reversed course, and drifted away, having weighed the odds of attacking us, and found them unfavorable. It was as anticlimactic a battle as I had ever experienced.

There were no whoops or hollers this time. The crew merely sat down, or leaned against something, completely dispirited. Their mood was at odds with mine. I was happy to be alive after the attack.

I jumped off the rigging onto the deck, and turned towards the captain. I lowered my rifle. "Ship secure." I said, exhausted.

The captain almost never smiled, and I couldn't expect one at a time like this, but I detected the barest glimmer of one cross her face as she regarded me. "Well done, lieutenant." she answered.

It was the first time she'd called me lieutenant. And for the first time since I'd met her, I brought my hand up in a salute.

"As always, sir." I said confidently and smiled briefly.

CHAPTER 19

For the next several hours, we saw no sign of our attackers. We had taken an amount of casualties that was manageable from my point of view. However, the way in which the victims died had severe effects on the crew's morale. Around mid-off-rhythm, I discovered just how much that had been.

The captain had left to her ready room, intending to write down and clarify her thoughts about turning around. It still appeared impossible at that time to reverse course, seeing as how we had a heavy frigate waiting at the other end, but she was prepared to do this in order to avoid further casualties. I heard from multiple sources afterward that she had been in the midst of drawing up a plan to run the blockade imposed by that behemoth.

I took the opportunity to go below deck and collapse in an exhausted heap. I hovered between sleep and wakefulness for about two hours before I had any indication that something was afoot aboard the ship.

That indication came in the form of a hard thump at the door of the senior crew's cabin. At about three minutes after mid-off-rhythm, I jolted myself awake at the unexpected intrusion into my sleep. I remember having locked the door, not really caring if the rest of the senior command objected to my occupation of the entire cabin. My hand shot to my revolver in an instant, before I remembered that I was out of ammunition. I cursed my luck as I switched gears to pull out a small knife I kept in my belt. The blade glinted in the light of the lantern I had left in the middle of the room.

A tremendous slam fell against the door, and I heard loud cries of "Heave at her, airmen!" going up from the other side. I scanned the chamber, looking for an exit, which didn't exist, or a hiding space. I discounted the idea of hiding immediately after I had it.

A third crash sounded at the door, then a fourth at which the door weakened on its hinges. I steadied myself, parting my legs in a fighting stance. On the fifth crash, the door finally caved in backwards, slamming against the floor as a throng of chaotic forms came streaming through the entrance. They surrounded me quickly, and began trying to grab me.

To my credit, I think I gave two of them severe stab wounds, another a black eye, and hit another hard in the solar plexus. It wasn't enough though against multiple pairs of arms in close quarters, and I found myself pressed against the floor of the cabin, my hands tied behind me, and a smelly bag forced over my head. After they had succeeded in restraining me, they roughly shoved me onto my feet and frog-marched me out of the cabin into the corridor. I could tell that they were taking me above decks, from which I heard a myriad screams and the clear sounds of isolated fighting.

***

The fighting above deck lasted only a short while. I heard scattered orders being given by the airmen first-class to their subordinates:

"Take him to the barbers, but make sure he doesn't escape from there."

"Diyndir, take these men into the brig and secure it."

"Hands on your head! Drop the rifle! Now!"

"Where's the captain?"

I was shoved to my knees, and heard muffled curses thrown at our attackers from my right. It was Yuri's voice.

"Get your hands off me!" he snarled.

"Yuri?" I inquired.

"Yeah?"

"I think I know what's going on."

"I think I do too. Have you heard from the captain?"

A sharp voice interrupted us, "You two, shut up!"

Yuri cursed at the voice, before I heard a loud thud of a rifle butt connecting with his body somewhere, followed by a gasp of pain. I gritted my teeth. "You'd better not hurt him..." I began to say.

I felt an unseen presence next to my head. "That's enough of that." I recognized the voice as belonging to airman Yudina. The one I had been in command of only ten rhythms ago.

Another call went out. "Yudina! We've got the captain, but

she's in bad shape."

A sudden shock of anger went through me. "What did you do to the captain?"

No response came from anyone, I heard footsteps walking away.

Five minutes later, the deck had still not calmed down, even though it was apparent that the mutineers had taken full control of the ship. The sound of fighting had disappeared, but it had been replaced with numerous conversations carried through the medium of raised voices. I closed my eyes at that point and tried to do what I could to determine what my surroundings on deck looked like without actually seeing them. I knew that there were guards from the noise their constant pacing made.

I also knew that Yuri and I weren't alone in being held captive. As time went on, I sensed an increase in the amount of presences being roughly pushed next to me. The one immediately to my left made an undignified grunt that betrayed her identity: it was Tian' Xi.

I waited for the guard in front of me to pass down along the line before I started whispering to the master of altitude. "How many are there?"

"Most of the crew." She replied.

"Do you have any idea what happened to the captain? Where are they holding her?"

"I can't tell you where they're holding her, but I was near her ready room when they came out of it. She's wounded."

"How badly?"

Tian' Xi waited to reply until the guard that was patrolling behind us walked along the line. "I saw blood on her chest. They were carrying her out."

I growled. "We need to find her."

"They're likely taking her to the barber's. It's best to leave her there for right now."

"You don't know that they'll be that kind." I said bitterly. "If she recovers, she'll try to take the ship back. Or speak against them at a court-martial."

"Even so, captain Nome is respected among the crew. I know some of these people. They wouldn't do that..." Her answer faltered despite whatever confidence she was trying to display.

Another person was forced down next to Tian' Xi. That made a set of six, including Yuri and myself. A thought struck me. "Where's

Pullnir?" I asked.

"I haven't seen him. I think he's somewhere in the engine room."

The first lieutenant's voice interrupted suddenly from in front of us. "You'd be wrong."

I hesitated. Why was he not in the line? The answer came to me just as Tian' Xi spoke up. "Do you have any news we don't?"

"Of course he does," I said with realization, "he's with them."

That statement hung in the air for a while before I felt a hand grasp the bag covering my head and rip it off. The change in light wasn't that extreme; we were still in the tunnel after all. My eyes adjusted to the flare of outlying magnesium torches at either end of the ship with ease. In front of me, Pullnir sat unrestrained and pensive. "Good guess. I was going to play along with Tian' Xi's idea, but there's not really much point now, is there?"

I kept my calm. "You realize they're going to want to turn around? I'm surprised. You felt strongly about getting us into this tunnel." I inquired.

There was no overt response from Pullnir, but I detected a hint of fear and indecision in his expression. It was gone in the blink of an eye. That didn't matter; I'd seen what I needed to see.

"You didn't want to be lined up here with the rest of us, did you?" I continued.

The lieutenant ignored me. "Where's Yensir?" He demanded while cracking his knuckles.

My poker face held. Nonetheless, questions flew through my mind. Did Yensir have a plan to get us out of this mess, or had he left the ship in order to cut his losses? No, that didn't make sense. "How should I know?" I answered truthfully enough. Yensir had avoided all my attempts to keep tabs on him.

Pullnir leaned forward. I couldn't read his thoughts. My instinct was that he didn't believe me, but how could I know for sure? "Yudina wants to know where he is. He's the only one we haven't accounted for. I'm sure you know every nook and cranny of this ship by now, seeing as how you skulk around below decks every chance you get. Where is he?" I sensed an insistence in his voice, and powerlessness.

"Sorry to disappoint you, but no, I don't know where he is." I smirked at the first lieutenant.

"I don't believe you." he responded. I spat in his face as he attempted to intimidate me by leaning in closer. The first lieutenant grimaced, and I sensed his calm façade slip. His hand clenched in a fist. He drew his arm back and gave a hard blow across my nose. I flinched as I felt blood gush out of my nostrils. "I could do much worse than that." He stated simply.

I laughed. I decided to go on the offensive. "So, you're answering to an airman first-class now, huh?" I said with venom. "How's that feel? A few hours ago you were playing captain. What a change of pace."

He gave one last glance into my eyes before nodding to himself. His expression changed and he abruptly stood up, shoving the bag that acted as a blindfold over my head again. "You don't know where he is." He walked away quietly and swiftly, no doubt to deliver a report to that mutineer woman.

"Haye, are you alright?" Tian' Xi's concerned voice finally broke the silence.

"Yeah, I'm fine." Pullnir hadn't broken my nose, just reopened a particularly annoying vein that didn't know when to stay undamaged. I let the first lieutenant think he'd broken my nose though. Didn't make any sense to understate my injuries in front of him.

"I can't believe he threw in with them. I knew he was a scumbag, but for an officer of the Aery to join in mutiny?"

"I'd believe it. He's a coward; that's all he is."

***

The Destiny had completely stopped. The back and forth discussion on deck had mostly ceased, but I could tell, judging by the lessened footsteps around us, that there was intense activity below decks. I knew what they were looking for.

Yensir had prepared for this. Only one of two possibilities seemed realistic: one, that he had hidden himself aboard in some place that even Yuri didn't know about, and two, that he had left the ship. If he had left the ship, he didn't stand a chance alone against the glowing blue creatures that had attacked us. Likely, he had taken this fact into his calculations. He was aboard. I didn't know where, but he was here. That left open the possibility of some sort of resistance against this mutiny.

The idea did cross my mind that he might try to work with the mutineer's command. That would be a long shot, since they effectively had competing interests. Yensir wanted to go forward, on to the sunward pole. The mutineers wouldn't have any of that.

I kept snorting out more blood until my nose stopped bleeding.

In retrospect, it was not a sound decision by the captain to delay her response to the crisis. We should have been as prepared as Yensir. I supposed that her faith in her crew was too strong at that moment of decision.

I just hoped against hope that she was alive. If not, there would be hell to pay. The ferocity of this conviction startled me. I hadn't felt that way about anyone for a long time...

After a long while I heard the aft hatchway open, and several pairs of footsteps clambering up the ladder. They lifted something up through the tiny portal with great difficulty. As they continued towards us, I heard pained groans coming from whatever they were carrying towards us. I recognized them as belonging to the chaplain.

They set the wounded man down gently at one point in the line. I detected reverent silence in the way they treated him. Figures. No respect for their senior command, but the chaplain had the red carpet laid out for him.

He was followed by a mute, unmoving body that I assumed was Dr. Hennir. I couldn't tell with my blindfold on.

Something echoed from far away and my head snapped towards it instantly, trying to judge what it could have been. It wasn't that far away in the tunnel. My mind raced to all the possibilities. Were the White Hats close? Had those creatures had come back?

I heard crew streaming out of the aft hatchway, some with the clatter of bayonets attached to their rifles. There were hushed conversations, but a weird quiet held between the members of the mutiny now. I tensed, waiting for something, perhaps a revolver against my skull.

In the same manner that Pullnir had ripped my blindfold off, someone else yanked it off me. This time, however, I saw the faces of my fellow captives. Yuri's face was bruised and beaten. Tian' Xi less so. Evinsir was also captive, as was Dr. Ininsir, the ship's company of midshipman, and three crewmen who I didn't recognize.

In front of us stood Yudina, flanked by two airmen. The rest of the ship's crew gathered at either end. It didn't strike me until now how many casualties we had received.

Yudina spoke calmly and firmly.

"So, as you may have gathered, I'm now in command of this vessel. All of you need to listen carefully to what I'm about to say."

She stepped forward.

"You are fourteen in total, we are fifty-six. Together, that's seventy souls aboard. Little over half of what we started out with. We took one dead going through the Great Range, nine dead at Dostwickr Basin, nineteen at the entrance to this tunnel from artillery fire, and *twenty-five* fighting down here, including my cousin Vickir. We can't continue like this. We need to turn this ship around.

"We can fight our way through those creatures. They're afraid of us now. At the point where we entered the tunnel, we can negotiate a deal with our pursuers, whom we have reason to believe are linked with the White Hats in some way. To put it bluntly, we are going to trade Haye Zintan, renowned sunward outlaw, for our lives and safe passage back to civilization."

Scattered murmuring erupted at this.

Yudina shifted her arms in front of her. "The captain did not see the situation as it exists. She has been removed from command. Unfortunately..." she paused, and looked back towards Pullnir as if confirming something, "During the confrontation with the captain, there was an act of treachery. It appeared as if the captain might have agreed to our demands peacefully, but the vile..."

My face twitched. I knew what was coming before she even said it.

Yudina was a great actor. She thrust an accusatory finger towards me, her face barely remaining stern, her eyes watering, her voice quivering just the right amount. "...the *darkward*, Haye Zintan, the cause of all of our troubles, shot her twice in the back before anyone could do anything." she stated.

I felt a palpable anger coming from the crew. It wasn't that heartening to know that they still felt strongly towards the captain, even in rebellion against her.

"I don't know why she did it," Yudina continued, "but the fact remains that I saw her shoot the captain myself. The captain is dead."

I felt as though I'd been stabbed in the gut.

***

"You lie."

The accusation didn't come from me. I turned to look, and saw the chaplain standing up on his legs with some difficulty. It amazed me that he was even able to remain conscious, let alone stand on his own two feet. Bandages were wrapped around his arms, and some parts of his chest. His head, was uncovered. I saw burns crossing his cheek, and moving down to his neck, something I hadn't noticed while he was a patient. They were in the shape of a lightning bolt, captured in mid-strike. The burns forked outward, snaking across his face up to his nose, and eyes.

His eyes were open wide. I saw a different man in them. It wasn't even the religious fanatic that had almost electrocuted the gondola in the lightning storm. This was different. There was a strange wild conviction written on his face that gave Yudina pause.

She acknowledged him. "Brother of the River, you are not well." she said.

The chaplain's voice was scratchy, as if he was parched for water, as he responded. "I am well enough to know that while the captain may have returned to the River, she did not meet that end as you said she did."

"You don't know what you're saying." Yudina motioned the crew to restrain the chaplain.

The chaplain, for his part, wasn't having any of that, and slapped away the hands of the crew. Astoundingly, they didn't try to seize him again. He tottered forward two steps, before he raised his arm and pointed outward towards the unseen darkness lining the ship.

"Behold a sign." he declared. "It is the sign of the land of Solandye. It is the River's chosen sign. Behold it now and repent of your folly, young one." Everyone turned to look, and I twisted my arms when I saw exactly what that "sign" was.

A lone blue creature was floating far off to the side of the ship.

It was signaling us. It danced about in midair, spinning slowly while waving its tendrils in strange and intricate patterns like an alien ballet. I couldn't recognize them all save one. I was very familiar with it. It formed three interlocking triangles with its tendrils.

Yudina shouted out the order, "Crew, rifles at the ready."

There was only one creature. I questioned in my mind whether it was the wisest idea to attack it and possibly anger others. Besides, it was clearly intelligent. It was trying to signal to us. If only Dr. Hennir was awake at this moment, she would definitely be able to understand it.

"Do not harm the messenger of the River." The chaplain

ordered.

Yudina countermanded him. "Sharpshooters prepare to open fire."

"The River judge you if you fire one shot at it." The chaplain's voice was laced with fury.

The crew wavered. I realized there were a portion of the mutineers who were going along with Yudina simply because they were afraid. The chaplain's words had a real effect on them.

Yudina looked back at the chaplain with an undisguised expression of annoyance. "Get him out of here." she said.

This time, the airmen behind the chaplain did comply. The chaplain grimaced, and I saw him barely contain his rage. "If you reject this sign of the River, and throw my guidance as to its meaning aside, judgment be on you. This is the sign of the land of Solandye. This *is* the sign!" He struggled fruitlessly with his captors. "Haye Zintan is innocent," he spat out, "and you are guilty of all you accuse her of. Haye Zintan is innocent!" The crew frog-marched him away before he could get in anything else.

I didn't know what would become of the chaplain, but at that moment I wished him well. It was strangely gratifying to have him stand up for me, especially when he didn't have to.

He was right that she had killed Nome herself, of course. At this point, I didn't care if it was an accident, or if Yudina had intentionally taken out the captain. My blood boiled, and I resolved to make her pay dearly for it.

The creature by the side of our ship suddenly stopped its posturing, and began retreating into the distance once the chaplain left the deck. I felt a strange loss at its presence, but also glad that it wasn't the prelude to a new attack.

The rest of the line was suddenly forced onto its feet. Yudina ordered us to be taken into the brig and locked away. I didn't pay much attention to her words. I instead locked eyes with her.

I wasn't loud; I didn't say anything she heard. But I let it be writ large on my face that she was not going to get away with this, if for no other reason than that she murdered the captain. I remembered Nome's face, and the image morphed from her to my mother and back again.

"I'll shoot you." I half whispered to myself.

A sudden whirl of activity exploded as we were pulled away. I got in one last look at Yudina before my view was blocked. Her expression was savagely triumphant.

CHAPTER 20

I pressed my face up against the door in an attempt to hear outside my cell. It might have been a futile exercise, but I had to gain as much knowledge about what was going on outside my prison as possible. It was only a matter of time before the crew made the necessary preparations and managed to turn the ship around. At that time, I had a few hours at most before I would be in the hands of the White Hats and their associates. I couldn't let that happen.

The ship hadn't moved yet, and a few other signs pointed in my favor. The crew had stationed only a small contingent of guards around the brig. I assumed that meant they were understaffed and couldn't afford to spare any hands for guard duty. That also meant that if I found a way out of this cell, I stood a good chance of coming out on top if I fought the guards. The trick would be to do it quietly, without informing the rest of the crew of my escape.

I was stuffed into a cell with the two doctors, as there weren't enough cells to hold the fourteen of us. Hennir still lay prone and comatose, and took up the only cot in the cell, a fact I was somewhat annoyed at. Ininsir, meanwhile, huddled near the back of the cell, trying to shut out the cold chill that had seeped into the room.

The Destiny's turbines had been shut off. That much was encouraging. I assumed Yuri had the good sense to disable the ship as soon as he became aware of the mutiny. I only hoped that didn't land him in even hotter water.

I needed to establish contact with the other imprisoned crew. I knew that getting off this ship would be easier with the whole group involved. And it felt wrong to leave Yuri and Tian' Xi.

Quiet had reigned for the time immediately after our escort had left. At one point Dr. Ininsir had tried to speak, but a rude command from the airmen on guard had silenced her.

As the minutes ticked by, however, it became clearer to me that the guards weren't off-rhythmers. I heard stifled yawns coming from the both of them through the door. Their drowsiness was only briefly interrupted when I heard two more guards arrive and unlock Evinsir's cell before dragging him out.

Their failure to use off-rhythmers was a huge miscalculation on the part of the mutiny's leaders. I made a note to exploit it when I got the opportunity.

Sure enough, after barely a half-hour, snores erupted from the airmen outside. I smiled quietly to myself. This mutiny was poorly led if they thought these men could be relied on. Yudina's inexperience with the crew showed.

A voiced whisper emanated through the hall between the cells. "I think I've discovered a structural fault in my door." The voice was so faint that I barely heard it even with my ear pressed up close against the crack under the bottom rail. Nonetheless, I could tell it was Yuri's voice.

I remained pressed against the door. "What does it look like?" I asked. There was no response, only muted whispering that sounded like an argument taking place between Yuri and his cellmates. I almost pounded on my door in frustration at not being answered.

"What's going on?" Dr. Ininsir asked.

"I don't know. Yuri says he's got something, but doesn't seem to be able to tell me what." I answered.

"Oh."

I glanced back at her. "Something wrong?"

"Yeah. What are we going to do even if we do get out of here?"

"The question is: what am I going to do. You'll be ok as long as you go with the flow. You'll make it back to civilization without problems. Me on the other hand..." I grimaced. "They're gunning for *me*. I have to get out of here."

"I'm beginning to think they're wrong about how safe they'll be if they hand you over. They fired on the White Hats. I don't imagine that group will be very forgiving of that fact."

"It's certainly worth it from the crew's perspective."

"Both the crew and you are in the same boat. I don't understand why they can't see that."

"Yudina has them blinded to that by their fear of what's coming up ahead." My eyes narrowed. Maybe she wanted the expedition to fail. Maybe she was in with the White Hats. And the organization they represented. It fit. She was a recent transfer after all.

Was I just paranoid, or did everyone on this ship have a secret motive?

Dr. Ininsir shook her head and stood up stiffly, trying to put a brave face on. "Where do you think they took the chaplain? And who did they take earlier?"

"Do I look like I know? Probably somewhere for intimidation." I regretted his loss, seeing as how he clearly stood with me. "And as for earlier, that was Evinsir. They likely think they need his navigation skills in order to get the ship moving again."

A low rumble sounded throughout the hull. The turbines were starting up.

My grimace grew stronger. "And it seems they convinced him somehow." I added. The fact that the turbines were starting up was dispiriting for another reason: it meant that Yuri hadn't disabled the engines, and we would be heading back down the tunnel shortly. Back towards my doom.

The ship listed sideways, and I felt as though we were changing direction. Simultaneously, I heard more voiced whispers from the hall, the exact content of which I couldn't determine.

A familiar drip echoed through our tiny cell. Frustration filled me. I needed to get out of here.

There were fits and starts to the ship's movement. I assumed this was partly due to the extreme darkness above decks, but also a result of Evinsir's attempts to slow our exit. Or so I hoped.

About twenty minutes into the ordeal of waiting I heard a stir from the cot. Dr. Hennir moved her arm, something that shocked both Ininsir and me. The younger doctor rushed over to Hennir's side, observing her keenly.

With a slow and uninterrupted effort, Dr. Hennir sat up. She blinked her blackened eyelids and glanced around her surroundings, attempting to gauge her surroundings. Neither Ininsir nor I said anything. I felt too defeated by our position.

Hennir opened her mouth to speak, and promptly started coughing. "Drink." She managed to get out between coughs. Dr. Ininsir held out a small metal hipflask presumably filled with what Hennir wanted. I thought at first it was spirits, but was disappointed when Hennir poured a small trickle of water into her mouth. She drained the entire flask, handing it back to her colleague after she was done. Dr. Ininsir leaned forward to check the skin on her arms underneath her bandages.

I saw lightning burns across her arms as her bandages were undone. It was clear to me that she had been weakened by her ordeal as much as the chaplain had been, since she moved with deliberateness that she hadn't been hampered by before she had been struck by lightning.

After managing to orient herself, she spoke. "Where am I?"

"The brig." I answered. "Long story."

"What happened?"

"There's been a mutiny." My voice was flat.

Her expression chilled. "I've been worried about that possibility. Where is the ship located and what is its status?"

"We're past the ocean. Both you and the chaplain survived the lightning strike, but we've encountered heavy losses. There's a ship that chased us into a tunnel, and strange creatures that attacked us. The crew finally revolted." Ininsir replied.

"The captain?" Hennir asked, turning to face the young doctor.

Ininsir faltered. "The leader of the mutiny says she's dead. She's trying to pin it on Haye."

Hennir processed this information in less time than I expected her to. With effort, she raised herself off the cot and stood up. "I've seen things." She muttered half to herself.

"Pardon?" Dr. Ininsir inquired.

Hennir shifted her gaze from Ininsir to me and back again. "I'll explain it later if I have time. Needless to say, the expedition must continue. We need to locate the captain and determine if she is actually deceased. If she is not, we must assist her in retaking the ship. If she is, then we must wrest control of the crew somehow for ourselves."

Ininsir gave the older doctor an incredulous look. "How do you propose *that*?"

"By first decapitating the mutiny and seizing the ship's weapons. It is imperative that we continue towards the sunward pole." She added emphatically, "Whatever the cost."

I abruptly stood and marched over to her, attempting to stare her down. "I'm on board with you up to a point." I said.

"And that being?"

"If you try to make us go through the interior of the sunstorm unprotected, we'll get torn apart, and I'm not going along with any idea that involves me getting killed. You'd better have a plan for the storm." I folded my arms over my chest. "You'd also need to have an idea for how to take care of our pursuers."

"I don't know enough about our pursuers to help you."

"Oh really? Yensir never let slip anything?"

Her brow furrowed in confusion. "What is that supposed to mean?"

I ignored her question. "We have three ships pursuing us along with the White Hats. Nobody knows this except Yensir and me. Yensir because he has intimate knowledge of the White Hat's activities, and me because I interrogated him privately when I overheard something strange. We can't go back because we'd get blown out of the sky. However, even if we reach the sunward pole, they're going to catch up with us. We have to make a stand."

"Yensir? How could he possibly know about what the White Hats are up to?" Confusion reigned on Hennir's face.

"If you really want to go sunward, and have some plan to deal with our pursuers as well as the storm *and* the mutiny, then I'm with you." I restated relentlessly. "And one more thing: going forward is going to be difficult if the captain is still alive. She had decided to backtrack before this went down."

Hennir slumped backwards. "Oh, Ila... You too?" She addressed her absent friend.

I added firmly, "We can go with your plan, or we can leave the Destiny and hide out here. They can't fit their entire fleet through this tunnel, so the White Hats will come by themselves. That's the way they prefer to operate. It'll be a rough fight, but a better one than dealing with them all at once."

"And leave the sunward pole?" Hennir shook her head violently. "Not after what I've seen."

"Hate to break it to you doc, but our priority right now is staying alive. Not the original mission. The expedition is over."

"Not yet." She clicked her fingers. "I don't have the details worked out completely, but I promise you, I have an idea. Please don't abandon this ship. We can regain control of this situation and meet all three issues. Trust me."

I didn't. But it couldn't hurt to try her idea, whatever it was. I knew in my heart that my thought of fighting the White Hats in the tunnel was exactly what they would like us to do. It would cripple our ability to flee them and get rid of our superior firepower, which had been the only thing that had held them at bay. They might even get the Destiny's crew on their side against the fourteen of us deserters. In a one-on-one fight with them, or even a three-fourteen fight with them in our favor, we would inevitably lose.

As I pondered this, the quiet hum of the ship was punctuated by the sound of thumping from outside. I turned back towards the door, but the thumping ceased. There were no other sounds. Curious, I went over to the door and listened carefully. I heard the rustling of keys and some hurried footsteps.

I backed away from the door as I heard someone step in front of it. The key groaned in the lock, and the door swung open with a squeal.

It was Yensir.

He was heavily armed. Around his shoulder hung a bandolier of rifle ammunition. I saw an almost hilarious amount of magazines crammed into the pockets of his trousers. Slung over his back were three rifles. I tried not to wonder how he had commandeered them from the crew.

He scanned us with his brown eyes. "Are we ready?"

"Yes, Yensir, thank you." Dr. Hennir said. I noticed she made no mention of what I had told her about Yensir's knowledge.

"Very good sir." He unstrung one of the rifles and threw it at the younger doctor. I figured that he trusted her.

When he turned to me, I saw a conflicted look on his face. Only for a brief moment, but I understood that he was judging whether or not I was the right person to be holding a gun. The pause was only a second long. He threw me the rifle. "I'll distribute the clips once we're in a more secure location. I took the liberty of preloading these ones. Let's try not to get into a firefight."

"Remind me to have a talk with you later Yensir. There's something I want to get to the bottom of." Hennir murmured, stretching and limping towards the door.

Yensir gave me a cold stare.

***

"What's our destination?"

My whispered question echoed through the access way. I was

immeasurably glad that Yuri had managed to seal off the way behind us. It would be several hours with the proper equipment before the mutineers could hope to follow us through the small, cramped hallway. I led the line, just behind Yensir.

Thanks to his efforts at concealing our movements, and the strange fact that the majority of this level below decks appeared to be deserted, we had managed to make our way deep into the interior of the Destiny, and were heading towards the ballast deck. I was half-tempted to pray to whatever supernatural forces existed this far sunward that we would make it to a place where we could plan our next move. For a moment, I even considered praying to the Archivist.

Dr. Hennir answered from behind me. I heard wheezing exhaustion in her voice. "To a meeting, if Yensir has succeeded in his preliminary activations."

Yensir, for his part, didn't answer. I found myself growing ever more worried that we would bump into one of Yudina's patrols. My grip on my rifle tightened.

Finally, however, we made it to this, the deepest point of the ship. I had never known the existence of the route we traversed to get there. We appeared from the side of the chamber, in amongst a narrow space between two blocks, exiting a hidden door that gave access to the starboard diesel pipelines. I breathed a sigh of relief. The ballast chamber was a place that Yudina wouldn't have the manpower or motivation to patrol.

This made the existence of a group of five airmen at its center a major cause for worry.

My sights went up immediately once I'd gotten a visual on them. They in turn swung around to face us, and I saw five rifles raised in unison. Around their lantern were three more rifles, balanced upright against each other and hooked into each other with stacking swivels.

"*Identify*." someone in the group whispered.

Yensir answered. "Reinforcements."

The group eased almost immediately, though it took me a while to follow suit. The people behind me rushed into the room, and the more able of them armed themselves with the rifles on the floor. Yensir stripped off his bandolier and flung it down, before emptying his pockets of clips. The midshipmen behind me fell to loading these with a speed I hadn't seen from them before.

Dr. Hennir fell down, clutching her side. For a moment I checked to make sure she hadn't wounded herself somehow, but she waved me off.

For the next few minutes, we recuperated. I leaned against a ballast block, my rifle still held firmly in my hands. My eyes were trained on the aft end of the corridor, ready to open fire on the first of the mutineers that poked their head into the ballast chamber.

A part of me hoped that the person who would first intrude on our hiding spot would be Yudina.

The senior staff gathered around behind me while I wasn't looking. Yensir called out to me in a hushed tone. "Haye." I wheeled about to grab the thrown clip just in time before it hit my head.

Yuri waved me into the group with a certain immediacy.

There were six of us. Both doctors, Yuri, Tian' Xi, myself, and Yensir.

Tian' Xi was the first to speak. "So what is this?"

Hennir had recovered enough to straighten herself out and regain some semblance of dignity from the hard march through the Destiny's interior. A look of determination manifested on her face. "This is the counter-mutiny, all extant members of it. I've been preparing this ever since the Destiny left her berth at Basilica City. I had some idea that there were certain members of the crew who would prove to be difficult. This group was supposed to be a last ditch option in the event that we were taken over by exactly this kind of an operation."

"How is it that you were prepared that far in advance? And how did you manage to recruit from the crew?" I broke in.

"These are all people I know from the dockyard in Basilica City. Nome authorized their transfer personally. It wasn't too difficult to persuade her that they're trustworthy." She smiled. "Nome and I have been friends for many years now."

"There's two too many secret plots aboard this ship." Yuri observed.

"Many more, perhaps." Hennir mused. Yensir's face remained blank.

"You can say that again." I observed quietly.

"In any case, my point is that this particular group of mine is at the tip of a huge iceberg."

Yensir continued for the doctor as she descended into a coughing fit. "You may not have seen it up above, but there's less support among the crew for Yudina than you think. Under the initial circumstances they may have bent because they lost faith in the captain momentarily, but they're wavering. That little stunt of the chaplain's didn't help Yudina either. In the past few minutes, I've heard snippets of discontent going against her, though they're much more subdued than they were against the captain."

"So you think we can regain control of the ship?" I asked skeptically.

"Yes. If we play our cards right. Our first objective must be to find the captain if she is alive. The crew still respects her, so we can't form some sort of leadership without her if she is alive.

"Our second task needs to be to find the chaplain. He's the only one who can get inside the crew's sense of superstition. With him on our side, we would be able to frighten them into following our orders. He can act as a moral authority."

"We're going to need to take out Yudina." Tian' Xi murmured. "The chaplain is most likely with her."

I furrowed my brow. "What makes you say that?" I asked.

Tian' Xi shrugged. "A hunch. She's going to need to take care of any potential threats to her personally. If she's caught torturing or intimidating him by any of her subordinates, that'll go around. That's risking the River's eddies against the ship."

Hennir interrupted. "First things first, we need to find the captain."

***

It didn't take long for us to find the captain. Two guards had been left in front of the barber's, which Yensir quickly and stealthily subdued. Again, these weren't off-rhythmers. I had a feeling that the majority of those were above decks, trying to help Evinsir fly the Destiny out of the tunnel.

We entered the barber's as a group only briefly. The barber himself had disappeared. I didn't know where he had vanished. I hoped that he hadn't fallen victim to Yudina somehow.

What awaited me in the dimly-lit room caused the knot that had been growing in my stomach ever since a half-hour back to explode.

The group stayed inside the chamber for a half-second, before an argument broke out between Hennir and Tian' Xi over what to do next. In the process, the rest of our small squad filed out. I don't think they wanted to continue to look at what we had found.

I should have expected it. I should have trusted my gut since when I'd heard Yudina say the captain was dead. Nonetheless, it hit me like a ton of bricks to see Ila Nome, captain of the Destiny, her lower body covered with a clean white sheet stained red with her own blood, deceased. Her face was white, and her body was as stiff as a board. On the cots at her side were three other airmen who had undoubtedly been killed during the mutiny.

I stood over the dead body silently. Only Yuri remained by my side as the rest of Hennir's followers filed out of the room.

We didn't say much. Yuri tried to break the silence, to fill it with something, anything. "I knew her for two ten-rhythms." he said.

"Me too." I replied.

"Still, she was a good leader."

"I don't know that I will ever follow her ethic as strongly as she did, but she did teach me to respect it." There were other things left unspoken. Other things I didn't say. Their magnitude was easily read in my silence though, especially by Yuri, who had known me for years. In that moment, I felt as though I had relived the time I had stood by *that* deathbed when I was young. I had missed the moment that my mother had died. We never had any final words. The memory was refreshed by Nome's death and I started to feel rage coursing through me as I watched her lifeless pale face.

Yuri plucked out three bullets from the breast pocket of his field jacket and wordlessly handed them to me.

I looked down at the ammunition in my hand. They were the same caliber as my revolver.

My hand clenched around them in a fist.

***

My twelve-shot had been drawn and reloaded with those three bullets. We had managed to make our way to the captain's cabin. I hadn't been here before. Captain Nome's general pattern of living meant that she usually could be found in her ready room. Yudina was here to keep the chaplain under her thumb, something she needed to keep private. This was really the only logical place on board for her to carry out that kind of intimidation away from prying eyes. Captain Nome's quarters still held a sort of superstitious significance in the eyes of the crew.

I locked eyes with Hennir. I was going in first. If she tried to argue with me, there would be severe difficulties.

She nodded her assent, and I crept up to the lead position near the door.

I heard muffled voices from the other side. Yudina cursing and swearing. I heard a voice I thought was the chaplain's, offering some sort of resistance. It didn't matter.

I drew my sabre quietly. I breathed out and started counting.

One.

A slam of a fist on some furniture, accompanied by cries filled with unidentifiable religious epithets.

Two.

I saw shadows move under the bottom door seam. There were multiple pairs. She had guards, but it was too late to back out now.

I would see her and her lackeys dead.

Three.

I burst through the door. Pullnir reacted first. I saw him move to grab a pistol. Unluckily for him, I am a much faster shot than he could ever hope to be. I didn't think much about the act; I shot him. First in the groin, and then higher up, close to his heart. He went down smoothly, and in that split second I congratulated myself on a shot well fired.

There were two other airmen in the room. Both had pistols like the first lieutenant, but fumbled. I ran one through with my sabre, and gutted the other. They crumpled like slaughtered animals, blood sputtering from their mouths. The squad coming in behind me made sure to keep the struggle quiet as they moved in.

The fight was over in less than five seconds.

That left only Yudina. I advanced on her, and held my twelve-shot to her forehead. She was unarmed. I saw her expression turn in quick succession from shock to outright horror. She floundered, trying to think of something to say.

"This one's for Nome." I growled through gritted teeth.

She finally managed to get the words out: "Haye, put the gun down, don't you see what effect this whole situation..."

I shot my last bullet into her skull.

I heard distant echoes of a rage-filled reprimand from Dr. Hennir. Again, I didn't much care. Even though I'd managed to kill the captain's murderer, I still felt empty inside.

CHAPTER 21

An immediate quiet fell across the room after Dr. Hennir's tirade. Jumpy expressions passed between our group. Half of the airmen departed in order to guard the hallway outside and to check for incoming crew. Three shots had been fired. No doubt someone could have been alerted to our presence.

Hennir shook with fury. "She was trying to surrender, what are you thinking!?" she demanded.

I holstered my twelve-shot and moved to wipe my blade off on Yudina's dirty shirt. A spatter of blood marked the opposite wall, staining the pristine arsenic wallpaper. "I was taking out an enemy. Sorry to infringe on your delicate sensibilities." I said sardonically.

"Don't shoot anyone else unless I tell you to."

"Doc, I'm getting tired of hearing you screaming your head off. You're not the captain, so stop acting like you are."

"I hired you. I'm in command."

I raised my eyebrows. "Nome was in command. You are not until you explain to us what you'd like to do with this ship. From what I know of the Aery, command should pass down to the lieutenant with the most experience. That would be the Master of Navigation. Or me, if I so chose."

"I'm the original patron of this expedition. Orders come from me."

"I'm done following orders from anyone who isn't captain Nome. If you want to do something, you're going to have to argue its case."

We were both interrupted by the chaplain. "I claim the right given to me by the revelation of the River. I am, by its will, in command of this vessel and all the souls contained therein."

"Shut up." Hennir and I glanced over at the chaplain.

"You came here because you needed my support for whatever plans you have, yes? I won't give it unless you hear me out." The chaplain folded his arms as he said this.

"Uh..." Yuri scrambled back as a flurry of movement from the crewmen exploded.

I swung my sabre in front of me. The crew loyal to Hennir raised their rifles in my direction. The three of them that were with us in the brig moved to threaten their fellows.

A calm voice interrupted us. "Technically, in the absence of Evinsir, since he is under coercion, I'm in command of the Destiny, so why don't you all put away your weapons and we'll sort this thing out." Having said this, Tian' Xi stepped forward.

Slowly but surely, the weapons were lowered on all sides. "All of you, secure this section of the deck. Leave us." It was Yuri. No one argued with the order.

The door closed, and again three officers, two doctors, Yensir, and one chaplain were left alone. We stood for some time in an uncomfortable silence, the odor of fresh blood intruding into the space between.

Tian' Xi was the one who started the discussion again. "So once again, this is the situation: the captain and Pullnir are dead. First order of business is the matter of who will succeed Nome. The generally agreed Aery regulations state that the lieutenant with the most experience onboard should take command of the ship. That's me, not counting Evinsir."

Dr. Hennir narrowed her eyes. "I will only accept this if you make it your business to go sunward." She said.

To my surprise, the chaplain nodded his head and speak up in agreement. "My position is the same. We must not remain here for long."

"Let's take a step back," The Master of Altitude continued, "and talk about where we are. We are going to have to fight or negotiate past that pursuing ship at some point."

Yensir spoke up. "There are three ships, plus the White Hats."

Everyone stared at him.

"I'll tell you all what I told Haye." He stared icily at me. "I am not at liberty to disclose how I came by this information. If I do, and it is revealed to certain people, a person that is very dear to me will meet an untimely end."

"What can you tell us?" Tian' Xi inquired.

"All three ships are heavy frigates. They are faster, heavier, and better crewed than the Destiny. I advise you trust me with that statement. It is an observable fact that unless we change the battlefield somehow in our favor, we will be killed to the last airman. There will be no mercy or quarter given by our pursuers."

"You kept this from me..." Dr. Hennir mused.

"I did nothing to harm you, sir." Yensir bowed his head at the doctor. "What you don't know at this point is better left unsaid than otherwise. I will however offer what information I am able to for the ship's defense."

"Three frigates..." Yuri sounded awed. "Who did we piss on?"

"The Yinda of Yin, for starters." Yensir stated matter-of-factly. "Others who back the Yinda as well. That is all I am able to say."

"We're going to have to fight them." Tian' Xi observed.

Dr. Hennir waved a hand. "Not immediately. We don't possess any advantage over them. We need to delay until we do." she said. "The easiest way to do that is to continue sunward. The maps from site 23 indicate that there is a series of passageways ahead much like this one that continue on into the heart of the Forebear city. They were originally for internal transport, or so we believe. We should be able to continue forward to the city safely protected from the sun storm."

"What about inside the city?" I interrupted.

"We will be inside the eye of the sun storm. That is where the storm is the weakest. There's one catch: We will have no protection from the sun. Temperatures will go up hot enough to melt the Destiny's hull, to say nothing of her crew." There was a series of protests and guffaws at these words before she added: "If the Forebears really built their city at the very sunward pole of this world, then they must have had some way of negating the influence of the sun's rays on their city. A shield from the heat, if you will. I remain confident that we won't die from the temperature."

"So you say." I retorted. "You can't guarantee that."

"It's likely. We should go ahead before you immediately discount the possibility."

The Master of Altitude interrupted. "Presuming that you're correct, that means that we still have a problem to solve; going forward only delays getting shot down by the White Hats. Anyone got any ideas?"

Yuri mused. "Those are heavy frigates, and by the looks of it, they're armed with Audir Cannons?"

"What are those?" Ininsir immediately questioned.

"Long guns with ultra-heavy shells. They're only used on the heaviest of ships, and set along the whole length of the vessel aimed forward. They can fire up to thirty kilometers fore of the vessel at standard holding height before hitting the ground. Each of them requires a gargantuan amount of powder to fire, and each shell has at least a ton of explosives inside. They've got to be storing that in some section of the ship."

I suddenly realized what he was saying. "You mean..." I began.

He grinned. "From afar, they're dangerous and deadly. Sniper's vessels. Up close, if anything ever so much as touches the powder, the whole ship goes up in a big boom." He gesticulated an explosion with his hands.

Tian' Xi nodded. "So our goal will be to close the distance." she said.

"And promptly get in range of the White Hats." I added.

The mood in the room darkened even more. Too close, and we risked getting boarded and massacred by the White Hats. Too far, and we risked being shot out of the sky.

"We'll have to see the battle space." Tian' Xi said finally. "But at least we know that their fleet likely has a weakness."

"What if they're storing their ammunition in the center of the ship?" I asked quietly. "We'd have to shoot through several layers of armor in order to reach it."

"We may yet be able to do that with our most powerful cannons up close."

"This is again assuming that we can convince the crew to go through with this." Yensir said.

"Yes, that." Tian' Xi replied. Turning to address the chaplain, she continued. "Sir, it appears we will need your help."

The chaplain stood stiffly. "It appears our interests coincide." he replied after some thought.

I eyed him with distrust.

"You said it yourself: Nome was the ship's captain. Nobody onboard has the same level of command experience as she did. I won't be following orders from you, Tian' Xi." His expression became even more solemn. "I have only one superior now, and that is the ever-flowing River."

Tian' Xi shot him an annoyed glance. "Have you lost your mind?"

"To one not attuned to the River's ebb and flow, it might seem that way. I can do no other." He bowed his head.

"Explain."

***

The chaplain shifted on his feet. "By the grace of the River, it has sent me a vision of two ways we, its streams, could flow into the future. The first of these is that which occurs if we do not obey its dictates. The second is that which awaits us if the reverse is true.

"In the moment that I was struck by the bolt from the heavens, I was taken within its folds to commune with it deeply, to know the secrets of this land we find ourselves within. I perceived that I was among the River, and its voice flowed through my entire being as it spoke to me. Never have I been so close to it, such as to be able to sense its innermost currents.

"While I communed with it, I learned of something that I had suspected before now, and that is this: the River is here.

"In this desolate, sun-blasted wilderness, the River exists manifested within physical space and flows from the edge of eternity's horizon to the core of our very world. Into and above the sky it stretches, past the darkest voids of the ether, into the furthest reaches of the cosmos. It is interminable, with length beyond reckoning.

"In this land, the River takes its endpoint. In this land, which was known in rhythms long past as Solandye, it first created our species among others, its outflows. Those creatures you witnessed in the tunnel are its messengers, sent to chastise us of our indiscretions that we hold within our hearts, and to test our faith in following its will. Just the same is true of the Ancients we found on the land that encompassed the Great Ocean. I say to you now that the River is desirous that we continue our voyage until it can divulge to us the truth of all creation.

"This is why we have been selected for this expedition. It is the reason this voyage was pre-destined to occur. The River will reveal to me the Ultimate Truth of creation at its base within the city that we were cast out of. I only need commune with it in that most sacred of places.

"If we do not do this, we face immolation by our pursuers. This I have also witnessed; the Destiny being torn from the sky, and her crew massacred by those Biehs' sons given human form. The River's revelation is too important for it to be wasted on unfaithful beings as ourselves if we turn back now.

"To achieve this end, it has given to me a new name to be known by. I am no longer simply your chaplain, nameless by the requirements of my order. I am now Zealot, son of Water. I am a different man than the one you knew before."

***

"You saw the same thing I did. And you are misinterpreting the dream." Dr. Hennir looked Zealot up and down as she said this. "The River didn't send you a vision, chaplain. You can spout your supposed chosen status from you fairy-tale River, or you can grow a brain and think. Perhaps eating those mushrooms of yours has addled your mind too much for that though."

Ininsir hesitantly spoke. "Dr. Hennir?"

"While I agree generally with his garbled accounting of the vision, it wasn't a vision from the River. The Forebears wrote in their records at Site 23 that there was a last record made of their existence, in the event that they faced extinction. I am convinced that this beam of light that we both saw in our vision, which *he* seems to have gotten the notion is his beloved River, is that Forebear record. We have been shown the way to extract the ancient knowledge from within. It was designed to be as simple to operate as possible. We need only walk into its beam.

"We should not let the Forebears' servants bar our way. Their initial reaction was an attempt to communicate with us that went awry. They wish for us to continue, as do their constructs around the Great Ocean, otherwise they wouldn't have helped us."

"Doc, is this really the time to be talking about..." I tried to interrupt.

"Yes it is!" Hennir's face hardened and her voice rose as she overrode my attempts to steer the conversation back towards our survival. "Whoever is pursuing us wants us much more badly than they want you, Zintan. No offense, but your presence on board does not justify the extravagance of sending three heavily armed frigates over the Great Range. This is much bigger than the Yinda's petty revenge. Until this rhythm, I didn't have an inkling of what could possibly be the cause of this. You..." She turned to Yensir. "You're trying to help us, aren't you? There are people back there who want us to succeed. And people back there who oppose us. Enemies of reason." She clenched her fist. "There are interests whose livelihood and worldview will be destroyed if we return with the technology of the Forebears. If we prove that humanity is descended from the Forebears, and as such has the birthright of our own greatness running in our veins."

Dr. Ininsir's face lit up. "You believe my idea then!"

"*Your* idea?" A look of utter condescension crossed Hennir's face, something I had never seen in all of this expedition. "It was my idea to begin with. You just took to untrustworthy and biased sources to attempt to prove it."

Dr. Ininsir looked crestfallen and hurt at hearing her mentor's words. "It was... my idea..."

Hennir continued, regardless of Ininsir's reaction. "We must press on. This will be our only chance for potentially several centuries to do what we are doing right now. The historical dialectic demands that we uplift our civilization. All of us, as a whole, are poised on the precipice of greatness, and if we turn back now, the enemies of reason win."

***

"You lie!" As I expected, it was Zealot who had said this.

This was the start of a very heated argument that spontaneously erupted between the two. As it developed, their voices grew steadily louder and louder, blocking all of our attempts to interrupt them and quell the distraction from our planning.

"I have said everything truthfully as I have interpreted it. You on the other hand are merely projecting the insecurities inherent to your narrative of the vision onto mine." Hennir's middle-aged figure wobbled slightly.

"You never saw anything. You deliver falsehood to them in the hope that they might be deceived into your hands."

"The beam of light is the Ultimate Truth, as it was called by the being we both met. That being was not your River, but a technological construct of the Forebears, utilizing psionic technology to contact us."

"You claim that technology can perform miracles? I would

merely pity your blind faith in material engineering, but such an act requires me to forgive your brazen attempt to lead this ship astray."

"I am trying to keep the ship on course for the Ultimate Truth. I am not lying, unlike you right now. I have but to enter into it and receive the enlightenment of the Forebears in order to disprove your belief in the supernatural."

"I say to you, the River will incinerate you if you approach it with the arrogance you display before us now."

"There is no River."

"As surely as the ether is endless, the world unshakeable, and the planets above set in their ways, the River exists."

"Stop."

It was Tian' Xi who had nearly shouted this, a look of annoyance crossing her face.

"This man," Hennir pointed an accusatory finger, "is going to stir up a religious frenzy if we let him. If left to his own devices, I wouldn't be surprised if he somehow destroyed the Ultimate Truth with his sheer ignorance."

"If you follow her, she will lead this ship to ruin. The River must be approached with submission, as one would to a parent. If the crew follows her example, then everyone's lives, including my own, will be forfeit by the River's wrath." Zealot countered.

Tian' Xi waved away these assertions, "Enough with the accusations. Honestly, I don't know if you've noticed, but what you've both said requires a huge stretch of the imagination to believe."

"You would place my *educated* interpretation of a real and vivid message from the Forebears on the same level as his!?" A look of absolute offense came over Hennir.

"All of the miraculous events that have happened to this ship, and all of the supernatural that you have witnessed, and still doubt clouds your mind?" Zealot's face grew somber and contemptuous.

I had to agree with him on one point: he was a different person. The old chaplain would have better disguised his feelings of disgust for a person's viewpoint underneath a cloak of good intentions.

I stepped in. "I've a way of settling this thing between you two. How about we start by assuming that either one of you could be correct, and go on to this 'Ultimate Truth' thing or whatever it is."

"Have you heard nothing..." Zealot started.

I held up a hand and talked over him to silence him. "Both of you will enter it at the same time. That way, we'll account for if the other person is wrong. If one person is right, whatever knowledge is revealed from this Ultimate Truth should settle that, yes?"

"Do you intend to tempt the River's wrath with this unbeliever's presence in our communion with it?" Zealot spat.

"He'll break the Ultimate Truth somehow. I don't know how, but he will." Hennir testily stated.

I turned first to Zealot. "Don't you think the River would be pleased if it could be revealed to an unbeliever like her that the River exists? Might be humbling to her. Might even cause her to take up the Riverrun. That might keep the River happy." I then addressed Hennir. "You said yourself that the Forebears made the Ultimate Truth as simple as possible to access. I doubt that they wouldn't have accounted for a simpleton like him accessing it. Seems like bad engineering if that is the case, right Yuri?" I asked without breaking eye contact with the doctor.

"Of course. Very bad engineering. Can't think why someone, especially a civilization with far better engineering than our own, would do something like that." Yuri said.

"Yes." said Dr. Hennir in a much quieter voice.

Zealot's response was much less laconic. "I will suffer this plan to go forward, but know it is a dangerous path you are walking, Haye Zintan."

I stretched my arms. "We're good then?"

There were restrained nods between the two of them.

"Can we get back to the question of how we assert control over the ship?" Yensir pressed.

Zealot stepped towards the door. "Leave that to me. I will show them the light of the River and the folly of their rebellion against it."

I relaxed slightly. I had avoided further conflict by forging the truce between the doctor and Zealot. I hoped that the city ahead would provide a way to defeat the enemy fleet.

***

Our unexpected arrival onto the main deck of the Destiny was an unpleasant surprise for the crew who were trying to work with the recalcitrant turbines. Almost the entire remaining crew were on deck, scattered among the rigging and across the gondola.

I led the way, bursting nonchalantly out of the aft hatchway. It took a few seconds before an airman noticed me. He hadn't been part of the core group of mutineers, and so stood dumbfounded and lost for words. I ignored him and helped Zealot up through the hatchway, trying my best to remain calm in the face of the unlikelihood of our regaining control.

When the third person came up through the hatchway, the airman was suddenly shaken from his stupor, and called out, "They're here!"

All eyes turned our way, and I heard various airmen commenting on our miraculous appearance on deck.

"Is that Haye Zintan?"

"And the chaplain!"

"How did they get out of the brig?"

"Where's Yudina?"

These first few questions gave way shortly to a storm of shouted orders.

"Get them!"

"Don't let them on deck!"

"Sharpshooters on me, take the high ground!"

I tried to remain as cool about the whole process as I could. By now, there were six of us on deck, and I heard rifles being cocked and turned in our direction. One airman even closed the distance and held a pistol against my head. I turned and gave him a withering look as his arm shook. "Stop!" He yelled in my face. I turned back to what I was doing.

He wouldn't fire. As jumpy as he appeared, he was too young to shoot someone.

"Stop, or you will be shot!" He bellowed out.

"There's no need for that, young one." Zealot commanded. I heard him gently lay a hand on the arm of the airman. Through hastily grabbed backward glances, the airman exchanged a look with Zealot, hesitate, and then lower his pistol reluctantly.

"You're going back to the brig, all of you!" came another shout from further away.

Zealot stepped forward, his eyes flashing in the light from the magnesium torches. The airmen nearest to him moved to enforce his arrest. Zealot in turn swiftly took up position at the highest point at the aft of the gondola, where he could look down on the majority of the ship's crew. He spoke with the force of a man convinced of the rightness of his own cause, something that while it may have been annoying to me earlier, I was glad he repeated in front of the crew.

"Brothers and sisters in the River, young ones, you the misguided, I speak for the River."

Every airmen recognized these as the words of one of the higher prophets of the Riverrun, even if they couldn't quote a single passage. A stillness fell across the deck. Some of the crew that were more loyal to Yudina tried to agitate their fellows to go and seize us, but their efforts were in vain.

"Why are you stopping?"

"Get them! Don't just stand there!"

The ship was mesmerized by the presence and voice of the Zealot. I admit that his speech took on a hypnotic quality that pulled me away from helping Hennir's commandos up the hatch.

Zealot continued. "You have fallen for a charlatan. A blasphemer of the River, whose efforts to deceive you and turn you against the River's rightful authority, appointed over you to decide whither your streams will flow, should give you pause. But lo, you are like undisciplined and flooded creeks before the path the River has established for you. This one was willing to end the path of another if I had not rebuked him." He pointed at the airman who had threatened me with the pistol.

"Why do you quarrel among yourselves? Why do you vex yourselves and fight those who act to bring you towards the River's ultimate and kind embrace? Why do you fight against its very messengers?

"Listen to my words, crew of the Destiny, and listen carefully, for I have much to tell you."

Zealot closed his eyes for a moment before continuing before the assembled crew.

"The one called Yudina is responsible for the captain's murder. Three others too, have fallen before those loyal to her. These three knew of the captain's true killer, along with myself. They were carrying me to her ready room when I witnessed her barbaric execution.

"You have been following a monster, who has taken by force that which is not rightfully hers. By the River, I declare this testimony to be completely true. Let any of you gathered here speak to contest this if you wish to tempt the River's judgment."

A hush fell among the crew. Yudina's agitators still tried to sway the airmen's opinion, but it was clear that the mutiny's remnants were wavering. The question hung in the air: who to trust? The new airman that promised a way out of their predicament? Or their beloved chaplain?

Zealot started walking down into the center of the throng, looking airmen in the eye as he passed them. His voice echoed off the distant walls of the tunnel, something which made him sound as though he was speaking inside of a cathedral.

"You, young and old, know me as a righteous man. I speak with the River's blessing behind me. For my life, I have chosen to walk in poverty and to even renounce my name in favor of leading a devout life. I am not your enemy, whatever Yudina has told you. I have received a vision from the River. Revelation has been granted to me. Yea, to me, a fallible creek like yourselves, but one whose eyes are always fixed on the Ultimate."

Murmurs passed through the crew. Even those who had been loyal to Yudina stopped what they were doing to listen to Zealot speak.

"If we return, the pursuing ships will destroy us. Yudina lied when she said to you that we could parlay with them for our lives. If we return, nothing will await us but the full fury of the demons that lead them. Those that are called the White Hats are naught but the chattel of Biehs, and some in fact are Biehs themselves. Hear you me; salvation lies not whence we came.

"Instead, we must continue forward. For the eternal River awaits us at the sunward pole! Salvation is at hand, young ones!"

There were scattered gasps.

Zealot continued. "In the River's embrace, we will find truth and protection from our enemies. In the River's embrace, we will be freed from our pain." He pointed at one of the airmen with an eye patch. "You, who have experienced much injury in the course of your life, you will be made whole once more."

He pointed at another. "You, who have suffered the advances of a Biehs, he will be driven from you."

And another. "You, who have doubted, will be given confidence in the River."

"All this and more awaits us thither. We need only proceed in obedience.

"This is now a ship of the River. I will deliver to you the path of righteousness, and you will be saved.

"Fail to heed my warning, and may the River have mercy on your souls. He will have none on Yudina's. She lies dead in the captain's chambers, killed by the River's intervention."

The last statement was delivered with an ominous low tone. I half expected some of the crew to take umbrage at being threatened in that way, but that was where I misread their character.

The crew was scared by Zealot's words. Among the rank and file, most were firmly religious, and trusted the word of their chaplain over the word of Yudina. When he had challenged her initially, that had been the true breaking point for them. All they had needed was some indication that the Zealot would succeed in overthrowing the mutineers.

There were two airmen on deck who did not feel swayed by the chaplain's words. They started pointing rifles in the faces of their comrades, demanding that they seize our party.

One fired into the air above the head of his comrade. This startled the one being threatened, and her head snapped towards the shooter, clearly deafened by the blast. Her confusion turned swiftly to adrenaline-filled anger.

In the span of two seconds, those who remained loyal to Yudina were sprawled on the deck of the ship, clutching where they had been punched into submission. Their former comrades carried them away below decks, where I hoped they would be guarded better than we were.

Slowly at first, but with a growing enthusiasm, cheers broke out on deck as the assembled crew realized that they had a trusted commander at their head once more. Many of those closer to Zealot lifted him up onto their shoulders and carried him about the deck. I saw a rare smile grace his face as he raised a lightning-scarred hand into the air. The patterns followed the metal ink of the prayer lines that he always wore, and had burned them into his skin. The image enraptured me.

The remaining senior command filed up next to me, satisfied and relieved for once at the ease of our success.

The walls of the tunnel gradually appeared. We had long stopped firing flash-shells, so the warm light bouncing around the darkened space surprised me. A crack of orange light developed ahead of us, slowly at first, but then growing much brighter in a very short span of time. I covered my eyes and tried to adjust to the new blinding light.

I realized with some amusement that we hadn't returned the way we had come. When my eyes adjusted I opened them and shot another glance at the navigation panel. Evinsir hunched over there with a restrained but visible smile on his face. When he saw me looking at him, he gave an easy, jaunty salute.

That brilliant bastard had kept us going in the right direction. He'd completely fooled his captors with his airmanship.

***

We rose out of the tunnel. The temperature of the air struck me first. I expected it to be searing, but it was mild. Everywhere hung the smell of dead air, like what I would have expected from a sepulchre. Orange light enveloped the ship and the ship's canopy cast a shadow directly downward onto the deck for the first time this expedition. I felt a tingle of anticipation. We were here, in the most sunward of all places. I stood where I had dreamed of going in my childhood's wildest dreams.

The walls of the tunnel widened as we continued our ascent, and the light from the sun grew stronger. We crested the upper edge of the tunnel and exited. I was not prepared for what I saw next.

An unending complex of buildings stretched for kilometers into the distance. Each one was built from the same underlying material as that tower we had encountered in the sunward forests that lay behind us. The structures extended away towards the horizon, with spires that reached far into the sky. The spires stood a half a kilometer high at the least. The largest were several hundred meters thick at the widest. They twisted in ornate shapes that flowed into one another in strange optical illusions. I could make out... windows? Not a single ounce of ruin was apparent on these mega-structures. They were completely sterile.

Along the ground, a hard and open gray slate floor extended across the length of what was obviously the city at the sunward pole of the world. The city covered a huge distance, but the majority of that space was found between its dwellings. This slate pavement was unbroken, and reflected the piercing light of the sun in such a way that it made my eyes water to look at it.

Every now and then, a small pinprick of light would flicker into existence on this titanic floor, and I would observe the air around the single ray of light that fell to this floor ripple with extreme heat before it dissipated. My gaze followed the sunbeams upward towards the sun.

Encompassing the entirety of the ceiling around the city, reaching a mind-boggling distance into the sky, were a gargantuan series of rings that were dozens of kilometers in diameter. They were the same slate gray as the city, and floated in midair above the pristine buildings below. The space between them was darkened, but I saw mottled spots of light along the underside of these places. Imagine a glass window that has been imperfectly darkened so that some spots are lighter than others. Then imagine that those spots are constantly shifted from one place to the next. I didn't have the faintest idea what the space between these amazing giga-structures was filled with. It was some amorphous substance that was held up by technology so far beyond even the glimmer of comprehension.

In the middle of these rings, the sun loomed in the sky. I felt a tremor of awe and fear pass through me at the sight of its orb hung stationary in the sky, like a heartless overseer beating down on all of us below it.

At the city's edges, the sunstorm swirled around us. The inside of the eye of the sunstorm was easily at least a kilometer in height. The clouds from the underside of the convection current swept inward, transforming from the sunward to the darkward tides in a rising column of air that carried giant clouds up to the highest part of the sky in a matter of minutes. Incessant but silent lightning flashed in gargantuan arcs from sky to ground, searing the floor beneath them. The sun had made rainfall impossible, but that did not rule out a cloud of flying debris. I saw what were obviously boulders the size of houses being thrown about in the sunstorm's wind. Yet here, just inside the borders of the city, and only a few kilometers away, absolute calm reigned.

So this was the stage on which we were to make our stand against the White Hats. The reverent silence that occupied the air unnerved me. I began looking at the many other tunnel entrances that were scattered across the city. Some of them were bigger than the one we'd exited. I knew they'd be here soon, in force. The battle would come to us sooner rather than later.

Most worryingly, a column of light was nowhere to be seen.

CHAPTER 22

We set down at the third or fourth hour on a nearby platform that jutted out from one of the towers. By this time I felt the effects of a lack of an off-rhythm's sleep. I didn't relish the thought of fighting under those conditions, so I made an exception to my rule of not sleeping on-rhythm. For the next three hours, while Dr. Hennir fell to studying the minute details on the side of the tower we had landed on, and Zealot attempted to contact the River in his prayers, and the rest of the crew tried to repair some of the damage to the ship, I slumped against a protruding slate pillar and attempted to nap.

Inevitably, I fell to gazing at our surroundings after I awoke. There were thousands of points across the city that provided fuel for my imagination. I found myself wondering what it would look like if I stood at them. Ledges, plazas, colonnades, and artificial mesas all caught my eye, all invariably slate gray. I saw no rivets or cracks that indicated that the city had been assembled from many different pieces.

I stood a good distance away from the platform's edge. There wasn't a single rail on the ledge. Part of me wondered if the Forebears that had built this place ever intended for anyone to be standing where I now stood. Were they as concerned about heights as I?

A sense of agitation flowed through me. Our pursuers were coming. In a few hours, we would be either dead or nearly dead. Our prospects were bleak to think about. My mind returned to the time I'd spent before our confrontation in Dostwickr Basin. Ultimately, the battle hadn't been the worst part of it for me; it had been the build-up to it. The time spent walking about and cleaning my revolver gave me ample time to think about the approaching tide of death back then. Now, that span felt even greater, with less hope on the other end of coming out alive.

When I got bored of pacing around and listening to the crew shout to each other, I sat down and crossed my legs. I saw Yuri and Tian' Xi approach me from the side out of the corner of my eye.

"Ah! She's awake!" Yuri said exuberantly.

Tian' Xi sat down next to me after nodding politely. She was troubled. I gave her another brief glance. "Something on your mind?" I asked.

"I've never planned an aerial battle before." She replied hesitantly.

"Never have I. There's a first time for everything." I yawned and stretched. "Did the captain ever invite you to do anything as a staff officer? You seem like the kind of person that she would have for that kind of job."

"Sure, but did you see that ship? That thing is built for war. Those shell blasts were much larger than any flack I've been through. And Yensir tells us that there's *three* of them? I've been a staff officer Haye, but never for anything like this."

"What about Evinsir?"

"I've been looking for him since we set down. Can't find him. I think he's still trying to untangle some issues with the Destiny's control systems."

"It's the new electrics." Yuri broke in. "They're going haywire with the discharges around here. The ship has manual backup for a lot of the lower-level stuff, but main control is being a major pain in the ass. Outside of my expertise; needs his looking-at. I don't think it's a good idea to disturb him. More important to actually be able to maneuver through the air with any ease than to have his input on our battle plans." I saw the engineer stuff both his hands inside the pockets of his field jacket. "Besides, I don't think he has that much more experience than Tian' Xi."

I pondered for a bit. "Well, the three of us are going to have to plan this thing carefully, but we can do this."

"*How* are you that sure?" Tian' Xi muttered bitterly.

"We survived the battle at Dostwickr Basin, didn't we?"

"And how many of the crew will die this time?" I heard sadness radiate from her. "Now I guess I know how the captain felt every time we did something like that."

I didn't know how to respond to that. There were ideas that

bounced around in my head but each one faded out with further consideration.

"I wish that I had known you better, Haye." Tian' Xi finally said.

I blinked before realizing that she was trying to get her goodbyes in before the battle. "You know me well enough, don't you?"

"I wish we had been friends."

"I'm right here you know." Yuri chuckled. "Weren't you friends with me, Tian' Xi?"

"Mind if I join you?" I recognized Dr. Ininsir's voice, and sensed her walking up on us from behind. When no one objected, she sat down on my right and stared out at the city with us. "Who's a friend with whom?"

"I am, to you all." I answered before anyone could get a word in edgewise.

"I wish we had more card games or... blast it, I wish we had talked more often." Tian' Xi said.

I rubbed my head, wiping sweat from around my eyes. "We're going to get back from this place. We'll have all the time for card games then."

"You may need to count me in with those games." Dr. Ininsir said bitterly. "It seems my mentor has completely forgotten about my existence."

"Hennir?" Yuri asked, eyebrows raised. "You two have a falling out?"

"I would have had a proper one with her, but she keeps ignoring me every time I try to speak with her. First she takes credit for my ideas, and now she won't even speak to me about it. It's like she's a completely different person now." Ininsir sighed.

"Her and the chaplain both..." I mused.

"I was a fool to trust her."

"I wouldn't say that. I don't think you're a fool for trusting someone. I think they're evil for fooling you." I stated plainly.

"There a person you learned that from?" Yuri asked.

"Yeah. Nome, towards the end. I'm starting to think she was right about a lot of things. I'm not sure though." My gaze towards the city became harsh. "Yudina was with the White Hats." I said, changing the topic to something I was more comfortable with.

"Are you sure?" Tian' Xi asked after a while.

"Yes. Yensir is part of a group that wants to find something in this city. Maybe it's the Ultimate Truth that Hennir and the chaplain are after. Maybe it's something else. I don't care. The point is, they have enemies, and the White Hats serve those enemies. Yudina was probably a sleeper agent that they got to infiltrate the ship. Yudina killed the captain. The White Hats killed the captain. We need to end them this rhythm."

"I have an idea as to how we might do that." Dr. Ininsir replied.

"How?"

The doctor pointed out towards the ripples of heat I had seen coming down from the city "ceiling" earlier. "I've calculated the temperature coming from those breaks in the city's protective shielding. To put it in terms you'd all understand, they are frighteningly hot. Remember when Hennir said direct exposure to the sun this far sunward would melt through the Destiny? Each of those beams act like heat rays, one of the quirks resulting from the breakdown of Forebear engineering. They're lenses that focus the heat of the sun into one point. If one of the enemy ships goes through it, it'll melt into their ammunition stores and ignite them."

"So we have a battlefield advantage."

"There's more." the doctor added insistently. "I have a hypothesis we can make a hole of our own in the ceiling if we shoot a cannon upwards."

The ridiculousness of that statement caused me to snigger before I understood that she was being serious.

"They're fast, but they're not maneuverable. If we open a sunbeam ahead of them, they won't be able to avoid it." She protested.

"How do you propose we do that?" Yuri asked confusedly.

"We do an extreme dive. The aft cannons will need to be exchanged for our heaviest guns."

"The forward battery." Yuri nodded as he started realizing the gist of this crazy idea. "Can we pull out of a dive of more than forty-five degrees?"

Tian' Xi nodded. "The Destiny has that up on these heavy frigates. We have more vertical maneuverability than they do."

I probed further. "What about the White Hats?" I wasn't fully convinced.

"They should be our first targets. If we take them out from a distance, we won't have to deal with them up close."

All of us sat and considered the idea. It sounded so insane, so dangerous, that it might actually work. There was only one glaring flaw in it.

"What if we bring the whole shield down on top of us?"

Ininsir replied only after some hesitation. "Then I guess we'll call it a draw."

***

The next half rhythm was full of whispered orders and preparations made in secret from the two sunward prophets who now agonized over where their precious Ultimate Truth was. I figured at that moment that we, the senior lieutenants, were in command of the ship, not them. Evinsir was the only one we informed, and he offered little objection.

The way from fore to aft needed to be cut open a little wider for their respective batteries to be exchanged. This process was helped hugely by Yuri's expertise. The crew that was assigned to our efforts moved quickly under his direction, and the job's comparative quick execution boosted their morale. By the time we had finished, I noticed something strange happening in the city.

It started out slowly. A lookout first noticed a single one of those gelatinous creatures we'd seen in the passages below floating slowly towards the center of the city. Almost a half-kilometer below, it looked like a speck of glowing blue dust. I felt only mildly perturbed at that time. One creature we would deal with easily.

That sighting was followed by another, and then another. The trickle of individuals became small rivulets of them, flowing out of those cavernous mouths leading into the underground. The rivulets in turn became streams. The Destiny's crew was placed on the highest alert as their number increased. Alarm started to spread through the crew.

By mid-rhythm, the city teemed with an unbelievable number of beings. Their ghostly blue forms flowed along the long-deserted avenues, each one's bioluminescence mixing with the color of the sun. At the same time, I heard and felt a weird alien song begin to emanate from them. It had the same monotonous essence as the song that we'd heard when we met the Archivist. Here though, echoed in the deserted hallways and abandoned buildings of the Forebear city, and "hummed" by uncountable millions of these creatures, it was distinctly louder.

I was captivated and worried at the same time. I desperately hoped that the city's sudden new population wouldn't rise up against us as we fought in the sky above them.

The crew shared my reaction. The information relayed from airman to airman took on a frenetic pace as time went forward. There were whispered rumors. They were wavering once again.

At exactly mid-rhythm, a golden light began to appear at the city-center. It rose slowly, stretching upwards into the sky. When it had reached its zenith, it looked as though it met the sun, although that was impossible. The crew stopped what they were doing and stared dumbfounded at the sight.

I understood what it was. The Ultimate Truth. The thing we were here for. The end goal that Jif Turndr, Alanin Dostwickr, and Ila Nome had died trying to find. Above the beam of light, a new pattern faded into existence that was maddeningly familiar to me by now. Three vast interlocked triangles, hanging stationary many kilometers above.

I heard an ecstatic cry and saw Zealot fall to his knees in frenzied reverence. His eyes bulged out of his head as he witnessed what he took to be his Creator. His lips moved in a strange and quiet ululation that I couldn't decipher any meaning from.

Then, he stopped. Maniacally, he jumped to his feet and whirled on the amazed crew who were watching him. He briefly snarled out a string of syllables that could have been some ancient language from the time of the Riverrun's founding. Then again, it could have been meaningless speaking in tongues.

His speech was finally broken by a fanatical call. "Young ones! Lost brooklings! Behold the River!"

The response to Zealot's words was an order of magnitude greater than any mass hysteria that had spread through them before. Airmen wept for joy and tore their shirts. Even members of the crew that I recognized as being aloof towards the Riverrun were noticeably moved, with tears running down their cheeks. In that single instant, Zealot's promise became an outlet for the crew's anxiety over the upcoming battle.

Zealot's voice could barely be heard over the din from so many crazed voices. "To the River! Let us rejoin our one holy and eternal source! Do not let those who come after us cloud your mind with fear! To arms! To arms! Set the sky on fire young ones! To arms!"

A blur of motion flared as the crew got underway. They rushed towards the Destiny, swiftly clambering up the ship's ladders onto the deck. I ran for the ladder after them.

The other lieutenants and I shouted orders at the crew to ready for departure. It was a futile attempt to cover up the fact that we had lost control again. Zealot had won them over for the moment.

***

The Destiny once again took to the air.

Her turbines, long soaked by nearly two ten-rhythms worth of rain, still roared with energy, but there were signs that she was not doing well. Sporadic coughs echoed from the turbines. The great airship sagged slightly as she flew onward at full speed. No doubt, despite our best efforts to repair her canopy, she was still leaking helium up above somewhere. Her hull too, was slightly warped from the impact of massive shockwaves from the Audir shells before we had entered the Forebear tunnel network. Scoring from past battles had been etched along the gondola's outer surface. On deck, a small handful of airmen helped keep the ship aloft. The casualties we had suffered had ended the anthill-like look that had characterized the Destiny when I first saw her back at Kinyu.

Below decks, in the warren of maintenance passages and accessways throughout the ship, small groups of crew hustled about, carrying heavy shells to the aft guns. Lighter calibers were either pushed aside or sent elsewhere in the hands of overworked midshipmen. The dedicated gun crew had been primarily assigned to the heavy guns, and I took command of them personally. I stood there at the main viewport looking down, waiting and fingering my revolver. I flipped it open and frowned at seeing my twelve-shot only half loaded. Six bullets. I'd better make them count if the White Hats managed to close the distance.

Before I went down, I glanced forward towards the Ultimate Truth. I didn't have time to gather detailed impressions of it as we approached closer and closer. Only its colossal size and brilliant gold color stuck in my mind. I turned back towards the aft hatchway after barely a second's consideration of our destination. As I hurriedly rushed to the entrance, my eyes met Yuri's on the way in. We exchanged a nod.

The Ultimate Truth was within thirty kilometers of us now. In less than a half-hour we would be at the very sunward pole of the world.

CHAPTER 23

There was a sudden call from above decks, a sighting. It reverberated through the ship via crew relays, and I heard the tension in the voices that forwarded the message. A general alert. My gaze darted to the outside of the viewport, and I scanned the horizon behind us intensely.

From massive tunnel exits aft of the Destiny and close to the ground, three gigantic shapes lumbered up into the sky. Now that I saw all of them at a closer distance, I could make out the fine details on them. The heavy frigates' hulls were dashed with white paint that formed symbols that I recognized as Aulan. Identification numbers. Their outer surface bristled with a mind-numbing amount of artillery, including the barrels of the two humongous Audir guns Yuri had mentioned. I saw a swarm of men and small arms on their decks. In between the frigates, two disgusting flying creatures raised their malformed heads and delivered a mournful shriek across the city. The men wearing furred caps that were riding them were all too familiar to me by now.

For the third and final time, the White Hats were here. This time, there could be no escape.

The frigates angled upward at a distance of a kilometer and a half to fire at us. Six massive artillery blasts opened up from their Audirs. I saw the bright flare from the cannon muzzles through the viewport and heard the whine of shells whistling past our ship. Moments later the sound of the guns being fired reached me. The roar was deafening.

The shells missed us. Massive explosions from the shell detonations burst into life ahead of us by a few kilometers. They reverberated through the aft gun chamber with a dull thump. The shockwave was much further away this time than we had previously experienced, a fact I had to deduce from my position below decks by the way the ship wobbled.

I sucked in a breath. That was much too close for comfort. They must have miscalculated the timers on the Audir shells. They had fired without changing them, hoping to down the Destiny by a direct hit.

Or had that been a warning shot?

It hadn't. I squashed the thought as the frigate crews scrambled to load another shot into the Audirs. Their forward momentum had been stalled briefly by the powerful blasts, and so the two Shaffengur came forward from their positions between them.

Their forms were in full sunlight this time. They were long and thin, but with sections that were lumpy from misplaced fat. Pieces of their armored skin hung by connective tissue. I couldn't tell if this was due to molting, or if they had fared so poorly in the sunward lands. Most of their atrophied limbs had been amputated, whether by their own action or the White Hats'. I saw patches of leather sewn directly into their wings in order to cover up a collection of holes that had been punched through them. Their heads were like an outraptor's, if that outraptor had suffered from generation on generation of inbreeding.

There were two of them. I saw a pair of the White Hats were astride the one to the Destiny's rear starboard, and one of them on the other.

I was mesmerized by the reappearance of my foes. It was as though the personification of death itself had materialized before me. As a result, it took the second time for the order to be called out before I recognized that the order had been given to brace for an altitude dive.

We were going to execute our battle plan. I glanced around at the big guns we'd taken from the Destiny's fore. They were firmly secured for the dive.

"All hands brace!" I repeated loudly.

Nothing happened. With growing confusion, I kept my eyes trained on the fleet outside the aft viewport.

Cries of panic reverberated from the fore of the Destiny. The Destiny lurched under me as I felt her make a sharp turn.

The air around me grew increasingly hotter and hotter. I heard muffled calls of panic from above deck. My view of the fleet became untenable as bright light filled the space just aft of the Destiny. I realized that this was one of the sunbeams we had seen open up in the city's alien shielding. It couldn't have been twenty feet astern.

The frigates had recovered from firing the Audirs at this point, and charged at full speed. Too late, their commanders realized that they would be flying directly through the center of the superheated air. The White Hats had successfully evaded, but the heavy frigates were far less maneuverable. The two at the flanks peeled off to port and starboard, but the middle frigate floundered before drifting into the sunbeam.

The metal of the ship's canopy melted from the heat. For a split second, she was falling out of the sky at an alarming pace. I saw the silhouettes of airmen set alight and writhing about on her deck for a mercifully short period of time.

Then, the heat reached the ship's ammunition stores. They ignited with a titanic sound that echoed throughout the entire city, and the ship disappeared behind the bright veil of the largest explosion I had ever seen.

The shockwave from that explosion easily eclipsed anything that could ever have been created from a single Audir shell. Shortly after the frigate's immolation, the wavefront slammed into the other two with a ferocity that nearly batted them out of the sky. They careened over to the sides dangerously, ejecting many of their crew over the city. Among the few of the luckier, I saw parachutes deploy to carry them to the ground.

Where they really so lucky? The ethereal creatures still waited below.

The explosion even bowled over the Shaffengur. They writhed in midair as they tried to right themselves. Horrific screeches erupted from them as their riders whipped them mercilessly.

The blast hit us within seconds. I barely had time to belt out "Brace!" before the deck violently jerked beneath my feet, setting me completely off-balance. The restraints on the ammunition from the storage behind me came undone. Shells went flying everywhere, thankfully with their fuses unlit. The flying projectiles did nonetheless injure a few members of the gun crew.

I stumbled and fell against the wall. The gondola finally stopped swinging, and I called out "Damage report!" as I went running to the deck. I needed air. Something had been released into the air below decks. I couldn't breathe.

Arriving above decks, I gasped for air. A storm of airmen followed me, abandoning the gun chamber completely. Pieces of shrapnel and melted hull propelled from the explosion fell in the Destiny's direction, and I still felt a heightened temperature above decks. I turned around, blinking, looking for the other members of the senior command staff. Nobody was visible in the chaos above decks. I saw airmen with ventilators file into the aft gun section, looking to stem whatever toxic fumes were leaking into the chamber.

The ship had been blown off course only slightly, had corrected its course, and we were speeding once again towards the city center. The enemy ship to our starboard had regained control and was chasing us down. It was probably in the process of reloading its Audirs.

That was when I heard Tian' Xi calling out. "Haye!" My head swung in her direction. There was a determined look in her face. "Take your gun crew below decks and man the starboard battery." Were we opening up a full broadside against our pursuer?

I yelled out, "Gun crew! Man the starboard battery!"

There was a rush of airmen below decks. I followed suit, quickly moving to the starboard battery.

When I arrived, four guns were lined up, ready to fire. I was extremely poorly staffed. There were only three airmen to each gun, and three airmen total to forward ammunition to the batteries. My heart sank as I realized the toll of our casualties.

The guns clanked as they were loaded. I peered out the starboard viewport and awaited the approach of our pursuer.

The heavy frigate was barely a kilometer behind us and closing fast. All six turbines fired at full impulse. They were decreasing distance to gain more accuracy. Surely they knew how vulnerable that made them? Amazement filled me as I realized the true suicidal intent that they had. They would either shoot us down or ram us.

Underneath me, the Destiny lurched again. Someone vomited in the corner of the battery chamber. We were changing directions, moving to starboard to cross the enemy's T.

The gray surface of an alien tower cut off my view of the frigate. I leaned back instinctively for a second, my reflexes triggered by its proximity. I shouted another order down the length of the chamber. "Timer for two seconds! Aim at five degrees, one-seventy to ship's plane!" For a couple of seconds the Destiny made its pass.

The tower fell away from my vision, and I saw the frigate loom in my viewport.

I didn't wait for an order. "Fire!" I almost screamed out.

The roar of the batteries at my side was puny compared to the earlier explosion. Shells whistled through the air between the ships, impacting directly on the hull of the frigate. One shell hit near one of their batteries. The massive Audir gun was rendered inoperable, and I saw a small hole open up in their port side, near the ship's fore. It was a small thing, but I knew it would provide a target of opportunity for us.

Then the frigate drew sideways to starboard, and my eyes were met with the terrifying sight of dozens of cannons ready to bombard us back. I've never regretted a decision as much as I regretted agreeing to broadside that behemoth. At the very least we should have aimed for her turbines.

There would be deaths. "Reload!" I called out.

The crew tried to reload in time. The airmen on reload duty scrambled to provide ammunition forward. For half of the guns, they were successful before the side of the frigate lit up in a cacophonous volley of fire. I flung myself away from the viewport and against the back of the gun chamber just in time. About twenty-eight shells exploded against the side of the Destiny, ripping the bulkhead in front of me to shreds. I saw airmen sucked out of the side of the ship or hit with shrapnel and torn into several pieces. Loud cries of pain went up from the newly exposed chamber.

I felt pieces of metal hit my body and dig into my skin. I would have yelled out in pain had I not had the wind completely knocked out of me. I remained slumped against the side of the gun chamber for a few seconds before a cannon blast from one of the remaining operable cannons gave me enough impetus to pick myself up again.

It was a futile round yes, but the airmen who fired it were still kicking enough to return fire, despite having been injured by the volley. That meant there must be some hope left.

The entire starboard side of the ship had been blown away in sections. What remained in place was pockmarked with holes from shrapnel. I was only a few meters away from a very precarious drop outside. Two cannons towards the ship's aft had been destroyed or damaged beyond repair. Most of the gun crew lay on the ship's floor, wounded or dying. Two airmen alone had fired the answering shot from one of the remaining cannon. My eyes swung towards the last cannon. It was loaded.

I sprinted towards it, ignoring the pain in my side. The other airmen got the same idea and had moved to that gun by the time I had arrived.

I looked out over the void between the two ships. The viewport was gone. I would have to manually judge the angle of the shot to the best of my abilities. The hole in their ship towards the fore was the best option open to me. My brow furrowed as I stared at it. I decided to wing it.

"Three degrees, one eighty-five to ship's plane." I coughed out.

The wincher worked frantically. All other sounds faded. The cranking of the cannon was the only sound I heard besides the air moving past the ship. I saw their cannons moving, tracking us. They would be ready to fire again any moment now.

The wincher called out "Ready!"

"Fire!" I yelled.

The cannon blast sounded. Almost as if time itself was slowing, I saw the shell sail through the air, and find its mark.

The ship's ammunition stores didn't go up in flames as I had hoped. Instead, I saw a section of the ship rip free and heave upwards into the canopy, puncturing a massive gash in it. The wound was deep enough that it must have gone through several segregated chambers inside the canopy, bursting them and causing the front of the frigate to jerk downward suddenly as gravity claimed its victim. The ship listed forward. Crew fell off the deck once more, and the ship remained suspended with its fore sagging at a very precarious angle.

Then, she began to fall out of the sky. I saw several of her crew intentionally jump overboard with parachutes attached. They knew what was awaiting them at the bottom of the fall.

I left my post. The starboard battery was no longer operational, so it made no sense at all to remain here. I passed by dead and wounded crew, and spared them only the smallest of glances. The barber would be overwhelmed, and there would be no saving these airmen. Not with these kind of injuries.

A few seconds later, the frigate impacted the ground. Another massive explosion like the first rocked the city. I was traveling up the

Heaven's Expedition

main hatchway when it hit. When I was above decks once more, I heard a gigantic crack follow the explosion from behind the ship.

I turned just in time to see another ancient alien tower, which had stood for millennia undisturbed before we had arrived here, keel over slowly. It buckled and broke into several pieces before impacting the ground with a titanic thud, scattering pieces all over the city beneath it, and sending a cloud of debris into the air behind us, masking us from view.

Apparently, it wasn't good enough. From out of the midst of this plume, I saw one of the shadow flyers exit the cloud, leaving a wake of swirling dust behind it. There were two White Hats mounted on it. One of them pointed at us, and the other whipped the flyer. It delivered another unearthly shriek and swooped forward.

***

From my side, I heard a sudden clatter of gunfire coming from an automatic rifle. Only one person aboard had that type of weapon.

Yuri muttered to himself as he opened fire on the creature. "Come on. Come on." His rounds only hit empty air. I turned and saw his rifle click empty. He dropped to his knees and reloaded. I noticed that his hands were shaking.

"Yuri?" I demanded. He gave no answer. I was only met with a frantic silence.

The shadow flyer came even closer. I saw its riders ready their pistols and aim them in our direction. If they managed to close that distance, we were as good as dead.

Yuri stood up again and stared down the sights of his gun.

"Yuri!" I yelled. He opened fire. It was a futile gesture at this distance. Yet again, the bullets missed their target. Yuri stopped before his drum ran completely empty. He cursed and continued to mutter to himself. "Come on. Come on..."

The crew around me ran for close-quarters weapons. I drew my twelve-shot and levelled the barrel with the flight path of the monstrosity. At about fifty meters from the ship, I heard Yuri suddenly scream out, "Come on! Come on! COME ON!" He opened fire again.

In the distance, the shadow flyer suddenly veered off course. Some of Yuri's rounds had finally found their mark. It screeched in pain, and tumbled to the side, knocking the White Hats' aim completely off their mark.

I hollered out, "Fire at will!" An assortment of rifle fire erupted from the deck. Most of the shots went wide, but the continuing cries of pain coming from the White Hats' animal gave me some indication that a few at least were hitting. "Keep firing!" I yelled again.

I felt the Destiny list slightly to starboard. Just that same instant, the unwelcome and oppressive form of the last heavy frigate cleared the massive pillar of dust behind us, and bore down on our ship.

A lone cannon blast rang out from below decks; it was from the starboard battery. The shell flew through the air again and hit the shadow flyer squarely in the center of its mass, shredding it completely and silencing its cries.

I was stunned for a second. Scattered cheers popped into existence on the deck at our amazing victories. I almost felt the crew's resolve stiffen. Yuri turned towards me and I saw a grim look cross his face. He was shivering.

My thoughts were interrupted by the concussive thump of an Audir gun firing on our ship. This time, only one fired. The shot was nearly spot-on, sending another shockwave through the air that raked the deck. The crew was prepared this time. Even though the hull buckled beneath them, not a single airman was tossed overboard.

The second shot happened soon after, passing in between the silk lines that held the gondola up. I felt a rush of wind as it flew among the rigging. Once again however, the timer was off. The shell sailed over several kilometers to port before exploding at a greater distance than the first one had. I offered up a thankful prayer to whatever force was watching out for us, be it the River, or just sheer dumb luck.

The Destiny was crumbling around me. The gondola was bent at an obtuse angle, and several lines snapped above us. One flew back violently, cracking through the air as it whipped against the deck. Two people were caught in the impact. I recognized one as the Master of Altitude. Tian' Xi fell with a pained scream, her leg ripped open from the force of so much released tension in the line. I ran over to her, attempting to help her somehow. Confusion and chaos once again had descended on the deck.

Another of those ear-rending Shaffengur cries rang out from the ship's fore. I turned just in time to see the last White Hat approaching from that direction. It was too late to stop him; he had already flung himself off his creature, setting it free to fly away from the ship. It sped away from the battle, putting as much distance between itself and the Destiny as it could. The White Hat's boots slammed into the deck and he stood.

He drew his revolver and started firing at passing crew. Two bullets hit nearby airmen in the head, pink mist spurting behind them. Those nearest to the White Hat immediately withdrew and started running in a panic for the aft hatchway to get shelter below decks.

This was it. He was here. My hand drifted to my twelve-shot.

Yuri had rushed over to Tian' Xi with me, and had fallen down. I saw him curl his short form into a ball, muttering "They're so quiet." to himself. I glanced down at him in disbelief and horror. He had the shell-sickness.

"Not now..." I whispered futilely into the wind.

A loud cry erupted from somewhere on my left. I whipped around and saw Dr. Ininsir standing unsteadily on her feet with a rifle in her hands. She fired once towards the White Hat. He had anticipated this movement with almost supernatural reflexes and dodged out of the way before she fired her shot. The bullet went behind him, and lodged in one of the ropes. I saw it strain.

The White Hat shrugged his shoulders, lazily raised his revolver at the doctor and fired once. She dropped to the floor. I couldn't tell whether she'd been killed or not.

The deck was emptied. What remained of the crew was huddled below deck. Even Evinsir's navigation panel had been left unmanned. We were free to list from side to side dead in the air. Only the White Hat and I stood there, watching each other from many meters away.

The deck lurched out from under both of us. In the front of the Destiny, the lines attaching the gondola to the canopy had finally broken, causing the White Hat to lose his footing and stumble forward. I used the opportunity that provided. I fired three shots in quick succession to keep him pinned down, and vaulted over to the navigation panel.

I knew a thing or two from my time spent quietly observing Evinsir while he was piloting the ship. I pulled the ship's altitude controls down. Within an instant, the ship was tilted forward as her diesel shifted to the front. We were in a dive, one made all the steeper by the recently severed lines at the front. As a final measure, I pushed our throttle to the maximum. I knew I had to keep the White Hat off-balance, otherwise there was no way I would ever be coming out of this encounter alive. We were speeding towards the ground at a breathtaking pace now. I saw the Ultimate Truth awaiting us just ahead.

That was when I heard the twin blasts coming from the aft cannons behind me. I crouched behind the panel and glanced over my shoulder just in time to witness the exhaust from the twin guns fly upwards. The shots followed a parabolic arc, but weren't aimed at the heavy frigate behind us. They gracefully curved upwards towards the great Forebear shield. For a second, I thought they would fall short. They didn't.

Two explosions, tiny compared to the sheer amount of explosive power I'd seen this rhythm, burst into life at the ceiling of the city. Seconds later, a rip appeared in the protective layer above us. I was momentarily blinded by the light.

For the third and final time, a massive explosion flared into life high above the city. It was larger than either the first or the second. I saw the last frigate completely ripped in half. What remained of its aft section spiraled away from us and fell back down to the city below.

The other half fell towards us. Within a split-second, it had passed overhead and was headed downwards at a terrifying pace. I heard an awful, sickening screech of metal ripping open metal. I felt the Destiny begin to plummet at an increased pace and knew that a section of the canopy had been burst. We were nearing free-fall.

I felt myself levitate from the deck. I twisted and turned, trying to right myself, but there wasn't a direction I could orient towards. Yuri scrambled for a grip as the wind rushed against us from our descent. He reached an arm out to catch Tian' Xi as she started to be swept backwards by the force of our descent.

A prone form swept past me. It was Ininsir. She slammed against the side of the ship's railing and remained stuck there. She didn't move. My head swiveled back towards the White Hat and I grimaced. He was moving towards the aft. His gun was leveled at me. I saw a shot flare out of the revolver's barrel.

The bullet hit my right ear, tearing its upper fourth off completely, and causing a steady stream of blood to start trickling down the side of my face. I gasped in pain and raised my twelve-shot to return fire, but I only managed to get one shot off.

More shots rang out from the White Hat. He was furious that he had missed. Three more bullets dug into the deck behind me as I yanked on a handhold and took cover behind a secured barrel that used to store ammunition. I'd fired four shots. I yanked open the revolver chamber to double-check and shut it again.

The White Hat had decided against wasting any more of his ammunition. No more shots were fired in my direction. I had the initiative. I eyed the warped surface of the canopy above and an idea popped into my head. I holstered my twelve-shot once more. I would need both hands for what I was about to do.

I pushed myself easily off the gondola and grabbed for a rigging rope while drawing my knife at the same time. More rounds were fired my direction, but I was moving too fast and with an unexpected trajectory, so the shots didn't connect. I slammed into the canopy's underside, and sliced through the already-weakened section of rope with a single slash. I held onto the other end, and felt myself being carried by the motion of the rope's tension, like a spring, towards the White Hat.

He'd fired three shots in that time. Or was it two?

Two more shots. These ones hit me this time. One grazed my leg; the other ricocheted off a rib. Too much adrenaline was running through my system at this point. I was supernaturally focused on the White Hat as the distance between us grew smaller and smaller. I saw the bounty hunter stand up to aim a shot at me full-on.

My boots smashed into him before he could pull the trigger, throwing his aim to the side. He pulled the trigger a split-second too late and the gun discharged harmlessly into the air. I brought my knife up to his abdomen and stabbed upward, my knife meeting hard muscle.

The White Hat's expression didn't change. There was a suicidal calm on his face as I stabbed again for a second time. Blood spurted out of his mouth. He pushed me away and brought his revolver to bear one more time.

He'd fired eleven shots. I closed my eyes.

Click.

My eyes shot open again. The White Hat's face contorted in anger, his moustache stained red with blood. A smirk broke out on my face.

He moved to launch himself forward at me.

I was too fast for him. My hand immediately went to my hip and I drew my twelve-shot again. I emptied it into his chest.

He lashed out at me with his foot as he flew past me. I gave his body a rough push to the side, and he sailed overboard. A howl of rage escaped him as fell to his death. It was eventually lost in the sound of rushing air and debris falling.

I returned with some difficulty to where Yuri was still hanging on. The pain from my wounds was starting to kick in. "They're so quiet." Yuri continued to whisper. He was still curled up in a ball in shock and fear.

I held a palm up to the side of my head, trying to staunch the flow of blood from where the top bit of my ear used to be. "They don't die quiet." I stated calmly.

I made my way past Yuri, the pain growing with each pull. I had to get to the control panel. If we didn't pull out of this dive, we'd be scattered on the city floor. Taking a brief glance ahead, I saw that we were within seconds of impacting the ground. I struggled to maintain my balance.

I couldn't vault over the panel again. I had to pull myself around its side, which took precious seconds. By the time that I'd managed to get to where I could reach the altitude controls, we'd dropped another thirty meters. My eyes flickered with fear over to one of the gauges that dropped precipitously. I yanked the control up, and the Destiny's drop slowed as the deck righted itself. At the same time, my side split with pain and I groaned, my vision growing blurry.

I looked up and nearly panicked. We were headed straight for the Ultimate Truth. Less than three hundred meters away, I saw a crowd of the floating creatures standing in a silent congregation around six giant pillars that lined the base of the light beam. It was blindingly bright now. I had to cover my eyes.

The bottom of the ship impacted the wide avenue below with a loud crunch, and I instantly felt the deceleration. Metal ground against metal as we slowed. The Destiny's canopy, now no longer holding up its own weight, keeled over to starboard, and the deck jerked to the right. I slammed against the navigation panel as I saw sparks and bending metal from the canopy. The last thing that I saw before I passed out from the pain in my side was the Destiny coming to a stop, utterly capsized, her journey complete.

CHAPTER 24

I drifted in and out of consciousness, amidst unidentifiable shapes and sounds, with only a partial awareness of the world around me.

My first solid memory upon waking from my torpor was of leaning against a broken piece of rock with an agonizing pain searing through my midsection. Movement magnified the excruciating pangs. I let out a distressed growl. In a flash, my view of the alien skyline above me filled with the concerned face of Yuri. "She's awake, doc," he observed.

"Good." Ininsir's voice cut through my remaining unconsciousness. I heard her limping towards me, a bandage wrapped around her midsection. "How do you feel, Haye?"

I groaned.

"Misery loves company." She gritted her teeth and laughed haltingly before coughing.

"How long?" I demanded.

"Not long. Parts of the ship are still on fire." She gestured ineffectually at it. "I think we've run through most of our ammunition though. We shouldn't have a problem with explosions. We're a safe distance away."

At the moment she said this, the sound of shells bursting ripped through the air. I turned to look at the source and saw the ship lying like a wounded animal several hundred meters to our side. Her canopy was torn open. Smoke and embers billowed out of gashes in the hull. As I watched, more shells went off inside her. She was slowly being torn apart by her own ammunition stores.

"It's a shame. She was a good ship." Tian' Xi's wistful voice interrupted my stare. I looked back to where she had melted out of the shadows, and sat myself up to take a better look at my immediate surroundings.

We laid at the side of the central plaza of the city, which easily spanned four kilometers square. All four of us had gathered underneath the eaves of one of the side colonnades, with support pillars to one side, towards the wreck of the Destiny, and a solid wall at the other. Immediately opposite me, I saw the Ultimate Truth. I blinked and it hit me just how many of the city's creatures had assembled in the center. They hung motionless in the air above the edifices that ringed the base of the Ultimate Truth, and floated in dense formations in the open space between the buildings. Narrow spaces separated gigantic blocks of them from the next, giving the illusion that they had lined up in preparation for a military parade.

I could not easily distinguish their forms from the blinding column of light that rose in silent majesty. At times it appeared as though the creatures closest to the Ultimate Truth melted into it completely.

I looked around to rest my eyes from the strain of looking in that direction and began to grow more uneasy about our predicament. We didn't have stockpiled supplies; those would be trapped within the Destiny, on fire or destroyed from the explosions. Three of us were wounded.

The lack of any crew in our immediate area worried me the most. "Where is everybody?" I grunted out.

"Dead, dying, or with the chaplain." Tian' Xi said.

"Dr. Hennir? Evinsir?" An angry thought echoed in my mind. "Yensir?"

"She and a small group of the crew followed him soon after he left. They're going to that place." Tian' Xi jerked a thumb over her shoulder at the Ultimate Truth. "I haven't seen Evinsir or Yensir."

"Neither have I." Dr. Ininsir added.

Yuri sat down next to me. "Everything's a mess. Fortunately, we have the rest of our lives to sort it out." His gallows' humor was wasted on me. My thoughts were elsewhere.

We were free of our pursuers. In the process the expedition had fragmented, and we were stranded here. There would be no regaining control over the ship's crew any time soon. Not with Zealot and Dr. Hennir each commanding what remained. My mind turned towards the future, whether or not we would last a single year, or even a single ten-day in this sun-burnt land. Death could easily come within the next few hours. There were certainly enough of the alien creatures around us that if they decided to kill every one of us, we couldn't stop them.

A part of my mind, one that had driven me to despair many years before in Mansu, came back to me. It would be easier to hasten death. I didn't have any bullets left, but I could find a rifle or something in the wreck of the Destiny when it had ceased burning.

I pushed that thought away. I had to do something, anything. Even though no practical tasks remained, I had to keep moving. I wouldn't allow myself to fall into that mindset again. I had to find Zealot and Dr. Hennir. If they started fighting, the crew would start fighting. It served no purpose to kill each other at this moment. I needed to prevent that somehow. If they had headed to the Ultimate Truth, then I would head there as well.

At least, so I told myself.

Something within me drew me towards the Ultimate Truth, the same feeling I had felt when I had first looked out from my childhood home towards the sunward lands and wondered what lay beyond there.

I stood up with extreme difficulty, prompting sudden anxious looks from the trio. "I'm going to go find them." I stated firmly.

Their initial protests died swiftly. Defeat was inscribed on their faces. The magnitude of the situation had begun to sink in. Yuri alone said anything after me. My eyes met his as he spoke. "We'll see you soon. Please come back safe."

***

The limp towards the Ultimate Truth felt as though it took several hours. I can't say how long it really took before I reached the base of that gargantuan beam of light. All the while, I travelled through the ghostly ranks of alien creatures, their forms melding into each other like some bioluminescent liquid. I felt more alone that whole walk than I have ever felt in my entire life.

When I stood within a short distance from the incredibly bright beam of light, I could discern the figures of several airmen standing between two of the obelisks that ringed the base of the Ultimate Truth. They had separated themselves into dual groups and were watching two people in their center. Those were obviously Dr. Hennir and Zealot. I quickened my hobble.

Nobody paid me much attention as I passed them by. Everyone's attention focused on the two figures that had led them to this point. They stood silently, each one trying to gaze on the object of their long obsession. They were having extreme difficulty in doing so; the brightness defied the eye.

My averted eyes traced triangular patterns on the metal ground. The perfectly level floor supplied a blank slate for my mind as I walked right up between Hennir and Zealot. I looked briefly at each one. They stood in reverent silence.

For a little bit, I couldn't do much else other than to join them in that stillness. Every bone in my body felt alive from the strange quiet that had fallen all around.

I kept my arm wrapped firmly around the bandaged wound in my side. "This is what you're here for." I coughed out. "Is it everything you expected?"

Zealot turned directly into the light and closed his eyes. "River take me. Flow well."

"I've been waiting for this for a long time." Dr. Hennir breathed out.

I interrupted them. "Whatever happens in there, whatever you see, you have to accept it as truth. If he's correct, doctor, you have to concede that the River exists. If she's correct, Zealot..."

We fell back into silence. Around us, all sounds had faded. Even the explosions from the Destiny's arsenal had faded. The air around me thickened with anticipation.

Zealot first took a halting step forward, which developed into confident strides forward, calm happiness developing on his face. He crossed the boundary from where I could see him, his form being enveloped by the light so completely that his shadow disappeared from this world.

Dr. Hennir followed soon after. As she passed me, I heard her mutter something about the fulfillment of the historical dialectic. She stepped across the threshold, and was lost from view.

Seconds passed without a sound, or any indication that the two were still there, meters in front of me. They could have fallen over and died, or been consumed by the blinding light, and I would have had no way of knowing. I couldn't see a single inch of them. Behind me, the pitiful remnants of the ship's crew pressed in, eager to see if the duo would emerge from the light beam again.

Minutes passed.

The crew grew restless. I knew that if they were left hanging much longer, some of them would go insane.

I shifted my gaze away from the Ultimate Truth in order to rest my eyes. It physically hurt to look at the beam.

After a moment I turned back towards the beam. One of them could always see something and say they saw another.

And besides, I was curious. There was one question that nagged me, and had ever since the captain first echoed my mother's words to me...

And so, I began moving towards the Ultimate Truth, determined to find out what we had come here for. My footsteps clacked against the ground as I limped along, becoming the only sound I heard apart from the beating in my heart. The world outside the beam faded, and I became only aware of my own body, walking forward through the intense golden radiance.

***

In the time before time began, there was no land but the mountain. The eternal river sprang from a well on this peak, and all things were held in its embrace.

All times must end, and all times before time must end, and so the first cause was born. With it, the River changed its shape. Its placid surface became turbulent, and the sides divided among themselves. In the land of the River, great channels were dug, and the waters of the River flooded into these places, swallowing them beneath their waves. These streams were made to flow side by side with the River, but some of them departed into unknown lands, where they were lost to the River. Their channels had been created in this way, but the majority of these streams continued to flow alongside the River.

Then the first cause came upon the River again. In the rhythm of rhythms and the first season, countless streams flowed from its folds. And the streams flowed forth, and multiplied over the land of Solandye.

Onward flowed the River, and as its descendants spread across the world in time, it flowed well.

And so it was and is and will be, for one future time, the River will be made whole once more. From the River, all things flow; without the River, nothing flows that has a source. Its peace shines in the darkness, and the darkness has not overcome it.

***

From the stars they came.

The Forebears, our ancestors, were shaped out of matter and energy by the forces of nature. They came to the shores of our globe from a distant world, dying in the reddening embrace of its home star. They shaped the ground to their own ends, crafting a great city in the land of Solandye. But the Forebears were torn apart by ceaseless strife and superstition. A great weapon, terrible enough to wipe out life, and leave structures intact, killed the greater part of those people, leaving others, less sophisticated among them, to rebuild on the far side of the world. Much knowledge was lost.

Ages and eons pass in the blink of an eye from the perspective of the universe. Stone becomes sand, and mountains are worn down and built up in cosmic seconds. One life in the face of the universe is over and done with in a nanosecond.

The invisible hand of history guides humanity, much as the invisible hand of evolution guides many more species as a whole. First comes one society, to be swallowed by the next, and the next. Eventually, that society shall return to the stars once more, and the great migration shall begin again.

For ours is the universe, in all its infinite and infinitesimal wonder. And that is all that is, or ever was, or ever will be.

***

Yuri first noticed my return. He called out to me, "Did you find them?"

I had walked through what felt like thousands of kilometers of space. Dazed, partly due to simple exhaustion, partly due to the unabating pain in my side, I couldn't concentrate on the storm of words that launched my way. I shuffled back into the last remaining group of people I trusted. They each said something in turn to me that my ears refused to comprehend. I merely sat down against the wall and collapsed, my eyes wandering from person to person.

At last I found the will to speak. "Yes. And no. And yes."

My response clearly bewildered most of them, so I closed my eyes for a bit before I tried to organize a better response.

"I found them. They've gone their separate ways. We're alone."

Yuri's head sank down into his chest. Opposite me, silent tears trailed down Dr. Ininsir's cheek. Tian' Xi wasn't so easily fazed however. She attempted to read my face. "What did you find?"

"Neither of them," I replied almost immediately. "And both of them."

"You just said..."

"I found Zealot and Dr. Hennir. What I can't say is whether I found out if either of them was right or not." I grumbled and tried to ease myself back against the wall.

"What do you mean?" Yuri asked the inevitable question.

I sat there, looking out at the pythonic city, trying to ignore the rapidly fading fires that burned through the Destiny. I had to answer carefully. Even I wasn't sure what I'd seen. The moment that the light had begun to fade into many confusing sounds and images, I knew there would be no accord between Zealot and Hennir.

Their accounts were exactly as I had expected they would be after that vision. Zealot naturally said that the great and ancient beings we had seen were the River's servants and the Biehs respectively held to exist by the Riverrun. Hennir said that they were the Forebears. The fact that they seemingly manifested supernatural abilities hadn't given her much pause.

Two parallel sets of doubt dominated my mind at this point. On the one hand, it was hard for me to believe Zealot's absolute faith in the unbroken chain of book copied from book copied from oral telling of the River's account. Over many, many centuries, the details of these things were more than likely to be corrupted by simple clerical errors and changes in language. That much of it I didn't trust.

On the other hand, it never ceased to amaze me how blindly the doctor placed so much faith in the power of her own pure reason. Considering the way in which the supernatural seemed to permeate everything this far sunward, was it still reasonable to insist on interpreting everything in natural terms?

Ultimately I could not say who knew the truth. I had hoped that the vision we received from the sunward pole would have been clearer. Maybe it had not been intended for us to comprehend. Maybe we had yet to comprehend it. Maybe in some distant future, others would hear of it and come to an understanding utterly different from ours. Or maybe there was a narrative within the broken, out-of-order vision, but one that would always be subject to dispute.

There was of course, one further thing. Something that only I had been able to extract from the stupefying revelation. After I'd seen it, and sensed its presence through everything, a change came over me, and infused into my deepest awareness of myself and the world.

The captain, and all of those on the Destiny who had held to the Beltlander ethic, were the only ones who I could say for certain were right. That was what I would take away from Heaven's Expedition.

So I told them. And after I'd told them what *I'd* seen inside the Ultimate Truth, everyone knew enough not to inquire further.

Yuri's question came a while after my words had a chance to be thoroughly considered by the group. "What now?"

My eyes remained closed, but underneath my lids, they twitched. The possibility remained of deciphering the Ultimate Truth before we inevitably starved to death, but that would require finding one of the men who had disappeared. The one man responsible for the whole expedition. We would have to track him, but I was fairly good at that. For once, I had a job within my usual expertise.

For now, though, I was exhausted. Finding Yensir could wait a few more hours. My reply to Yuri was quiet.

"For now we rest. We'll see what next rhythm brings."

GLOSSARY

Aery: A military/mercenary order of ships under the command of a Grandmaster, typically called on by governments on Sunlock to augment their air navy capabilities

Andironback: Beast of burden, known for a large hump on its back that is used to carry luggage in non-industrialized areas.

Aula: The greatest of the Octant Empires

Basilica: An institution of science and learning, doubling as a forum for the resolution of international disputes, also formerly the home of the Riverrun hierarchy

Beltlander: Anyone who comes from the temperate 'equatorial' regions

Darkward: Towards the side of the world that faces away from the sun

Drei: An Octant Empire to the "west" of Aula

Forebear: Enigmatic prehistorical civilization on Sunlock, commonly assumed to be non-human in nature.

Great Ranges: A gigantic mountain range that rings the sunward pole, shielding it from exploration.

Ijritan: An Octant Empire to the "east" of Aula

Off-rhythm: The portion of time that the majority of humans are asleep

Off-rhythmer: Person that spends their time awake when the majority of people are asleep

Outraptor: Reptilian creatures often used for reconnaissance or other cavalry-related jobs

Nordecker: One of the Octant Empires just darkward of Yin

Rhythm: A circadian rhythm, used in lieu of the concept of "day" to keep track of natural human sleep cycles

The River: Ancient incomprehensibly natured being found in the Riverrun religion, from which all souls are generated and to which all souls return

Riverrun: A religion originating around the shores of the Ambrosian sea, that focuses on the teachings of a nameless master who encountered direct experience with the River. It is the predominant religion of Nordecker and Aula, and has a strong presence in Drei and Ijritan

Shaffengur: Flying mounts of the White Hats

Sunward: Towards the side of the world that faces the sun

Unknown Seas: Three seas – Nemasia, Anti-Nemasia, and Ambrosia – that provide the only source of saltwater on Sunlock, each comparable in size to twice the size of the Mediterranean.

The Veil: A mystical barrier that separates direct experience of the divine from everyday life in the Riverrun religion

White Hats: A trio of bounty hunters feared throughout Yin for their precision and accuracy with pistols, and immediately identifiable from their furry white capsized

Yin: A steppe-filled land sunward of Nordecker, widely regarded as being politically unstable and home to wild gunslingers and desperadoes

Printed in Great Britain
by Amazon